THE DEAN RETURNS
From the Dead

THE DEAN RETURNS
From the Dead

#4 in the Briarpatch College Series

William Urban

2010

iUniverse, Inc.
New York   Bloomington

THE DEAN RETURNS From the Dead
#4 in the Briarpatch College Series

iUniverse books may be ordered through booksellers or by contacting:

iUniverse
1663 Liberty Drive
Bloomington, IN 47403
www.iuniverse.com
1-800-Authors (1-800-288-4677)

ISBN: 978-1-4502-0542-9 (sc)
ISBN: 978-1-4502-0543-6 (ebook)

Printed in the United States of America

iUniverse rev. date: 1/21/2010

In *The Dean is Dead* Professor Donahue and Chief Biggs solved the mysteries surrounding the demise of Dean Wooda, who died "accidentally" in an insurance scam designed to resolve the college's perennial financial problems. Six months later they had it all to do over again when Floyd Boater was murdered by the late dean. (!) At the end of *The Dean is Still Dead* Flo Boater was college president and Stanley Wooda had become the youngest dean in America since the 1850s. In *The Dean is Dead Again* yet another underhanded financial scheme, hiding the sale of South American artifacts, was frustrated. Now in episode 4, yet more problems arise.

This novel can be read by itself, without having enjoyed the earlier ones. However, the more one knows about the persons (who have become more than characters) in the novel, the more the reader will appreciate the nuances of speech and behavior.

The situations and personalities are universal in higher education, and were especially so in the Nineties—when common sense fled before the onslaught of ideology. The "types" in this novel should not be understood to refer to actual living or deceased individuals—they were everywhere!

This novel began as a play in 2003, based on a fictional college and fictional characters created in the early 1970s. In the summer of 2003 I was on the staff of an Eastern Michigan University travel-study program in Europe; evenings, when the students went off to observe the locals relaxing, I sat down with my laptop and wrote novels.

Reality has a way of outdistancing reality. In the summer of 2009 I read of a small liberal arts college, currently doing well, being offered the nearby courthouse; financial limitations prevented the president from accepting that architecturally attractive poison pill. Had he read *The Dean Is Dead*, the decision would have been easier.

What else can this novel teach? A wise administrator of a century ago said that knowledge obviously does accumulate, since freshmen bring some in and seniors take none out. But such cynicism, even with that touch of wit, is off the point. Small colleges similar to Briarpatch (and even great universities) survive because generations of alumni look back on their educational experience with fondness and believe that it was well worth their time, money, and the myriad forms of stress that life can bring to any adolescent. Memory has a way of turning moments of anxiety into years of joy.

Cast of Characters
From the preceding novels

DO Donahue—former cop, now instructor of Sociology

Mary C—assistant professor of Spanish, tenure track (she hopes)

John Justice Biggs—Middleville chief of police, looking forward to retirement

C. Wooda—late academic dean of Briarpatch College; dead, but not forgotten

Stanley Wooda—current academic dean of Briarpatch College, young and ambitious

Floyd Boater—late president of Briarpatch College

Flora Boater—widow of above, now president of Briarpatch College

Lill—professor of Theater (Theatre), formerly acting-president

Lily—professor of Theater (Theatre), formerly acting-dean

Salvatore Iva—former chemistry professor, former lover of Flo Boater, imprisoned for conspiracy to murder Dean Wooda, hoping for release on parole

Molly—adjunct instructor (part-time) in English, once married to the late Dean Wooda, close to becoming engaged to Sal

Jay Bird—former janitor, pled guilty to assault on Dean Wooda, now Superintendent of Buildings and Grounds

Jenny—adjunct instructor in Music, closely attached to Hiram Jason Bird

Maximilian Stout—head of the English department, with ambitions to advance

The Creep—head of the History department, with similar ambitions

Miss Efficiency—the president's secretary

Windy Burg—Athletic Director and football coach

Choir director—a married man with a single-minded dedication to music

Dean of Students—a young replacement for a long-term administrator whose motto had been, "if we didn't see it, it didn't happen."

Ms. Gates—the librarian, old as the hills, with books to match

Miss Fox—professor emerita of Spanish, house-bound by age, eager to have visitors

Luci May Mankiller—president of Arcadia College, Briarpatch's main rival

Bambi Prudence Purdy—former Vice President for Financial Affairs

Jones (JJ) and Smith (Smitty)—students too busy to study, half-heartedly scheming their way toward graduation

Ellie (L.E.)—transfer student from Arcadia; bright but bored

Unnamed assistant dean—still to be hired

College motto: *Hic etiam jam sumus*

Prologue

"Stanley," the historian said, peering inside the dean's office. His hold on the door handle was soft, a softness bespeaking the quiet way he had slowly and silently opened the door. There had been no secretary to announce him—financial austerity still precluded such a luxury—and he had not knocked. He could perhaps have stopped across the hall, where Miss Efficiency handled telephone calls for both the president and academic dean, but he had sensed that both lines were busy. And knocks were so rude.

"Dean Wooda, if you please," the young man responded, putting down the telephone with a sigh, "it's more professional and less likely to lead to slips in public that, well, are unprofessional." Actually, he was unhappy at the assumption that he could be addressed like a student. Just because he was only slightly older than the average senior. Hardly older, yes, but much better traveled, and he *had* been named academic dean. He knew that his visitor, who want to be academic dean himself, rarely missed an opportunity to call attention to his inexperience; hence, "Stanley" came over not as an attempt at friendship—the visitor had no friends—but as a, what, put down? But did the visitor really have the brains or personality to attempt a put-down? As Stanley Wooda thought about it—with lightning quickness, as always—he decided that he was really more miffed at his rail-thin visitor having almost slipped into his office unnoticed—and wondering if he should have been nicknamed the Creep for that habit rather than for his cold, wet handshake. Recalling that the historian acquired interesting information that way, he tried to remember exactly what he had been saying to President Flo Boater and whether it made any difference. Right at the moment he was more concerned with a slight rumbling in his stomach. This interview was not going to help. And the restroom was downstairs, on the first floor. No elevator.

1

"Dean Wooda," the historian said, his lips twisted half-way between a smile and a smirk, "I have a problem." He took a seat without being invited, then added, "I assume you have time for serious problems."

The dean almost sighed, but only said, "Of course, I can take time. What is it?"

"Well, it's like this. You know that we have an honors system."

Stanley Wooda thought before answering, "Tell me more." In truth, he really didn't know there was an honors system. His student days at Briarpatch had been few in number—as a freshman he was off to an off-campus program before he was on campus; when he returned as a senior, who would have bothered to tell him about it?

"Our students are not supposed to cheat. They monitor each other…" At this he could not help sneering, "non-punitively."

The dean's eyebrows raised, "Oh?" Apparently this was not a program the historian was fond of.

"That means that we don't have to proctor tests or check for plagiarism."

The dean's eyebrows narrowed, "Donahue does."

"Well, what can you expect? He doesn't buy into anything we do around here."

The dean, though wondering when the historian bought into everything either, nodded in agreement, "You're right on that. But back to the point. You have caught students cheating?"

"Yes, Smith and Jones."

"Smith and Jones? Are they in your class?" The dean found that hard to believe. "I thought they were in the honors program, where they don't have to take tests." There was more of a hint of sarcasm in his voice than he intended, but he shrugged mentally to himself—no matter what he said, or how he said it, the historian would improve upon it in the retelling.

"It's still an *unofficial* honors program," the historian reminded him. "And you are right, Max Stout doesn't believe in exams; and, yes, they are sort of in my class. That is, they signed up but they don't attend."

"They signed up for your class?" Stanley Wooda was well aware how few students passed history classes, and how even fewer bothered to attend. What was so unusual here?

The historian sighed, rolled his eyes heavenward, and explained, "Yes, they can only take *one* honors class, so they have to take other classes, too."

It was the dean's turn to roll his eyes, but when his gaze returned to horizontal, all he asked was, "They cheat on papers?"

"No, I don't think so. In my classes only students who want an A or a B have to turn in papers. As long as they can pass the exams, they get a C. Some get a C+, but not Smith and Jones."

"So, they are satisfied with a C."

"Yes." After a moment's pause, he added, "though I have reason to suspect that they will turn in their papers late and want full credit."

"Is that the problem? Easily solved. Refuse to accept them."

The historian sighed, "I'm not sure I can. No one turns in papers on time."

It was again the dean's turn to sigh, after which he asked, "So, you've caught them cheating? On papers? That's easily proved."

"Not on papers," the historian responded, "but on exams." After a pause, he added, "At least I think so."

The dean furrowed his brows, "You've given an exam already? This is the first week of classes. Nobody gives an exam in January."

"I'm speaking about last semester, but they're enrolled again."

The dean suppressed a grin—any student taking a second class from him must have had difficulty finding another 10 AM class. "And you suspect they cheated?"

"I'm sure they've cheated."

"You've caught them?" The dean smiled—for months he had wanted an excuse to throw Smith and Jones out of school.

"Ah, not exactly *caught*, but *suspect*."

The dean's smile vanished, "Oh, that's harder. What are they doing?"

"It's like this—I give take-home exams."

"Oh, and nobody is supposed to look in the text."

"Actually, I don't mind if they look in the text. That way I at least get them to read it."

"How do they cheat then?"

"I have the students correct the exam in the next class. That way they learn what they got wrong."

"Fill in the blank? Multiple choice?"

"No, mostly short identification, some dates, map locations."

The dean thought a moment, principally about how he would have taken advantage of that. If he had known about it, he would probably have signed up for the historian's class… and not bothered to attend, either. He asked, "So they *do* attend exams?"

"Yes, I give seven or eight exams in each class."

"Exams?" He mentally calculated that a semester had forty-five class days. This would mean an exam every two weeks. Surely he meant quizzes.

"Yes, fifty minutes."

The dean looked upward for help again, wondering if this was the Creep's way of avoiding preparing lectures or trying to get a discussion going. He asked, "So they do what, write out the essays there?"

"Oh, no essays. Just what I said before, with some fill in the blank questions."

The dean hesitated, "Fill in the blank? And they fill them in right in front of you?" For fifty minutes? And didn't he just say that he didn't give that kind of question? Oh, well, he said to himself, maybe not every quiz… exam… was the same. Don't get distracted, he said to himself, or he'll be here all morning.

"Oh, it's not that blatant. The next class period I have them swap exams with the person next to them, then they grade each other's exam. Then I collect them and record the scores."

The dean smiled, "That must save you a lot of time."

"Oh, yes. I'd recommend it for everyone."

"No essays?" he repeated.

"Oh, no. No student knows how to grade an essay exam properly."

The dean refrained from rolling his eyes. Instead, he leveled his gaze on the historian, "How do they get away with it?" Observing some questioning in the Creep's usually stony visage, he explained, "The cheating."

The historian slumped in his chair and sighed, "Well, it's a big class. On that day, it is. And Smith and Jones sit way in the back."

"And their answers are always exactly what you read out?"

"A handout, to be precise. I read it out loud, slowly. I'm sure they copy from it then."

"You can't see them copy it?"

"I told you—I'm reading the handout aloud, so that everyone… well, you know, some students would just glance at it, then throw it in the trash later. It's better pedagogy, to go over the exams carefully."

The dean sighed. It was so true. "So they get exactly the same answers, exactly what you wrote out? You should be able to nail them for that!"

"I should, but they are not very good at copying. And Smith always gets a better score than Jones." After a pause, he added, "Smith is dumb as a post."

The dean's eyes narrowed, "I thought both were."

"No, Jones has imagination."

The dean thought a moment, remembering that the Creep was pretty good at reading personalities. After wondering what he thought about him—a young upstart inexplicably promoted to be academic dean—he shook his head to turn back to business, then asked, "Jones grades Smith's exam…?"

"Yes."

"Then you should be able to tell by the handwriting."

"I suppose, but neither one's is legible, and it's only a few words. Nothing long enough to give them away." He paused to take a breath, "Worse, it looks like they've mastered a common script. Not what they usually write, I guess or, maybe, hope, but a special *confound the professor* language. I can't even tell if they misspell a word."

"You can't read it at all?"

"Almost not. Only the numbers, and I add them up again myself." He paused for a moment before adding, "The total is usually wrong, but always slightly lower than what it should be. I can hardly complain that they are cheating there."

The dean thought for a moment, wondering if the boys were really so clever. That was smarter than he gave them credit for. "I don't know what I can do. At least you get them to attend class when you hand out the exams, then again to grade them." He could not resist a smile.

"Only to grade them. They make photocopies of another student's blank exam."

"Blank?"

"The exam has spaces for writing in the answers."

The dean leaned toward him, "Maybe you should number the exams."

The historian sat up straighter, "That's a good idea."

Then, before his guest could decide whether or not his smirk was insulting, Stanley Wooda stood up and escorted him to the door, "That's why we have deans. Sometimes we can help with difficult problems." As he sat back down he sighed, "At least that is one grade they didn't have to buy."

And there was the crux of the matter. The story of grades for sale, whether myth or moth, was eating holes in the college's reputation. The dean was still shaking his head when the next visitor appeared—once again without an appointment. It was Maximilian Stout, chair of the English department.

Stanley Wooda sighed. The Creep was an annoyance, but Stout was a force of nature—nothing could discourage him. Moreover, he, too wanted to be dean. Well, maybe not, but he always wanted to tell Stanley Wooda what had to be done. Well, here he was again, "Hello, Max, good to see you." Yes, he thought with a smile, using the first name might just put him in his place... as much as that was possible with Max Stout.

When Stout reached over to his desk, picked up the calendar and turned December 1996 to January 1997, the dean knew that his ploy had failed.

Stout's request was a simple one. The experiment with having Donahue on Stout's hiring committee for the new assistant dean had worked out so well—from Stout's viewpoint—that he wanted the dean to appoint Donahue to the search for a replacement in English. "First of all, he doesn't see any point in making waves when he knows he will be outvoted 3-1, and since 'Miss Curves' has taken another job...."

The dean interrupted, "Yes, I'll... that is, *we'll* miss her!" That was an awkward point—several faculty members had left in December. Staffing this semester's courses was a problem. Middleville was not a community rich in potential part-time instructors. Moreover, women liked Stanley, especially women who understood that Flo Boater had warned him against romantic entanglement—danger enhanced romance, and the lure of power over the powerful was potent, too. (A student—a "mere woman," but just realizing her attractiveness— enticing a professor into risking his career combined both the sense of danger and empowerment; while a faculty wife or staff member expected some kind of repayment.) He knew that the former Dean Wooda had gotten himself into trouble that way. Well, perhaps not romantic entanglements, but something more fundamental and physical. And with his boss, too—Flora Boater—that was one of those things that everyone knows and no one dares mention. Hence, her alertness to any slip on his part. And her encouraging beautiful female instructors to move to places with a better selection of potential male partners. "Yes, we'll miss her."

Stout broke into his daydream, "What about my search committee?" It wasn't quite a question.

The dean stared at a corner of the ceiling with his eyes half-closed, "I had rather hoped that Donahue might fall for her, then follow her away."

Though slightly annoyed, Stout continued, "I'll appoint other committee members, people Donahue never agrees with. That will annoy him so much that he might even resign."

The dean knew better, "No, not as long as Mary is here."

Stout was annoyed again. He had from time to time imagined himself as making a conquest of her. Nothing permanent—he could not imagine putting up with any woman for more than a few hours—but he had disliked being turned down. Rather rudely, too. Just because… well, some women liked being talked to that way. His thought was interrupted by the dean, who though still looking into space, said, "I doubt that any one insult will do it, but the Chinese water torture might work on in the end." No point in trying to get rid of Mary, they both thought. They'd tried that and failed… failed embarrassingly.

"The water torture," the dean continued, "and some people think that torture doesn't work."

"Yes," Stout agreed, with an impatient toss of his head, knowing that the dean was referring to him, or maybe Mary. It was one of those many beliefs he had in common with her. Something to work on, maybe, he thought, but what he said was. "Drop by drop is probably all we can do right now. We can have him do all the telephoning again, checking on credentials, that sort of thing, wear him down so that he won't have time to make trouble."

"Trouble?"

"Well," Stout said after a moment's hesitation, "you know that we are proposing a major restricting of the trustees' role in the management of the institution."

It was Dean Wooda's turn to hesitate, "No. Tell me more."

"As you know, the trustees are almost all businessmen, who have their own agendas for using higher education to prepare robots for their future workforces, graduates who don't know how to think, at least not think correctly, but only have technical skills that they could get at a junior college."

"Not at Arcadia College, not any more. Lucy May Mankiller is transforming that campus into a new Antioch!"

"Yes," Stout admitted. "She is trying, but she told me the other day that she was finding it harder than she expected. Too many people think they are still at a junior college. Faculty, too. And state education money... hopeless. She's discouraged."

"You talked to her the other day?" He almost asked if Stout was applying for the position of dean that was being advertised, then he did ask.

"No, not really. Just sizing up the lay of the land. But my commitment is to Briarpatch." He paused before adding, "If I can bring it into the twentieth century."

"Oh," the dean thought, "you aren't quite what she had in mind. Too forceful, perhaps." But what he said was, "How do we bring our own institution into, what did you say? The twentieth century is almost over."

"Technically, we are at the end of the century, but the trustees' efforts to push their theocratic, capitalist crap on us is more appropriate to a hundred years ago."

"What are they pushing? I guess I missed it."

"You missed it?"

"At the last board meeting, they agreed with everything that Flo and I were doing."

"I heard that, but that's just for public consumption."

"Max, I tell you, all they're interested in right now is the budget."

"Stan, that's what I mean—they have no interest in the curriculum, a curriculum we need to revise to meet the needs of our times."

"OK, Max, lay it out for me."

Stout sighed, then explained, "First of all we need faculty representation on the board."

"That's a non-starter. They won't go for it."

"Stan, you're making my case for me. They have a monopoly of power and won't let it go. That's why we have to seize it, to expropriate it."

"OK, but let's move on. What's point two?"

"We have to see that every professor and instructor, and the staff, too, understands how important the progressive agenda is—world peace, universal health care, more control of the right wing media, less interference in private drug use and immigration, and more support for higher education."

The dean jotted down some notes. "Might be useful someday," he thought, "in a speech, to the right audience, of course." But what he said was, "This *would* annoy Donahue."

"Absolutely, and that's why we have to guarantee freedom of speech by finding ways to shut him up."

Stanley Wooda, now alone again, wondered what to do about the former detective. There was more to it than shutting him up. When Donahue's insights were combined with Chief Biggs's common sense, that was enough to make Stanley Wooda sweat. His ambitions for a future career in Washington... those were hanging on, what? On no corpse showing up? A year ago he'd have laughed at the idea, but since then there had been nothing but one newspaper headline after another. There was nothing he could do about the chief—his position was secure. But Donahue.... They'd tried to get him off campus, tried to get him to quit, nothing had worked. Maybe they could arrange for him to apply to a better college? But how? He wouldn't leave Mary as long as there was some hope.... Maybe arrange for a lover? Someone to sweep her off her feet. No, not practical. He might have a chance himself, women used to fall for him pretty quickly, but not her, not now. Too much history; she knew him too well. Also, he was younger, too much younger, and she was a very practical woman. Politically, not very practical, but in her personal life, she was practically a nun. Too bad she wasn't Catholic. That might be an out—getting her into a convent. But, hell, not even Catholics went into convents now.

The dean stood up to pace his office floor. Maybe Donahue had nothing against him personally. Could he just ignore him? Nah, he thought, Donahue was a threat to Flo Boater, whom he suspected of involvement in two murders, first her lover, then her husband. And without Flo Boater's help, Stanley would still be stuck in a classroom, trying to finish his BA degree. Afterward who would give a Briarpatch graduate a chance in the political world? His future seemed to depend on doing something about Donahue.

As it happened, at that very moment Donahue had just gone into the coffee house, the Japanese-style structure so ill-suited to local winters. When he saw Mary, his heart sank—she was apparently depressed. Unless she was just cold. No. Depressed. By the time he reached that decision, however, he couldn't turn around and leave—she had probably seen him. Making the best of it, he walked over and said, "Hi, Mary, nice to run into you."

"Oh, hi, DO," she responded without enthusiasm. She had barely looked up.

"What's up?" he asked, "or, rather, what's down?" He hadn't seen her since mid-December. Maybe he could make the new semester go better. Jolly her up at bit. That would be a good start, maybe get back to the warm relationship they had enjoyed before—before he suggested they get married. She gave a wan smile at his effort at humor, then replied, "It's Irene…"

"Your new colleague. She's in English, right?"

"Yes. We're short of offices, and since Flo didn't replace the two instructors in Spanish who left, there was a free desk in my office."

"Yeah, I don't understand that, but there's a lot here I don't understand."

"You're not alone, but that's not the problem."

"What is?"

"Irene just got her first exam back. She spent what must have been ten minutes staring at one blank page. I asked her what the problem was. It seems that she was trying to figure out what the student was telling her."

"Can't be that hard, can it? Either she didn't teach the material very well or the student didn't study."

Mary frowned, "You make it sound so easy."

"Well, which was it?"

"She's not sure. She distributed a handout. She's fairly sure the student was there that day."

"She isn't sure? This is only the third day of classes."

"She wanted to get an early feed-back on how well students study."

"She doesn't take roll?"

Sharper than she wanted to, Mary said, "One isn't coercive nowadays."

He nodded, indicating that he understood, but he was aware that she saw through the subterfuge. He thought for a moment, then asked, "Does she ever have students turn in their notes?"

"Turn in their notes?"

"Sure, to see what they are putting down. Don't you... no, of course not, Introductory Spanish isn't that kind of subject. But in Sociology, maybe in English, too, it helps to make the students aware that they are supposed to write down the main points. At least the main points."

"The main points?" she asked. "You mean what you write on the board?"

"Do they?" he asked, though he wanted to say, "More than that, much more."

"Well, I guess I don't know. Anyway, doesn't that stifle the students' creativity?"

"Creativity? In note taking?"

"Why not note taking?"

"Why test then? If creativity is the criterion, isn't anything they write appropriate?"

She sighed, "It took you long enough to figure it out—the student left the page blank."

The rest of the conversation didn't go much better. At length Donahue offered to buy her a cup of coffee. When she declined, he realized that it was time to leave: male/female miscommunication—men saw a problem as something to solve, women saw it as a manifestation of a deeper trouble that had to be talked about. Mary's reaction was just like that of the women in his class last semester. When he had proposed the theory, the men agreed, the women did not.

What was going on, he asked himself as he left. Was it true that feminism killed romance? He saw no reason why it did, unless no thinking person could also have emotions. Was marriage really slavery? Mary Wollstonecraft thought so, but she was a slave to passion, too—twice attempted suicide over a man. Ancient Greeks believed that women were prone to fits of mad passion (and indeed, he thought, that was when they went prone most quickly). Phaedra and Medea, and the worshippers of Bacchus (what was his name in Greek? Oh, Dionysius, god of wine and insanity). So they kept the women almost locked up and away from alcohol. Such a marriage, yeah, that was almost slavery. Certainly, they didn't want women educated. But that's not true any more. There was a day when American women saw marriage as a type of freedom. Of course, maybe the ring was just the symbol of adulthood, the entry into a sisterhood. Maybe there's an article in that? On the other extreme is the idea that the more free from men a woman is, the more authentic feminist she is. Well, more lesbians might mean fewer children, which would resolve one world problem; and schoolteachers who complain about empty classrooms can't be authentically feminists, anyway. He had to smile at that argument—his own classes might be empty, too.

And what did all this have to do with Mary? She was bright, funny, passionate about whatever she found important at the moment, but basically just nice to be around. Most of the time. If only she weren't in that "herd of independent minds," all trying to be exactly alike, each wanting to be more progressive than the next. Only she isn't. She doesn't wear black, with black eye shadow, and she blushes at some of the exaggerations—like "all men are out to subject all women, to kill them if necessary" or "sex is really rape." But she'll argue that there are underlying truths there, then we'll quarrel again. Either I'm "trying to force my ideas on her," or if I give in, it's a "passive-aggressive ploy."

Aloud, but quietly, he said to himself, "Maybe I should have gone to the convention, to see what jobs are out there." After a moment he responded, in a mental dialogue, "Maybe I *am* trying to make her into a conventional wife. Ancient Greek style? I don't think so—Plato wanted to educate women to be the equal of men, to share in governing his Republic. DeTocqueville said that American women were the freest in the world, but they gave it all up voluntarily to be wives and mothers. It was an admirable thing, the most admirable thing in America." He smiled at the thought of a Frenchman saying that the best thing in America were the women. "How very French, but DeTocqueville was hardly a typical Frenchman. Maybe that's what Mary's afraid of. Of giving up all the freedom she's worked so hard to get. Freedom through education? Does she see tenure as the only guarantee of that freedom? But if that's the problem, why doesn't she just do what is necessary to get it? Drop everything else, even me—or is that what she is doing?"

Mary would have said, "Typical male problem-solving."

Donahue wondered if Miss Fox's advice had been best: "Move on, get on with life! Women are too much alike to think that any one of them is *that* special." When he asked her why she had never married, she had smiled, "I was asked, but I was waiting for somebody special." She had added, "Don't you make that mistake." Then she went on, "But *unlike* does not mean *all the same*. Don't just marry the first gal who throws herself at you."

It was his turn to smile—he'd been there and successfully escaped. Anyway, nobody was throwing herself at him right now. When that happened again, it would be just another problem to solve. Meanwhile, Miss Fox was right—he needed to make a decision.

In the Administration Building President Flo Boater was trying to make a decision, too. Her gala inauguration would be a fine opportunity to attract media attention, potential donors, and, well, show off the college. But when to do it? Right after Commencement, when the weather is good. Or at the start of the fall semester, when students and parents would be around? Fingering a calendar, she thought she saw two appropriate dates, when she noticed that she had chewed off a nail.

Chapter One

Three weeks into the semester Donahue looked around the campus and sighed. Another summer and autumn had passed into early winter. 1996 was now a memory, having fled before his eyes, not even leaving the occasional dust devil as proof of its swift passage. All summer rain would have been welcome, but now there was rather more than convenient; Christmas went without mistletoe and New Year's without a date. That's the way it was. Mary C, having faced the likelihood of leaving for Latin America again without visiting her mother, had decided that, since that unwelcome opportunity for research in the jungles and mountains was removed—a sword of Damocles, she had called it, "without the pleasure of governing under its shadow"—just such a visit was now called for. Donahue had not been invited to accompany her. Ah, well, better to think of the lost potential of the summer of 1996 than the reality of January, 1997. He'd hardly seen her since classes started.

The first weeks of the fall semester had dragged, with his mind divided between classes and his unsuccessful effort at courtship. There had been intense heat in August, but the weather soon changed suddenly, being far cooler and wetter than customary, after which normal temperatures returned. He hardly had time to notice these changes, much less enjoy them after the disappearance of Miss Bambi Prudence Purdy, the college financial officer, claimed his attention. When Miss Purdy reappeared, having been on a business trip to investigate financial irregularities, it came out that President Flo Boater had thrown away the note informing her of the trip. Flo Boater never read notes from staff, faculty or students; this was a lesson that she seemed slow to learn, preferring a clean desk over information. Miss Purdy had left to avoid a subsequent embarrassment, having been discovered in the wee hours of the night, perhaps clothed and perhaps not, in the clutches of Professor Stout, or vice-versa.

In those weeks Mary C had worried about being exiled to South America, the only way that Flo Boater would promise her tenure—a status that guaranteed her life-long employment unless she did something very out of character, like sticking up a bank or selling grades. The anxiety now passed, only to be replaced by the need to write up her past research on Andean cultures into a scholarly publication—and Mary was suffering from a writer's block of mountainous proportions.

"God, I can't do this! She complained to Donahue.

"Sure you can. You just need to put something on paper."

"What, for example?" she replied, a bit of hostility in his voice. Writing came so easy to him. It wasn't fair.

"Well, maybe your main idea."

"The introduction or the conclusion?"

"Either one."

She almost cried, "I don't have a main idea."

He paused for a moment before making his next suggestion, "Then perhaps an anecdote. Something you saw in the village. Something interesting."

"And where would I use it?"

"Oh, it'll come. If not, you haven't lost much. But it'll get the manuscript started."

She hardly paused before replying, "Maybe. After I get my exams graded."

He sighed. There was always something else to do first.

He had things to do himself. There was some hope of getting the long-promised museum of Latin American Culture, though that would have to await some major gifts for renovating the Music building after constructing a suitable place for concerts. Donahue was the likely curator, though he disclaimed having the background or interest for such a project. His friends, nevertheless, pushed him to push the project—it would become a selling point for Briarpatch College in the competition for the best students throughout the region. Like an Honors program, the Admissions director said, students liked having something special around, as long as they didn't have to participate in it.

Donahue smiled as he thought of her last report to the faculty, in early December, with her obvious wooing of Max Stout, praising his unofficial Honors program, which was immediately followed by Stout's effort to get scholarships for it. At this point, their paths diverged. After a glance at Flo Boater, whose almost imperceptible shake of her head indicated "no way," the director pointed out—delicately—that most Briarpatch students weren't Honors program material. Donahue had chosen not to become involved in this discussion, but had he done so, he would have asked where most students were, except at those lucky colleges with huge endowments—in short, not at Briarpatch. When the director went on to note "how desirable it would be to have a really good Honors program someday," she managed to offend both Flo Boater and Max Stout—the former disliked any suggestion that Briarpatch was not first rate in every way (unless she herself said it) and the latter thought he already had a fine start on turning the institution around.

Donahue whispered to Mary, seated on his right, "Someday I've going to have to have a long talk with our director, to see what she thinks she is selling." He smiled when Mary replied that the director was doing exactly what she thought Flo Boater wanted, but that figuring out Flo Boater was probably harder than keeping up with the changing tastes of high school seniors.

Anyone trying to follow campus politics needed a lot of patience—stoic patience. But Donahue was used to it. That is, anyone courting Mary needed *a lot* of patience. And as for his academic future, his first publications, insignificant as they were, suggested that he would not have to stay in Briarpatch forever. "Yet," he thought, "Briarpatch is where Mary is. Also where a murder occurs almost every semester." An exaggeration. While he had been on campus three semesters, there had been only two bodies total—Flo Boater's husband and her lover, that is, the president and academic dean, who expired in reverse order, both under circumstances that suggested the dean might have been responsible. Or, as some speculated, if Flo Boater was the *éminence gris*, the hand behind the dagger—to mix a metaphor—she had never employed such direct methods. She forcefully denied any involvement, of any kind, in those "accidental deaths," first because the trustees would have turned out any administrator they believed guilty of murder, and second, because she looked better in black than grey. Those who heard this declaration were struck by what they thought might be the unexpected appearance of a sense of humor, but were soon relieved by learning that it was merely a lack of familiarity with the French term.

There might be three bodies soon, Donahue had thought just before classes had started in January, when Stanley Wooda decreed that there would be no one-person departments, and that the senior professor of the combined departments would become his chair. He had shared his concern with Lill, who not long before had briefly been assigned an acting-chair who knew nothing of Theater.

She took a deep breath, "Oh, my! I hope it isn't the Creep."

"Oh, yes," Donahue replied. "He told me himself."

With a wry smile Lill suggested that Donahue's background in homicide might be useful, "You, better than the rest of us, should understand the criminal mind."

Donahue had laughed, but he was not alone in contemplating homicide, perhaps even double homicide—why leave off with the dean, if the president would still be able to harass Mary? But as he reflected on the past summer's heat, he decided that if he could survive that, he could survive this, too. It was no accident that the summer heat came to mind when criminal mentality was mentioned. The heat always seemed to be at its worst just as classes started in August, and Briarpatch College had no air conditioning except in the administrative offices and the cafeteria. And Donahue had just asked his new chair for morning classes for the coming academic year, was told that students wanted Sociology classes in the middle of the afternoon, so that is when he would be teaching the next academic year—at 1, 2 and 3 PM—except for two night classes; he was certain this was harassment, but just as certainly somebody had to teach at those hours and he was the youngest member of the newly formed Social Sciences division; in fact, he was the only Sociologist/Anthropologist, and the heavy teaching load was justified by the college's difficult financial situation. Rumors of an increase in the president's and dean's salaries were neither confirmed nor denied by official announcements.

Donahue had not recovered from learning of his future teaching schedule before an additional job was thrust upon him—to make preparations for converting the Music Building into an Anthropological Museum. He had to do that without a budget, a time-line, and without the Music faculty leaving the building. The musicians, mostly local people working part-time as instrumental instructors, having discovered that the mold and asbestos problem was non-existent, had moved back in before they bothered to inform the dean of their intentions; now they resisted every effort to remove them. The dean, in his wise understanding of such people, made it known that he would not attempt it himself nor ask anyone else to do it—that task he left to Donahue.

Such was the miniature universe of Briarpatch College, an educational institution much like many others—except for its exceptional lack of money, its not having anything approaching a favorable geographical location and or friends in the regional media. Only its football team gave promise of extraordinary achievements, but even there most observers expected a return to its losing tradition.

Briarpatch may have been forgotten by much of the world, certainly by the state department of highways, but it was not lacking in interesting people and disturbing events. Perhaps a certain isolation is necessary to truly cultivate those personality traits which we called 'character,' much as English country life provided authors more enjoyable eccentrics for literature and mystery novels than the dirty slums of Sherlock Holmes's London. Briarpatch lay more or less in the center of Middleville, which was surrounded by land less densely inhabited than any English countryside since *Wuthering Heights*. More trees, of course. It is hard to beat a moor for lacking trees. But fewer sheep. It barely had a golf course—probably the best use ever devised for worthless pastures. For greater sophistication, enthusiasts had to go to Arcadia, one county over, a small town slightly larger than Middleville, but still a rural community at heart; or to Zenith, the largest city in the region, a long drive away at the legal speed limit, a restriction that few drivers honored, and the younger they were, the less they honored it. It might take less time to get to Zenith next fall, since the legislature had recently promised to make it easier for rural customers to get to Zenith businesses.

Donahue had occasionally talked with Miss Fox about why Briarpatch had more characters than he knew in graduate school, "It is really Briarpatch, or just my being more aware?"

"Probably the latter," she had replied, a twinkle in her eyes. "You get to know people better here."

"I don't know. Some people I know, but only very superficially. The cliques are very strong here. You meet people on a professional level—except some of the scientists. They don't have much to say to a sociologist."

"You're probably not asking the right questions. The Creep manages to learn everything about everyone's personal life." It was not a particularly happy observation. Both knew that the Creep used every opportunity to bring up Lill's relationship with Lily.

"I guess so. But he's also an eavesdropper and a snitch."

"But he's a character. You've got to admit he *is* a character."

Another character, though very different, was Ms. Hogg. She was so secretive that almost nobody knew anything about her personal life except that she had a mother no one had ever met. For many years she had worked part-time for History and part-time for Education, with the history classes in the evening so she could travel during the day to area schools, supervising student teachers. As a result, opportunities to drink coffee with other instructors—the most important social activity at Briarpatch—were limited. She was a large woman—small colleges tended to have more large women and skinny men than universities—and she was shy. Perhaps there was a connection there that hurt such individuals' chances in interviews at more prestigious schools.

That was a matter that Donahue had been thinking about looking into. It might be a great research paper. However, could he write it in the incomprehensible post-modern style now expected by the standard journals in his fields? "Ah," he thought, "it can't be harder to learn than Spanish. And I'm making progress there." He would be making more progress, he knew, if he could spend more time with Mary. And if she would help him more.

Was Ms. Hogg really so large? Not really. Through great efforts at dieting and more exercise, she had reduced her weight significantly in recent years. But slow changes are hard to notice, and her rare outburst against "Sizeism" reinforced old memories and the successful camouflage of her baggy clothes to make people think of her as outsized. Her name did not help, though it had an honorable ancestry—an indirect but still provable connection to Governor Hogg of Texas, one of the greatest men to preside over the fortunes of the Lone Star State, and the possessor of one of the largest chairs in the Union

As a result, Ms. Hogg did not seem like a person destined for success, or even promotion. It came as a surprise to everyone, therefore, that in the middle of the fall semester President Boater had asked her to become the registrar; it was an even bigger surprise that she accepted— classes had already started, and she had always said that students came first, meaning students in classrooms, not students in dorms or bars, where they actually spent most of their time, and certainly not students as numbers in a registrar's bureaucracy. In this she was a typical faculty member—administrative work was a necessary evil, or perhaps not quite as necessary as evil. As soon as the semester's grades were processed, she failed to appear for work. Her disappearance came so suddenly, or perhaps so slowly, that almost nobody noticed; it was as if she had blown away with the last autumn leaves. She reappeared the week before classes started, but once the students had made the inevitable changes in their schedules, she was gone again. No one noticed at first. Who was there to notice? And who could have imagined her being blown away, this time with the snow flakes? A woman without friends, there was no one to worry when she did not call or come by. Besides, the Purdy crisis had absorbed everyone's attention. The paperwork was still carried out by her staff, who had been conditioned by her predecessor to expect long and unannounced absences, and she had left a note, "Carry on as before until I get back." She had not been involved in campus politics, so despite her reputation for rigorous honesty—a trait she owed principally to giving an occasional B to student teachers instead of the obligatory A that was necessary for them to have any chance on the job market—she had never spoken for or against any of the strong personalities who sought to dominate the campus political scene—so nobody inquired about her opinion on the latest crisis. There was always a latest crisis, just as there was always a clash of personalities over the ways to deal with it.

The most serious of these clashes was between Flo Boater, now president of the college for several months, and Lill, who didn't seem to have a last name that anyone can remember. That is, there are some characters so powerful that they only need one name. Two would diminish rather than augment. Lill was one such personality. Only a year earlier she had been acting president. There was no issue, however large or trivial, that now escaped becoming entangled in their feud. Neither exhibited anything sheep-like in her nature, other than a desire to be the ewe who lead the rest of the flock over the fence.

Not long ago Donahue, at one of the "seminars" that Lill hosted at the coffeehouse, two tables pulled together for faculty and students who wanted to talk, had asked her if she wanted to be president again. The question caught her by surprise. She was still searching for the proper words to indicate that she really only wanted to get Flo Boater out, but without providing anything quotable that the president could use against her, when Lily said, "Damn straight."

"Why?" he asked.

"The illusion of power," she replied. Looking around, she saw that not even Lill understood what she meant. So she explained, "In our profession, you see a lot of semi-competent deans and presidents. There are jokes about those who can, do, and so forth, suggesting that deans and presidents were just failures as professors. That isn't true. Sure, some went into administration from the start, but most of those who started in the faculty were pretty good. Some very good." She paused to see if anyone could see where she was going. No one could, though they hoped she had a point coming. Lily was an excellent teacher and had been an adequate dean, but sometimes she allowed her odd sense of humor to take her far afield. So she continued, "When they see the incompetence of their deans and presidents...." At this point she stopped to make sure that her audience was hooked—Lily was very good at this—and then proceeded with a sly grin, "They thought—like we all think—that surely they couldn't be any worse themself!" When her hearers smiled, recognizing themselves in this picture, she finished, "They thought they might even do some good."

"Where does the illusion of power come in?" someone asked.

The voice came from behind Lily, from a student who had pulled up a chair from the next table, and Lily, unable to turn around easily to look at her, could not identify the voice other than belonging to a female. She could see that the students knew who it was and didn't show any signs of surprise, so she addressed them, saying, "Human beings—among whom I count faculty members—often share semi-humorous misperceptions of reality," she started, with a smile. "They may believe that if they held 'power,' they could make changes. It was too much work to become a politician, and getting rich took too much time, but anybody could become a dean and then maybe even a president. Surely, *they* could make a difference." Lily's sly smile baffled her listeners, partly because they were not used to subtle humor from her, and partly because they agreed with the reasoning—surely a faculty member moving into administration *would* make a difference."

"Doesn't it sometimes?" the 'someone' asked. "Ms. Hogg is making a lot of changes in the registrar's office. She came out of the Education Department."

This time Lily knew recognized that the voice belonged to Ellie, who had transferred to Briarpatch from Arcadia because that campus lacked intellectual spark and student interest in changing the world—while Briarpatch at least had its twice-a-year protest demonstrations. Her transfer had come as a bit of a surprise, since Arcadia administration—President Mankiller—with the encouragement of outspoken faculty members, was trying to make Arcadia another Antioch (though Evergreen, a state college, was a better comparison), but the student body was so local and so lower Middle Class (or even Poor) that there was little interest in Great Ideas. Not that Briarpatch was that much committed to the "life of the mind," but no place nearby was that much better, either. Ellie had said dismissively, "There is nothing here to attract a thinker," though Lily suspected that a certain boy, recently only an undergraduate named Stanley, but now Dean Wooda, had something to do with it. Lill half rose out of her chair to see Ellie better before saying, "That's in office procedures, isn't it? Not policy. Lily means changes in the way we all think and act."

"Isn't that the point of education? At least, the point of Education as a major," Ellie challenged her. "In order to change the way students think, you have to pay attention to structure. If your structure is sound—if you can repeat the words other people write out for you, then trick your students into memorizing them—it doesn't matter much whether you know your subject or not."

Lill smiled, wondering if Ellie had become an Education major, "There is something to the principle that you will learn a subject best as you teach it. But I doubt that Ms. Hogg would appreciate your summarization of her department's methods." She smiled to herself involuntarily when she thought that Ellie was the perfect example of a person who liked to talk without knowing anything about the subject. "They call them 'goals and objectives'."

"What's the difference? Goals, objectives, methods?"

Lill thought for a moment, "Good question. I've wondered about goals and objectives myself. Rhetoric, I imagine. Methods are clearer—those are the means employed to reach a goal."

"But I've read the goals and objectives, and if I understand them correctly, that's what they say—that if you understand how people learn, you can employ the right techniques to communicate knowledge and ideas. That runs against common sense—not everyone learns the same way. They make the teacher, the 'learning facilitator,' the center, not the student."

"You may be right," Lill conceded. "But my memory is that they simply rewrote the mandates from the State Board of Education. And judging from what I had to do to get state approval for the Theatre program, my impression was that the 'goals and objectives' were so complicated that nobody could honestly achieve all of them. That is one reason that I eventually became so cynical—surely *anybody* could do better than this, but *nobody* who gets on the state board is unable to make much difference." She thought to herself the conflicting recommendations about whether to spell the department *Theater* or *Theatre*, so she had used both. Nobody noticed.

"That's the reality," Lily added. "Also, there are financial constraints." Everyone nodded. Briarpatch was the poster-child of financially-strapped small liberal arts colleges. "But more important are the institutional restraints—committees, faculty resistance, traditions. The poor blokes…" No one knew why she suddenly became an Englishman (did English women ever use this term?), but no one was ever too surprised at anything Lily did. "They found that they were as helpless as those people they had once mocked. Now," she concluded, "they understood that their power was an illusion. Hence, 'the illusion of power'."

"How about Ms. Hogg?" Ellie asked.

"A very good point," Lill conceded. "If we start from the viewpoint that we can achieve nothing, why even make an effort? Obviously our lives and our actions make a difference. What I mean to say is that our goals should be realistic. Like Ms. Hogg, that she can bring order to an office noted for chaos. I think she can, and I support her wholeheartedly. That is different from, say, a belief that you have to change the entire college before you can put the records in order." At that she paused, because she wondered if she really believed that or not. Fortunately, she was spared trying to explain that at this moment, before she had thought it through.

Lily jumped in: "That explains a lot, including Lill's belief that she can do better than Flo Boater."

Everyone agreed with that observation. The students were astute in many judgments of people they knew—Ellie pointed out that Lill would never have murdered a lover and a husband, never have wasted money on redecorating the president's office, never have tried to get rid of her enemies (though, she thought, maybe she should have). Lily agreed, wondering how Ellie had managed to learn (and remember) all this, but she only reminded everyone that Flo Boater was now president, not Lill, and that was because Lill had been unwilling to do what was necessary to defend herself.

This brought protests as well, but Lily pointed out several ways that Lill and Flo were similar. Both were competent people, both possessed a Ph.D., both were ambitious—Lill only newly so, but she was being corrupted, too This charge brought a blush to Lill's face. Still, after a moment's thought, she grudgingly admitted to it, though she quickly added that she was not proud of it, and her ambitions were for the college more than for herself. Lily smiled, then went on—neither had children or wanted any. Neither could be long satisfied with hobbies—Flo was an excellent cook whose cookies had been famous until the unfortunate poisoning of the late Dean Wooda; Lill had her motorcycle, which she rode less and less nowadays.

Lily could have added that each had a 'sidekick,' a dependable associate who was almost always in her company. Flo's was Stanley Wooda, the youngest academic dean in America, Lill's was Lily, whose short term as academic dean remained only an amusing adventure;

Lily had often said that she would assume that office again only under the unlikely circumstance of the trustees begging her to do it and, most importantly, if that was the only way to keep that skunk, Stanley Wooda, from stinking the college up. Both sidekicks were intelligent, courageous, and occasionally more insightful than their leader. Occasionally, but not usually. Today was one of those occasions.

They each had their problems, too. Lily's was the persistent rumor that she shouldn't be allowed to use the "women's restroom," Stanley's was a persistent stomach upset that the Old Doc, the only physician in Middleville, said was "just stress."

The stress had led to Flo Boater's decision to hire an assistant dean. Not to help Stanley—though his frequent speaking engagements off campus ("the youngest academic dean in America" was a great advertisement, as was "the youngest Black dean in America," though he wasn't really Black) meant that he could not make committee meetings or appointments, and his paperwork was falling behind. The assistant dean was to read Flo Boater's correspondence, then decide which should be forwarded to her, which to her secretary, Miss Efficiency, and which to the various deans. Miss Efficiency could have done it all, but she lacked an advanced degree (as did Stanley Wooda), and Flo Boater wanted someone with a Ph.D. tacked to his name. She almost insisted on hiring a woman, but drew back when she remembered that if she did so, she couldn't complain about the number of men in the administration. Women needed more incentives to come to Briarpatch, she said, reminding everyone of the obstacles she had overcome to attain her position (and not mentioning the fact that her late husband, Floyd Boater, had named her academic dean only days before his own death). She was also not happy with the applications she saw—the women were clearly ambitious and outspoken. Her brief telephone interviews confirmed her initial impressions and also indicated that most of the applicants knew nothing about Briarpatch College. One of them might emulate that legendary former dean who walked around the campus one morning, then put his resignation on the president's desk. She needed someone more desperate.

The person she had hired was a former dean who had unwisely married a non-traditional student. Being divorced was forgivable—it was becoming almost a requirement for a successful administrator—but he should have married a professional with an advanced degree of her own. Worse, his former wife had become a cabbie. After using the free tuition for spouses program, she had divorced him rather than move to a smaller university town where he was to fill in only temporarily for an assistant dean on medical leave. His second wife at least had a BA, but not an advanced degree. Clearly, he had demonstrated poor judgment in both marriages. That had disqualified him for most deanships, but it had enhanced his chances with Flo Boater. Moreover, knowing that his job would end shortly, he was desperate. She could count on his being utterly under her thumb.

His name was also awkward—Cross Threshold. Cross was a family name. Threshold was, too, but rather unavoidable, being that of his father. Cross had endured decades of jokes about being almost ready to enter into something important or exciting, but could not get over the threshold; that was perhaps instrumental in his career choice—if his childhood friends had called him "Butch" or something else masculine, he might not have retreated into his books. But that was a different era, before "Butch" took on a different meaning; in *his* socio-economic ghetto, it suggested a tough guy. (If he had grown up in the Nineties, he would not have welcomed that nickname.) Had he been tougher, perhaps he would have been better as an administrator in his last job, but had he been tougher, he might have succeeded in the rough and tumble competition for teaching jobs. He would certainly not have met his second wife, Mabel, who had been employed herself in a large Student Services Empire before moving to aforementioned lesser-known university as an associate dean to an assistant dean—the title was more important to her then than the salary, though she quickly learned the advantages of a sizeable paycheck. There was an opening in the Briarpatch SSE, but Flo Boater had warned that she would soon take steps to discourage "nepotism" in college employment. Though disappointed at not even being interviewed, Mabel did not complain when the male "partner" of a new female instructor was given the position. She took a job at the local diner, a choice that was criticized as much as if she had become a cabbie. Middleville, however, had no need for a second cab driver. Moreover, the owner of the diner thought Mable was a great name for a waitress.

To everyone's surprise, Cross and Mabel seemed happy. His office was on the ground floor in the Student Services Empire, so climbing the stairs twenty times a day to confer with Flo Boater or Stanley Wooda did much for both his appetite and his waistline. Students tried to call him "Dean Cross," but the effort soon died—his job was too obscure for him to offend anyone, and those who met him socially were pleased to discover that they liked him. Even Flo Boater nodded agreement when anyone praised his efficiency and friendliness to her, though there was something in her eyes that indicated that something must be wrong.

The most unhappy pair on campus consisted of DO Donahue and Mary C. They had quarreled in the late fall. At least Mary had started an argument and Donahue had declined to do the traditional male thing and agree with her. Mary was concerned about her future.

Donahue had tried to persuade her that this was foolish, "You've got Flo Boater's written promise. Tenure's a shoo-in. In any case, worry just wears you out."

"You'd worry, too, if you thought you'd lose your job and didn't have something to fall back on." She meant that *he* could become a cop again, but that *her* only choice might be to marry Donahue. That vision, drilled into her at countless "feminism conferences," was, to turn a phrase, "a fate worse than death." Sex was okay, her colleagues told her, even good sometimes, but not marriage. Donahue thought marriage was okay, even good, and having already taken the leap from a steady job in the police force to the unpredictable world of Academe, he worried less about his economic future than did those who had never had to look for what he called "real work." That phrase, in fact, was the one which had set Mary off—she had burst out that she wasn't going to flip hamburgers. He avoided his usual mistake of reminding her that she had never flipped a hamburger in her life, either professionally or privately. Instead, he suggested that if she did take such a job, she would quickly be on the management fast track and be sent to run a chain of restaurants in some Spanish-speaking country. "You do teach Spanish and Latin culture, don't you?" That did it. If Mary hated anything more than menial work, it was the possibility of being a successful capitalist pawn. As Mary stormed off, Donahue sat down on one of the benches that lined the campus's curving walks and glumly observed the beauties of nature.

It had actually been too cold to be comfortable, but that had not stopped him from remembering that day not much earlier when it looked as though Mary would actually fall for him. It had been a perfect day, one of those rare occasions when everything was as God had intended it; God in a good mood, at least. So was Mary—lively, funny, cuddly. It was one of those days that alums remember fondly—partly from the beauty of the campus, partly fond memories of friends. The trees had turned their fall colors—more brown than orange or yellow, and very little red, but still very attractive—and no wind had yet arisen to blow them away. Clouds built up higher and higher, but the weathermen—if they were to be believed—predicted no rain, again. A short frost had slain most of the flies and mosquitoes, so that students lying in the warm sunlight could enjoy the Indian Summer fully, and picnickers could spread out their food without fighting the usual swarms of insects. Donahue sighed at the memory. The fall of 1996 had earned its place in history. The football team had run up the score on Accidental East so quickly that the coach, Windy Gale, had sent in the second team in the middle of the second quarter, then in the third quarter sent in instructions to punt on second down; he wanted this opponent available at *his* homecoming next year, and he feared that ruining their homecoming might make them reconsider making the long trip to Middleville, but his players had rebelled. As he explained to an alumni group later, "At least they didn't throw no passes." His team's spirits were too high. The players had gloried in the shuttle ride on the private airplane and their high spirits at this moment were a carry-over from the excitement of traveling first class to a place more distant than most of them had ever imagined; or it might have been their youth—most were freshmen, fresh off the farms, and fresh from the small town pool halls, that is, and they couldn't believe that the coach would order them to punt! At last he resolved the crisis by putting last year's starters onto the field. The contest was immediately equalized, and by the end of the day the hosts could claim a moral victory. The final score 35-7. On the flight home, the owner of the optical supplies empire—hence his *alma mater's* unofficial nickname, Old Eyewash—was pleased not only with the coach's sportsmanship, but also with the potential he saw in Middleville, dropped a hint that he might open a plant there. The *Middleville Weekly Moderate*, pointing out that labor was plentiful and environmental restrictions insignificant, suggested that a new football rivalry was in the making. Perhaps just as important were comments by knowledgeable observers that this was an unusually talented team and that next year the squad, reduced by transfers and flunk outs, would surely return to its normal mediocrity. Also, Flo Boater had hinted to the visitor that the college was looking for a Commencement speaker, an invitation usually accompanied by an honorary degree.

But that had been only one game. In a more important contest, at least in the eyes of alums and townsfolk, the 'Pricks" had scratched out a win over Arcadia College, the first victory in the long series of contests between the schools. Painted slogans appeared all over campus, 22-21, and on the Arcadia campus as well (courtesy of some 'real pricks'). A song was composed with 'twenty-two, twenty-one' as its hypnotic refrain, and it seemed likely to carry over into basketball season and beyond as the new school fight song. Losing the last two games by narrow scores hardly dampened the spirits. After all, it was a young team, and young teams make mistakes. As Windy told the alums, "Just wait till next year!"

Donahue had to smile at the memory of Windy's most innovative move—to guarantee that every good player would be eligible, he had enrolled them in the unofficial honors program, and each had gotten the lowest grade that Professor Stout gave—a B. Windy had gotten some brief national attention for having so many players in the Honors Program, and he had manage to distract the press from asking Professor Stout for his assessment of their talents. Moreover, having heard that Stout's emphasis in the spring semester would be on group work, with an A for everyone who attended class, he was overjoyed. Class met 10-12 on Mondays rather than MWF or TT, so it would be relatively easy for Windy and his captains to see that every player was up, dressed and in class. Awake was another matter. Worse case scenario—another B.

The cross country team also came up with two improbable victories thanks to terrible downpours and heavy winds. The Briarpatch "Pricks" were too large and too sturdy to outpace their opponents on a dry day, but they were incredibly effective "mudders." Lastly, a team of young debaters coached by Lill, her first experience in this job, placed fourth in the regional competition at Arcadia. True, there were only eight colleges involved, but no Briarpatch team had ever placed higher than seventh, and this time there were only a few points difference between the first and fourth teams. Best of all, Arcadia came in fifth, and Zenith University sixth.

The impact of the resulting publicity in the regional newspapers was seen in two ways—first in a modest increase in monetary gifts, an increase aided by the climb in stock market values; second, in prospective student visits to the campus, with an expectation that approximately half would eventually enroll. (Seniors who found a reasonably comfortable college would not bother to visit another one, and Briarpatch was reasonably comfortable—visitors whose talents were demonstrably mediocre saw that while they might be somewhat challenged, nobody would expect more than moderate efforts; late bloomers understood that they would not be rushed into flowering too quickly.) More students meant more tuition money, more filled beds helped pay off the ancient debt on the dormitories, and the central sidewalk packed with students hurrying to classes gave the impression of a healthy and vibrant institution.

The prospect for an improved financial situation made everyone happy at Briarpatch College, especially Flo Boater; happy, but less enthusiastically so were those who resigned themselves to having her as president for years to come, unless she parlayed her successes into invitations to interview at more prestigious colleges (or even minor universities). The gala inauguration would be expensive, of course, but it was an opportunity for trustees to feel good about themselves; and happy trustees are generous trustees.

Everything seemed to be going well—except for Donahue's courtship. He fretted about Miss Fox's advice—what if she was right?

It was against a much less glorious background that Flo Boater and Stanley Wooda were walking across campus. They exchanged a few words about how dreary January had been and how much easier it would be to recruit students if they only had a better climate; neither had a plan for improving it.

"If it were only warmer in the winter," she had complained.

"And cooler in the summer," he had replied, though he knew this was unimportant except for the opening weeks of the fall semester, when hot classrooms and hotter dorms always caused a few students to leave before it was too late to enroll in a local junior college.

She was silent for a minute, reflecting on the possible impact of heat on her gala inauguration. May seemed more and more attractive, though that might crowd the celebrations associated with Commencement. Her thoughts were interrupted by Stanley Wooda musing about what do be done to make the dead of winter more attractive. He stumbled a moment after saying "dead," because it reminded him of the unfortunate events of recent semesters.

But President Boater hardly noticed. She responded that winter sports were no cure-all—snow and ice were too unpredictable, and the gym was inadequate even for the sports that the college already offered. But, with everything else going well, she said, "We can't complain too much. In any case, we must always emphasize the positive." They then continued their walk in silence.

In accordance with that apparently universal rule of human behavior that accords most credit for success to whomever is at the top of an organization, whether it be military or its exact opposite, a liberal arts college, those who are in charge also have to accept some of the blame. It was a refreshing change for Flo and Stanley to get *some credit* rather than *all the blame*, because Briarpatch College had experienced so many setbacks for so many years, that almost nobody on campus knew how to deal with success. Flo and Stanley, however, had planned and dreamt about this for months now, and the fact that very little of it came from their own efforts or their encouragement did nothing to stifle their pride and self-satisfaction.

They were also free from the tedium of grunt work. This allowed them more time to reflect and even to think. Flo Boater even conceded that her late husband, Floyd Boater, was correct in declaring that higher education needed more assistant deans. She had backed away from that claim when delivering his scheduled speech to the assembled presidents and deans of local institutions of higher education. That was, she now thought, a mistake. Higher education did need more assistant deans, or associate deans—if she could remember what the difference was.

The most obvious outward manifestation of their new confidence in the future was their appearing more often in the coffee house, the goal of their stroll. This free-standing Japanese style structure was the most striking building on the campus. The administration building was graceful in its own way, and a few of the academic buildings bordered on pleasant, but the coffee house caught every visitor's eye. Its cluttered interior—all sports trophies, bulletin boards and tables occupied by students deeply involved in a wide variety of conversations—contrasted with the elegant simplicity of the exterior lines. Offended by the winter drafts, Flo Boater wanted to modernize it—get rid of the athletic bric-a-brac, remove all signs, abolish the time-honored "pay monthly, drink forever" policy on coffee, and bring back juke boxes—but the faculty, backed by a student threat to strike, had forestalled her plans. The usual protestors she could ignore, but she had to take the football players' threats seriously.

Flo Boater never quite understood football. She attended games, but she saw them as opportunities to greet alums and parents. While everyone else was hoping for touchdowns, she was working on donations. Whatever she might think about the game, the players or the coach, she was not going to disturb the goose that was laying golden eggs. Basketball was another matter. It was more difficult to climb around the seats to speak to people. A year ago, that would have been easy, but this year the crowds were too large. Even the students, normally far more apathetic about sports than the alums, were attending. The basketball team, in fact, was the principal topic of conversation at this moment. JJ's surprising decision to try out for the team resulted in the even more surprising revelation that he was a devastating three point shooter. However, his unwillingness to get in shape, or attend practice, and his illogical demand that Smitty be named to the starting team— despite a deplorable lack of height, speed or quickness—resulted in his being benched. Then they had both quit, saying that they needed to concentrate on studies.

Flo Boater's motivation to visit the coffee house was similar to her appearances at games, she wanted to meet people she could persuade to support her policies. This meant a handful of students and those faculty who were not acknowledged supporters of Lill and Lily.

Her bright eyes dimmed when she saw the senior historian sitting at a table alone. "The Creep" was the only person sitting alone. It was not sympathy for him that caused her such mental anguish, but he had caught her eye and motioned toward vacant chairs. She joined him, telling Stanley Wooda to get them coffee, with lots of cream, sugar and a little cinnamon. She had been to Vienna once and had never recovered from the experience. Whenever she could, she even had her coffee in exquisite china cups with a K&K motive. It fitted well at home and in her office, where her fine porcelains were on display, but what she served to visitors was nothing like the thin brews of the coffee house—her exotic beans, fresh ground, produced a thick coffee that had to be diluted by large portions of cream. Visitor unaccustomed to tiny cups usually declined the cream—to their regret—and who those who swallowed the entire cupful rather than sip at it often began gasping for breath. Flo Boater's disapproving stare made most of these unfortunates turn down the cool offer of a second cup. Lill and Lily understood how the rest of the world drank coffee, but she never offered to "pour" them a cup.

By the time Stanley Wooda arrived with a tray filled with coffee in Styrofoam cups and the tiny sugar and pseudo-cream packages, Flo Boater was spreading her hands out helplessly toward the historian and saying, "There's nothing I can do for you." She glanced at the coffee, frowned, then turned her attention back to the historian, who appeared to have shrunk significantly.

With a shake, the historian sat up, took a deep breath, and whispered, "What if I can do something for you?"

His wheedling voice caused Flo Boater to grind her teeth, but she only nodded, noncommittally, meaning, "Then we'll talk again."

He stood and offered a limp hand to shake. She managed to control a shudder, knowing that if she took it, she would have to get out a tissue to wipe off her palm. She managed to avoid the crisis by waving at two students, who quickly turned and ran out—for good reason, certainly, after the articles they had written about the disappearance of Miss Purdy for *the Zenith Apex* and *the Arcadian Woodman*. Also, although it was unlikely the president would ask why they had quit the basketball team, the dean might inquire when they were going to start attending classes. Trying unconvincingly to hide her smile, she looked over at her young dean and with her eyes called his attention to their retreating backs. As the historian withdrew his hand with a sigh and began to slink away—perhaps remembering the interview that he had provided Smith, an interview that had been twisted in ways he should have anticipated from prior experience with student reporters—she half turned to say, "Nice speaking with you." But before he could respond, she was concentrating on mixing her coffee properly. After taking her first sip and reminding herself that she was not there for the coffee's quality, she sighed with satisfaction and said to Stanley Wooda, "Here we are. Everything quiet at last." This was not a reference to the noise level in the building.

Guessing her meaning, Wooda said, "No demonstrators."

She nodded agreement and added, "No police."

Wooda sighed contentedly, "No telephone calls from trustees."

"Or the press."

"No missing VP for FA." Use of initials was almost required for administrators, in this case meaning Vice-President for Financial Affairs.

"No Prudence Purdy." Her heart sank at the thought of starting another search. Replacements were so hard to attract to Briarpatch. Happily, Jenny was doing a credible job as a temporary replacement. Too bad she couldn't keep her, but if Jenny and Jay married, they would be in violation of her not-yet-announced anti-nepotism rule. Moreover, without her the Music department was short-handed; her colleagues had agreed to cover her classes themselves only after the president had promised she would return as a full-time assistant professor. Flo Boater barely suppressed a sigh—running a college was so stressful.

At that moment Wooda leaned across the table to say softly, "I've got to give you credit, President Boater, you really pulled us out of a tight spot."

Flo Boater leaned back in her chair, took a deep breath and realized that he was right. She looked about her little kingdom to see if anyone was watching them, then moved closer to him to say, "Stanley, we both did well, very well, indeed." When he nodded, she added, "Stanley, you really did a great job with those demonstrators!"

Wooda came as close to a blush as he ever did, "Nice of you to say so, President Boater."

Touching his arm, she said quietly, "Stanley, you should start calling me Flo." After glancing about again to see who might be close enough to hear, she added seductively, "At least when we're alone"

Alarmed, the dean moved to the side slightly, "Whatever you want, uh, Flo. Whatever you want. Meanwhile, meanwhile, what about those promises you made?"

She had to stop to think, "The promises.... You mean tenure consideration for Ms. Canary?"

He had read her thoughts, "Mary? Do you think we *have* to give her tenure?"

She did not answer directly, "It's Donahue I'm really worried about."

"But you renewed his contract."

She hit her fist into her palm hard enough to attract momentarily attention, but soon the students went back to their own, more important business. She explained, "Had to! Had to settle that last murder charge, that disappearance or whatever it was. He made me believe that he had rescued me from being involved. Or something. It was so confusing, I really didn't know what was going on, but I couldn't say no." She paused to determine whether the background noise was sufficient to assure them absolute privacy before adding, "He tricked me into giving Lill and Lily their department back, too."

"I thought it was something like that," he said. Inwardly he said to himself, "Of course, I do. I was there."

She did not like to confide in Stanley Wooda. He was so swift in thought and deed, that she could maintain control only by denying him information. And by not getting too close. That is, too close in an intellectual sense. In the common understanding of the thought, well, that wouldn't be bad. He was very good looking, and men are such fools when romantically entangled.

Wooda knew this, too. But he also knew that he wasn't an ordinary guy.

She told him—not for the first time—the basic outline of the plot last spring by which Lill had swapped vital information about the late dean's sale of artifacts for a continuation of their contracts, information which had the effect of showing that she was not involved in the scandal and thus had less reason to commit murder.

"That's a nasty combination of enemies," Wooda said, barely suppressing a yawn. He had often wondered to himself why four puny little professors were worth worrying about. He nodded that he understood now why she was concerned, but he carefully refrained from suggesting that she should remove everyone who knew the inside story of the two poisonings; he equally refrained from saying that she was over-reacting.

Flo Boater then surprisingly expressed what he was thinking, "There's only four of them." When he nodded, she added, "It takes five to make a cabal."

He didn't understand the reference, "A what?"

"A cabal is a secret conspiracy." She had to search her memory before adding, "Five people were in the first one." She then indicated that she'd like another cup of coffee.

When the dean returned, he asked, "Why'd they call it a cabal?"

"The word was made up of the first letters of the conspirators' names. Some time long ago."

Wooda took a sip of coffee and leaned back, "Not a problem here. As you say, there are only four of them." MDLL. Not even a vowel among them. Unless one wrote it MDOLL.

She shook her head at this, "That's silly, but you have a point. There really are five in the cabal. We have to count Molly as the fifth." Molly was an instructor in English, part-time but always full-time; that is, they never gave her contract until they were certainly that there were classes to teach, and they paid her by the course—at the academic equivalent of minimum wage. Flo Boater hated her, remembering that she had stolen a professor of chemistry, Salvatore Iva, from her; if anyone had asked why she felt this way, she couldn't have explained—after all she had been married to the president of the college at the time and the late Dean Wooda had been her lover; but there was something so very attractive about anything one has lost, even when one didn't really miss it. With Sal going to prison for conspiracy to murder—and her being the person conspired with, though not convicted—the weeks she spent in jail awaiting trial should have erased any last lingering fondness for him, but of course they hadn't.

She was brought out of her daydream by a voice: "Even worse," the living Dean Wooda was saying, "was MMDLL. It doesn't even make sense as Roman numerals." Unable to do anything with that combination, Wooda dismissed the idea, "She's in Music. She doesn't know anything about campus politics. No registrar has ever done much except respond to complaints, much less a temporary one."

This came as a mild shock to Flo Boater. Her dean was—if that keeping that M in the formula meant anything, not replacing it with a J—confusing Jenny with Molly, and he had her job wrong, too—Jenny was directing the Finance office. It was the first time that his tendency to skip over details had been so painfully obvious, but her discomfort was partly offset by the pleasure of correcting him. Pompous know-it-all wimp! A good dancer, she heard, but still a wimp. And his usual defense! That it is difficult to tell one middle-aged woman from another. That was just unacceptable. But all these comments were purely mental—he was as proud as Satan, a phrase that only the rare readers of Milton still understood as almost a compliment, and he would likely find some future opportunity to revenge himself for any unnecessary insult, as if there were necessary insults. She conceded that he had not had much contact with either one, but reminded him that Molly might be a relative by marriage—she *was* the late Dean Wooda's widow.

This Stanley Wooda remembered well, his having said that once to Molly. She had responded in her crisp English-teacher style that "widow" presumed being married to the deceased, while she had been divorced, and happily so. After that, he couldn't remember having spoken to her privately again. Every contact with the English department was through the chair, Prof. Stout, who despised those members of his department who lacked the "doctor" title. Moreover, Stout returned from every meeting of the Regional Modern Language Association with a new set of demands, none of which fit into Stanley Wooda's budgetary projections., and with ideas for courses that almost no Briarpatch student would voluntarily enroll in—"Queer Theory in Computer-Generated Poetry" and a team-taught one, "The Post-Modern African Renaissance" (knowledge of French required). Stanley had questioned this last one, since the French instructor was part-time and had not read any African novels, and Stout did not speak French—Stanley had ascertained this early on by trying to start a conversation with him. Inspiration from the most recent MLA conference had prompted Stout to demand changes in the graduation requirements that would assure that such "consciousness-raising" classes would be filled. All this had taken only a fraction of a second for Stanley Wooda to process. He said, almost bursting out. "I know who Molly is. She sings in the choir and participates in plays. The late dean hated that."

Flo Boater only cocked an eyebrow at this. Why was that important?

Without her asking, Wooda explained that no other member of the English department would ever sink to performing in public. Lastly, wasn't she away all the time, visiting Sal in the state minimum security prison or going to the state capital to petition for his release? He then dismissed Molly as being a 'bit player' in campus politics. This was a sly reference to her roles in campus theater productions, a joke that went over the president's head—Flo Boater never attended local plays or concerts.

The president had no patience for such rambling. Leaning forward to emphasize her concern, she said, "She's learning. Just like Mary, learning fast."

"What do you mean?"

"You've heard of the problem with grades?"

"Slightly."

"You'll be hearing more, I'm sure. Ms. Hogg was turning the registrar's office upside-down. Some nasty secrets may come to light." She gave him a meaningful glance.

"Grades, you think? Not purchases of artifacts? Miss Purdy...." Something in the way his voice trailed off suggested that the scandal was not yet buried.

"Artifacts? In the Registrar's office?"

"I guess you're right," he said, "I should have thought of that." What he was thinking—again—was that it was dangerous to have Jenny in the Financial Office—if another invoice for artifacts came in, she would see it. Anything irregular would be instantly communicated to their enemies, whereas the sale of grades would not be obvious—that was all in the past, the distant past.

More worrisome for Flo Boater—why had the dean thought Jenny had replaced the registrar? She gave him a sideways glance. Stanley was usually quick to see connections. What was going on? Did he already have a plan?

He thought a second, remembering her earlier comment, "What has that to do with Molly?"

She sighed, somewhat in disgust, but somewhat anxiously, "Molly was the late dean's former wife. She might know more about this than she realizes."

"You mean 'connecting dots?' Dots she doesn't realize are dots?"

"The dots lead directly to your office."

Suddenly concerned himself, more about his having missed an important development on campus than the danger Molly might represent, he asked, "What do we do, then?"

"Get rid of them!" Then, remembering her protégé's bully boys, she said, "Not the way you're thinking. Legally." The weight-lifters had been useful once, but Wooda's influence over them had declined drastically after Chief Biggs had threatened to call their mothers. (Briarpatch was that kind of backward college where mothers still exercised more authority than a professor.)

"But how? We don't have a legal leg to stand on, and the college can't afford another murder."

"We'll work on that, Stanley, we'll work on it."

"Ms. Hogg. Can't you just fire her?"

"Probably, but since she had tenure, it would cause a firestorm on campus."

"Wasn't she part-time?"

Flo Boater sighed, "Strange things happen at Briarpatch." In short, it made sense at the time and it wasn't her fault.

"She didn't lose tenure when she became an administrator?"

"We could make that argument, but we tried it with Lill and Lily, and it didn't work out well." She smiled slightly, remembering her triumph in removing them from the offices that she and Stanley now held, then frowned at recalling her inability to keep them from returning to the Theater department. "

Stanley, reading her face carefully, answered only, "I see."

"I hope so. You need to get a feel for this type of situation. Otherwise, we'll have the faculty demonstrating."

"Maybe," he cautiously suggested, "we could find a new job for her, maybe a study of the curriculum. We're always doing that. Or to help in Admissions. They always need more people." He glanced over at his boss, then concluded, "As soon as she comes back, that is." He almost expressed a wish that Ms. Hogg just disappear, but instantly remembered that such an event would have Chief Biggs snooping across campus again.

Flo Boater sighed. "We can't afford to pay her for doing nothing, and as for going back to Education, we missed that chance. Maybe we could do it for next fall, but that's a long way off."

"If it's that important, we should do it anyway."

"Not without a good excuse," she reply, sighing. "It would suggest she had been a failure. Who knows how she would respond? And it would mean a cut in pay. And we don't have a replacement in line."

"And we can't make up an excuse? Something like health? Maybe stress?" he half-queried, thinking of his own stomach.

"Maybe. When the time comes. Meanwhile, you find someone to do her job, temporarily."

He smiled, "Will do, boss."

She winced slightly at the "boss", then mused about when it would be proper to suspend Ms. Hogg's pay. A temp's pay would be much more affordable.

Stanley Wooda was thinking that pay for a registrar was a wash— one out, one in—just like paying a new finance officer. But fitting Jenny back into *his* budget, as seemed inevitable, counted as an addition. Her part-time substitute had been very, very cheap, but incompetent; and a replacement might very, very eager to get a job, and perhaps even be attractive. So might a new registrar. As he thought of this, he sighed— the turnover in that office was unlikely to change, and Flo Boater was likely to be vigilant about fraternization with the staff. Staff, he thought, was a strange word. At Briarpatch there were relatively few male administrators....

His daydream was interrupted by the president's voice, "Not yet. Any registrar's office runs pretty much on routine. You know, record grades in the computer, file professors' reports, then eventually shred them. It's not a high stress business until May, when the list of graduates have to be made and those who fall short have to be notified."

"Her absences?"

"Not sufficient, yet. We'll find out if that's a reason when she gets back, but we'll have to do it one step at a time. Start a rumor, perhaps."

He gave her a satisfied grin, "When do we start, and where?"

She smiled, "Right now, let's concentrate on getting the insurance payment for my late husband's CEO insurance policy." That, she thought, might cover the expenses of an inauguration if she couldn't get a trustee to make a special donation.

He returned the smile, "And the settlement for the late Dean Wooda, too."

This stopped her for a second before she commented, "Yes, too bad you weren't really related." There might be, she thought, some money still hidden somewhere that family members could help find.

Wooda shrugged and said, "I've got my grandma working on that now. There can't be too many Woodas in the world."

In a motherly manner, she responded, "It wouldn't matter, Stanley, you're one of a kind." Looking around before he touched him on the hand, she asked, "Anything you think we should attend to?" Privately, she was wondering when he had come up with a grandmother.

In fact, he did have something. He pointed over to a student she did not recognize. A quieter fellow than the rest, with a deeper tan, perhaps a bit taller and thinner. Perhaps a good center on the basketball team, she thought, not knowing much about centers other than their pushing other players around under the basket and liable to foul out at the worst possible moment. She understood better when Wooda explained that he was the college's first fully Native American student in years, and that he had approached the dean's office for a complete remission of tuition and board and room.

"What?" she exclaimed, then was stunned into silence by Wooda reminding her that the very name Briarpatch was of Native American origin, and therefore, he was claiming that this was tribal land. Since the college was occupying Indian land illegally, the student had argued, or at least immorally, the least the college could do was give him free tuition and full room and board. That meant, of course, that it would be awkward if he chose to play basketball—it would look too much like an athletic scholarship, which was forbidden in Division III.

All she could do was to ask his name.

"It translates as 'Golden Arrow,' but legally he's called Flechadoro."
She sighed, then asked, "What tribe's he from?"

"Ah," the dean responded slowly, "I don't believe he said."

"You sure he's a First People."

The dean hesitated before saying, "He must be authentic. He has some federal financial support the admissions director has never seen before."

Flo's mind began to race. It was no surprise about the admissions director—she had hired her cheap, and her experience was minimal. But a lawsuit? She glanced up, then down before turning back to Stanley Wooda, "This might be less a disaster than an opportunity."

The dean thought so, too, "The Chinese have a saying…"

She cut him off, but not before he was mentally composing a note reassigning Jenny from Financial Affairs to Acting-Registrar.

Dean Threshold soon found himself with a new assignment, too—checking the land titles to the college land, and collecting everything he could find about the new student's tribe.

Meanwhile, Chief Biggs had a problem. A female corpse in the copse of poison ivy alongside the gym. A quick check of student dorms established a short list of persons unaccounted for.

Chapter Two

The body was not identified quickly, but after several parents were frightened almost out of their wits, their daughters were located—two at motels in Arcadia, with boyfriends, others innocently studying at the library (the last place anyone expected to find them), two doing technical work in the theater, others at local bars and, last of all, two roommates waiting for the Japanese coffeehouse to open. The announcement that every young woman at the college was accounted for hardly quieted all parental heart-flutters, but it instantly calmed what could have become a campus-wide panic. Faculty members were harder to track down—some didn't answer their phones and had to be visited at home by patrolmen. Could it have been Ms. Hogg? Not likely. Too thin. Death seems to have been accidental—too much alcohol on too cold a day. Chief Biggs finally concluded that the victim was a tramp (his description, a reference to her presumed mode of transportation, not her morals). The town buzzed briefly over the news. Were there still tramps? Not a single one had come on the railroad in recent years. And a female tramp? Was women's liberation getting out of hand?

"A tramp?" Donahue had asked.

"Well," the chief responded, "She had no money, no bag, not even a warm coat. She seems to have come in on the train. And it doesn't have passenger service."

"How was that possible? They don't have open boxcars any more."

"No, and they watch to keep people from hanging onto ladders. But when heavy equipment shipments come through, there are opportunities to squeeze in. Particularly if the person is small, as this one was."

"You sure she came on the train."

"Yeah, there was some grease on her clothes, smudges typical of the dirt along the track—there are still traces of coal there. Scratches indicate she got off the train before it had completely stopped—you know how it slows down on the big curve. And the woods are on the

way from the tracks to the campus. Getting off that way suggests she
was not thinking right. Probably too cold and exhausted. Unless there
was foul play, she just wandered off the path. Couldn't make it any
farther."

"You think she was headed for the college?"

The chief stopped to think, "Hard to tell, since she'd have pass
through the campus to get to town. Certainly, she wasn't interested
in the nearest houses, on the other side of the tracks. I think she was
looking for somebody."

"Oh?"

"There was a part of a message, stuck deep in a pocket of her jeans,
'Looking forward to seeing you.' It was so small we missed it at first.
No name of sender, just a 'your friend.' And, luckily, her email address.
That allowed me to locate her—missing from a program for the, what
do you call it now, 'developmentally handicapped?' She apparently used
a library computer, so we couldn't find out who she was writing to."

"Well," Donahue said, "apparently they didn't meet. At least
nobody came forward." He wondered who would. At Briarpatch almost
nobody had email yet.

"No, nobody has asked about a friend who didn't show up. I find
that strange."

The chief had called the state police, which tracked down her
computer to Zenith, then contacted the director of a home for battered
women where she had been living. The director agreed to drive down
to make an identification, but she had no ability to transport the body
back to the institution or funds for a burial. Consequently, the chief
persuaded the local funeral director—a cousin of his late wife—to
do what was necessary until he could locate relatives—the director
had a name, but no address to send the body. He could count on the
Middleville Moderate giving the incident publicity, with some chance
that locals would recognize her. He smiled when he wondered if he
should call the historian's mother in to look at her—she knew every
sordid incident of the past half-century or so. Surely she'd make a good
guess on this one. But he decided that the newspaper story, together
with the photo supplied by the director of the home, would be enough.

Newspapers across the state might pick up the story as human interest or another reason to increase funding for women's causes.

The students held a well-attended memorial. Briarpatch College was good in that respect. Death was rare on campus, but students were aware that all humankind was somehow connected. True, it was not always easy to show a connection, but a death in the campus woods was obviously one such tie to the wider world.

The coffee house was becoming quieter. Across the course of a day, it had its high and low moments. It opened early enough for students to get a bite before their 8 AM classes, then remained almost empty except for the occasional faculty member who hurriedly grabbed a plastic cup of coffee and carried it across campus, cursing at the college's inability to foresee that the stock of Styrofoam cups was running out. There was a rush of students just before nine, after they had groggily crawled out of bed and stumbled toward class; this continued for more than an hour, as the students emerging empty-headed from their early class (although nutrition experts have preached for years that people who eat breakfast learn much better, folk wisdom among young people stressed the importance of the last fifteen minutes of each night's sleep) and those headed toward their 10 o'clock classes filed in through the opposite doors.

Lill and Lily entered shortly after the rush was over. They had already been at work for four hours. Unlike most theater people, they were early risers. (They hinted that they took frequent naps, although when this happened—except at faculty meetings, with eyes open—no one could imagine.) They had arranged a breakfast nook in their work area, where they could enjoy a Continental breakfast with large cups—almost flagons—of strong coffee ground on the spot from "fair-price" beans that Mary had urged them to buy. They stayed up late, as was necessary in their profession, and strong coffee first kept them alert, then helped them to instant deep sleep. Today they were dressed in academic grunge, but carrying their motorcycle helmets, leading everyone to believe that they would soon be dashing down seldom-traveled back roads, when their actual intention was to slip home and close their eyes. It was too cold for a joy ride. The coffee house was on the way to the distant parking lot assigned to motorcyclists.

"Hi, Lill," one student said as he hurried exited.

"Oh, JJ," she responded, then tried to say more, but he was already gone.

Lily laughed, "Some things never change."

Lill looked around and, sighing, said, "Well, here we are again. Back in the coffee house and it sure looks familiar."

Lily felt the same, "In less than a year the wheel has turned full circle. They talk and talk and never reach a conclusion."

No space at any table opening up, Lill remarked, "The students are doing well without us. Though God knows what they're talking about."

Lily laughed, "Sports and sex."

"The women, too?"

Lily laughed again, "Oh, they're gaining there, and on cigarettes they've positively taken the lead."

Lill waved her comment off, then looked around before remarking, "I thought there was to be a demonstration."

"Me, too. Though I don't know what about."

At that moment they saw Donahue alone at his distant table. Glancing over at Lily to get her approval, Lill led the way through the chairs until she could take a seat and say, "Nice to see you, DO. It's been weeks."

He nodded agreement and indicated the empty chairs, "It's hard to imagine, Lill." He straightened up slightly before saying, "Strange. I was just thinking about you."

Lily, straightening up herself and raising a hand to check her hair, drawled, "Oh, that's nice."

Lill gave her friend a sigh, then asked, "What were you thinking."

"The irony of life." He paused before explaining, "How you were acting president, then fired, then rehired."

With a frown, Lily agreed, "We're back in Theater, at one-quarter the salary." That was it. She had anticipated the presidency being short-term employment, but she had been surprised by the 'temps' effort to make their jobs permanent. She had hired them on the understanding as soon as the trustees conducted a search for a new president and dean, she and Lily would return to Theater. However, the temps had not anticipated that Lill would be demoted so quickly. Having persuaded themselves that they had stumbled into long-term employment, they were pleased when Flo Boater told them not to worry, that they'd be able to keep their jobs.

Lill echoed this in a depressed voice, "And no perks." She had enjoyed the travel to trustees' meetings, the rent subsidy and free lawn mowing.

"It's your own fault, Lill," Lily observed. "If you'd kept the maid and garden service, you'd really have enjoyed the perks while you had them." Her smile indicated that she anticipated the joy of a spirited discussion.

Donahue attempted to cut that off, "You let Flo Boater to stay in the presidential manor."

Lill started to say that Floyd Boater was just on medical leave, but Lily broke in, "She'd have liked it better if Lill had provided lawn mowing services, or paid the water bill."

"Lily's right," Lill laughed. "She wanted the lawn cut three times a week and watered daily. Flo just saw my budget cuts as a conspiracy against her."

"Come on, Lill," Lily countered, "the only conspiracy was hers—to murder the dean, or maybe her husband."

"Or both," Donahue interjected with a smile.

A moment of silence followed. Much had changed since Flo Boater had become acting-president, and as far as Lill and Lily were concerned, it was a very mixed picture.

Donahue tried to lighten the atmosphere by observing, "Well, at least the Creep is no longer *your* chair." It was a mock serious comment, with a suggestion that he had gotten the worse of a swap when the historian was transferred from head of the Fine Arts Division to Social Science. No one knew where History really fit, anyway. Donahue indicated with a slight movement of his head a small figure several tables away, half-concealed behind his newspaper. Most people at the coffee house who read papers—and there were only a few of them—folded them back to the article of interest and laid them on the table, bending over to read, sweeping away crumbs onto the floor to provide employment for the janitor. Not the senior historian. He held his paper out proudly, occupying not only his space, but the places which could have been occupied on either side of him. It was clear that his ears were as fully employed as his eyes—he was Flo Boater's most important campus snitch.

At that moment a group of students began talking loudly, a few of them scooting their chairs back for imminent departure. The commotion allowed Lily to ask, "Where did *he* come from? I didn't see him sneak up."

Lill replied loud enough to be heard, "It's a shame the way we treat historians. Nobody ever pays attention to them. Those who ignore them have to repeat their classes." At this, the historian folded his newspaper and left without even a nod of his head.

Donahue sighed, "He's not just in History; he's in charge of Social Sciences."

Lill watched him pause a few moments to overhear some student conversation, then said, "It won't last. He doesn't wear well. Even Stanley Wooda will see that."

Lily made light of this, "We're almost as bad off. Who listens to the *head* of Theater?" This was meant to annoy Lill. Lily always used the word *head* as something one flushed.

Ignoring her, Lill said reflectively, "There were some nice aspects to being president."

Donahue played the innocent, saying, "Such as?"

"The reserved parking space," Lill said.

Lily was less reserved, "Do you know that Flo Boater won't even allow our motorcycles on campus now! We have to park in the 'distant lot'."

Donahue was surprised, "Did she say why?"

"Lily thought it was funny," Lill said, "to rev up right under the president's bedroom." Since the presidential manse was set back from the road at least fifty yards, this was indeed impertinent. It was impossible for Flo Boater to tell one motorcycle from another, so the most the Chief was willing to write down in the complaint was "loud and abusive nuisance, unidentified rowdies." It was highly unlikely that motorcycle engines could be heard from the presidential office, which was on the campus side of the administration building; and the dean, who could hear the street noise well, was not believed when he claimed that motorcycles were worse than pick-ups firing out of parking places, wheels spinning. That was a public space, the Chief had said, and it was a matter for the city council. Both knew that the city council was not recovered from its displeasure over the fall's student demonstrations— too many TV cameras and newspapermen with negative stories that reflected badly on the town and its citizens.

"People need to lighten up," Lily complained. "'Rowdies,' the chief called us."

"Still," Donahue said, "I can see Flo Boater's point." He could imagine the scene. What he did not know was what they had done to Flo Boater's cherished English lawn. Short green grass was almost impossible to grow. It required careful nurturing and lots of water. Lots of water. And a motorcycle can chew it up beyond imagining.

Resignedly Lill sighed, "We were not going to have much influence anyway. You can't put any college president under suspicion of murder three times and not build up some ill will."

Lily responded with her usual passion, "Especially if she may be guilty of at least one!"

Donahue was quick to dissent, "We thought Miss Purdy was dead, and that she had done it! That was certainly jumping to a conclusion."

Lily replied in a mock disbelieving voice, "Surely you don't believe her story about finding the blood 'accidentally?'"

Lill added, "Flo was breaking into that office as surely as we're sitting here."

Donahue, holding up both hands, urged more calm, "She did have keys and she was authorized to be there."

Lily didn't agree at all, "But that wasn't her story!"

Donahue conceded, "The truth was never Flo Boater's strong suit." But his concession was almost drowned out by another table of students leaving.

Touching his arm to get his attention, Lill thanked Donahue, "A good thing that you got her to promise Mary tenure."

"In writing!" Lily enthused.

Donahue was almost ready to blush when Lill added, "And that you didn't ask anything for yourself." That did redden his cheeks. He reddened even more when he thought about what his former colleagues at the police station would have said about him blushing.

His friends, however, hardly noticed. Lily was already saying loudly, "She would have been quick to call *that* extortion!"

With a smile, Donahue brushed this aside, "Good thing I didn't have time to think the situation over. Given time, an angel might have been tempted."

Nodding, Lill said, "As the Good Book says, 'deliver us from temptation'."

Lily took umbrage at this, and lightly punched her friend on the arm, "Let's not take this too far!"

At this moment something caused Donahue to look out the window and say, "There goes Dean Wooda."

"Thought he was ill," Lill said.

"Diarrhea, I heard," Lily replied. They leaned over to watch him slowly making his way toward a group of students.

"The demonstration," Lily exclaimed. "It must be about to start."

"What's the demonstration about?" Donahue asked.

As usual, it was Lily who acted, "Grab your cups and let's find out." They went the nearest door, but, not able to see clearly what was going on in the distance, they put down their coffees and set out at a brisk pace toward the administration building, almost overtaking the dean. They saw the demonstrators dancing and yelling, and as the students espied the dean approaching, their yelling increased in volume and joy. The dean put up his arms in a Nixonian victory sign. The cries, "Wooda, Wooda," echoed off the administration building. "One less week, one less week!"

As Donahue and Lily looked at one another, Lill turned away, "I don't even want to know what *that's* all about." She had already turned back toward the coffee house when Lily suggested they go on and cause some trouble.

Lill growled, "Don't tempt me." Then she grabbed Lily, who was already headed toward the crowd. Donahue, meanwhile, stopped two students on their way to the assembly, "What's going on?"

They hardly stopped, but they explained quickly, "Dean Wooda's going to change the grading system."

"Not the calendar? One less week?"

"No," the students replied. "We'd like that, but we'll settle for higher grades."

"How? How better grades?" Donahue managed to ask, his voice choking.

"*How?*" one laughed. "You sound like Flechadoro!"

"Dunno," the other said. "Maybe eliminate exams." With a laugh, they hurried in the direction of the dorms. They were saying something about no more classes this morning, maybe not all day.

"Eliminate exams," Lill fumed. "He gets the credit for innovation and reform, but we'll have to clean up the mess." After a moment she added, "We'll sure look great when the Accreditation visitation comes."

Lily mulled the matter, "I know of places that write essays about student progress. They always get away with it"

"Yeah," Lill agreed. "They might have to write another explanatory essay, when what's needed are more *student* essays."

Donahue just laughed, "I know places they give away A's." When they looked at him, he explained, "Look, the average grade nationally is now a B. The elite schools claim that their students deserve higher grades than, say..." He paused briefly before adding, "students at Briarpatch College. And the dean is just following their example." His joke was acknowledged by smiles.

"Nice try, DO," Lill responded. "He's just playing for student sympathy. The question is, 'What is he up to?'"

"Now, Lill," Lily interrupted. "He might be only justifying what our colleagues are already doing."

"Sounds like one of Stout's initiatives," Lill concluded. "Either way works fine for the unofficial honors program. She turned away, saying, "Don't let Dean Wooda cross my path today!" The others followed her after they watched the crowd carry the dean ineptly away on their shoulders.

"That can't be good for his diarrhea," Lily observed.

Walking back toward the coffeehouse, Donahue laughed, amused, "The youngest dean in America, and he's got the trots." He suggested another cup of coffee, but Lill and Lily were not enthusiastic—the coffee house brew might have contributed to the dean's problem—but they agreed when they saw Mary at almost the same instant she saw them and waved an invitation.

Lill and Lily exchanged a meaningful glance at each other as Mary asked enthusiastically how they were doing, but said nothing to Donahue except a quiet, "Hi, DO." He responded in kind, "Fine, just fine. How are you?" No fire in either one, and certainly nothing in either voice to light one.

They were seated at a central table, still speculating on the dean's motives, when a number of students entered, apparently from the demonstration. Not knowing any of these students, they were reluctant to ask what they had learned, and all they could gather from the loud remarks was that Dean Wooda was a fine fellow.

Lill groused quietly, "Flo Boater should at least have made him graduate first."

"Maybe that's it," Donahue suggested. "Without exams, he just might get a degree."

Lill was smiling again, when out the window, she saw Flo Boater crossing the campus. Her frown returned, "There goes Her Majesty, getting ready for her coronation."

Lily was more malicious, "Flo Boater, the grieving widow of the late Floater."

"She doesn't look grief-stricken to me," Lill said.

"For her grief is breaking a finger-nail." She had noticed one was shorter than the rest.

"Give her a break," Donahue said.

"Okay," Lily responded, "It was the dean who drowned, not Floater."

Donahue sighed, but the late Floyd Boater's nickname had always provoked disparaging jokes. He then looked over at his friends, then asked, "I wonder if she saw us?" His unasked question was whether they would be blamed, but what he asked next was if their fear of the president was perhaps making them too cautious.

Lily's mood immediately lightened. She gave him a friendly punch on the shoulder and joked, "That's right. We're all such dangerous people it's unwise to be seen together."

Donahue knew she was making fun of him, but he still said, "Lily, I didn't mean it that way." He glanced over at Mary, who, he knew, still worried about tenure. She seemed unconcerned right now.

Lill, ever more practical, said, "Sure you did, DO, you just didn't mean to say it like that." He was crestfallen. There was some truth in her observation.

Recognizing his embarrassment, Lily gave him a slight hug, "But that's ok, big boy. We know your heart is in the right place." For once, she refrained from trying to locate it. She might yet have done so, but she saw Molly enter with Chief Biggs. She released him and called out, "Hi, Molly. Hi, Chief."

Molly was obviously excited, with news to share, "Did you hear? Sal is out of prison!"

"No!" Mary exclaimed. "That's great." Indicating two free chairs, she stood up to hug Molly, while Donahue more soberly shook the chief's large hand.

Lill asked, "When'd you hear about Sal?" Everyone remembered how disappointed Molly had been after her last round of interviews with judicial officials, newspapermen and prison officers. Lily gave her no time to answer, needing to get her hug in, too. Consequently, it was the chief who answered, "Yesterday. We went right up and drove him back to town ourselves this morning." He was proud of it. Apparently, he had played some small role in the effort. Maybe not so small a role.

Donahue did a quick mental calculation, "They must have opened for business early!"

The chief allowed as how the prison officials wanted people out the gates with plenty of time to get home before dark. Everyone nodded, except Lill, who asked "Where is Sal now?" Molly was still tied up in Lily's hug, so the chief answered, "He wanted to ask the personnel manager about a job. His parole requires that he find work."

Molly, now releasing herself from her friend's muscular grasp, gushed enthusiastically, "He knows he can't teach here any more, but he'd do anything. Cut grass, deliver mail... night watchman."

"What will the personnel manager say?" Lill asked, "Any guess?"

"Too risky now, I imagine." Molly conceded. "Flo Boater would find out and his 'ass would be in the can.' Those were his words when I asked earlier, but Sal wanted to hear them himself." Seeing questions in their faces, she explained, "It's sort of a measure of his being forgiven."

Lill changed the subject, "How'd the release come about?" She knew that Chief Biggs had some influence statewide, but not that much—he'd not been able to get the original sentence reduced to time served when the jury had found his alleged co-conspirator, Flo Boater, not guilty.

The chief confessed as much, saying, "Flo Boater's letter. It came just as they were discussing over-crowding in the pen."

Molly gave him a one armed hug, thus able to show him off to the others, "You're just too modest. But whoever gets the credit, it was great!" She glanced at the clock and said, "Got to go. Sal is on campus somewhere, probably at the registrar's. He wanted a word with her, too."

Donahue interrupted, "She's not on campus."

"No," Lill added, "Nobody knows where she is."

"Oh, I knew that," Molly responded, speaking more rapidly with each sentence. "But it's still probably the place to look for him. I'd forgotten all about Miss Hogg. I guess I should say Ms. Hogg. Anyway, I should have told him. I still need to find him and he should be finished at the Personnel Office. That's on the first floor, so I can check there first anyway. Well, I suppose I shouldn't have come here, but I just had to tell you myself. You all have been so wonderful." She gave each a hug, including DO, then said, "Bye," and left with the chief.

Lily said to DO, "I guess the hint you dropped Flo paid off."

Donahue was not comfortable admitting to his role in extorting concessions from the president, so Lill jumped in, "Sal and Flo were lovers. That might have something to do with it, too."

Lily gave her an enthusiastic puppy-like push, "You old romantic, you." Then she started to get up for coffee, stopped to think for a second and sat back down, leaned closer and said reflectively, "It's a strange world. We go down, while Flo Boater…"

As usual, Lill finished the sentence, "…becomes president."

"And Stanley Wooda is dean." Having said that, Lily fell silent, apparently despondent.

Mary, losing enthusiasm for more conversation, said goodbye and left. It was worrisome that her usual pleasant mien was now totally absent. At the last moment, Donahue tried to wave goodbye, but he failed to catch her attention before she was gone.

Watching her depart, Lill sighed and said, "At least Mary got a promise of tenure out of it."

Donahue tried to encourage what optimism there was, saying, "I've kept *my* job, too."

But Lill would have none of it. Eore-like, she grumbled, "Just for the time being. Flo Boater is just too busy to take care of you."

"She'll get around to it," Lily warned.

Determined not to allow this to degenerate into a bitching session, a word that might have lightened the mood considerably had he been bright enough to use it, Donahue proposed, "I suppose I had better update my résumé?"

Amused, Lill asked, "What are you going to put on it?"

With a smile, Lily suggested, "Solves campus murders…."

"Accuses college administrators…"

"But can't convict them."

Lill laughed, "That's going to catch the eye of any search committee!"

Donahue shrugged and smiled, "What else can I do?"

Teasingly, Lill suggested, "You might try getting some publications." She knew that his articles were in demand, but in popular magazines, not professional journals. Only those counted—whatever the public learned was unimportant. And essays in the *Middleville Moderate* would have counted negatively if any faculty member had read the local newspaper.

Lily, moving hands like a fortune-teller, prophesized, "I can see the title of your book now, *Latin American Artifacts for Death and Profit*."

Donahue said seriously, "There's no future in that one."

Lill retorted, in a friendly tone, "The late Dean Wooda thought there was."

"And he successfully did in Floyd Boater," Lily added. The suggestion hung in the air that there was more to the president's death than the $5,000,000 insurance policy. Each was aware how upset the president had been the day before the dean's death, and why he had been considered a prime suspect right to the last moment.

Donahue, with a warning finger half-way off the table, reminded them, "We still don't really know what was going on!" But each was aware that the dean might have been plotting the president's death to prevent an investigation into his activities. In short, there could have been more to the dean's motives than money. And Flo Boater might have been the one to put the dean's ideas into action, with Sal Iva as an unwitting accomplice.

Lill accepted this, and helpfully suggested, "I still think there's a story in there."

Lightly, Lily suggested, "At least a play." Then with one hand she theatrically covered her eyes and raised the other toward an imaginary heavenly spirit, and said, "I can see the title, *The Dean is Dead.*" They all laughed at the improbability of the idea.

Attracted by the laughter, the senior historian stopped in his tracks as he rounded a corner, then stepped back out of sight. This conversation seemed interesting. At his last meeting with President Boater he had little information to pass on. That would not happen again, he had vowed to himself. At least, not if innocently overhearing a loud conversation could prevent it. He strained to hear as Donahue said, "You have more confidence in me than I do myself. Or are you pulling my leg?"

Lill answered sardonically, "*Us,* pull your leg?"

Lily followed up seductively, "DO, I'd love to pull *your* leg."

"What did she say?" the historian wondered. Lily had spoken too softly to hear. For Lily that was unusual. Nor could he hear clearly when Donahue laughed, "Mary's got dibs on that!"

It was Lill's turn to quip, "If you can ever persuade her to." Looking at her watch, she indicated that it was time to go.

As Lily stood up, she suggested, "You need to warm that girl up."

Donahue agreed, "I'll work on that. If Flo Boater decides I have to go, I'd better have a place to stay. At least Mary has tenure." That the Creep heard.

Lill delayed her departure to warn, "Promised is not delivered."

Lily's last words were, "Not on this campus."

"That sounded more encouraging," the Creep said to himself, but "promised" what? He had to slip closer. Affecting nonchalance, he moved quietly around the corner and took a seat behind a pillar.

This time Lill saw him out of the corner of her yes. Whispering, she told Lily, "Be quiet now." But when her friend started to look behind her, Lill shook her head, then, shielding her hand with her body pointed to his hiding place.

"The snoop?" Lily said under her breath.

"The spy," Lill elaborated.

Donahue said quietly, "Warning taken. But I think I'll still go look for Mary. I really need to talk with her. And I might bump into Sal and Molly."

"Good luck, fella," his friends said at the same moment. And meant it.

Once Donahue left, the conversation lagged until Lily whispered, "Let's give him something to report to Flo Boater." She nodded toward the snoop.

Nodding, Lill said, "It's too bad what they are saying about the head of the History department."

"Oh, what are they saying?"

"I just can't believe it."

"Believe what?"

"That they are saying that."

By this time the historian was about to fall out of his chair, so dangerously was he leaning over in an effort to hear around the pillar.

"Come on, Lill, what are they saying?"

"You haven't heard?"

"Apparently not. No one has talked about him in years. Well, months."

"They're talking now."

"About what?"

"I just can't believe it myself."

"What?"

"Well, you know he's on the personnel and retention committee."

"Of course."

"And so is Professor Stout."

"Sure."

"Well, I just don't believe it."

"Believe what?"

"That they've agreed not to retain anyone who's not, well, you know."

"No, what?"

"Use your imagination, Lily. Think of Flechadoro!"

At this Lily began to giggle. This spread quickly to Lill, who sputtered out one final, "I just don't believe it," then gave Lily a hug, after which they exited laughing.

The historian, whose face had almost turned beet-red, followed them at a discreet distance, but without much hope of ever figuring out what they were referring to. "What the hell was the reference to Flechadoro?" he asked himself, uncharacteristically using a vain oath. "As far as I know, he isn't anything, much less 'well, you know.' And what do I have in common with Stout? Or is Stout 'well, you know' with our 'noble red man'?" The contrast of his reddened visage with his normal ultra-pallid complexion caught the attention of by-passers, even of students. "Do I tell this to the president or not? Can I even ask mother? She wouldn't even understand what 'well, you know' means. I'm not even sure I do."

Dean Threshold's report was not good. The courthouse had burned in 1849, literally sparked by so many emigrants heading for California that those remaining could make claims on the "vacant" properties left abandoned by the gold rushers or rented out until their return (presumably loaded with valuable nuggets). Once people realized that the property records had gone up in smoke, they filed claims on the "abandoned" properties. "Squatters' rights" lawsuits were not resolved until decades had passed, and locals were still suspicious of any inquires into old records. Indian rights had already disappeared when the last members of the local tribe, those few who had not been murdered by ancient rivals, sold their lands and moved west, but local rumor confused claims on those lands with these "more recent" ones.

"All of them?" Flo Boater asked. "They all moved away?"

"Maybe not. The county history, 1886, suggests that some 'survived'."

"Survived?"

"That's what they wrote. You know, a few men lived in the country, hunting for a living. Some women became wives; the children, though locally accepted as White, became formal members of the tribe."

"They made the children into tribal members?"

"Very common among Native Americans, I'm told. Often no blood tie at all. Whatever was needed to keep up the numbers of warriors, but in the end a losing proposition. Too many deaths from disease… alcoholism… that sort of thing."

"The local children died out, too?"

"No, nothing like that. The relatives who had already moved west never lost track until much later. There was a small annual federal payment, which they increased by counting everyone they could think of as tribal members. At least until the Indian Bureau caught on to the scam."

"It was illegal, then?"

"On the edge. Anyway, they kept in touch with relatives here for quite a while, then even the western members dispersed and disappeared. Locally, people just didn't pay much attention to their origins, and now they have too little Indian ancestry to qualify as Native American, though there might be some who married others descended from the tribe. That could up the percentage. I haven't been able to check that out, yet."

"So," Flo Boater concluded, "they disappeared, their claims disappeared, the courthouse burned down. So nobody can make a claim on the Briarpatch campus."

He hestitated, "Not quite. The property on which Old Main was built..."

"Yes," she demanded.

"The college only has a hundred year lease. It is up next year."

She looked at him a long while, "Who holds the land title?"

He hesitated again, "That's not clear. It appears that the grantor died intestate, without children...or a will."

"I know what intestate means," she snapped.

"He may have been a Native American."

"One of the children?"

"No, the real thing. The last 'noble redman,' according to the obituary. Never married, no children."

She thought a moment, "Who have we been paying for the lease?"

"Nothing. It was a 100 year lease, one dollar a year—cheap even then—paid in advance."

"Why so cheap?"

"A historian said..."

She interrupted, "Our historian? Not *the Creep*?" She almost laughed at the thought.

"No, at the state university in Zenith. Anyway, he suggested... purely a guess... that the owner wanted cash for alcohol."

"A drunk Indian."

"He said 'First American.' Prone to alcoholism. An excuse for moving the tribe west, to protect them from people like us. But this one stayed behind."

"He didn't want to be protected."

"No."

Flo Boater thought for a moment, then asked, "What happens next year? When the lease expires."

He hesitated, "The county recorder said that probably nothing would have happened if we hadn't made the inquiry. It was tax-free land, but it might revert to the county, now that they know about it." He began to sweat as he explained, "The county needs money."

"So? Isn't there some good will to exploit there?"

He began to sweat, "Thirty years ago we flunked both the county clerk and the recorder out of the college. They laughed at me."

She pondered the matter a moment, "Isn't there such as thing as 9/10th of law or Finder's Keepers?"

Dean Threshold smothered a smile, "I think an argument can be made on those lines, and you might want to consult the college attorney."

"Bottom line. What's the bottom line?" Flo Boater demanded.

The dean squirmed, "A good lawyer could make trouble for us. If not for the descendants, then the county. The college isn't very popular with potential jurors."

Flo Boater's eyes squinted as she studied him.

The choir director was not particularly a lonely chap, but he was too busy to join in most of the activities that brought faculty and students together, or even just faculty. He was present at many of those events, but he was providing the entertainment. Consequently, he missed out on the principal entertainment of any small campus—gossip.

Only rarely was he sufficiently moved by something he heard— usually from one of the students in a musical group—to inquire further into it. At this moment he was spurred to do so by sighting Lill on the sidewalk. "Lill," he called out, proud of himself for remembering her name, "Could I have a moment."

She laughed, "Certainly. Even longer if you want."

"I've got a question. An important question, I think."

"Fire away."

"I've heard that your former chair, that historian chap, you might remember..."

"Oh, how do I!"

"Well, I've heard that he has a new theory about the origins of our Native Americans."

"New to me."

"Well, you know how Mormons believe that the Native Americans are the descendants of the Lost Ten Tribes of Israel?"

"Certainly."

"Well, he told one of my students that the choral piece we are doing gives the wrong impression."

"How so? And what piece? I didn't hear you were doing anything about Native Americans."

"Oh, it's not really about Native Americans, but about the Hebrew people in exile. Verdi, you know. But when my student mentioned it, this fellow criticized him for over-emphasizing the importance of the Jews in history."

"And one thing led to another."

"Exactly. He didn't stop until my poor student was thoroughly intimidated and confused. I really don't understand it, or why he wanted to make a 'big thing' of it—that is what one says, isn't it? Verdi doesn't usually cause much controversy. Not for a hundred years."

Lill puzzled over this a moment, "How does this get to the Mormon beliefs about Indians?"

"Well, it's this way, if I understand correctly—he says that the Indians are really Islamic immigrants. There may have been a few pre-Adamite inhabitants here and there, but their culture didn't bloom until the Moslems arrived." After a moment he added, "That's why Kennedy was shot, he said, because he was about to expose the whole conspiracy. It was the Italians—that is, the Mafia—because it would expose Columbus as a fraud."

"Come again?" she asked.

"Columbus learned of the existence of America from the Moors in Spain, who had an oral tradition about their settlement of America."

"And what has this to do with the Jews in exile—in Babylon, if I remember."

"Right. It's not about the Jews carried away by the Assyrians, nor the Babylonians, he said, but the Arabs. This music reflected our anti-Arab prejudice."

"Edward Said's name come up?"

He squinted, hoping that would squeeze a memory out, but he got nothing more than, "That name sounds familiar."

"Chomsky?"

"Oh, yes. Definitely that one, whoever he is."

Lill refrained from laughing, "I'd say that collection of theories is right on par for our historian, but I'd also say that the student probably got it wrong. At least, he… it was a *he*, wasn't it?"

"Why yes, how did you know?"

"Oh, because the Creep is afraid of women. I doubt he would ever work up the nerve to correct one, or even think that it was worth the effort."

"Really! I suppose I should be happy that I've never met him."

"If you had," she responded, "you would remember him, and you'd understand why you shouldn't take him seriously." She thought to herself that even the choir director would not forget that experience! And he had the worst memory of anyone on campus.

"So I shouldn't worry about it?"

Lill thought about this for a moment, wondering whether to tell him how close the Creep came to being chair of the Fine Arts Division—and thus the choir director's boss. She chose to say only, "Nah, ignore him. Everybody else does." She almost corrected his use of Moslem—it was becoming obligatory to say "Muslim"—but she was sure that he wouldn't remember.

The college's sole Native American, Flechadoro, learned of the dean's visit to the courthouse and county library within hours. His time spent tracing down distant relatives was thus well-rewarded—they were pleased to learn that their ancestors now included famous warriors and to meet such a noble representative of their tribe.

Thanks to local inbreeding, he was sure that he could demonstrate that at least a quarter of the town's citizens had Indian ancestors. But while Flechadoro smiled at the thought of what an "Original Settlers Association" could do, he was concerned that this might undermine his claim on the college property: "What belongs to everyone belongs to no one."

He smiled again at the memory of last night's vision—following the late dean down the hall of the Administration Building. Maybe it would come again—if he had more peyote.

Chapter Three

Donahue awoke in a sweat. A terrible dream. Not the same as before, but with the same theme. He was in a revolution again, this time in China, probably in the Twenties, and he was responsible for a large railroad gun. The enemy, whoever they were, had an even larger cannon mounted on the first car of their armored train. Because normal artillery bogged down in the mud of the endless Chinese roads, these armored trains were the decisive weapons of war. Rarely did they meet face to face, but somehow his train was within a hundred yards or less of the other. Donahue realized that his crew had fled, leaving him alone. The enemy was directing small arms fire against him, and infantry was moving in on the flanks, but their large artillery piece remained silent. Were they trying to capture his train without destroying it? Why wouldn't his own gun fire?

Losing the gun intact would be a worse disaster than having the train destroyed. What should Donahue do? Glancing out the aiming port, he saw that the opposing train, coming slowly toward him, was almost exactly in his gun's sights. Twisting the aiming wheels with all his strength, he moved the barrel the few inches necessary to aim it directly at his foe. Now he opened the breech. Able to see the approaching armored train through the bore, he began the laborious process of bringing a large shell down the loading chute, then after almost dropping it several times, small arms fire all around, managed to insert it and close the breech. He looked one more time at the enemy train. It was not there! He awoke with a start.

As Donahue rinsed himself off, he knew that the dream had nothing to do with Chinese revolutionaries. It required no advanced degree in Freudian psychology to understand that the true message lay deeper, somewhere behind a Chinese wall.

Later that morning Donahue wondered if the symbolism of Chinese revolutionaries had not been highly appropriate. He saw the demonstrators marching past the classical façade of the administration building with signs proclaiming, DOWN WITH COMPEITION, END CAPITOLIST RULE, NO GRADES. Surely the incorrect spelling and lack of logic meant the end of civilization as he knew it. The Red Guards of not so long ago had marched their teachers and professors to public humiliations, then sentenced them to "reeducation" camps. Presumably, the camps were run on a "pass-fail" system, and he was guaranteed to fail.

He was impressed by the hardiness of the protestors. The weather was more conducive to staying in. Of course, the protestors probably did not care whether Green Bay or the Boston Patriots won the Super Bowl. The football team did, but they were too busy in the weight room to carry placards. With a shiver, Donahue turned toward the coffee house.

Flo Boater, coming onto the scene from a crosswalk, her head shrouded in a shawl, almost stumbled into the midst of the protestors; she thought briefly of confronting them, then decided that all that would come out of it was more bad publicity. Besides, she was cold. Not long before, she would have marched right up to them, then been out-shouted, and finally have to retreat in ignominious defeat. But since then she had attended presidential training seminars that advised giving into student demands, not matter how ridiculous, as long as the issues were inconsequential ones—freedom of speech, for example, was to be allowed for 'dirty' language, but not for speakers known to hold views that would hurt people's feelings—like advocating Christian beliefs or questioning abortion on demand. The line had to be held on the vital issues, however, which always meant "the money." In effect, she would control the cash, and her dean had to somehow control the students—her young Academic Dean, not the new, also young, Dean of Students. Meanwhile, she would just slip into the administration building by the less used of the side doors.

She had hardly vanished before the real action began. Stanley Wooda came charging out, without a coat, looking for one of his intimates, someone who could tell him what was going on, but he didn't see anyone he knew. All she saw were strange faces, students from God-Knows-Where, chanting NO GRADES, FAIRER TESTS.

Off to one side was Flechadoro, not participating, but watching. It was not idle watching, but he wasn't participating.

Not knowing what else to do, the dean began shouting, trying to be heard over the chants, "What's going on here? I thought we had an agreement." Then he saw Smith. Dashing over, he repeated his question/demand.

Smith stopped, put down his sign and yelled to the others, "Hey, it's *Stan* Wooda." As the chants died down, Jones joined them and explained, "That was over *Boater*. We're not demonstrating against *Boater*."

Wooda was too angry to take it in quickly, too angry even to react to the insolent *Stan*. "Well, what is this, then?" he asked. "This is the administration building. It sure looks like it's against Flo Boater."

Jones reacted to the shouts by replying loudly, "We are against the grading system! Competition is evil, tests are irrelevant to learning, consider our feelings, our self-esteem! We want the registrar!"

Wooda stepped back, stunned—grades? The registrar? And this from one of the students who wanted to buy grades from him? Smith's light push helped his backward motion, but more important, he felt his bowels loosening. Still, he was able to shout, "The registrar is off campus. Anyway, she doesn't give grades; she registers them!" He was relieved to see that this argument seemed to sink into Smith's brain; he began to relax—if he could persuade Smith, he could persuade any of them. He then looked around, saw Jones, and appealed to him, "I promised we would discuss the whole grading system. We can, we will."

"Discuss," Jones said dismissively, "that's just evasion. We want action."

Even more loudly, Smith hollered, more for the benefit of the demonstrators than for the dean, "Yeah, it's unfair!"

The lack of connection between action and unfairness brought a sudden stillness to the conversation. Even the bystanders quieted, listening for an explanation.

Shifting from foot to foot, Wooda asked, "What's unfair about it?"

Less loudly, but still audible to everyone who wanted to hear, Jones barked out, "It is all based on competition; worse, it's *corporatism*! Its foundation is pure dog-eat-dog capitalism."

Smith seconded him, "Yeah, we're against dog fighting."

"Corporative dog-fighting," Jones sneered. There was a murmur of background agreement which prompted him to add, "And we're the *cats*, caught in the middle!"

Wooda tried to explain, "No, it's about competence. You have to demonstrate competence."

"Competition, competence, corporations," Jones said, "I can't tell them apart."

"Me neither," added Smith. "But I know all 'bout demonstrating." More murmuring in the background.

Wooda thought the ideas sounded familiar. Perhaps something he learned in France. Hard to tell in translation. Harder yet to explain anything to this kids. Yes, he thought of them as kids, though he couldn't say that. What came out was, "You know, we aren't much different in age."

"No," Smith taunted him, "but we haven't sold out."

"We're not Oreos, like you," Jones added.

"Hell," he shot back, "you aren't even a little bit Black. But that's not the point." Nothing cowardly about Stanley Wooda, unlike the crowd surrounding him. Besides, though it was cold, he was wearing only a jacket—proof of his manly hardiness. His aggressiveness won him enough time for an effort to lead them aside a bit, to work his personal magic on them: "A diploma means that you know how to read and write, that you have mastered a subject, completed a major, that you can stick with something for four years."

While Smith and Jones thought about this, the clock struck. Several demonstrators hurried away to classes, exclaiming, "Off to biology," "O My God, my paper was due today," "See you at supper," and "God, my feet are frozen." Smith tried to stop them, "I need to write a story for the paper!" But even he saw that the numbers were now so small that it wouldn't qualify for a front page story. His editor had made it clear that she wanted significant news, not spontaneous pranks. He sighed. He knew that he had gotten the assignment only because the student newspaper rarely sent female reporters to cover events happening out of doors. This was not sex discrimination, but gender balance—for time out of mind, only coeds—as Flo Boater quaintly called them—had been editors, and the men did the leg work for them, especially in January, when the wind was brisk. This was a phenomenon that some serious scholar should have investigated, but social scientists were too busy explaining curious social customs in distant lands or long ago.

As the last demonstrators waved to Smith and Jones and departed, Wooda glanced up to see Flo Boater nodding approvingly, apparently very happy with his success at having dispersed the protest so completely, so rapidly. And so undeservedly, though he wasn't going to tell her that. His heart thrilled to realize that he could complete his triumph if he could only win the leaders over in the next few minutes; if he failed, however, they would be back. And soon!

"Why the demonstration over grades?" he asked. "Almost everyone leaves with a diploma. That's all that really matters—demonstrated competence."

With a sneer, Jones retorted, "If a diploma meant competence, how come the football players graduate?"

A very hostile Smith, oblivious to his supporters melting away behind his back, shouted for their benefit, "Yeah, how come?"

Wooda sucked in his stomach before responding, "This is Division Three. No General Education majors, no jock dorms. Athletes have to study."

Jones was unbelieving, "Oh, come on!" He didn't study, and he was more of a scholar than most of the "Pricks" he knew. Moreover, he had never seen Stan with a book in his hands.

Smith waved his hands dismissively, "Yeah, don't give us that." Smith was no prodigy, but he wasn't born yesterday.

Zooming in with the "killer comment," Jones exclaimed, "I've never heard of any athlete worrying about losing his scholarship here."

Dean Wooda, sweat breaking on across his forehead in spite of the cold, explained, "In Division Three we don't give scholarships!" The cold wind was getting to him.

Jones responded, "Woo, woo, woo. Another fairy tale."

Smith pretended that the dean couldn't see him. Turning halfway to an almost imaginary audience, he pointed at the shivering dean, "He does look a bit like a fairy. Look at him dancing; listen to him singing!" Smith had just learned this technique in a Theater class. That was amazing for several reasons. First, he hated theater; second, he rarely went to class; and lastly, he rarely stayed awake when he was in class. Of course, he was in Lily's class, and she had been known to go to students' rooms before class and awaken them. Keeping them awake in their seats was another matter. But she usually succeeded. In Smith's case, now, she had succeeded too well.

Wooda, stung by the reference at his efforts to dampen his intestinal rumbling, was outraged, "We don't allow sexist or genderist comments like that."

Jones was right in his face, "What are you going to do about it?"

Smith joined him, "Yeah, you don't want another demonstration."

Wooda, shifting from foot to foot, looked around for any of his "brown shirts," but didn't see any. Maybe later, after finding a john, he'd go by the gym. That Austrian body-builder might be hanging around; not Hollywood quality, but pretty impressive for Briarpatch. If not, he'd check out the dorm, where the exchange student watched *Terminator* over and over again. Nobody in sight. Realizing that he would have to handle this himself, and he had already lost valuable moments in thinking about what to do, Wooda was feeling truly ill. There was no time to think, just to act. Hurriedly, he agreed, "No, we don't. You'll just have to learn to clean up your..."

Jones cut him off, "Dean for a few days and Woody already acts like one!" He was clearly not impressed. "*Stan—ley*" he drawled, "another sell-out."

Smith sneered, "Sold out *fast*."

Jones added, "Probably for Cold Cash." His smile indicated that he was better clothed for the weather than the dean was.

Before Wooda could answer, Smith was on him again, "You know what you represent?"

"No, he doesn't," Jones interjected. "*Tell* him!"

"You represent the masculine force in society." He looked over to Jones to see that he got it right. Jones formed an O with his thumb and index finger.

Wooda was halfway happy that he was no longer a fairy, but he suspected that what was coming would suggest he was screwed.

Instead, Smith proclaimed, "We represent the feminine force, the healing, curing, caring force that is the future." He then glanced over to Jones again. "Just like Native Americans." With that he made a gesture toward Flechadoro, as if asking for confirmation.

Jones nodded with approved, then added, "You, in contrast, just think in straight lines."

Smith jumped in, "And we aren't straight." Then his argument fell apart, because he knew that he and Jones were not gay. They just couldn't get a date. At that moment Flechadoro made a gagging motion and left.

This was the moment for Wooda to retake control of the conversation, "Well, what does the feminine force want?" He was tempted to quote a famous philosopher, "What does a woman want?" But he suspected this would go right over their heads.

Jones pointed to his sign, "Can't you read? NO EXAMS."

Wooda was puzzled, as well as more frantic than before. He himself had been the most non-traditional student he had ever met, but he had never been that radical. "How can you have a college without exams?"

"You, yourself, "Smith taunted, "said we didn't need grades."

"Well," Wooda began defensively, "that would eliminate evaluation." He didn't want this discussion to move onto payments for a revised transcript.

Jones moved closer, and puffed up his chest, "Evaluate what?" he asked.

"Why, your…uh…education. To see what you've learned."

"If you've got enough beer, you'll get an education."

This was even more puzzling. Wooda had been non-traditional and unconventional, but he had always had a goal in mind, "How will that qualify you for a job?"

"A job!" Smith exclaimed. "We'll get jobs." What else are parents for?

Jones was even more optimistic, "By the time we find jobs, we'll get paid for not working."

"Not working?" Wooda asked.

"That's the future, man! This is the Nineties!"

"Welfare?"

"Nah, just tax rebates. You known Congress did something or other. No welfare any more."

Wooda tried to explain, "You can't get a tax rebate unless you pay taxes."

Smith tried to think about this—he couldn't see why not, but words failed him. It wasn't necessary to explain, anyway—as always, Jones came to his rescue, "Okay, we'll get a job of some type, for a while, then we'll retire early."

"How early?" Wooda asked, almost with a sneer, imagining (probably correctly), that they were thinking of twenty-five or so.

"Hell, man," Smith said, interrupting. "Can't you share the vision? Don't let the facts get in the way. Isn't that true, Jonesy?"

His friend picked up the cue, "Stan, don't you know the stock market is going up, and up and up? We'll be rich in four or five years, maybe less."

"You're going to be a stock broker?"

"Why not? All we need is a diploma, and you can give us that easily. You're our model, *Stan—eley*!" The implication was that they should get one without finishing their senior year, which was, in fact, almost true for Stanley Wooda—the dean still did not have his degree.

The dean, not wanting to go into that discussion and not knowing where to take this one, was ready to throw up his hands and leave, when he heard Jones say, "The *real* Dean Wooda got us grades."

This definitely got the young dean's attention. He turned and asked, "the *real* Dean Wooda?"

To Stanley's surprise, Jones gave a sensible answer, "Yeah, the *dead* one."

"What could he give that I won't?"

"With the *real* Dean Wooda, if you had the *green*, you got the *grade*."

Smith agreed, "Yeah."

Stanley, despite the implication that he was somehow not the *real* Dean Wooda, was now beginning to believe that the rumors were not just wild marijuana dreams, "You mean he really did sell grades?"

Jones sighed deeply, "Oh, how little you know."

Smith chimed in, "Him and that fat assed registrar."

"Ms. Hogg?" Wooda asked, unbelieving. He even forgot, momentarily, about his stomach troubles.

"Nah, not her. She's lost weight. The old one. The guy without hair."

"And all the others. New one every semester."

Wooda began to understand they meant her predecessors, "You mean the former registrars sold grades?"

Jones sighed again, "Don't be silly. The dean sold them. Like you said, the registrars recorded them." There was a pause, then, "Or something like that."

Wooda picked up the ambiguity, "You mean you, *you*, yourself bought grades?"

Proudly, Smith boasted, "How do you think I got to be a sophomore?"

Jones, who knew that they were both almost seniors, scoffed, "Yeah. Look at him, a real sophomore. After only four years here."

Very interested now, Wooda asked, "What courses did you buy grades for?"

Smith began counting on his fingers, "Biology, math, Spanish.... chemistry." Clearly he had forgotten with whom he was speaking. Had he been more clear-headed, he might have spoken to 'Dean Stan' anyway, but clear-headedness had been a rarity recently.

Jones laid his hand on his friend's arm, but Smith, who had been counting on his left hand, added one more, "History."

With this Jones disagreed strongly, "Na, nobody ever had to buy grades for history."

Smith stuck to his story, "I had to, I couldn't stand attending classes." When he saw Jones looking at him, he asked, "Or was it Sociology?"

Wooda broke in, "How did this, uh, scheme work?"

Jones shrugged his shoulders, as though there was no point in denying anything now, explained confidentially, "*Everybody* knows professors forget."

In a stage whisper, Smith added, "Bad memories."

"So?" the dean asked, logically. Everybody knew that.

Jones made a face, then spoke slowly and clearly, as if to a child, "You *attend* a few classes, *take* the exam...." As his voice trailed off Smith shrugged and finished the thought "...and you flunk."

The dean was mystified, which was what the boys expected.

Jones whispered confidentially, "A few months later you *pay* the dean, he *changes* the grades."

"*Everybody's* happy," Smith said. "The student, the parents, the college."

"Another potential failure saved," Jones concluded triumphantly.

Wooda was a bit dazed by this. He had been around, but he'd never heard of anything like it. All he could think to ask was, "The registrar didn't object?"

Jones explained dismissively, "They changed so often that they didn't notice."

"So," Wooda said to himself, "the registrar may never have been in on the scheme!"

Meanwhile, Smith had added, "And the professors never checked."

"Except maybe a *chairman*, looking at majors' grades," Jones quickly amended.

Smith reflected on this, "Yeah, Woody would never give a *passing* grade in a student's *major*."

"No?" Wooda asked.

Suddenly more sober, Smith explained, "That was real awkward, too. How would I, or anyone, graduate without C's or better in their major?"

Jones added more detail, "He just won't sell *good* grades. And not in the major, either—nada!"

Smith corrected him, "Except in choir. Everyone gets A's there."

"Yeah," Jones agreed. "A *C* would really stand out there."

Wooda suggested a reason for the late dean's restraint, "A professor might notice in a major. Departments are small."

Jones agreed, "Probably not, but too much risk, anyway."

"Some professors did check," Smith blurted out. "You had to avoid them."

"Concerned about their students?" Wooda asked.

"Maybe," Jones agreed.

Reflectively Smith said, "Mary C. was."

"And Lill," said Jones, who barely knew her.

"And Lily," added Smith, who remembered that her classes were ones he hated to miss, but he did anyway. After all, the one he had signed up for was too early in the morning. 10 AM. She had even come by his room to wake him up, which had required him to find alternate lodgings on Mondays, Wednesdays and Fridays.

Jones confided, "Sequential courses were too dangerous, too. But electives! And those 'integrated studies' that no one was in charge of."

Smith agreed, "Wow! The sky was the limit! Nobody ever checked those grades."

And Jones added, "But we didn't buy those. Everybody got a C anyway."

"Unless you disagreed with the professor, and we never did!"

"They have their secular theology, and we have ours. So whatever they said, went."

Smith, seeing the dean was confused, explained, "We never attended, so we never disagreed."

"That," Jones clarified, "made everybody happy."

Enthused, Smith added, "If they want socialism, that's okay with us, as long as we don't have to take part."

Wooda had a vague sense that he was a tenderfoot in this academic wilderness. Not certain whether they were telling him the truth or a version of the local tall tales, he led them into the coffee house and had them sit down with coffee before asking the next question, "What kind of grades did he sell?"

Smith winked at his companions and whispered, "Free coffee." They were more accustomed to stealing it, the pay-by-the-month program working on the honor system.

Jones took out a small flask, poured some brown liquid into his coffee before taking his first sip. He offered some to the dean, who declined without inquiring what it was. Jones then confided, "He never gave good grades. C's, a D here and there."

Smith added with a laugh, "For girls, a B."

Jones then shared a remembrance, "He used to joke that he saved the scarlet A for very special girls." He hesitated a moment before adding, "Smitty, ever wonder what that meant?"

Smith said that they had never figured that one out. He frowned when he saw Jones's smile.

The crisis passed when Wooda, shifting to another foot, leaned forward to whisper, "What if someone raised a question?"

Jones snickered, "Clerical error."

Smith added, "Or Hacker."

"Anyone but the dean," Jones summarized.

Suspicious, Wooda asked, "Why are you telling me all this?"

Jones reacted as if this were unbelievingly obvious, "If you don't know about it, how are you gonna start it up again?"

"Yeah," said Smith. "We wan'ta graduate."

Wooda, noting some lack of conviction in Smith's voice that tempted him to take the conversation in another direction—perhaps towards Smith's parents' desires—asked cautiously, "So the dean's death brought it all to an end?"

Jones nodded, "Yeah. Dean Lily wouldn't do it."

"She wouldn't?"

Smith agreed, "Na. Real hard ass."

"She knew about it?"

"Nah, when someone asked, she laughed at them."

Wooda's brows furrowed, "You mean, she didn't take them seriously?"

Smith nodded, "She thought I was joking."

In a confidential tone, Jones said, "She was about to look into it when Boater got her removed."

Smith nodded again, "The second time somebody asked, she got suspicious."

"Suspicious?" Wooda asked cautiously.

"Yeah," Smith said. "She told me to stop halucinaring, or something. Such a scheme would be too complicated, too many people involved. The registrar and computer director would have found out."

Jones added, "The student newspaper would have heard." He didn't remind the dean that Smith was the star reporter (which says much about the newspaper's quality). "*The Penprick* knows everything."

"But she began to snoop around," Smith said. "Till she got distracted."

"Good thing she got fired," Jones concluded.

This was interesting, Wooda thought, "And you want....?" It was time to get to the bottom line.

Jones finished his sentence, "You'da get back with the program."
"Yeah. We wan'ta..."

It was Wooda's turn to interrupt, "I getja." It was, he thought, a good parting line, and he made ready to run. This was a form of humor appropriate to peers, and by the reactions, Smith and Jones indicated that he was no longer their peer—he had sunk to some form of swamp-dwelling mammal, or reptile. A dean. He didn't even know what was going on. He had sold out to the "system."

Jones was nevertheless sufficiently practical to ask, "Whad'ya think?" That stopped the dean in mid-turn, his foot already lifted to walk away.

Wooda stopped, his head turned toward the boys, but his reply was evasive, "I think... I think I'd better talk to President Boater." And with that, shivering the moment he felt the cold wind, he hurried to the administration building.

Jones shouted after him, "You do that! You make her see what's good for her. Or we'll be back under her windows!" Then he marched off.

Smith, hurrying after Jones, added eloquently, "Yeah." That pretty much summed the situation up.

An hour later Lill entered the coffeehouse with a sigh. A quick glance around confirmed her suspicion—the usual crowd was totally absent. Lily was in class, as was Mary. DO she wasn't sure about. She was disappointed, but she understood that her friends could not be there waiting for her whenever she might show up—professors had lives of their own, hard as that was for students to believe, and most were busier than most people imagined. She smiled at that thought, "Some are almost as busy as they think they are." Normally, she wouldn't be free at this hour herself, but the power had gone out in the theater temporarily. Fried squirrel, she believed. It wasn't practical to work outside, because of the cold, so she had taken the students to the foyer, where there was at least more light, then divided them up into groups to prepare oral reports (she knew they had not done the reading, and even she found the text on set design utterly boring), and gone off for a cup of coffee. No point in even checking the coffee machine in her cubbyhole, since it was never left on unattended. Fire hazard. And why put temptation in the way of others? As for the lack of heat, their sweaters would do for an hour or so. As she took off her winter coat, she spied Professor Stout in a corner. He made eye contact, then indicated a chair.

With a sigh (and a shiver she attributed to the draft racing through the building), she gave him a nod, poured herself a cup of coffee and joined him. It was warm and that was all she really needed, but it would steel her for a conversation with a person who always had an agenda. "What was it this time?" she wondered.

"What brings you her at this hour?" he asked.

The question was a revelation. She had no idea that he came in often enough to know who was a regular and who was not. "Power outage. What brings you here?"

He laughed. It was that same semi-bray that so irritated Mary, a noise that did not quite convey an expression of mirth. More akin to contempt, though that was clearly not what he intended now. "I tell my honors students to meet me here when they have problems."

"Do they?" Seeing his brows furrow, she explained, "Come here."

He brightened, "No, actually, not often. So it gives me a chance to read my mail."

"DO does that, too," she noted.

He frowned slightly, "It's a good idea. There's no telephone here. Fewer disruptions."

She wondered if that were an invitation to leave, but quickly remembered his gesture to join him. "It is a good place to meet students." She wondered if he were aware of the raucous gatherings of her students here later in the day.

"And to think about the mail…." He paused before adding, "Like this letter here, from Lucy May Mankiller."

"Oh, yes, the president of Arcadia College. How's she doing?" She knew that Stout was "in tight" with the president, whatever that meant. Nothing romantic if she knew Lucy May.

He thought for a moment, then answered, "She's planning a nation-wide speaking tour. You know, Pittsburgh, Milwaukee, Boise, Des Moines… places that value her brand of cutting-edge feminism."

"Oh, interesting…." Lill replied.

"Boulder, too."

"Oh, yes. Boulder, too." Lill paused, but getting no response, asked, "What else does the letter say?"

He hesitated, then said. "She's got a problem." He stopped to think, waiting for Lill to say something. When she waited, too, even shifted her large frame a bit closer, he continued, "She wants to speak on the subject, 'never get laid again,' but she's not sure it will go over well."

Lill's eyebrows went up slightly, "What's her argument?"

Stout brightened at the question, apparently pleased that there was no ridicule in Lill's voice, "Women have to worry about stress, disease, pregnancy...." His voice trailed off.

"Humiliation," Lill suggested. She had heard President Mankiller speak to the subject before, only with a title that got less immediate attention.

"Oh, yes, humiliation. Certainly, humiliation." He fell silent again. How could he have forgotten that one?

"Something she must know from experience," Lill thought, but what she asked was, "What's the problem?"

"The problem? Oh, she wants my advice on the title. I think it's, it's a bit 'pop,' you know what I mean?"

"Yes," Lill laughed. "I think I do, and I think you're right. Something else would be better." At that she finished her coffee, studied the dark stain at the bottom of the cup, then explained that she needed to get back to see how her students were doing. At the door she turned and suggested loudly, "How about 'Sex without Fear?"

Stout reddened a bit when students turned to look at him, but quickly recovered. He thanked her quietly for her advice, but said that it would be easier to do away with the sex than the fear. "But," he said with a smirk, "that's the point of her talk."

Lill agreed. But she reminded herself that the potential for danger was one of sex's major attractions. At least for the unmarried and for adulterous relationships. The other attraction was familiarity and comfort, but no audience would rush to hear that. Maybe laziness, too, she thought, then wondered if Stout had heard her laugh. "Never get laid again," she said, almost choking. "That'll sure attract women!" Then after a pause, she smiled, "But if she wants publicity, it'll draw reporters."

As soon as Lill was gone, Stout began to mentally compose a reply, "On the matter of the title, it is of utmost importance to catch the audience's attention at the very onset of the talk. No, before the talk. The advertisement sets the tone of the entire event. Your title, though some might think it provocative, will certainly draw in a large crowd…." He smiled at having phrased his thought so well. Now, he wondered, how was she going to persuade young women that getting laid was so bad? He had just assigned his students a paper on the advantages of free love. What would she think if she learned of that? Then he smiled. He could deflect any questions by reminding her that since every student got an A, it really didn't matter what they said. He could imply that the really bright kids (yes, his mental reply had said "kids") would automatically react against any kind of authority. They would write against free love! Then he frowned again. President Mankiller was in favor of free love, just not with men. "Women who are truly emancipated," he remembered her saying, "don't need men for anything." Perhaps the maintenance of the species, he thought, but he then remembered that she was in favor of negative population growth. With a grunt, he pushed his half-empty cup away, awkwardly moved his chair back, and stood up. "How did I gain this extra weight," he wondered. "I guess I need to play tennis more often." He slung on his Florentine overcoat, noticing as he left the building that it was designed for a milder winter. Wondering whom he could persuade to play tennis, rain caused him to look at the sky. Rain, not snow. Light rain, but still rain. As his face moistened, he sighed again. Not today, not today. Not even bundled up. What else could one expect at this time of year? What did he mean by that? If he'd been asked, he couldn't have said, though his overcoat shed the moisture perfectly. More important, he saw that the lights had come on across the campus. Maybe he could chase the pickup basketball games off the court and put up the net in the gym. Surely there was someone willing to endure a beating—he needed an emotional boost right then.

Dean Threshold's inquiry into the census records went much quicker than President Boater had expected. He had a college friend at the regional archives of the US Census in Zenith who had immediately dispatched two interns to look through the indices, then into the actual records themselves. Alas, they could not confirm Flechadoro's claim to be a descendant of that defunct tribe—there had been lists of tribal members, but that particular Indian census was lost somewhere in a warehouse, or perhaps in the great fire that consumed the census of 1890. However, the census of 1900 indicated that families named Flechadoro—perhaps his great-grandparents—lived across the Midwest; some were white; others were colored; none claimed to be Indians, "Uh, Native Americans."

"Was there any connection to Middleville?" Flo Boater demanded.

"Maybe," the dean said hesitantly. "The elder family members were all born in this state."

Chief Biggs made the rounds of Ms. Hogg's neighbors. None had heard anything from her, and nobody, on or off campus, had any idea where she might have gone. He asked where she had been the morning the body of the young woman had been found. "Oh," they said, "she was gone long before that."

Chapter Four

The coffee house was abuzz with the usual midmorning conversations. Lill and Lily sat at a central table, with their customary collection of students around them. Some wanted to discuss "politics," but Lill had reined their enthusiasm by insisting that they talk about "issues" rather than expressing their "emotions." Some of the freshmen didn't know the difference yet. Some wanted to talk about the "patriarchy," the topic of the decade—with opinions unreflectively recycled from high school and other classes; and drugs, the issue of the era. On the whole their ideas reflected movies they shouldn't have watched, MTV, and favorite professors' opinions. Lill let them talk, as long as they spoke to the philosophies that underlay their chosen styles of life—which Lill feared were too often self-destructive—until a well-known transfer student asked passionately, "Why do old men in congress forbid us from using recreational drugs?" Everyone was nodding in agreement until Lill explained, "Because so few of them have the courage to face a mother whose child had died from drugs."

After a stunned moment, the young woman asked, "That can't be. Women have no influence in politics."

Suppressing a smile, Lill replied, "Women vote."

"But Stout says that women are naturally conservative, and easily led astray."

At this Lily, who had been uncharacteristically quiet, began to steam. What she wanted to say was, "Your comment is proof of that!" But, instead, she asked, "Oh, so he says that women are stupid?"

"Don't exaggerate," Lill warned, *sotto voce*, then explained. "He was just saying that he could make coeds believe anything." At that she winked at the student. Everyone knew that Stout had no interest in seducing students—the student grape vine would have passed along any suggestion about his "availability."

Lily missed the signal, "He thinks we're stupid."

"Yes," Lill responded. Then, putting a hand on her friend's arm, she explained, "Every poll suggests that women are more likely to vote for Democrats than for Republicans, that they support social programs more strongly, and they oppose any kind of military action, even in Bosnia and Kosovo, where rape is used for ethnic cleansing."

"Or so they say," Ellie interjected.

"Yes, so they say," Lill responded, then added, with a slight smile, "You can't trust the left-wing media."

"Left-wing!" Ellie countered. "It's all owned by millionaires!"

"PBS?" Lill asked, knowing that Ellie considered the Clinton administration hopelessly conservative, then asked another student what he thought of Stout's assertion—or, rather, the assertion attributed to him. She was careful to remind them that it was easy to misunderstand what someone had said, or meant. As the debate became more impassioned, Lill suppressed a smile at seeing her students struggle with conflicting beliefs that women were easily misled, had no influence, elected Bill Clinton, wanted health insurance and whether it mattered what happened in distant lands they had never heard of.

When the topic of drugs came up, Ellie remembered what Lill had said: "All these other things are irrelevant, at least to us right now." She looked around before sputtering, "You just said that mothers were against drugs. How can that be? Women take lots of drugs, persuaded by the pharmaceutical mega-monopolies that they will cure everything!"

"Ellie," Lill responded, seriously, "women are as complicated as men, but as mothers you can count on them to protect their children."

Ellie slowly stood up, turned, and left. As obvious as the explanation seemed, she hadn't bought it. Her parting statement was a challenge: "I'll think about it."

"That's what college is for," Lill responded to her retreating figure. She said to the others, "The answers change, but the questions remain the same."

Lily's brows puckered, "Isn't that what DO always says?"

Lill laughed, "What's your point?"

"I guess I don't know."

"Maybe that *even a man* can be right now and then?"

"Okay, I'll give you DO."

"If he were your's to give, that would be interesting," Lill laughed. "But what do you think about our dean, or our head historian?" She turned to the students, "You didn't hear that."

"Dean W's not a man," Lily croaked, pretending to gag on his name. She knew that Stanley was popular among the beer crowd and the girls, but she said it anyway—it wouldn't hurt for them to think about what being a man meant.

"The Creep?" one student asked.

"Not a human," another said.

This part of the conversation—hardly a credit to the Leather Lesbians—was ended by the students heading for their next class. They left, whispering to one another, some discussing the personal comments, the rest the ideas.

Lily, relaxing, smiled over to her friend, "Well, about half got the point on women's influence."

Lill smiled back, "50% will win you the batting championship in the American League any year." After a minute's reflection, she asked, "When will women stop complaining about the past and do something about the present?"

"Or listening to people like Stout! He calls himself a feminist, too."

"Yeah," Lily agreed grumpily, "Our colleagues announce that they won't take domination by men any more, but they give in the moment he raises his voice."

This incipient discussion was cut short by the sound of Molly's voice at a nearby table. "Who," she was demanding to know, "is that woman in my department who is being proclaimed 'teacher of the year?'" None of her companions—Donahue, Mary and Jenny—could answer because she wouldn't give them a chance. It was a reasonable question, she thought, since although English was the largest department on campus, it wasn't that large. Moreover, 'teacher of the year' was usually chosen in the late spring, by a hotly contested student vote, not so early in the semester; moreover, Molly, who understood that Lily or Mary would usually win any fair vote, knew that both were ineligible this year. Therefore, she herself, for the first time in years, stood a good chance. But here she had been beaten out, without having known the contest had started, by an unknown! A person who was apparently in her own department—a stealth candidate.

The conversation was not disturbed by Lill and Lily moving to join the group. They left their coffee cups behind, but two students at a nearby table gave them their chairs and even offered to get fresh coffee. That was one of the nice things about Briarpatch—students were still polite. Still, Lily grimaced at the thought that they were taking pity on two old ladies.

Mary asked what the person's name was and when she had been hired. At length, Jenny, too polite to break into anyone's half-started sentence, managed to say that Jay had mentioned there was something strange going on, but he didn't know what. This puzzled everyone, since Jay was the most knowledgeable person on campus about people and activities. As Lill's glance ran from one of her friends to the others, they spoke up, each providing a new detail. A story began to emerge.

The "person in question," as they described her, apparently taught a night class and rarely appeared on campus during the day. No office, but her name was in the campus directory—in the few copies that were distributed—and the students were properly registered. She used the "group method," giving everyone in the group the same grade—usually an A. Her students had apparently been individually encouraged to start the "teacher of the year" nomination and Dean Wooda had approved it, though technically part-time adjuncts did not qualify. Molly voiced some suspicion about this. The instructor wasn't particularly attractive, but the dean wasn't—reputedly—"choosy." At least not in recent months, she'd heard. No, no one had been approached, and knew of no one who had, but, as students were saying, "everyone knows…."

Lill broke in at this, *"Everyone knows* means that no one has proof." Meeting some downcast eyes, she asked, "What does Professor Stout say about it?" This brought about some smiles, because his honors program routinely gave out A's—as he explained it, at every opportunity, less time spent on tests meant more time available for learning.

To Lill's surprise, Professor Stout apparently knew nothing about it—he hadn't been on campus enough to notice the new instructor's presence until recently, and the dean had hired her during one of his absences. She had been given the award because students had endorsed her strongly, writing to the president, the trustees and the student newspaper! (The editor hadn't printed the letters, but had passed on the "widespread student endorsement" to Flo Boater.) This campaign had been quietly organized by Flechadoro, who had, in effect, bypassed Stout, who had told several students indignantly that they should have consulted him.

"What about student freedom and initiative, his favorite themes?" Lily asked, somewhat maliciously. She smiled when she heard that Elllie had asked that very question, only to be told that there was a time and a place for everything, and that people needed to remember who their friends were.

At this Lill made a mental note that the matter should be investigated, and she decided that Donahue would be the chief investigator.

Mary wondered if they were talking about Irene. She couldn't imagine her participating in something underhanded, and she would have described her as attractive. But there were more adjuncts than she could name, and they all seemed more popular than the tenure track faculty. So she kept her guess to herself.

At the far end of the building, pretending not to notice, Flo Boater was dictating letters into a recorder for Miss Efficiency to rewrite later. (Miss Efficiency, who was now secretary for her third president, would always put her thoughts into the correct words before laying them before her employers to sign. No one dared make changes in a draft, or saw the need to do so.) Mary and Molly observed this, saying to one another, "There she is, in her 'office,'" and "Yes, out here she can avoid appointments."

Mary shook her head, "How can she claim to be 'available' to students? No one ever goes near her."

"It's a brave student who'll sit down with a college president! Especially if they are obviously busy."

"I feel the same way!" Mary confessed, "and I know her."

"Watch this," Molly said, and pointing discretely at Flo Boater sorting the mail. Letters she put in one pile to open later, junk mail she threw in a trash can, and faculty communications and committee minutes joined the junk mail. "That's why you never get an answer to a note." To herself she wondered why the president hadn't learned to read the notes, but she could not formulate a better answer than "habit" and "human nature." She asked the others, "Why doesn't see get someone to look at the notes we sent her. I'm sure that one she just discarded was mine."

Lill responded, "I've heard that Dean Threshold is responsible for sorting through them."

Lily could not resist a joke, "She's just making his job easier."

Mary felt her spirits sink. She had written to inquire about action on her tenure process. She had the earlier note promising presidential support, but there had been no faculty action yet, much less an announcement by the trustees. A flush came to her face thinking about this. It was all Donahue's fault. He had gotten Flo Boater's signature on the letter guaranteeing tenure, but forgotten that tenure was awarded by the trustees, not the president. Or, rather, there was no time to negotiate with trustees. Was Flo Boater using that excuse to keep her dangling? Was her inquiry about a decision among those now in the trash?

A few minutes later Flo Boater looked at her watch, reluctantly put her papers and recorder into a briefcase, signaled to Jay, the chief janitor, to dispose of the trash, looked questioningly at her "enemies" drinking coffee together, and, tugging the collar of coat closer around her neck, walked down the long curving sidewalk to the administration building. There, in Miss Efficiency's office, she found Salvatore Iva waiting for her.

She moved toward him, laying her coat on a chair and spreading her arms for an embrace, "Sal, it's so good to see you!"

To her surprise, he rebuffed her, "That's all over, Flo."

She stepped back—almost no one refused one of her hugs. Not that everyone wanted a hug, but no one wanted to offend her. She looked at him questioningly, glancing over at Miss Efficiency, who was busily pretending to be typing something onto the computer screen, and led him into her office. He looked around at the massive space, so greatly changed since Floyd Boater's days. But she left him no opportunity to look at the remodeling, despite his having no intention of doing so long. She led him to the PC (the "power circle" of chairs for intimate visitors), sat him down, then took a seat opposite and asked, "Over?" With a bemused smile at his lack of reaction, "Are you sure?"

He nodded and said firmly, "Molly is my woman from now on."

Almost taunting, she asked, "Isn't she a bit old for you? She *is* the dean's widow."

Sal observed quietly, "She is younger than you." This was quite a change from his usual studied politeness, but it did build the invisible fence he wanted between them. Still, it was not quite a challenge—prison had beaten that out of him.

Archly, Flo Boater retaliated, "Not by much, but she did stick by you better than you stood up for me."

"That's not fair, Flo!" Sal protested, with more of a whine in his voice than he wanted.

"Not fair, how?"

"I went to prison because of you!" He felt better for having said it, then stood and walked to the nearest window.

Flo Boater followed, turned him around and gave him a great slap, shouting, "You tried your best to send me there, too! Some loyalty!"

Sal turned back toward the window, "But you were guilty! I wasn't."

"Now think about it," she growled. "You never had to say anything. If you had only bluffed it out, as I did, you would have never have been convicted." Rolling her eyes, she led him back to his chair.

He took deep breaths before complaining, "The plan never included killing anyone."

Laughing quietly, she said, "Floater did in the dean, not us." She leaned over to touch his knee. "Not that he intended to. The dean—my ex-lover, as you know, before you, well, you know." She wasn't going to say, "took me away from him." That would make her look weak. While "before I seduced you" made her look manipulative. Her compromise was: "Woody probably left that little pill on my husband's desk, assuming that Floater would take it right away, but it had gotten mixed in with some other pills. So he resorted to Plan B—you remember. But by then Floater had recommended some new pills—you remember what a hypochondriac Woody was! He swallowed his own poisoned pill! Isn't that a scream?" She laughed and invited him to join. But when he didn't, she removed her hand and continued, "Six months later my idiot husband presses the worry ball just right, the poison strikes. Not enough to kill him, but he dies of fright. Just popped off." She sniggered before continuing, "Both of them should have paid more attention to what they swallowed or passed around." She leaned over to pat his knee as she said, "You had nothing to do with it. Neither did I."

Sal, shaking his head, asked, "How can you even talk about it like that?

Flo Boater playfully answered, "You think I'm afraid? What if the worst happened?" She rose, invited him to the window again and asked, with a wave toward the campus, "You think my running all this is an accident? I didn't plan those deaths, but I worked hard to prepare myself for this job." Getting no response, she continued, "I didn't expect to be president yet, but I knew I'd be dean." Then she stopped suddenly enough to make him turn toward her, "Say, are you wired?" As he protested no and turned around, hands on the window sill, she patted him down, starting professionally and ending with a soft caress. "This subservience," she thought to herself. " He isn't the Sal I used to know." She smiled as she walked way, then turned to croon, "If know, if you had been wired, it wouldn't make any difference what I said. I've already been tried and found innocent."

Following her back to the chairs and sitting, Sal said in a quivering voice, "The Board of Trustees...."

"He's got no backbone now," she thought. Exploiting her advantage, she playfully moved behind him and put her hands on his shoulders, "I was just playing you along." When he did not respond, she began to give him a soft massage, "To see what else you might have been up to."

At this Sal stood up, "Flo, I didn't come here to be teased."

"Then why? For 'old times' sake?'"

Subdued again, he croaked, "Not that, either."

"Then?" she asked, learning forward.

Shaking his head, he said softly, "It sounds so silly now." Unsteadily walking the length of the room, he grasped the back of a chair at the giant conference table, then sat down, his head in his hands.

Flo Boater knelt down, took his hand and said, "Come along, Sal. What sounds so silly?"

"Students wrote me while I was in prison."

She let go, stood up, and walked over to the window, where she looked out onto the campus before answering, "I should have expected that. Some of them were very fond of you." When he did not answer, she moved behind him again, putting her hands on his shoulders— an awkward move, given the height of the chair—and whispered seductively, "After all, I was."

His response was cold, "You didn't write."

Playfully, she said, "Now, that would have been foolish!" And she tried to knead his shoulder muscles, those she could reach.

Surprised, he turned to ask, "What? How foolish?"

"That might confirm that we had been... well, that we had been...."

"I see."

"Far too dangerous, far too risky."

"You mean you might have gone to prison."

She moved back to the window. After a moment's silence, she turned again, her voice raised, "And you would still be there. After all, it was my letter to the parole board that got you released."

"I suppose so."

Recovering her businesslike attitude, she faced him again, "Now what did these students write about?"

"They wanted to know about their grades, whether I had graded on a curve, or what?"

"Had you?"

"No! In chemistry you have to know the material. If you are only right seventy percent of the time in mixing chemicals, you'll harm somebody."

Looking out the window, she responded calmly, "That makes sense."

"I never graded on a curve. You can't turn out chemists who haven't mastered the material."

She thought a moment before her next question, "So, why did they ask?"

"Because some of their friends got better grades than they did, and they couldn't understand why. One blonde even got an A! That's what they wrote. Impossible. She couldn't have remembered the formula for peroxide!"

Suddenly agitated, she led him back to the chairs, then asked, "What did you tell them?"

"That I would check it out. They gave me a couple of names. Non-majors. I didn't remember them coming close to passing."

Suspiciously, she asked, "Why have you come to me?"

"I still had my grade books. I wanted to compare those grades with the registrar's files."

"Ah, I see. You couldn't see the students' records without her permission. Privacy."

"Exactly," he replied, hesitatingly slightly because he had almost replied in Italian—a habit that prison had almost broken. A moment later, he added, "And because I'm no longer employed, I can not look at them. Miss Hogg could make an exception, but she is away. Only you, or perhaps the dean, could give permission to see them. I don't know the dean, so...."

"I had rather hoped you'd just come to... well, say hello." When he didn't respond, she said, "If you'll give me your grade books, I would be glad to check them out for you." She extended a hand, as if she expected him to have his grade books with him.

Suddenly Sal was suspicious. "No," he said. Then after a pause, waiting for her to speak, he added, "I don't think that would be a good idea." What he didn't say was that he had left them in his office; since he had not been replaced by a new hire, the office was still unoccupied and probably not even the locks had been changed. If she knew that, they might not be there long.

With an excellent pretense of surprise, she asked, "Don't you trust me, Sal?"

Sal was confused. He did not want to offend her—that would ruin any chance of ever getting a job at the college again—but he was not going to surrender his grade books. If he had thought ahead, he would have made a copy, but how could he have imagined being arrested for murder? All he could do was to stammer, "I think, I think I'd better do that myself."

"You just want to see the grades the registrar recorded?"

"Yes, *esatto.*"

She smiled at his lapsing back into Italian, as he did under stress or in lectures. She nodded that she understood, but she was firm, "I don't think I can let you...after all, you are no longer on the faculty... it could so easily be misunderstood."

Sal was not so easily persuaded, "I don't see how. Who would know?"

Instantly she retorted, "Sal, think about it. How many secrets are there on a small campus?"

"Well," he argued, "no one knew about us."

"Sal, *everyone* knew about us." That wasn't true, but there were, as a rule, few secrets on a small campus, and they had agreed to stop meeting in order to avoid a scandal. "Except my husband, and he was as dense as a post."

"And Dean Wooda."

She responded playfully, "Ah, yes. Dean Wooda." Then she laughed, "Well, deans are too busy with paperwork and committees to keep track of what goes on."

Sal was unbelieving, "*Everyone* knew?"

"Everyone who counted."

"Molly, too?"

"Almost certainly," Flo Boater remarked, then continued. "When it came out in court, it doesn't seem to have surprised her."

A hand on his heart, he gasped, "*Dio.*"

"Don't take it so seriously," she advised. "She's probably forgiven you long ago." Then she added, "On the other hand, our seeing each other again, so privately..."

He shuttered, "She didn't want me to see you."

"Maybe you underestimate her," Flo said, with a smile. "She probably understood that I couldn't possibly let you near the registrar's office."

"I wanted to ask for a job. At the Personnel Office."

She smiled again, "Be realistic, Sal. You know that would be impossible."

"If you won't help," Sal said. "I will go to the newspapers. They will be interested. Grades for sale."

"Do that," she responded quickly, "and I'll pick up a phone..." With a sly smile, she imitated dialing a phone, "and talk to the parole board." She put the imaginary phone down and said, "Once I tell them of your threat, you'll be back in the pen faster than you can get into a stripped suit again."

Sal replied, "Prisoners wear orange now." After a blink, he added, "That's blackmail!"

"Call it what you like," she said. "It's college policy."

"I will find a way," he said.

Leaning over to touch his arm, Flo said, "Sal, calm down." After a moment he broke free and turned away in a sulk. She leaned forward, saying loudly, "Sal, if I hear one word more about this, you go back to jail." When he didn't respond, she grabbed his arm, turned him around and said, "A woman was found dead near the gym not long ago."

He didn't understand.

"If you had been employed here, everyone would have wondered if you had murdered her."

"She was murdered?"

"No, but who could tell. Your just being around would have been suspicious."

"They would have suspected me?"

"Of course. You are an ex-con." Watching till his blinking stopped, she asked, "Now do you understand?"

He answered morosely, "Yes, I understand."

"You are not to talk to anyone about grades. Not your grades, not Molly's grades, nobody's grades."

"Yes, I understand," he said, rising as if to leave. "Yes, I think."

Standing up to face him, she said quietly, "Sal, let me explain." Not being able to make eye contact, she spat out, "Sal, it's not a cover-up."

"No?"

Holding him firmly at an arm's length, she explained, "No. It's a matter of protecting the college reputation." When he seemed to doubt her, she added, "We've had some hacker problems. Someone has broken into the system. We're on top of it. We think we can correct all the changes in time. But we don't want the story broken until we've caught the culprit. Do you understand?'

Glumly, he mumbled, "I suppose." It was not an explanation he could disagree with. Certainly, it there had been someone breaking into the computer system, the problem would have been kept as quiet as possible. Also, that would explain the discrepancy between the grades he remembered giving and what he had heard reported, and it suggested that the administration was working to find the culprits and correct the changes. In short, she had him boxed in. Moreover, if she reported to the parole board that he was making himself unwanted on the campus, they might chose to reconsider his release. After all, her letter had been very important. Presumably, a suggestion from her that she had made a mistake would be... well, it didn't bear thinking about. That just had to be avoided at all costs.

Flo Boater saw that she had made her point. She smiled, saying, "That's good. Now give me a hug and we'll forget all about it."

Sal returned the hug reluctantly, but he could hardly refuse. He muttered, "I am pleased you explained."

"I'll look into your grades."

"Thank you."

In a motherly voice, she said, "Okay, now run along. I've got business to take care of." It sounded strange even to her ears, since they were so close to the same age, but her slight push cancelled that out. When he had his hand on the doorknob and turned half-way round to look back at her, she added seductively, "Don't be so long in making your next call."

Sal opened the door slowly, said, "Good bye, Flo," and left.

Within minutes, Flo Boater asked Miss Efficiency to tell Ms. Hogg to come to her office. She was surprised to learn that the registrar had not yet come back to work. She was even more surprised to learn that Jenny was doing her work.

When Dean Threshold appeared at Miss Efficiency's office, he was puffing from his dash up the stairs. "No," he told the president moments later, "I have no experience in a Registrar's office."

"That's okay," Flo Boater responded, "it's pretty much common sense."

When he stared at her, obviously wondering what that meant, she explained, "I don't know that we'll need a replacement for Ms. Hogg, but I'd like to send Jenny back to Music. So I'm thinking of having you take over, temporarily only, just till we can conduct a search. Only part-time, of course. In addition to your regular work for me." She paused a moment before adding, "It wouldn't be hard, it's right down the hall."

His eyes widened as he thought of the long stairway from the ground floor. He was already going up and down more times than…. This on top of the assignment to circulate the photo of the young woman, that poor soul who had frozen to death in the wood. He understood why the chief thought it possible the young woman was trying to reach one of the students—a friend, perhaps, or a sister, someone the same age—but why he had to go up and down the stairs, up and down the halls—rather than pass out flyers to dorm residents. Oh, well, this was Briarpatch College, and if the president wanted to limit publicity, that was her business.

As for Flo Boater, if the grade scandal flared up again—Sal couldn't be relied on to let it lie—she wanted someone reliable in the registrar's office. Jenny was too close to Molly, and Molly was practically engaged to Sal. Dean Threshold? She couldn't read him very well. But he seemed to be doing a good job with the mail. And what other choices did she have?

And that rumor—that the dean's ghost was haunting the building. She'd have to get Jay to tighten the floor boards. As if a ghost had weight!

Chapter Five

Flo Boater reached across her desk, picked up the phone, then spoke a few words concluding with, "Yes, right now," and leaned back. Within seconds Stanley Wooda was coming through the door, saying, "Thank God you're finally here." She signaled him to close the door and sit down. As soon as he was composed, sitting bolt upright, she explained, "Stanley, we've got a problem with Sal."

Wooda ignored this, blurting out instead, "We've got a bigger problem with students. They believe that grades are for sale."

She rolled her eyes. "Why me, God?" she almost said, but she recovered enough to say only, "They were." The two problems were connected—Sal and grades, students and grades.

The dean slumped back into his chair, asking, "I've been hoping it wasn't true."

Calmly Flo Boater said, "It *was* true. Perhaps until very recently, until Dean Wooda, that is, the late dean, died."

Young Dean Wooda gave a low moan. It was too soft to be an exclamation and too loud to be an escaped thought. He looked hard at her. This was not something she had just learned. How long had she known? What was getting himself into?

She ignored his body language, "That was why Sal was here, to find out what was going on."

The dean sat slowly up, trying to formulate a question. Finally, he asked, "What did you tell him?"

"A cock and bull story about some hacker breaking into the computer."

"Will he believe it?"

"Not for long," she said. "We've got to get him out of town. That probably means getting rid of Molly, too."

That reminded him, "Speaking of Molly, she wants to see you." His eyes indicated that she was in his office, waiting.

With a resigned sigh, she said, "Bring her over." Replacing Jenny would have to wait.

Donahue could not remember having ever been so depressed. His last conversation with Mary C. had not gone well. She had come very close to telling him to leave her alone, but at the last instant, she had not. It had been back and forth. Yes, she liked him; yes, he was what every sensible woman wanted; no, she was not ready; no, she did not want to talk about it. The only people he could think to ask what to do were Lill and Lily, who, despite their eccentricities and lack of personal experience with the kind of marriage he wanted, were astute observers of the human species. Moreover, they were in Theater, and more psychological problems appeared in plays than anywhere else (except perhaps soap operas, which, he had often told students, were only extended plays in which all the problems of an entire community were foisted upon a small number of characters).

He found them in the theater 'lounge,' as they now called the breakfast nook . This was officially a small seminar room, but mornings it was a 'nook,' and inevitably Lily came to make a joke out of it). They wanted to banter, but Donahue's face sobered them up quickly. He held his coffee in his lap, leaning back into a comfy chair. "What is Mary's problem?" he wanted to know, "Or is it just me?"

Lill glanced at Lily, who nodded. At this Lill indicated that he should closer, until their knees almost touched. That way nobody could overhear. There were students working not too far way—not many, most having faded out after the all-nighter, but among them were a few much like Smith and Jones, whose ears were famous for picking up private information. Smith and Jones themselves usually came in only for "breaking down" the sets, since it was traditional to have a great party once the place was cleaned up, but it was so early in the semester that they had only begun hammering and painting. Lill wouldn't have stood for that if they had bothered to enroll in the Technical Theater class, but she tolerated absences among volunteers.

Lill took a careful look around her. This was clearly a very private matter. She took a deep breath before starting, "What has she told you about her family?"

"Nothing," Donahue admitted, "and that has bothered me a bit." He sighed, "No, it's bothered me a lot."

"It should," Lily said, for once not making a joke, "people need to know a lot about one another before they get too serious."

Donahue admitted that he had been remise, "It's particularly bad for a detective not to check."

"Hell," Lily said, "she wanted her privacy, and if she'd found you were snooping.…"

"That's why I didn't. Getting caught would be fatal." It would also have been ungentlemanly, and, he thought, unnecessary.

"It's like this," Lill said. "Canary's not her real name."

Lily interrupted, "It's her real name, it's just not her birth name."

Donahue broke in, "I've always wondered about that, why anyone would put those two names together."

"That's how we learned the story," Lill explained. "We asked about it."

"Her real name was Woolworth or something like that," Lily interjected.

"Woodward," Lill corrected. "Her father was a bank examiner, or the equivalent, working for some very large firms."

"Constantly on the move," Lily added, "Off to this place for three or four days, there for a week. Away from home all the time."

"He tried to get his wife to join him on some trips," Lill said, "but she wouldn't."

"Some nice places, too," Lily commented, reflecting briefly on the potential holidays that Mary's mother had passed up, "but she wouldn't leave the children even for a weekend."

Lill sighed at this, "In the end, his secretary got him. There was a divorce. A good settlement."

Donahue wasn't sure what this meant, so he asked, "How old was Mary at that time?"

Lill looked at Lily before answering, "Six or seven." Lily nodded.

"A sensitive age," he noted.

"All ages are sensitive," Lill stated, then looked at Lily, who added, "Only in different ways."

"What then?" he asked.

Lill sighed again, "A year or two later he was killed in a car accident. Together with his new wife and their baby."

"A real tragedy," Lily said. "He really was a good man. That much Mary told us years ago."

Lill agreed, "Mary learned that even good men can bring heartbreak. Commitment has its risks." With that she gave a meaningful glance at Lily.

Lily responded with a slight smile, then continued, "It was very hard on Mary's mother." She paused for a moment to think of the right words, "and afterward she didn't even have the child support."

"No insurance?" Donahue asked.

"There were a lot of debts," Lill explained. "He had two mortgages, two families, and he hadn't reached that point in his career that the salary was really good yet. He had dropped some insurance rather than ruin his credit rating; the rest went pretty fast."

Donahue pondered this before continuing, "Then her mother met Mr. Canary?"

"Yes," Lill said, "when Mary was about fifteen. Isn't that right, Lily?"

"That's my memory of it. They had to move to a new community, new school. Mary didn't really like him, but it wasn't her choice."

"Why did she take his name, then," Donahue asked.

"There was this Canary Foundation," Lill explained, "that guaranteed every family member a college education. It was a very good program."

"It ought to be!" Lily exclaimed, "to change your name to that!"

Lill hurried to explain before Lily launched into a monologue, "Lily means that it started as a small family program...."

Lily interrupted, "...begun by a great-great uncle or something, who felt that he could have been a real success if he had only gone to college."

Lill finished her thought, "It was a nice sum, but it grew larger after several bequests came in from people who were interested in bird protection. They saw the name of the fund, then drew their own conclusions."

"Large bequests," Lily broke in, "so the family made arrangements for a pet store to take in ownerless canaries. It became such a popular attraction that they had to add onto the building, then they had to add to the parking lot. Make room for school buses, that sort of thing. It was a big-time business success."

"What Lily means, is that older people could enjoy their pets, knowing that there would be a place to send their birds if they became too ill to care for them or if they died. Most often, the younger birds would be adopted, not sold, and elderly birds could be kept in an environment that suited them. Well, you know, stimulating, caring. The owners could even visit them."

"The upshot," Lily gushed, "was that the foundation got more and more money."

"So what had started modestly, as a college fund," Lill persevered, "expanded to several cities and came to include even more distant relatives. Only those bearing the name, however." She paused for a second before continuing, "On that point, they were very strict. Even those who had married were excluded."

Donahue, massaging his lips, commented that this seemed to benefit the men more than the women.

Lily agreed, but she was still enthusiastic about the program, since it discouraged early marriages, which were usually unwise. "Also, it paid her tuition for a very good school. She had some scholarships, of course, but the main thing for her was to go far away."

"What did her mother think?" Donahue asked.

Lill thought about this before saying, "I believe that she told Mary that it didn't make any difference. One day she would be changing her name anyway."

Lily sighed and observed that it was an old-fashioned practice, but it had its practical points—you could keep track of who was who, especially if there were children, and at parties you could put pairs together so that you won't say the wrong thing to the wrong person. But today, with divorces and multiple remarriages...; in the Spanish-speaking world a woman at least kept part of her identity.

"Mary was, of course," Lill said, returning to the subject, "sensitive about the rhyme. People made fun of it, and she was shy to begin with."

"I've always wondered if that isn't why she studied Spanish," Lily said reflectively, "because in that language her name automatically defaults to Maria."

Donahue nodded, then asked, "Couldn't her step-father have paid the tuition himself?"

Lill was embarrassed when she answered, "DO, he was a cop." Nothing more had to be said. But there was more. She continued, "And in her senior year he was killed in the line of duty."

Dean Threshold went down the steps, wondering why he had been given his next assignment, before he had finished the first, and why he had been warned so strongly not to tell anyone about it. Not even his wife. He wasn't sure he could do it—he told her everything.

Chapter Six

"Her mother took it very hard," Lily said.

"I see," Donahue said. "No risk, no pain."

"Exactly," they agreed.

He pondered this, knowing that his friends were observing him silently, trying not to look at his face. At length he asked, "What do you suggest I do."

"Dearie," Lill whispered, "If we knew, we'd have told you long ago."

Flo Boater told Miss E to have Molly wait: "I have some important business right now, but it won't take long." If lucky, she told herself, Molly would become tired and leave. Meanwhile, she had her nails to do. Ah, if only she had time to have a professional do them. But in Middleville, the only professional always let her know how unpopular the college was in the community.

Her eyes drifted to the windows. Light rain, instantly freezing.

Smith had just met the girl of his dreams—Ellie. Not for the first time, but now he had fallen hard, tripping over the thread of hope she had strung out in front of him. He had seen her at the demonstrations the previous year, but he had failed to get beyond an occasional short conversation—she had come over from Arcadia and he had no car, so he couldn't even walk her back to her dorm or offer her a ride back. She had transferred to Briarpatch, expecting to have a lively political debate every day, but she was soon disconcerted to learn how much alike most colleges are. There was an appalling lack of intellectual challenge— that is, most students at Briarpatch, but most of all Smith, saw the demonstrations as political theater and, therefore, were not interested in debating the issues; demonstrators were interested in action, not thought or talk. She couldn't say specifically what else she had expected to find, she said. Stanley Wooda, of course, Smith suspected, was one of Briarpatch's attractions, but she said that Stan had gotten somewhat stand-offish after he became dean. Flora Boater's influence, most likely. Jealous. Most older women were, especially the ones struggling to keep their weight down. While Ellie had no problem—she remained slim as a rail without effort. More importantly, Ellie had seen that Arcadia College under Lucy May Mankiller was so politically correct—if that new term had any meaning on a campus so liberal—that there wasn't anything to protest against without becoming a conservative!

Ellie had initially dismissed Smith as a light-weight, but she was amused by his clumsy efforts to seduce her. She also liked his five-minute documentary for Lill's television production class, a study of the last season's demonstrations. It didn't have much content, but it was lively. It had caused a sensation in Arcadia, both because it was done at Briarpatch—where such talent was unexpected—and because that handful who had driven to Briarpatch to participate in the rally were proud of the brave blows they had struck for freedom of expression.

Reality in the form of classes hit Ellie hard. The classes weren't that difficult, but the adjunct professor in Philosophy was actually criticizing her writing style instead of praising her imagination. Although she had listed herself an English major, she didn't take any literature classes because she was too advanced and too sophisticated to study novels and poetry (and she suspected that the English faculty felt the same way). Instead, she enrolled in Sociology, Theater, Philosophy and a course in general science (on the assumption that she might need to make soap someday if she decided to live in a commune). On the whole, those classes were not much of a challenge—she aced the first exams, then began to cut classes. She loved the coffee house chats, the morning give and take between Lily and her worshipping students. That was what she had wanted, though it was disappointing to discover that Lill considered Derrida a relic of the past—and never really understood outside California and its East Coast subsidiaries; also that the class met so early in the morning. She had no memory of meeting either of them on the campus earlier. But that was to be expected—she had been so sleepy, and so high on excitement that she had just passed out.

And that was why Smith had not been able to find her after the last big demonstration had broken up—she had gone to sleep. Splendor in the grass. And her group had forgotten about her, so that when she finally awoke, she had a difficult time finding a ride back to Arcadia. At last some poor guy took her home in his broken down pickup, and for his efforts he barely got a thank you. Nothing close to a kiss. And nothing at all like what he had thought she had promised. Or, at least, hinted at.

That was what had so elated Smith now. After two years of not even holding a hand—contemporary dance didn't even permit that—here was a girl who hinted at the date of a lifetime!

"How did I ever manage to meet her?" he wondered. "And what was different this time?" Accidentally, of course, and who knows? Like Smith, her preference for sleeping past noon had made it just too difficult to attend the coffee house seminars in the fall. Or even many classes. But the previous evening she had seen her in the line at supper. Jones was asleep again, prepping for a party that evening. Cutting into the line and politely excusing himself to the largest football player he had ever seen, Smith introduced himself again. She pretended, he thought, to not remember him, but they fell into conversation easily.

"How are things going?" he asked.

"Okay, I guess. But with the registrar gone, I can't get my transfer credits straightened out."

"Bummer," he said. A period of silence ensued, while he tried to think of something to say.

"Registrar's a bitch."

He thought for a while, wondering if he dared tell her how to resolve the problem, but the gigantic athlete was watching them, well, her, carefully; and hanging on every word. Besides, he had recently had a confrontation with a half-wit considerably smaller than this one, and the guy had literally hung him on a coat rank. He flushed at the thought of how his feet had almost touched the floor, but not quite. He noticed that she noticed, and blushed at the thought she must think he was blushing.

She glanced up now and then, but remained silent until the giant said, "Yo, you gonna move the line 'long or just stand dere?"

Once Smith had invited the giant to move ahead of them, Ellie spoke up. Looking at the huge guy now standing in front of them, she congratulated Smith on breaking into the line so suavely and resolving the crisis so cleverly, then whispered, rather loudly, "Most men here are just dumb jocks; all they think about is obeying the rules."

"One thing about me," he had answered, "is that I'm neither dumb or a jock."

When she said, "That's fine," Smith had added, "I defy all conventions, all expectations!"

"I agree," she had gushed. "There should be no limits on what we can think and do."

Smith certainly wasn't going to mention her to Jones. Or take her to the party. What did "no limits" mean? And what did it mean that she said that to *him*? But how to keep her a secret? He and JJ were like Siamese Twins. It was a miracle that he had wandered down to the cafeteria alone tonight and managed to meet this marvelous creature—he almost never ate supper this early. But she if ever saw Jones. No, "seeing" was okay. But if she "listened" to Jones, and if she liked brains… then it was all over for *his* chances!

Across the campus, Flo Boater was settling into her new "power chair." It was the latest "must have" item for "rising administrators." She was as sure that it would impress the trustees as she was that faculty would seize upon it as a symbol of misdirected expenditures. What could she use as an excuse? A bad back? Maybe. She was in good shape, given her dislike of exercise, but the "power diet" had kept her reasonably slim. Ah, if only she could wear stripes without causing sniggers. But even pin-stripes caused people to call them pen-stripes and glance quietly in her direction before laughing among themselves.

She picked up the phone and called Miss Efficiency. If would have been possible to walk to the door and speak to her secretary, but that would involve getting out of this marvelous chair—not exactly an easy task—or she could have called out, but that might have seemed "un-presidential." "What is my schedule for the rest of the day?" She had some appointments. Quickly, she ran through them in her mind. The first was Molly. Oh, yes. She had managed to put that out of her mind, but there she was, waiting. What could Molly want? A problem in the English department? No, that would be the dean's job. It had to be Sal, Molly's "gentleman friend." This could be awkward. Flo had been very "close" to Sal herself. That had gotten him into prison—conspiracy to murder the late Dean Wooda—and almost landed her there, too. Best to take control of this conversation from the start. She told Miss Efficiency to send Molly in.

Flo, after a moment of struggle, sprang out of the chair the instant Molly appeared and hurried over to greet her, "Molly, I want to congratulate you." Her hug concluded, she led her over to a comfortable chair.

Suspiciously, Molly answered, "Yes?"

Flo Boater seated herself opposite, then enthusiastically rambled on, preventing Molly from saying anything. She paused only after saying at last, "I'm especially pleased that you brought Sal to see me! He looks marvelous." At this moment she adopted a serious mien, then proceeded thoughtfully, "After all, a year in prison should be hard on anyone." Almost to herself, she added, "especially on the complexion. The tan would be ruined." Looking up at Molly, she asked, "What can I do for you?"

Molly asked hurriedly, lest this opportunity be overwhelmed by another avalanche of words, "Did Sal ask about a job?" She waited for an encouraging look, and seeing none, volunteered, "Any kind of job." Seeing Flo Boater's impassive visage, she explained, "I told him not to ask, but his parole requires him to look for work, and he knows nothing but academic…." Seeing no reaction at all, she offered, "He would even sweep the floors." After a moment she added, "Some fine men sweep our floors. It's honest work, and Sal's an honest man."

At this Flo Boater looked up, raised a finger to her mouth and said, "Ah, yes. I understand." In the back of her mind was having employed Jay, who had been involved in the dean's death, too. He had been welcomed back as a janitor, but he had been a janitor before. She shook off the furrow in her eyebrows, then looked at Molly and shook her head, "No, working here would be awkward." After a pause, during which Molly's morale collapsed, she explained, "The trustees wouldn't understand. The publicity, you know." Realizing suddenly that she was mimicking a well-known public figure, she went on, "Besides, the money isn't there, you know." Damn, she did it again. But she persevered, "We have a hiring freeze. We may be letting people go." She paused, looked upward reflectively, and played with her hair, "Good people, you know." She glanced at Molly before adding, "Friends." Dropping her hands into her hands, she concluded, "So hiring Sal is out of the question. At least right now."

Molly was disappointed, "Yes, I understand." But she recovered quickly, "It's just that there are so few jobs in this little town, especially for a man with a record." She paused before adding, "Even if he didn't deserve it."

Flo Boater did not like the direction this was leading, toward her former romantic relationship. She cut the interview short, saying, "I'm sure something will work out. I assure you, you'll be the first to hear." She almost smiled when she thought of the one job that she could not persuade anyone to take—secretary at faculty meetings—but it was neither full-time nor suitable for Sal's talents—he was so meticulous that the minutes would never be good enough.

Seeing the president indicate the door, Molly stood up and began to move away. But she turned instantly when president called after her, "Molly, one more question."

"Yes?" she asked hopefully.

"Are you and, uh, Sal, a ... uh... couple? Going to be one?"

Alarmed, Molly said, "Oh, no. There's the age difference. After all, he's young and I'm almost your age."

Flo Boater was less than happy at that thought—Sal wasn't *that* young and she certainly wasn't *that* old! They were both in... She thought a moment before coming up with the right phrase—*the prime of life*. She couldn't say that, but after a moment she was back on track, "You're not, what we used to say, back when we were ... uh... young... *sweet* on him?"

Molly quickly said, "Just good friends. I did visit him in prison, but I felt...that because of my ex-husband.... uh, Dean Wooda's involvement.... that I owed him that."

Flo Boater knew that, strictly speaking, this was not true. Molly's relationship with Sal had grown closer over the months just before the dean's death and had, by ironic coincidence, become very close on the very morning that C. Wooda was found dead in the swimming pool. They had, in fact, been one another's alibi. Flo Boater saw that this was an opportune moment to end the conversation. She stood up, extended her hand and advised, "Good, good, keep it that way."

"I thought you'd think so," Molly said.

"Oh?"

Hurriedly, Molly added, "And so do I."

Chapter Seven

Her next appointment being Mary C, Flo Boater leaned back in her chair, sighed, rubbed her eyes and prepared her thoughts. Then she rang Miss Efficiency to ask if Mary was there. She was. "Send her in, please." "Please" was counter-productive with Stanley Wooda—a sign of weakness—but it went a long way with Miss Efficiency.

As Mary entered, Flo Boater stood up and went to meet her, saying enthusiastically, "Mary, I want to congratulate you!" She then indicated that they should sit in the small circle of chairs reserved for more intimate visitors.

Mary did as ordered, suspiciously asking, "Yes?" There had been no indication that the president had read her note; she had just been told that the president would appreciate it greatly if she could drop by for a "chat."

"About your research prospects for tenure."

"My Sabbatical work?" Mary asked. Maybe she *had* read the note.

"Yes, yes. It's perfectly marvelous. You're sure to get tenure the moment it's published."

Flo Boater exuded pleasure and good will.

Mary, disappointed, asked meekly, "Published? Not till then?" This was not the agreement they had reached earlier.

Waving her hand, the president dismissed this "quibble," "Purely a technicality. We will have the trustees approve the arrangement and the moment the article appears in print, you'll have tenure."

Mary leaned forward to explain, "Journals are slow. It could be… it could take a year or two, maybe more. And I haven't even written it up yet." By the time she finished and straightened up, she was out of breath. Her chin sagged toward her bosom. She obviously had not communicated properly. "Your promise," she added weakly, "was that I'd get tenure."

"Oh, that," Flo said with a wave of her hand. "Yes, of course, that."

"Yes?"

"Well, that was, of course, subject to your meeting all qualifications." Seeing Mary wilting, she hurried to add, "And so far, you've done marvelously. Just marvelously." After pause, she added, "So far."

The ensuing quiet was broken finally by Mary asking, "Published, you said?"

Flo Boater, standing up and walking back to a large window looking over the campus, where ice hung from the branches, both sparkling with hope and causing limbs to break. She waved toward the dual nature of beauty, observing, "Winter is indeed a magical season at Briarpatch." She half-turned to see if Mary now regarded her as softer and more human. Seeing no sign of that, she assured her, "Don't worry. We can make out a special contract to cover it. Purely a technical matter." At that she came slowly back to her chair, sat down carefully, not removing her eyes from Mary's, and told her that she had not really invited her in to talk about the article *per se*, but rather because, "We want to upgrade our academic status. From now on the trustees want faculty to publish in high class journals before they give tenure or promotions."

Mary was dumbfounded, "High class? Such as... what?"

Flo Boater relaxed and motioned toward heaven, which was appropriate for a room with as lofty a vaulted ceiling as her office had, "As high as you can think, but don't worry about it." She leaned forward and put the heavenly hand on Mary's shoulder, then said consolingly, "You are the first person on the new program, so we can be a bit forgiving." Leaning back, she sighed before commenting, "Besides, *who knows* which archeological journals are good?"

Mary was becoming frantic, "I was going to publish in a modern language journal."

Flo Boater dismissed this, "Oh, *none of them* are any good. They'll print *anything*." Mary knew that there was some truth in this, but she was unconvincing in arguing that a number were still "high class journals." Flo Boater's only concession was, "Well, maybe there's a good one somewhere, but we'd rather see something in a real archeological quarterly."

Mary could only think to say, "The best ones in archeology only print articles by established scholars." Besides, while her work might be vaguely anthropological, it was not in any way archeological.

"Oh, don't worry so," the president advised. "Archeology is a fast-growing field. There's sure to be an appropriate one out there."

With a barely audible sigh, Mary suggested that she could send it to *The Journal of Obscure Cultures.*

Flo Boater had no idea what that journal was like, but it sounded like the sort of off-beat enterprise that her late husband tried and was rejected by. Then it came to her—she remembered Floyd complaining that a spin-off from *Agamennon at Bay* was just too mainstream for its readership, or so the editors had said; they wanted something new and cutting edge. Whatever Mary wrote, she thought, would reflect current thinking of several years earlier, what she had learned in graduate school. That is, out of date. Hitting her fist in her hand, she exclaimed "That sounds like just the place." Standing up, she offered her hand to Mary, who took it and rose. Saying, "So, you are right on track now. Again, congratulations," the president led her to the door. "Now, you think of some way to introduce yourself to the editor."

Mary turned and said, "I suppose I could write to her to say that I need this published to get tenure." She had heard the editor speak once at a conference, but all that she remembered was her denunciation of tenure as a male device for dominating women, a kind of "chastity belt," though she had never quite understood how the two ideas fit together. Was male domination aimed at keeping women from sex? DO had laughed at this, saying that the speaker's point was that if you give away the key, you lose control. Other than that, he had said, the point was backward—tenure was to keep people out, not lock them in, while the chastity belt was to keep women in and men out. When she tried to argue that tenure guaranteed protection from administrators, Donahue had agreed that people like Flo Boater were a threat to anyone who disagreed with their policies, but not so much freedom of thought or speech; tenure was also used to protect lazy, insolent and dishonest faculty members. When she had protested that no Briarpatch professors were like that, he provided a short list of names. If tenure was to protect teachers—and he did say "teachers"—then it should be applied to everyone, not just those who had managed to "hang around" for seven

years; the decision should be based on competency and congeniality—
yes, he did say congeniality, as though that was important. He added
that, from what he had learned from colleagues in other schools—and
he did say "schools"—administrators should be able to make decisions
on young instructors after a year or two; since they didn't do it, the
tenure decision was often made on the principle of "he's been here quite
a while, he has a lot of friends now who are a lot like him. Why pick
a fight?" Also, at small colleges, where departments often consisted of
two people, it would be better to get outside counsel—that would cost
money, but it would be cheap in the long run. Mary's cheeks beginning
to burn from memory of this exchange, she repeated more forcefully, "I
think I could write her."

Flo Boater, delighted, went over and pumped her hand
enthusiastically, "Yes, you do that! I don't imagine that anyone else
would have thought of that." Mary started to turn and leave, but the
president kept a firm hold on her hand. Gesturing with her free hand
while she prevented Mary from retreating, she exclaimed, "Be *bold*!
Stand up to the editor if he hesitates! Women have been held back
for decades because they lacked *confidence*. This is the age of *the new
woman*. Be bold!"

Mary wondered how the president had gotten the idea that the
editor was a man, but correcting that seemed less important than
straightening her own shoulders and managing to summon from
somewhere a more confident voice; she then stammered agreement,
"Yes... be bold. I think you are right. Women need to be bolder." She
took a deep breath and promised, "And *I* will be. I will grasp the key."

Flo Boater wondered what this meant, but chose to not ask;
releasing Mary's hand, she looked upward, as though enlightenment
might be found there. Mary's eyes followed hers upward as she heard
the president's encouragement, "And don't worry."

Mary turned to make her way out, but she hadn't reached Miss
Efficiency's door before the president called her back. Mary almost
didn't hear her, busy as she was shaking her head and repeating quietly,
"Be bold. Be bold." But when Flo Boater's words broke through her
concentration, she heard, "By the way, you'll soon have an opportunity
to demonstrate boldness—the Dean of Students has an idea I'm sure
you'll find exciting."

When Mary came back to listen, Flo Boater outlined the new co-curricular program and Mary's critical role on the committee assigned to develop it. Mary almost didn't remember to nod toward Miss Efficiency when she left. All she could think about was the contradictory orders to work full-time on her publication and, at the same time, on the co-curricular program. When she learned that Donahue had been given the same assignment, her heart sank again.

Mary passed Stanley Wooda in the hall without noticing him, or her paying much attention to him. He was on his way up from the men's room to the president's office, shivering from the cold drafts that seeped through the panes. He had no time for pleasantries. When Flo Boater summoned him, he knew that she would be mentally timing how long it took him to cross the hall. She was well aware that Stanley always wanted to visit the restroom before he saw her, so that he would not have to hurry away. When he was cold, haste was always more necessary. In the contest between Nature and Nuture, Nature lost.

Flo Boater checked the secretary's office to be sure that Mary had left, then closed the door, walked over to the sacred circle of chairs reserved for the most important visitors, sat down, looked at him curiously, then asked, "Any idea why I wanted to talk with you?"

"Ms. Hogg, I thought. People are getting concerned." He was pleased that the president's office was warm, but he would just as soon have been elsewhere.

"No, no. She'll show up. Don't worry."

As his stomach gave a twitch, he asked, "Maybe we should report it to Chief Biggs?"

"That idiot!" she exclaimed. Then, more calmly, she said, "Keep him off campus as much as you can."

Realizing that her statement was a warning as well as a policy, he said, "No, I don't know why you called me."

She smiled, "Didn't you see Ms. Canary just leave? Can't you guess?"

He shook his head slowly, "No, I saw her, sort of, but I didn't pay any attention."

She took a deep breath of disappointment, then asked, "Stanley, what do you know about *The Journal of Obscure Cultures?*"

"I've tried to read a few articles—assigned by my professor in Paris. Typical French post-modernism—pure gibberish. All made-up words and jargon. The sort of thing Prof. Stout likes. Otherwise it wouldn't be in our library."

Leaning forward to emphasize her seriousness, she asked, "Would Mary be able to publish her research there?"

Wooda thought about this before answering, "Probably not. Not that her work wouldn't be up to the quality required, but I understand everything she writes. Opacity seems to be the journal's gold standard. That and leaden prose." He let a moment pass before adding, "But she's got the right politics. Maybe she would stand a chance." Reading the president's face, he asked, "Why? Is it important?"

Flo Boater stood up and walked to the window, gazing out onto an imaginary Rose Garden—filled with Iceberg roses—and after a dramatic pause, said, "She is going to send an article there. And if it's published, we'll have to give her tenure."

Getting up to join her, and, looking out the window, imagining himself in the real Oval Office—if he could only overcome the problem of his foreign birth—Wooda asked, "You are sure she's sending it there?" If the point was to prevent her from publishing, he would have picked a journal that accepted only end-of-career summaries of contributions by senior scholars.

"I talked her out of a language journal."

"Why?" He could think of several reasons, but he was interested in hers.

"Because there are so many of them. One might accept it."

He nodded agreement, "The weaker journals do get desperate."

She turned back to the chairs and sat down again, "Even the good ones sometimes."

After joining her, Wooda suggested that he could call the editor.

"You know him?"

"No, but he might not know that."

She had to smile at his moxie, but she was almost instantly serious again, "What good would that do? I mean, how would you persuade him to not publish an article that looked good?"

"I could say that we are investigating her for plagiarism and ask him to hold the manuscript until our investigation is completed."

Intrigued, she asked, "Why not just say it really isn't very good?"

"First, the editor might read it and like it, whereas if we ignored it, the chances are that he won't get past the first paragraph. Second, if he rejected it, she would just try another journal." He gave her a wicked grin, "This way the manuscript doesn't even get as far as peer review."

Standing up and pacing with her hands behind her back, Flo meandered as far as her late husband's folly of a gigantic table at the far end of her huge office, where she stopped and frowned, then turned around and walked back. Wooda followed so closely at her heels that they almost collided when she turned suddenly to exclaim, "Brilliant. The outside readers wouldn't even be contacted until it was too late." Excitedly she repeated, "Excellent! Excellent." Putting her hands on his shoulders, she said, "You're a genius, Stanley!"

At this Wooda moved away, concerned about where her hands might go next, or, worse, that she would give him a hug. How would he respond—exhibiting repulsion or farting. Either could be fatal to his career. His stomach churning, he decided to give her something else to think about, "But what is the point?"

This time she followed him, explaining excitedly, "I am going to give her a contract requiring publication within a year. When she fails to publish, I'll give her a terminal contract." Gleefully, she laughed, "Two years from now we'll see the last of her!"

Wooda saw the point, "And if she goes, so will Donahue!"

Less enthusiastically, she responded, "We can hope."

He began rehearsing all the problems, then asked, "What if she makes a complaint?"

"We blame it on the trustees. That's what they're there for."

Flo Boater had her hand on the door when she remembered something else, "And also, Stanley, I've put Mary on the new Co-Curricular Program Development Committee—the CCPDC. Together with Donahue and the new Dean of Students."

His attention stirred at the mention of the new dean, but all he dared ask was, "Co-curricular? How's that different from Extra-curricular?"

"Oh, Stanley," she responded. "It's in all the journals. It's about making the Extra... that is, the rest of each day, after classes are out, making the student experience holistic."

He thought a second, "You mean education 24/7?"

"Not quite that, just combining what students *have to do* with what they *want to do*."

"Sounds tricky. You mean getting professors to work extra... co-curricular activities into their classes?"

"Why not? It sounds like something we could sell."

He reflected on that while she took her seat again, "Yes, I think we could sell it. Off-campus, that is. To parents and trustees."

"Stanley, that's all we need. The professors never cooperate and the students ignore us."

"Then why should we do it? It sounds like a lot of work to set up."

"Ah, that's the beauty of it. Mary and Donahue can do the work, and when we announce it... that is, present it... to the faculty, they will get all the blame.

Stanley Wooda gave her one of those smiles that had worked so well in the past, but which had become rare recently. Life was good again.

Dean Threshold discovered that although the name Wooda was not common, that made it no easier to find information about its holders—only less confusing. He tried phonetic variations of the name, without coming up with anything plausible. Why had Flo Boater wanted to know about her dean's ancestry and any possible connection to the late dean Wooda? Wasn't he born in the Caribbean, where records were not kept regularly and where he had no contacts? He didn't even speak Spanish. However, neither did Dean Wooda. Stanley Wooda's family were Taino, he had said, and—he suspected—India Indian. Most Tainos were on northern Spanish-speaking islands—Santo Domingo, for example—while Indians were found in more southern British colonies, brought in as laborers, but had quickly given evidence of a South Asian interest in education and professions.

When did Stanley Wooda become a citizen? Or his father? His draft board would not help, and his high school was defunct. The courthouse personnel in his home town were downright rude: "Don't you know we've been sued for violating privacy rights. Who are you anyway? His draft board?"

Inquires to credit card companies? No help. Who didn't have credit cards? He knew people who had forty or fifty. No, they wouldn't release information about Woodas in general. Relatives? There was that grandmother, wherever she lived and whose name he didn't know—other than maybe being a Wooda. No—apparently on his mother's side, since—according to President Boater—she knew little about Stanley's father, or so she believed. Ah, it would be so easy if he could only ask the dean, but he had been warned not to let a word slip about the inquiry. Thank goodness, he could trust Mabel to keep his worries private!

Meanwhile, Flo Boater had called the Dean of Students in. The dean was new, her predecessor having found a better job at Zenith University, supervising the After-Hours activities program—their equivalent of the CCPDC. Her credentials were slim, but she had a recent degree in Student Services and experience as the assistant to the assistant of a student dean in one of the largest universities in America. That had impressed the hiring committee—which had consisted of the former dean, Stanley Wooda, and Maximilian Stout. She had never heard of the policy, "If we don't hear about it, it didn't happen," but she understood its meaning. But now she was confused—she was getting mixed signals.

"President Boater, I really don't understand the college policy right now. Dean Wooda is telling me to let the students enjoy life, but also to keep them quiet, and to get rid of troublemakers, but not let the enrollment drop. How do I do that?"

Flo Boater smiled, "First of all, don't worry about Stanley Wooda. I'm your boss, not him. Every dean reports to me."

"Why does he give me these… uh, instructions, then?"

She smiled again, "Well, let's say that you are young and attractive, and that he is young and attractive, and it is natural for the male of the species to… well, you know."

The young woman paused. She wasn't that attractive. In fact, she hadn't had a serious boyfriend since she was a freshman ("freshwoman" or "first year enrollee" she remembered were preferable words, though whatever parents said was correct) and that didn't work out all that well. "I don't understand. What are you telling me to do?"

The president became more serious, "Stanley was exceeding his instructions. I'll tell him to lay off you."

"Exceeding his instructions?"

"Why, yes. He's Academic Dean, not Dean of the College. I suppose he forgot this momentarily. We do often talk about potential strategies. You know, brainstorm about various ways of dealing with campus problems, not all of which deal with instruction. You can see how this happens—I have to bounce ideas off people. Stanley just went too far, thinking that we had agreed upon some policies."

The young woman thought a moment, then asked, "Could you give me some examples? I mean, clarify what you want me to do."

"Well, uh, naturally we can't afford to lose students who might be saved, that is, taught how to behave like, like good citizens. You've, I understand, instituted training programs for the student dorm councilors and obligatory lectures for all students regarding behavior."

"Yes, though it is difficult to get the students to attend the lectures without some type of incentive, positive or negative; and they ignore the dorm councilors. They know they won't be kicked out."

"Ah, yes. And what have you decided to do about that?"

"I moved into a dorm myself, as you suggested."

"I suggested that? Well, I guess I did mention trying to be creative. Uh, how did that work out?"

"It was good for the dorm I was in. There were plenty of empty rooms, so I could change floors each night. Just move my sheets, that sort of thing. That helped, but I couldn't be in every dorm at once."

"No, of course not," the president replied. She thought a moment. "Back when I was a student, actually just before I was a student, we had house mothers."

The dean thought a moment, "I've heard about that. They seemed to work. Why did college stop hiring them?"

Flo Boater smiled, "My late husband, Floyd, used to talk about that. He was, you understand, a bit old-fashioned. He thought it was because colleges were competing for young people who wanted more freedom, and wide-open dorms were the way to guarantee them."

"Spoiled boomer kids," the dean suggested, thinking of her own undergraduate dorm at Zenith. She frowned, remembering how she had missed out on the fun. If it was fun. She wasn't sure. She had known a couple unhappy "popular" girls.

"Earlier, actually, I think. Floyd said it was the GI Bill men. After fighting their way across the Pacific, they weren't going to be treated like they were eighteen."

"I thought the Fifties were quiet."

"I believe you are right, but the principle was there. The Sixties just revived it."

"And that explains it?"

"No, there's more to it. More young people were coming to college who needed jobs—the lower classes, you know, moving upscale. And housemothers wanted to be paid. Bed and board weren't enough. We weren't in the Thirties any more. Dorm councilors fit the bill—and they were cheaper than house mothers. Lastly, let's see, what did he say? Oh, it was getting harder to find that perfect combination of loving and disciplining—even mature women were beginning to think that the rules were old-fashioned."

At this point the dean broke in, "My Women's Studies classes—that was my undergraduate major—also said that women no longer thought of being a widow at fifty was the end of life, but just its beginning! And more women were professionals now, or then, and so they were becoming college professors, not house mothers."

"Right you are," the president responded. Then she began to wonder if she could retrofit some professors back into dorm managers. Her mental imagine was Mary C and DO Donahue. Maybe that would persuade them to resign. Then she had a thought. She had almost stood up to escort her young dean to the door, when she sat back down and said, "You remember our last conversation… about 'co-curricular student programs?'"

The response was enthusiastic, "Oh, yes. The recognition that what students do outside of class is as important as what they do inside. I'm finding a lot in the literature about them."

Flo Boater smiled, "The profession is catching up with the students."

"Pardon?" the dean said. "Catching up with the students?"

"Well, don't they already consider their social life more important than studies?"

"I guess they do. I just hadn't thought of it that way."

"How had you thought of it?"

"Oh, it's providing lectures and workshops and off-campus programs for spring break and such. To make them aware of the world and its problems in ways that their professors never do." She concluded with a smile.

Flo Boater smiled back, but kept an almost voiced ironic comment to herself. Instead, she formulated a suggestion, "I'm going to ask two young faculty members—one male, one female—to assist you in drawing up a proposal for such a program. Try to make it as detailed as possible, but within reasonable budgetary constraints. We'll find money for it, of course, but we have to be reasonable." She smiled again, thinking that such an assignment would drive Donahue nuts; Mary, of course, would gladly join in.

"Oh," the dean responded. "That's nice, but I already have one volunteer, Max Stout. I was talking with him about your idea. He says that it will fit in nicely with his Honors program." Her smile suggested that Max had other attractions than ideas. "There is also an adjunct…"

"Dearie," the president said, interrupting, a bit more drily than she intended, "Max isn't quite what we need here. He has a hard time thinking inside the budgetary box." To herself, she wondered how the subject had ever come up, and whether she should tip the young woman off about Max's history with women. She shook the last idea off. She needed to concentrate on the main goals—to keep the students too busy to join in a demonstration and to persuade Donahue to resign. The CCPDC might just do the trick.

Flo Boater then explained that adjuncts should not be brought more fully into institutional governance—they might get the idea that they are more a part of the college than they should be.

The dean left mildly depressed. What would she tell Irene? She had been so enthusiastic about the prospect of replacing essays with group discussions and service projects. And she was, the dean had noted, very cute, too. "Ah, well," she said to herself, "cancel that dinner… no, *postpone* it… to discuss the project." She'd already bought the wine. No point in letting that go to waste. Maybe she could invite Mary?

It was an opportunity to discuss the new program, she told herself, and surely Mary had the time. It's not as though they were at Zenith University, where everyone was trying to publish and qualify for tenure. Or so she was told by a close friend, a friend unfortunately recently married and therefore unwilling to come for a visit.

She sighed, "Few do get tenure, anyway. Zenith is trying to move up in the academic world. Not giving tenure is proof that it is serious." She had learned that when she applied for a minor job at her *alma mater*— they didn't hire their own graduates. So there she was, in Middleville, with no prospects social or intellectual in sight. Single women didn't hang out with single deans, and there were almost no single men. And here she was getting mixed signals from a domineering president and a sex-starved dean, or, she wondered, was it the other way around?

Chapter Eight

Entering the coffee house by a side door, Donahue looked around the crowded tables until he spotted Mary. Going to the counter, he poured himself a cup and paid. Grousing to himself about the presidential edict ending the pay by the month program, he walked over to her and inquired, "May I join you?"

Without enthusiasm, she responded, "I suppose."

He opened with what he hoped would be good news, "You heard that Sal is free."

This worked as he had hoped. Mary's mood improved instantly, "Isn't it marvelous?"

Taking a sip of coffee and being slightly offended by burned taste—from sitting too long atop the coffee-machine—he said, "Yes, but it would be even better if Flo were just getting out of prison, too." Normally, he made no notice of coffee, just whether it was strong or weak, but this potion bore evidence of budgetary cuts having gone too far.

More passionately than was necessary, she exclaimed, "It is unfair. *He* pleads guilty to conspiracy to murder and goes to *prison....*" At that she was unable to think of an appropriate ending.

Donahue began to suspect that there was more to her anger than Salvatore Iva, but he finished her sentence, "while a jury lets *her* off."

More calmly now, Mary asked, half to herself, "I wonder if he's angry about it?"

Taking another sip to gain time to think, Donahue finally said, "I suppose I'd be bitter." His choice of words was inspired by the coffee.

"I know I would be," Mary said, then tried to finish off her cup so that she could leave.

Donahue did the same, then raised his cup in mock piety and intoned, "Lord, remove this temptation from us."

Mary recognized that he was referring both to Sal's situation and the coffee. She laughed at the odd combination, "If thoughts could kill, the world would be empty."

As Donahue looked at her, wishing the time was not yet over, he glanced past her shoulder and said, "Hey, look who's coming!" It was Lill and Lily.

Lily sidled up and said seductively, "Hi, DO." Turning to Mary, she drawled, "Wow, it looks like I have competition!" Then Lill pulled her off to get coffee.

"She knows how to treat a man." Donahue said, but without getting a response. They remained silent until Lill and Lily sat down.

Lill, after looking from one to the other, indicated Lily with a shift of her head and remarked good-humoredly, "Don't worry about it. She's that way with every man."

Lily pouted, "A girl just wants to have fun."

"Especially when she isn't a girl," Lill joked, elbowing her in the ribs.

With a wave of the hand, Lily dismissed this, "Oh, you. You're just jealous."

Donahue broke in to ask, "There's been a rumor about that." It was, in effect, a question: was it true?

Lill rolled her eyes, "Lily started that as a joke. The late dean took it seriously."

The conversation then settled down. Lill took a deep breath before saying, "We've got a more serious concern."

"Yes," Lily added. "Sal tells us to watch out."

In a confidential tone, Lill warned, "Something's up."

"Any idea what?"

Lill looked over as students entered to get coffee, then leaned close to whisper, "He didn't want to say."

Mary whispered a reply, "Why is he so secretive?"

"I don't think he knows anything specific," Lill said, and Lily added, "But he's picked up vibes."

"*Vibes?*" Donahue asked. "What kind, and where?"

Lill looked at Lily, who said, "People who've been away are sometimes more perceptive."

"Yes," Lill continued "...than those who are too close ..."

"…to the situation."

Donahue began to think aloud, "He picked up vibes so soon? Not likely. He must have heard something when he was in prison."

Lill hesitated a moment, pulled even closer and said, "Probably. But he went to see Flo Boater. He may have heard something, or sensed it."

Donahue was now leaning forward about as much as he could, "What did he want with her?" Anyone observing them would know that something was up. Just what would be the only question. That, in fact, was what the senior historian was thinking. He had come in through the far door, unobserved, and, having smelled the coffee, had decided to order tea. For that he would have to wait several minutes. Other than Mary, who was now learning to like coffee, nobody at Briarpatch drank hot tea.

Lily said, "We thought that was suspicious. Why would he even want to see the witch…"

"…who sent him to prison."

"That's the question."

"And we'd like you to find out why."

"And what's going on."

Donahue had to think about this, but after a moment he agreed, "OK, no problem." But he asked seriously, "You really think it's better that *I* ask?'

Lill explained "People are afraid to talk to us."

Leaning close and cupping her hand, Lily whispered, "We're being watched right now."

A few moments later the historian drifted over with his tea and sat down nearby. He gave no sign of recognition, made no greeting, but concentrated on the difficult task of stirring his tea with the proper mix of sugar and milk. At this Lill stood up and said, "It's good to see you again, DO. I'll look forward to seeing you when you get back."

Donahue and Lily looked puzzled, but said nothing. A gesture hidden by her body silenced everybody. As Lill and Lily reached the door, Lily whispered a question, "*What* was that about?'

"DO's trip?" Lill responded.

"Yes. I didn't know he was going on a trip."

"He isn't, but we have to give the Creep..."

"I gotja," Lily said, "...something to report."

"Something so incorrect that his standing with 'the boss' will be undermined." She then glanced back to see the historian moving quickly toward the other door. He hadn't bothered to finish his tea.

It was at this point that Mary asked Donahue, "Are you going somewhere?"

"Not that I know," he laughed. "But around here there's a lot I don't know." Then looking over at Lill and Lily laughing and pointing, said, "It must have been a joke for our eavesdropper friend."

Lill came back to explain: "He wants to be chair of the Theater department again. History and Sociology aren't enough for him."

Lily added with a sneer, "He thinks if he can keep us under his thumb, Flo Boater may make him dean someday."

This surprised Mary, "But she's got a dean, Stanley Wooda."

Lill leaned over between them to explain, "Stanley's going places. Nobody expects him to stay here long."

Lily leaned over Donahue's shoulder, giving his collarbone a light pinch and making certain that Mary saw it, "Stanley is either going to Congress or to jail."

"Or both," Lill added.

Donahue, relaxing, agreed, "Men in a hurry cut a few corners.'

Mary, frustrated, turned to Donahue, "And what do *you* say when Flo Boater asks about what Lill said?"

"Make up a story, I guess." Having said that, he turned toward Lill and winked. Lily waved enthusiastically as they left.

Mary, who had been too busy looking at her hands to see his head move, now jerked her head to look at him and asked, "What kind of story?"

Slyly, he said, "I suppose something about going to South America."

"Don't you dare!" she warned. "She might start that all up again. Grants and exchanges. That silly idea to send me back to the jungle again." She shivered involuntarily, "No showers, no toilets. My mother bugging me about not marrying somebody who can't speak English."

Donahue could only laugh, "But lots of mosquitoes and large hairy bugs."

Mary was exasperated that he thought it was funny. She slapped the table and exclaimed, "Think of something else."

"There are other jobs."

She sighed in exasperation, "Do you know how hard it would be to get a job after teaching at Briarpatch!"

"Oh, lots of people leave. Most of them find jobs."

"Damn it, DO. They haven't been turned down for tenure!" She scowled at him, "Everybody known that you have to be really bad not to get tenure at Briarpatch."

He laughed, "Most people don't know anything about Briarpatch, or even if it exists." He then explained, "Your resumé is good—successful teaching, research in South America, a paper well started—a slight exaggeration is always forgiven, but you could use material for your formal presentation. As for why you're on the market, you'd just have to say that, well, maybe you're looking for a place closer to family."

There was a long silence before she calmed down enough to ask, "What would you do if they fired you? You wouldn't get a good recommendation." What she wanted to say was, "I wanted to get away from a former boyfriend!" But she couldn't be that cruel. Not now, but maybe the next time!

He thought a moment, "Back to police work, maybe." As Mary hung her head, he explained, "I've got the experience. Might be a job somewhere doing the anthropology of criminal catchers." He was half-way into saying, "Or the mentality of pigs in blue," when he was interrupted.

Everyone stopped talking when Lill and Lily reappeared and took their seats again. "Just saw Chief Biggs outside—he was looking for Jay, to ask if anyone has seen Ms. Hogg. Apparently a neighbor heard her kitty whining and discovered that she hadn't been fed recently."

"Recently? Has she been feeding it, without anyone seeing her?"

"No, apparently she had an automatic feeder and some kind of hook-up for water."

"I'm surprised it didn't complain from day one about being lonely."

"I suppose it did, but the noise level went up when the feeder malfunctioned."

Donahue thought about this before asking, "Who's been running the office?"

"Staff," Lill said. "Flo told them she'd be back soon."

Donahue sighed, "Another Miss Purdy disappearance."

"No college business this time," Lill said. "Registrars may go off for a couple of days to compare notes on newest computers and such, but no request for a car or anything. I checked."

Donahue congratulated her for having the instincts of a detective, to which she responded that she had been a college president—she'd learned how to get information. With nothing further to report, the conversation turned to the all-time faculty favorite topic: gossip.

When Mary mentioned tenure decisions, Lily had an idea. Speaking to Donahue, she exclaimed, "Flo might want to write you a good recommendation. Just to get rid of you. Then the pressure would be off Mary."

Seeing that Mary was not getting the joke—the rumor Lily had planted on the Creep, that Donahue might be looking for another job—Donahue signaled the others to give up. Guardedly, he told Mary, "I don't know that I could fake an interview. Or pretend to have published anything serious."

"What's left?" Lill asked.

He shrugged his shoulders, "I could say that the rumor was untrue. A misunderstanding."

"On the other hand," Lily suggested, "if the story got around that you were leaving, it might provide an opportunity to speak with some people who want to purchase grades."

"How would that work?" Donahue asked.

"Oh, we'd say you need some walking out money."

Donahue employed his hands to ward off that idea, then said lightly, "On the other hand, going off campus to 'interviews' might allow me to speak to some graduates, if we can identify the right ones. They might not talk about themselves, but they might know who to talk to."

Lill got a twinkle in her eye, "I think Jay could provide us with a few names."

"Huh," Mary said. "Could be expensive. We've no money for travel this year, again."

"More to the point," Lily asked, "Would they talk?"

"Perhaps, if promised immunity," Donahue said. Turning suddenly serious, he said, "We could promise to keep their names out of the whole business if they cooperate. But if the investigation goes public, they or their friends could lose their degrees."

"Can you do that?" Mary asked. "You're not a cop any more."

"No, but they don't know that, and perhaps 'promise' wasn't the right word."

"It sounds like a plan," Lill said.

"Yes, that's it," he agreed. "A plan."

Mary, more practical, suggested that he couldn't just make up an interview. Flo Boater was likely to check up, to see if there was any way she could help."

Donahue laughed, "You've got us. That plan is fatally flawed."

"So," Mary said, "if Lill and Jay can provide you with names, you'll want to leave for a few days. What will you use as an excuse? As I visualize this, it can only be done face-to-face, catching the alum by surprise."

He shrugged his shoulders, "I guess there's nothing left but family and friends."

Mary looked around at them, "Well, when students want to take a trip, someone's always sick, aren't they?"

Lily agreed, "That's right. My sick aunt, my cousin's wedding."

Lill stood up straight and said, "Any one of those will do."

Lily also straightened up before warning, "Nothing too serious, or she will want to send flowers."

"A suggestion would be welcome," Donahue observed,

"Just borrow an excuse from the last student who asked," Lily suggested. Then she offered brightly, "You know the statistics, how dangerous mid-term exams are to grandmothers."

Even Mary had to smile at this, "Yes, the students just have to hurry home and miss the exam."

"But attend a dance," Donahule offered.

"Or hand the paper in late," Mary countered.

Lill said reflectively, "I knew a student who actually had a sick grandmother." Of course, she did. They all did. Grandparents were at an age when serious illnesses were common, and most students were sincere in their concern. But the more real a problem is, the more likely the excuse is to be abused.

Donahue and Mary stood up now, ready to leave, but he had a request, "You can't just send me off to find people who will talk. Jay might provide names, but I've got to have some leverage."

"The specific courses, you mean?" Lill asked as she and Lily stood up as well.

"Exactly."

"Can't you ask the registrar? When she shows up, that is."

"Can't you yourself?"

"No, President Boater has surely warned her about me. Probably about you, too, for that matter. Besides, she's disappeared."

Donahue thought a moment, "Maybe we could get someone on the staff to talk, someone who wouldn't be suspicious."

"No. They've been taught to keep quiet."

"How about faculty? They'll talk about anything."

"Stout, you mean?" Lily quipped. "I'd love to see him involved with another of our administrators."

"It wasn't such a big thing," Lill commented, half laughing at the thought of Max Stout pinned under the finance officer, Prudence Purdy, his clothes half-torn off.

"Miss Purdy was *a big thing*," Lily retorted. "And Ms. Hogg isn't much smaller."

"You should speak," Lill shot back.

"With me, it's muscle."

"Anyway, Ms. Hogg has lost weight."

"I could, too, if I wanted to."

Donahue interrupted, "So you don't think Ms. Hogg will show up soon."

"No, not soon," Lill said. "Moreover, she's a very secretive type. And we don't know why she's disappeared. Maybe she's involved."

Lill sighed, "I'd be surprised. But at Briarpatch anything is possible." With that she shrugged, indicating that she had nothing more to say.

Mary reached over and touched her arm. "Thanks anyway. We'll ask around."

"We'll see what we can find out. Who knows where it will lead?"

Lill reached over to Donahue, "And thanks, DO." Then she and Lily left the building, waving at one group of students, stopping briefly to talk to another.

Mary was ready to depart as well, but Donahue touched her forearm lightly and pointed to some students dragging along protest signs that said, NO EXAMS, NO GRADES. She wanted to ask if this was a co-curricular activity, but decided that he had not yet been informed about the CCPDC.

Donahue studied the crowd for a moment. He recognized Smith and Jones and Ellie. Smith and Ellie looked happy; Jones, the usually enthusiastic organizer, was not. As they went up to the coffee bar, Donahue said, "I had better go look for Sal"

Mary, following him, asked, "You think he's still on campus?"

Donahue stopped to think, "I'll go check the science building. He might have gone over there." Turning to her, he asked, "Mary, do you think you could mingle with the protestors?"

"Sure, but why?"

"To find out what they are really talking about."

Mary snapped him a salute, "Mary Canary, star reporter on assignment." It was the first real enthusiasm she had shown for anything in weeks. Perhaps, Donahue thought, what she really needed was to be involved in something important.

Dean Threshold was perplexed. According to his wife, who had asked people at the diner, almost nobody knew anything about the late Dean Wooda. He kept to himself, except when chatting up attractive women. They didn't like that: "College people should keep to themselves. They don't have any morals, anyway. Should keep away from our women." Well, the women didn't say that last part, but even the farmers had heard about his philandering. If he had eaten at the diner, they would have known more, they were sure, but he generally ate out only in Arcadia and Zenith. Maybe she should ask at the country club. Mabel didn't know where that was. Dean Threshold had to ask.

He learned it was at the golf club and the food was at the same level as the greens—mediocre. He also heard a rumor that the Administration Building was haunted.

Chapter Nine

Professor Stout did not keep up on campus gossip as well as he could have. Such was his admission when he informed Chief Biggs, "I'm off campus too much to attend lunches and coffee klatches where they swap stories. Cheap gossip. I prefer the life of the mind."

"How about beer parties," the chief asked. "I understand unmarried faculty have quite a few of them?" When Stout just starred at him, he posed another question, "You do drink beer?"

"Occasionally," he answered, "but not like that." He was, in fact, often the host of parties for selected individuals; offering a lavish, but informal spread, he served only imported beverages—French wines and German or Czech beers available only in Zenith. Young professors and wives who read *The New Yorker*—and they all did—imagined themselves transported into a world they had only dreamt of, sort of like local boys reading *Playboy*. "Not like that," he repeated.

"Like what?"

"Like, you know, losing control. The younger crowd tends to do that."

The chief did not give up, "You are, I believe, unmarried?"

At this Stout puffed himself up a bit, snorting, "Well, yes. Of course. But I don't have time to listen to stories…."

"Or complaints about the registrar?"

"Well, yes, everyone knew there were problems."

The chief leaned closer to ask, "What kind of problems."

Stout actually stepped back in order to put his hand to his chin. It was a practiced gesture, one intended to indicate thoughtfulness. "I've heard something about selling grades." Observing the chief's interest, he hurried to add, "Not in my classes, of course. Bright students don't have to buy grades."

Chief Biggs relaxed. Once Stout allowed himself to be more at ease, the chief said, "I never suspected you." As Stout began to smile, the chief added, "I understand that almost every student gets an A anyway."

Dean Wooda was also asking the same questions, though not to the same people. Once Smith and Jones had confronted him, he had gone straight to the source whence flowed all relevant records—the registrar's office.

The registrar was not there, of course. What her small staff told him—and they were more willing to talk to an academic dean than to anyone else, even to an adolescent dean. After all, they had seen him around, and when he spoke at meetings, he seemed to know what he was taking about—expect when he touched on things they understood. But he *was* new. Like Ms. Hogg was new. In fact, they considered almost all administration officers except the dean of students new, and that was because she was so new they didn't know the former dean had been replaced. But they respected Ms. Hogg. She was not so new as to be totally ignorant; after all, she had taught Education courses for years; and nobody was more concerned with grades than Education students. They had known her when she was thinner. Not so long ago, it seemed. And they had known her when she was heavier—again, not so long ago. Her wanting to be registrar was a surprise, though it was a full-time job and paid well by Briarpatch standards. If she had not asked detailed questions during the interview process, they told him, that was understandable—it might seem "pushy." But on her very first day of the job she had discerned that not all was well in the record-keeping department....

That surprised him. They already suspected that something was wrong!

Chief Biggs came away from his visit with the same impression.

Chief Biggs had learned from Stout that Ms. Hogg had immediately talked with Flo Boater about her misgivings. "That was a mistake," Stout said. "She should have waited for a few weeks until she had more evidence. As it was, the president had told her 'to work with what she had' and that they 'would look into the situation later'."

"Go on," the chief said.

"Consequently, she had been in a mood to talk when I appeared in her office to ask about the process of revising grades."

"You went to see her... about grade changes?"

"Actually, no. I had wanted to reappraise some overly harsh grades I had given the previous semester." Reacting to the chief's raised eyebrow, he hurriedly said, "Contrary to the word on the street, I had failed fifteen of sixteen students in our required freshman tutorial."

"The honors program?"

"Not by any means. These were ordinary students. They were..."

The chief interrupted him, "Still, fifteen of sixteen? How did the word on the street get it so wrong. Your grading policy...." At this he hesitated, then vainly tried to recover, or cover over, his words, "I guess, it was like you said, the word on the street...."

Stout sighed, "It's true that students in my honors program generally make good grades. But they are all outstanding students, and giving exams just gets in the way of learning."

"I don't understand," Biggs said. "How is this other class different?"

"Oh, that's because we are required to give exams, and some of the questions are factual, the same questions as all the other freshman sections."

The chief fidgeted, "I guess I still don't understand."

"The students don't do well on that material because I don't spend any class time on it." He paused to collect himself, then continued, "The books are nineteenth century trash. Dickens, Aristotle and that sort of thing. I won't lower myself to teach something not based on *Theory*. And besides, they don't write well."

"You mean the freshmen?"

"Of course, it's not my job to teach writing."

"I thought you were in English."

"Yes, certainly," he said, puffing himself up again, "but it's old-fashioned to think that English departments teach writing any more. We have a writing-around-the-curriculum program now. Everybody teaches writing, so the English department can concentrate on ideas. At least, in the honors program."

"So you flunked fifteen of sixteen?"

"Yes," Stout admitted, "that was unusually high, though several of my colleagues have congratulated me and said that they only wished that they had the courage to do the same."

"Interesting," Biggs said. "Then you had second thoughts about the grades."

"Well, my dilemma was complicated." He squinted—he certainly wasn't going to mention the fact that one of the fifteen was the grandson of a trustee. "I wasn't planning to do anything right away, but I wanted to understand the parameters of the situation. Ms. Hogg was, in fact, relieved at not having to make a potentially momentous decision on the spot. She had said that the usual process would be to send a note to the dean, indicating the changes to be made, and the dean would then instruct her to 'bump up' the grade."

"And what did you do?"

"Nothing." In fact, the student most in question had legitimately flunked. To pass him, he would have had to persuade his colleagues that everyone, in every section, had to pass.

Dean Wooda found that the "nothing" was more than that. The registrar had told her staff that Stout had said that in a few days he was going to a "feminar" in Zenith, that is, a program on feminist theory, and she might want to consider sharing the ride. "Pleasant conversations made conferences so much more enjoyable than driving alone," she quoted him as saying. She had promised to think about it. The subject attracted her very little, but the prospect of getting out of town, especially in the company of a charming male colleague, was something else.

The staff had been amused—but not to her face. They had assumed that she was a committed old maid. Maybe even a lesbian. But after discussion they decided that she was an old maid. Definitely old maid. Otherwise, she would have remained a faculty member.

The dean thought briefly about a question that had come to him in the middle of a daydream—who was to call the CCPDC together? As academic dean, surely he should work together with the dean of students on that. The thought made him smile. Then he frowned. What if Flo Boater wanted to launch this vessel herself? If he acted too quickly, she would not be pleased. Moreover, he might end up pointing out some obvious gaps in the intellectual framework—like money. He reached out to write her a note, only to remember that Dean Threshold now read all the president's correspondence first. She might not want this idea out there yet. Better let her decide when and where to begin.

When Donahue arrived at his office the next morning, he found Flechadoro waiting for him—inside.

"Oh, hello. You looking for me?" It was a bit surprising, because the young man was not in any of his classes, and he thought he had locked the door.

"Yes. I have something to talk about. Privately?"

"Okay," Donahue responded, before giving a friendly warning, "My office is so public that it is practically private."

"What?"

"Well, people can see us, but the noise from the hall drowns out anything we say."

"If you say so… But can we close the door?"

"That would look suspicious."

"What?"

"Today no wise professor ever closes a door when talking to a student." He paused, but he saw that Flechadoro didn't get the point. With a sigh, he pushed the door almost shut and said, "Take a seat. What's on your mind?"

"It's about the sale of grades." Having said that, the young man looked toward the door before continuing, "I've heard some students say that it's an urban legend, but I think it's true."

Donahue leaned over to close the door more, then asked, "Why do you think so?"

"The registrar refused to talk about it."

"That's understandable. No administrator would talk about such a sensitive matter to a student. Besides, she's…uh. When did you talk with her?"

"Days ago. I wanted to go back, but she's been gone. She acted really, uh, strange."

"Strange," Donahue asked? "How strange?"

"Well, if there was nothing to it, why didn't she just say so? If a person has nothing to hide, why not say so?"

Donahue paused to frame an answer, then suggested, "Perhaps she thought it was none of your business." He worried that his response might bring an end to the conversation, but he wanted to get around to why this student was asking the question.

"In my culture," he explained, "we have no secrets."

Donahue smiled in spite of himself, "In your tribal culture, is it the custom to tell the truth all the time?"

Flechadoro smiled in return, "Not quite, though that's what we tell ourselves."

"Well said. In our culture, the normal reaction of an administrator is to deny that any problem exists."

"Then why didn't Ms. Hogg?"

"Perhaps because she hasn't been an administrator long enough."

"So, she's still learning?"

"That, but your original guess may be right. She could be looking into the matter herself, but isn't ready to talk about it with anyone." Seeing Flechadoro's questioning glance, he added, "Certainly not me."

"I understand. But I have reasons to believe that something is going on."

"Such as?"

"My uncle says so."

"Your uncle? How would he know?"

"He's a distant relative of the late dean. When he attended Briarpatch, the dean said that he could arrange to improve his grades."

"Your uncle attended Briarpatch?"

"That's what I said."

"But I thought you were the first Native American to attend in years."

"He's as white as anyone. You think we only marry one another?" There was a hint of sarcasm in his voice.

"No, obviously not. I just didn't think."

"That's how I came to Briarpatch. He recommended the college to my mother."

"Your mother?"

"In my tribe the women make the decisions. My mother made mine."

"I see."

"I hope so. But one of these days we'll enter the modern world and Indian men will be able to make choices themselves."

"I see."

"You probably don't, but it doesn't matter. My tribe is not like any of the others. The important thing is to keep this thing from ruining the college."

"You're concerned with the reputation of the college?" Donahue did not have to fake his surprise.

"Of course, don't you know it has a Native American foundation?"

"No, and I don't think anyone else does, either."

Flechadoro smiled at the honesty of Donahue's response. "You don't speak with forked tongue," he said, then smiled again.

"Thanks."

"I suppose if anyone knew about it, the college would have an Indian mascot. I wouldn't like that. Paying for the land would be good, paying for the college's use of our name would be better, but neither one will happen unless the college's reputation is kept pure."

"Well," Donahue conceded, "your concern certainly makes sense." He thought to himself that the tradition of Indian eloquence was certainly alive. Flechadoro's short sentences, the monosyllabic responses, had all vanished. What was his game?

"It's the only college my tribe has a connection with. We even gave it the athletic nickname."

"The Pricks?"

"That's what the other tribes called us. We call ourselves 'the people,' of course, and the others are just non-people. That's why they're jealous."

"I don't know about the nickname. I heard it was of more recent origin."

"Another effort to eliminate all references to Native Americans. If you knew more about my people, you'd know they were the original 'pricks'."

"I'm afraid I don't know any of your people but you, and you don't seem to fit the description."

"Thank you, I think. But the point is to save my tribe's reputation from the potential scandal. I think you are the only person who can do it."

"Well, thank you, I think. But I've not been able to find any evidence that grades have really been sold."

"The dean suggested he could find ways to pass all my classes."

"The present dean?"

"Yes."

"Your uncle knew the earlier Dean Wooda."

"Yes. Like I said, he was a relative somehow. On the White side."

Donahue thought a moment, "Your uncle bought grades?"

"No, the offer was like a gift. But he didn't need them."

"And the current Dean Wooda, what did he offer?"

"Help."

Donahue hesitated, "Help studying?"

Flechadora smiled, "I could do that on my own."

"Give you the tests?"

Another smile, "Less work than that."

Donahue buried his chin in his hand for a minute before asking, "This Dean Wooda?" From the late Dean Wooda he could believe anything. But Stanley was more cautious.

Flechadoro did not hesitate in his response, "Yes. He said we weren't related, or he could do it for free."

"Were those his words, or was he more specific? What did 'it' mean?"

"It was a bit vague."

"Was he joking?"

"Maybe. White men are hard to figure out sometimes. Like saying we weren't related. All Woodas are related, I understand."

Donahue nodded, "He's said they might be, I've heard him say that, but he doesn't know how."

"That's why I thought he wanted money. You know, not being family."

"He didn't mention a payment?"

"Not in so many words, just that he could see that I passed all my classes."

Donahue thought about this for a moment. "That's not much to work on. The football coach says that all the time."

"I thought this was different."

"You are a scholarship student, aren't you? Do you have the money to buy grades?"

"Right now, I've no money, but if my tribe gets to open the casino, I could become wealthy."

"A casino? Where?"

"In Zenith. We have identified a park downtown where we used to have a campsite. Arrowheads, all that kind of stuff has been found there."

"Your tribe?"

"Who else would live in this area? Anyway, all that crap looks alike."

Donahue had to smile, "So, if you say it's yours, who's to say it isn't."

Flechadoro smiled a confirmation.

"You'd build a casino there?"

"Most likely, Zenith would swap us for a suitable building in a rundown neighborhood along the river. We could buy up the entire area, put in restaurants, a Native American Museum (with a federal grant), and maybe a branch campus of Briarpatch College."

Donahue stared at the young man, wondering, "You've really thought this out, haven't you?"

"My mother has, actually. With the aid of my uncle."

"How many are in your tribe?"

"Only fifteen, but that makes it easier to divide up the money when we get it. If necessary, we'll declare some distant relatives who 'went white' to be members, too, if we can find them, and maybe join with a couple other 'vanished tribes.' Congress will give us what we want. Bill Clinton wants to be remembered as 'the Red Man's Friend'."

"I don't remember him using that phrase."

"Only in private, only in private. He is from Arkansas, remember?"

"Yes, they have more Native Americans there than most people realize."

"Exactly."

"So," Donahue asked, "what do you think we can do about grades being for sale?"

Somewhat later Donahue was asking himself how the late Dean Wooda might be related to American Indians. In the case of Flechadoro's family, by marriage, but he heard that some descendants of French Canadians were 95% Indian or more—only their names were French. And the Wooda name was certainly unusual. He could fit it into any of the usual ethnic categories. On the other hand, if the late dean had known of Indian ancestry, wouldn't he have exploited it somehow? He did everything else. Maybe the government had just not gotten around to compensating the Indians for taking advantage of their inability to read contracts? Treating them like taxpayers. No, more like credit card users. The current Dean Wooda was a descendent of India Indians, and perhaps Caribbean Tainos, too. He couldn't remember where he heard that. Probably not important. But it was just another illustration that America was one giant melting pot. He smiled, thinking that not even the Donahues were pure Irish. They just thought they were.

Dean Threshold continued to find occasional leads among his various searches into the family histories of the Wooda clan and more Indian tribes than he had ever imagined had once lived in the Middleville area. The drive to the university library in Zenith was becoming tiresome, but he hesitated to ask Ms. Gates for more interlibrary loans—she was giving him odd looks as she handed over the dust covered books, or, more often, notices that the books were too rare to be put into the mail. The internet had some promise, but not for genealogical research. Something for the future, he thought, but he needed results now. Feeling the pressure of time, he began to wonder why he was supposed to sort the correspondence for the president and dean. He asked his wife, "What's going on? Miss Efficiency could do all that herself."

His wife just rolled her eyes. Opening letters beat working at the diner.

"That's really the only job I have. This 'secret' genealogical study. What's it for? What if Stanley is somehow related to the late dean? It's not as though he lied to a grand jury."

She rolled her eyes again. There he was, making dangerous comparisons to politics. Who knew what Flo Boater thought about Bill Clinton? With a sigh, she explained, again, "Just don't take any risks. This job, this *great* job, it's all about sorting the mail, isn't it?"

"I guess."

"Then *never*, *ever* bring it up! That it's all crap. That's between us. Whatever Flo Boater wants to do is *always*, always right. And don't you forget it!" She thought to herself that she understood why his first wife became a cabbie. Really!

Dean Threshold, however, couldn't just let the matter slide. It ran against his sense of workmanship. Sensing from telephone calls that the president was discarding faculty notes without answering, he began making a summary of the content of the notes that he read. In the future, he decided, requests for money should be returned with a scribbled note; that would eliminate the telephone calls, he hoped. He chose his moment carefully, "President Boater, I think we can handle these requests easily, without committing ourselves."

"Oh, God, not now." She was already on her way out.

"I'm sorry," he had stammered, deliberately. "It's just a small issue, I thought we didn't need to talk about it, not really." He followed her into Miss E's office.

"Oh, what's it about?" she snapped, turning to face him.

"I think we could just tell faculty that requests for money would be taken up in future budget hearings."

"Future hearings?"

"You have hearings every spring."

"No one attends." She looked over to Miss E for confirmation, which she obtained.

"All the better," he replied. "But everyone will think they are being listened to."

She sighed, gave him a mumbled authorization to do whatever he wanted. He would have preferred written instructions, but this was not the time to annoy her. Budget talks were coming up, and his salary was one of the top items for discussion. At least Miss E was a witness, whatever that was worth. She was known to be very competent, but she wanted to keep her job.

Chapter Ten

The historian was so excited when he entered the president's office that he almost forgot to sit down and wait for her to start the conversation. Impatience was written all over him, a fact that Flo Boater realized immediately, "I gather you have some information to share this time."

"Oh, yes, I think so."

"Important?"

"I'm sure you'll be interested. My mother was."

Flo Boater resisted the sickly feeling in her stomach. Keeping her face immobile, she asked, "This came from your mother?"

"No, oh no, but she confirmed it. The story is all over town."

"What story?" She leaned over the desk and put her forearms on it to steady herself; involuntarily she reached for a facial tissue. She had, without realizing it, put the box on the desk rather than back in a drawer when she heard that he was her next visitor.

"It's about Golden Arrow. You know, Flechadoro."

"Yes, what about him?"

"You may have heard that his tribe is going to reclaim its ancestral lands." It was not a question.

"Yes, Stanley told me about that."

Crestfallen, he continued, "That is one story."

"There's another?"

"The lawyers in Middleville have heard that his tribe has filed suit for prime real estate in Zenith to build a casino."

She leaned back to contemplate this. "Do they think he, that is, his tribe, has a chance?"

"Oh, yes. A *very* good chance. My mother has a cousin who's a lawyer, and he thinks so."

"That is very interesting. But how does this affect the college?"

"The college?" he asked.

"You haven't heard that he only wants the land the college is on?"

"No, nothing that specific. But I can ask my mother."

"You'll do no such thing," she said firmly. "We have enough problems without that rumor going around, too. Now, tell me, how does this affect Briarpatch College, other perhaps that being able to ask the government for some money? We could use a major gift to renovate, say, the Museum of Native Americans." She did not mention the fact that all the materials gathered by the first Dean Wooda were from Latin America, or the state running a significant deficit, or Republicans in Congress criticizing the "waste of taxpayer dollars."

"Museum of Native Americans?"

"Ah, yes," she said, then, realizing that she was imitating him, she started again, "You may have heard it called the Ethnological Collection or the Anthropology Collection. It's your responsibility to know this—you are in charge of the Sociology program, and Donahue is the likely future director. For an appropriate donation, sufficient to either build a structure or remodel an existing building, we would be willing to consider renaming it." She then ground her teeth, realizing that she was imitating the presidential style of her late husband.

"I understand," he said hesitatingly. Then he ventured a question, "Naming it what?"

Flo Boater was slightly taken aback. She hadn't considered this. "Well, maybe the name of the tribe or, perhaps, its most prominent chief."

He hesitated before venturing a comment, "I don't think we'd be able to do either one. I've looked into the records—a hundred years ago we had a good collection on Ind… Native Americans…." A prolonged "ahh" and a slight blush followed.

The thought came to Flo Boater that this was the first sign of color in his face that she had ever seen. Still, she barely refrained from drumming her fingers or saying, "Get to the point!"

He finally broke his silence, saying, "Ah, uh, the tribe's name is unprintable, uh, and it doesn't seem to have had any prominent leaders—it was a matriarchy, you see, and the men who signed the treaties were, well, uh, just 'front men'. The names of the women have been forgotten."

Flo Boater sighed before asking, "What else did you learn? That is, you and your mother."

"If his lawyers can prove the tribe's right to the land in Zenith, there is every chance that they can get a law through Congress to make Briarpatch eligible for funds through the Indian Affairs Bureau... or whatever it is called now."

"Your mother's cousin's lawyer or whatever thinks that?" She found it odd that nobody locally had connected this with the claim on the college property.

"My mother's cousin thinks so. He lives in Zenith. It could mean a goodly sum over the years."

"How so?"

"Perhaps for scholarships, certainly for a chair in Native American Studies."

"A chair would be nice. But I have a hard time imagining Briarpatch students taking that kind of courses."

"Oh, I think we could make it a graduation requirement."

"Ah, yes. I imagine that Professor Stout would be *very* pleased at that."

"Immensely so," the historian continued, missing the sarcasm. "As would I. Surely you would need an associate dean to administer the program."

Flo Boater looked her guest over carefully, "I shall give that some thought. Please keep me informed about this." As she wiped her hands, she wondered why anyone would think that Briarpatch College would be able to get money for such a program rather than Zenith University. Was there somewhere a memory of the tribe's presence on college land? And how would that work? Would the college be expected to pay the tribe off, then skim off enough from a casino to restore financial stability? She shrugged. It sounded like the kind of scheme that the late dean would have thought of.

Across the campus in the English building, there was a similar excitement. But the topic was very different. Sal was speaking quietly but quickly, "Molly, did you talk with Jay?"

Molly looked out in the hall before closing the door, then whispering. "He says he can't help you. There is so much trash around, he could use another janitor. Classrooms, campus. But he can't get you into the registrar's office right now. He's being watched."

Remembering the hallway, Sal agreed, "Yes, the buildings are a mess. The administration saves money by cutting janitors."

"It's a job that needs to be done. The professors are as bad as the students. Sometimes worse! And the demonstrators, they are as bad as a football crowd." She thought briefly that the football crowd had not been a problem before, but now the team was winning.

Sal gave her a quick hug and opened the door, "I'll see you later, *cara*, I have some more people to talk to." He then darted into the hall and disappeared.

Meekly, Molly called at his receding back, "Yes, I'll be home." She sounded exhausted.

Hearing her voice break, he turned back and whispered, "*A piu tarde.*"

Understanding him to mean "soon but not too soon," she answered, "OK. Good luck."

On his way toward the coffee house, he bumped into two students who were jauntily taking up the entire sidewalk, their heads turned halfway around to gawk at the hottest girl they'd seen that day—the only girl, too, since they had just crawled out of bed. How they knew she was hot was a mystery—she was thoroughly covered with heavy coat, woolen cap and scarves.

One turned to ask, "Who was that guy?" It was Jones who asked, then added, "He's in a big rush!" He was also dressed rather lightly for the weather, too lightly to walk slowly.

Smith thought a moment, "He looks familiar." They stopped walking and turned to watch him moving away. He was more interesting even than the coed, who had stopped to chat with some football player whose neck began at the top of his arm; she was too far away to see well now, anyway.

Jones scratched his head and asked, "Isn't he the guy whose class we always missed?"

"No way *you'd* recognize him!"

"I was in class the first day."

"So was I," Smith responded, "but way in the back. And asleep."

Jones was now certain, "No, really. He's the *chemistry* prof!"

Smith tried again to see the disappearing figure, "The class we passed?"

"Yeah," Jones explained, "but we *bought* the grades."

"I've heard someone was asking around about that."

This was alarming, "Him?"

"Dunnow. But it's scary. I don't need the grade now. Not after getting the Lit exam back today."

Jones looked sideways at him, "Don't you need the chemistry grade to meet the science requirement?"

"I'll get around it," Smith assured him. "There's always a way, Stan said."

"You've spoken to Stan?" Jones couldn't imagine that Smitty had done anything without consulting him.

"Yeah, back when he was a student."

"Oh," Jones replied, reassured. "What did he say?"

"Independent study or something. Off-campus program without going away. Something."

Jones nodded his head. He had never thought of those possibilities, and he had studied the catalog with a thoroughness that would have gotten him an A in any class. "I hope so," he said. "If I'd known you could pass English Lit without reading the books, I'd have majored in it right away." He hadn't met Professor Stout at that time, but now he was a disciple. "I could've skipped that chem class."

"And if I'd been told that in Environmental Studies all you had to say was 'Stop the Growth,' I'd never have taken Chem, either."

"Maybe I should take that." Jones was impressed again—Smith had never seemed this sharp. Had something changed?

"I dunno. I think it's a ten o'clock class."

"Well, that wipes that off." Too early in the day. Jones was relieved—this was the good old Smitty he had relied upon to provide predictability in an uncertain world.

"Something will come along." Smith was an optimist. "It always does."

Jones changed the subject, "Stout says that next year we can take Indian Lore. Everyone will pass."

There was something in Jones's voice that seemed to imply that Stout was being sarcastic. Smith had rarely been able to tell when his friend was putting him on. So he asked, "Everyone?" Smith was becoming a cynic.

"Everyone who agrees with him." Jones was already a realist.

"What do you have to agree with?"

"With Stout it's easy. America is always wrong."

"I can remember that," Smith responded. "I've heard it before." Then he furrowed his brows, "I didn't know we offered that class."

"Oh, not yet, but Stout says it will be part of the new museum. He'll be in charge. Everyone who enrolls will pass."

"What about papers?" Smith wrote occasionally for the student paper, but his editor corrected his grammar. Would Stout do that for him?

"I think we just write letters to Congress."

Smith thought about this for a moment, "That means we graduate?" His voice lacked any suggestion of optimism. In the back of his mind was a potential separation from Ellie.

"Without doubt." Jones was thinking of graduate school, where, he had heard, talking was more important than studying.

"Would it count for science?" Smith asked. "Sort of an alternate view of reality, like alternative medicine or Noam Chomsky."

"We could ask," Jones responded. What did Smith know of Chomsky? Only Ellie ever read *him*. In fact, she was probably the only student on campus who could spell his name—or pronounce it—other than Jones himself.

Smith wrinkled his eyebrows: "Stout will be teaching Indian Lore? I thought he was English, or English and Honors and Tennis."

"No, he'll get someone else to teach it, but he'll be in charge."

"You *sure*?"

"No, but he *sounded* sure."

"Well, he's gotten *everything* he wanted. I think we can count on it then."

Jones gave a sigh of relief, then frowned. This was an awfully astute insight for his friend to have. But he shook it off, "Too bad we spent all that money on grades. I could use a beer right now. And Dean Wooda is dead now; he can't help us any more."

"The new Dean Wooda can, but we don't need him, you say?"

"Nah, he's just a fall-back guy, in case we need him."

Smith frowned, "You mean he's selling, but we're not buying." He paused to think, then added, "Unless we really need him."

Jones nodded agreement. "I dunno if he's really selling right now. I heard that Golden Arrow is asking around about that. Maybe he's keeping his head down. Worried, maybe."

"Me, too." Smith responded, "What if they catch us now? Now that we haven't done nuthin? Not recently."

Jones agreed. "It was a mistake, that chemistry grade."

"What about the others?"

"Maybe, but they don't matter. Chem is different. What's-his-name is on our trail. We'd better do something about that now. Like, make it all go away."

"Kill him??"

"No, silly. Get rid of the grade."

"What? Change the grades back?" In the back of his mind, somewhere barely accessible, he was wondering about how he would meet the science requirement.

Jones gave him no time to search, responding, "Yeah, like that."

"But how?" Smith asked, "The dean is dead." The old Dean Wooda was predictable, and he took care of everything.

Jones ignored him—he had an idea. "Didn't you used to work in the registrar's office? Can't you work something out there?"

"Like what?"

"You could fill out a change of grade slip and fake the instructor's signature."

"How would that work?"

Jones explained, "You told me all about it. We put the grade in the hopper—just like the registrar had done it herself, or some professor— and her assistants will put it into the computer."

"Just turn in the form?"

"Put it in the IN hopper. It goes automatically from there. The registrar won't even notice."

"She isn't even around now."

"That just makes it easier."

Smith wasn't so sure. "You mean go over right now? They'll see us." The IN file was way in the back, by the computer.

"No, silly. We break in about ten-thirty, before the night watchman makes his rounds." He knew this well. Ever since Smith and Jones had broken into the financial office, Flo Boater had rehired the night watchmen and tightened up security everywhere. "I know his schedule."

"Break in!" Smith wasn't so sure of this. It hadn't worked out so well before. Well, it had, but there had been tense moments.

"We won't break anything. That would make everyone suspicious. I'll drop by the registrar's office now and unlock a window. No problem. We slip in later."

"What it someone locks it again?" It was winter, and the old windows let in air unless latched down firmly.

"No problem," Jones said "All the locks in the doors are old. We'll get in."

"It's on the second floor. They replaced the main doors."

"We'll get in."

"I don't know. Those are new locks."

"I can handle them. That's why my name is Jimmy."

Smith's response was uncharacteristically long: "Well, it's an 'unacquired' skill, they say. You have it when you're young, like learning a language. But you've grown up." He paused for a moment before adding, "And you're out of practice." He wanted to ask why they'd come in through a window when JJ could pick any lock? It sounded like something out of *Huck Finn*. He hadn't read it, but his high school teacher had said that someone people just can't do things the easiest possible way, but have to do it "by the book."

Jones didn't wait for Smith to put all these thoughts together. He interrupted, saying, "You're just jealous. Sometimes you can't get into your own room. And you have a key for it."

"If I could hold my liquor well enough to remember which dorm I lived in, it would be a snap! Besides, you're no better! The other night…"

"It's the administration's fault!" Jones exclaimed. "The dean of students kicks us out of one dorm after the other. How am I to remember where we belong?" After a pause he added, "Besides, I usually get us home somehow."

Dean Threshold knew where he belonged. Among the assignments piling up on his desk was a report on Jones's parents and the likelihood they would make a major donation to the college—after he graduated.

Actually, it was not on his desk. Flo Boater had phoned him and given terse orders.

"Why not ask the director of development?" he had asked.

"If I had wanted to involve him, I would have." Flo Boater was nothing if not direct.

"How the hell," he asked himself, "do I get that kind of information?" He could not ask around, and he certainly couldn't ask the kid—as if he had a clue. Maybe he should just call and ask.

"What will you say to them," Mabel asked. "Just: how much money do you have?"

He smiled. She was so direct. Being a waitress was giving her a tart tongue. "No, I think I could suggest that we are reviewing his financial aid information. Update it. That sort of thing."

"Isn't that backward? Parents always pled poverty."

"I've thought of that. Something more like a genius-award, say for that mural he almost finished in the Administration building. You know, the one opposite my office."

"Oh, *that* one!"

"Yes, but before we could even consider such an award—which doesn't exist yet—we need to make sure that their—his parents'—income is such that he doesn't need financial aid."

Chapter Eleven

Flo Boater's voice raised more than she wished, "What is it Stanley, that you have to see me in such a hurry? Couldn't it have waited?"

"President Boater, this is a real emergency." He was still panting from running up the stairs. "I almost shit in my pants, I was so upset."

"First of all, Stanley, calm down. Now, then, call me Flo." Getting no response, she added, "When we're alone, like now." When he nodded, she continued, "We are, after all, colleagues... comrades in arms. We ought to be on a first name basis."

"Yes... Flo."

"Now, tell me about this emergency." She was relieved to see him relax...somewhat.

"You've heard the demonstrators?"

"Of course, they were right out there until lunchtime."

"Have you heard what they want?"

"No. I don't listen very carefully."

"This is serious." He squirmed as he began to wish he had stopped in the washroom on the way up.

"Stanley, it's always serious. But it's also *information overload*. Demonstrations are very effective when they are rare. Here it is a daily occurrence. No one pays any attention any more."

"Yes, in general."

"So...why should I pay attention to this one?"

"This one is about grades!"

"Stanley, students have demonstrated about grades since the 1700's. Besides, you told me about that earlier."

"This is more serious." His hand began to tremble slightly.

"Golden Arrow again?"

"Partly," he said half-way, changing it to. "No, worse."

"Worse? How could it be worse than his wanting us to give the campus to him? 'Back to him,' he says."

"Forget the land. This is about grades. Two groups!" He started to sit down, then jumped up and went to the window, looking out at the demonstrators.

"Two?"

"One group down there—Smith and Jones, I think, are in charge—want to be able to buy grades again! Golden Arrow's crowd wants it stopped. The two groups are getting larger by the minute. There could be a fight, then there'd be television, all that all over again."

Flo Boater stood up to take her dean by the hands and said, "Now, Stanley, calm down," she tried to nestle his head on her bosom. But he broke away and turned back to the window, "I'm okay now. It's just... so...frustrating. I'm trying to do a good job, and all these students...."

"Golden Arrow I think we can handle. If my information is correct..."

"The Creep?"

"Yes," she responded, involuntarily reaching for a tissue. "Maybe we can create a special committee to investigate, quietly and discretely. Put him on it. That could tie him up for months."

"How about the others? They want grades now."

Soothingly, she suggested, "Your former friends..." and came toward him again, to assure him that he was safe with her. He, however, quickly darted to one side and sat down. It was a graceful movement, one that was not lost on her. But when he commented that, "All they want it is to get through college without doing any work," she gave up and sat down herself, commenting dryly, "That's nothing particularly new."

He, however, was angry and wanted to say so, "I've worked my butt off, and they want everything I have without lifting a finger."

"Unless the finger is around a beer can," she said. She knew students well, or thought she did. Besides, Stan hadn't worked that hard.

Not quite getting the sarcasm, he exclaimed, "Exactly! Are there no standards any more?" He stood up and threw his arms toward heaven. This was a gesture that had worked before. Younger women loved it—it demonstrated passion, ambition, and anger. And it had an effect on Flo Boater as well, though hers was modified by an ironic awareness of what he was doing.

She stood up, and moved toward him again, but when he turned away, she ordered, "Stanley, sit down." Once he was back in his chair, she looked down on him and inquired, "Now, Stan, how old are you?"

"I'm twenty-one," he said. "You know that."

"It's a rhetorical question. What does twenty-one mean in terms of experience?"

Spreading his hands, embarrassed, he admitted, "Not much. That is, not much experience."

"Stanley, when you're my... when you have more experience, you'll realize that human beings are not perfect."

Peevishly, he exclaimed, "I know that. I've known that since I was a child."

Flo Boater detected something important in those words, but she decided to ignore them. With the voice of a concerned mother, she spoke soothingly, "People are not perfect, but they are predictable."

"Yes?" he responded.

She continued quietly, "The students, having heard... somehow... that grades were for sale... they want to have the same... opportunity as students used to have. It's perfectly normal."

Exasperated, he retorted, "You make it sound like a civil rights issue."

Hurriedly, but quietly, she said, "No, no. The issue not comparable. But the human reaction is." Seeing his puzzled expression, she stood up and walked around to think, "We've got to make people believe that this is a misapprehension."

Turning his head to follow her, Wooda agreed, "Okay. How do we correct this 'misapprehension?' And when did you first learn of it?"

Stopping to face him, she said, "I was aware of it long ago." Turning toward the window, she moved to where she could look out. Eventually, she said, "It was one of those things I was going to correct as president."

Wooda asked, "Why hadn't I heard of it."

"You were always on off-campus programs. And, to be frank, Stanley, you never needed to buy a grade."

I guess that makes sense," he observed. Then he furrowed his brows and asked, "You knew about this at the time?"

Confidentially, she responded, "Not the point. Selling grades was the issue that got the board to appoint me president."

"It was?"

"I might as well tell you now. You'll hear about it anyway. This way it won't come as a surprise at... an awkward time."

This left Wooda confused, "An awkward time?"

She turned toward him, then gazed upward, as if the answer should be obvious, "Say, a trustees' retreat. I don't want it to come as a surprise. It's much better than we are all reading from the same page."

"The trustees knew?" He was amazed. In fact, he was amazed by the fact that she still could amaze him.

"I told them," she admitted, somewhat boastfully.

"When?"

"When I heard that Lily suspected it."

"You went to the trustees then? Why?"

"I explained that if the leather lesbians were left in charge..."

His legs shaky now, he sat down, "Lill and Lily...."

".....that a misunderstanding would be blown into a major scandal."

At this he jumped up, "But you said that it wasn't a misunderstanding."

Flo Boater was now ready to give him a good shaking, "Let's get agree on what the story line is here! What we know and what the trustees want to hear are two different things."

He was suddenly subdued, "Okay." He understood *Realpolitik*. Then he suddenly became aware of what she had implied, "You mean the trustees really didn't fire them because of their sexual orientation?"

Flo Boater spoke almost apologetically, "Well, their motorcycle clothing helped, of course. But no, that wasn't the real reason." As she sat down, she added, "Obviously, they couldn't tell anyone the real reasons. That's a basic rule of administration—never tell anyone anything that isn't to your advantage!"

Sitting down and staring at his lap, Wooda could only say, "I'll be damned."

"Maybe," she said. "Certainly, for sure, if you turn out to be a good dean. But that's not the point. What every good administrator has to do is play the game well."

"What game?" he asked.

"Call it the game of life, it you want. It may be a serious game, it may not be.... Sometimes it's hard to take higher education seriously." With a look at Stanley, he continued, "Anyway, it's a many-sided game, and those who want to be successful have to pit the rest of the players against one another and against themselves."

"Against themselves?"

Waving her hand, she said, "People want contradictory.... things."

"Such as?"

Sitting down next to him, she explained, "The trustees, for example. They want to be included, but they usually don't want to be bothered. They love the ceremonies, the prestige, the feeling that they are doing something worthwhile."

"And the college *is* worthwhile." He said this with a passion that even surprised himself.

Putting her hand on his, she explained, "Yes, but it is not a simple operation, and they hate complexities. Most importantly, they abhor scandals."

"So you play the one desire off against the other?"

"It's actually not that hard. Just like dealing with Golden Arrow. Give them the illusion of participation and something to do."

"And the other students?"

"If we pass the word to a small number of students," she explained, "Smith and Jones, for example, offering them a special opportunity...."

"We buy them off?" He had a vision of Smith's newspaper article the previous semester. What an embarrassment. Not a person he'd trust!

"In a sense. They are also buying us off."

"I don't understand," he said.

"This is also a way to offset the budget deficits, silly." Watching his reaction, she smiled, "Think about it. Smith and Jones are the only two students who pay our listed tuition; everybody else has a scholarship, most quite generous ones. If they weren't such a nuisance, we'd want to keep them here forever."

"So, we should help Smith and Jones make 'progress'—slowly— toward graduation? Then they'll let us alone?"

"It's a practical matter. It gets both trustees and students off our backs!"

He was not persuaded, "It just doesn't seem right. How can we get away with it?" By "right," he meant getting away with it.

She agreed, "It's not right. In the conventional sense."

"Would Ms. Hogg go along?" He sounded doubtful.

"I don't think I could persuade Ms. Hogg to change any grades. Certainly not without plausible reasons. I don't even want her to catch wind of it. Anyway, that's not an issue until she turns up. A lot can happen before then."

"If it's dangerous, why not stop it?"

"First of all, it could resolve part of our retention problem."

He was baffled, "Retention?"

"We can't afford to have students flunk out. Each student means *money*!"

"Oh." Now he understood.

"It's a question of doing this so quietly that… well, how did Woody do it? Nobody really suspected while he was alive."

Stanley Wooda began to think about this as more a puzzle than a threat. "We really need to find that out?"

"And how do we do that?"

"I think the first step is to compare grades on the transcript with grades on the professors' sheets. That's easy. We could just ask the staff to pull those items… or could we? They might wonder what's going on and compare them themselves."

Flo Boater's eyes rolled, "Not another late night break in?"

"Either that or during a weekend. How much of a hurry are we in?"

She glanced toward the window and the unseen demonstrators outside, "A lot, I think."

An hour later Stanley Wooda was back in the president's office, "How long will we have to run this scam? Just till Smith and Jones graduate? Or till we get caught?"

She leaned back in her power chair and put a hand to her chin, "Getting cold feet?"

"Yes. It's the sort of thing that is impossible to keep quiet. Someone is sure to talk."

She laughed, "That's right, but we're sort of stuck. One of them just might talk to the press if we say no. We've got to ease it out of existence at the right time."

He plopped down on a chair, "It *is* out of existence. They want it brought back."

"So we do that," she said, then as he relaxed, she added, "But only temporarily. Only for those students who *deserve* it."

He admired her nerve and her nerves. He commented ironically, "Who *earn* it."

A mocking tone was more than she would tolerate. Rounding on him, she insisted, "*Yes*. Those who help stop the demonstrations."

This was something new. "I think I get it now. Only for those two, maybe a few more, but not anyone new. Even Golden Arrow might understand that."

"Let's not push it. He may turn out to be honest."

"The way he gets scholarships, I think he understands the system."

"We'll deal with him later. Right now you get out there and talk to the right students, the ones you suspect of having bought grades. Take them for a beer. Find out what they know, what they'll settle for. Find out, if you can, who else has benefited." She paused before adding, "No specific promises. If they want to hear something definite, they're idiots anyway. Say nothing you can't deny. You might think of recording the conversation—they'd never think to suspect."

Stanley Wooda was not pleased to hear these orders. Sullenly, he objected, "That means starting with Smith and Jones. They're behind this whole thing and I don't trust them."

She waved a hand at him, "Trust? Trust in what sense?"

"They lack good judgment. They could talk."

"Anybody who knows them knows that. You'll have to persuade them that it's in their best interests to keep quiet."

"What does that mean?"

Dismissively, she sneered, "You are an imaginative boy. Do I have to do *all* your thinking for you?" As he left her laughed to herself, "If it all goes wrong, I'll say that we were just investigating—a kind of sting operation. In fact, I'll write a note to that effect now, then let Miss

Efficiency mail the letter to me. Not here, Dean Threshold would read it. But to my home, with her signature and today's date on the back. The postal date should persuade even Chief Biggs that it's all on the up-and-up. If Stanley gets in over his head, I can pull him out...," she thought with a smile, "on the condition that he cooperates in, let's say, 'other ways'."

Only later did Stanley Wooda remember to ask about the missing registrar. "Oh, well," he said to himself. "Tomorrow, maybe."

Ellie asked Smitty what the demonstration was all about. Why insist on grades being for sale when they are so easy to earn—good grades.

"Easy for you to say," he thought, but he remembered Jones's instructions: "This is how we call attention to the problem." And that is what he told her, adding a thought of his own about athletes getting grades they hadn't earned. She frowned, realizing that the kernel of truth in the statement did not add up to an oak tree. At Briarpatch College there were as many professors who graded football players down as who were sympathetic to "their special needs."

Smith breathed a sigh of relief and practically swelled with pride at having remembered not to tell the real reason for the demonstration— to bring pressure on the dean to erase their chemistry grades.

Chapter Twelve

Tomorrow always comes, and it usually comes much as it was yesterday. But today was a bit different for Flo Boater, at least. She was yelling, "It's about time you got here! Why are the police always the last to get to the scene?" She was standing beside her desk, shouting at Chief Biggs the moment he crossed the threshold. Young Stanley Wooda, who looked out his door when the noise began, cautiously slipped back inside his office.

Biggs answered apologetically, "I only received your call a few minutes ago. Sorry."

He stopped and looked around, wondering if he should stand or sit. He decided that she meant him to stand until she was finished.

His answer was far from sufficient for Flo Boater, who commented sarcastically, "One would think that a town this size would have a better communications system for the police."

The chief responded defensively, "The town isn't big, but I have only five policemen. I can't expect them to 'jump to' except for emergencies."

This was not satisfactory, "You should still have a better reaction time."

His retort was grim, "For serious matters, we do. But you only told the dispatcher that you wanted to see me."

"When *I* want to see *you*, that *is* serious business!"

"We've always treated the college president like just another citizen."

"Then that's a policy you have to change. The college is, after all, one of the largest employers in the county."

With a sigh, the chief conceded, "I shall so instruct my dispatcher."

She followed up with a sarcastic comment, "You find my request odd?"

He barely controlled his temper, "Your husband, the late president, never put it that way."

"Put it what way?" she demanded to know

"If there was an emergency, which was rare, he would say so."

She knew this was not an apology, much less an abject one, "I bet you jumped when Lill was acting-president."

"I don't remember her ever asking me to hurry over. She was...." His voice trailed off while he sought to find the right words.

Flo Boater prompted him: "Better organized?" As she paused to await his response, Biggs shrugged his shoulders. She snapped, "I rather expected that." Indicating that he should sit in the uncomfortable straight chair placed directly in front of her desk for unruly students and faculty members with suggestions, she took her place in her "power seat" and said, "You don't like me very much, do you, Chief Biggs?" When he didn't answer, she offered, "Off the record."

"Okay, off the record, I didn't agree with the jury when it found no connection between you and Dean Wooda's death, and I was suspicious of your husband's."

"And the Vice-President's 'murder?' Last semester."

"That was an accident, of course. Miss Purdy was okay, but for a while we didn't know what had happened." While he had suspected foul play, he had been very careful not to accuse Flo Boater of being involved with it, even if she had found the blood. "Why did you ask me to come here? Surely not to discuss... ancient history."

"As you wish," she responded. "This is the point: I'm *very* upset."

"About something I did?"

"It's about what you don't do." She paused for effect, then said, "First you let these students protest."

He sighed, "We've been over this before. As long as they don't violate any law, I can't do anything. It's up to you to enforce college policies."

Sarcastically, she said, "To the extent they are legal."

"Yes. That's correct," he agreed. "But there is much you can do within the law... if you want to do it."

She didn't like this answer, "Yes, but the blame always lands on me, and you, the representative of law and order, won't help me maintain order."

He indicated his helplessness with a shrug, "If they violate the law, call me." As he began to rise, he asked, "Anything else?" Not getting a response, he turned to leave.

At that, she snapped out, "Yes. There is one more item" At that she paused, and with a gesture signaled the chief to sit down and hear her out. When he was once more on his uncomfortable chair, she gave him a smug look and continued quietly, "Sal Iva is out of jail and back in town."

This was not news, "Yes, he's been released. Not surprising after that strong letter you wrote to the appeals board."

"That was Donahue's doing," she snapped, "and you know it."

"It was still a generous thing to do."

"I never expected him to come back here. I thought he'd be too ashamed."

The chief sucked in a breath. Wow, did she change moods fast! But he said only, "Conspiring to kill a dean is a serious business."

Her nostrils flared at the implied insult, "I thought we agreed that I had nothing to do with that!"

Firmly Biggs held his ground, "It is odd that he was convicted for conspiring with you, and you were found not guilty."

More quietly, she explained, "That's why I'm afraid of him."

His response was quick, "Get a court order to keep him away from campus and your neighborhood."

She hurriedly rejected this "I don't want him to know I don't trust him." She tried to appear vulnerable before she added, "He could be dangerous if he found out." The pose was not successful.

The chief once again made ready to leave, "Then I can't help you."

She challenged him, "You'd help Lill and Lily."

He looked back to answer, "Not if they made a request like yours."

She called after him, "You might as well go, then."

At the door, he turned back to say, "If you need me, just call."

She yelled at his vanishing form "And your dispatcher better give me highest priority!" But he was already on his way down the stairs, too far away to hear.

Flo Boater was still shaking thirty minutes later when Miss Efficiency came to the door to ask if she was ready to see the next appointment. It was Ellie, she mouthed, trying to avoid being heard by the others who had just arrived to see the president. The line was longer than it used to be, because the faculty had begun to sense that she rarely read their notes and memos—from Dean Threshold's replies they had figured out that if was wasted effort to try to catch the president's eye; to be heard, they had to get her ear. Therefore, they wanted to speak with her personally, but in her office, not in the Japanese Coffee House, where everyone could see them. She, in contrast, was afraid that they wanted to lead her by the nose. Why didn't anyone come to see her except when they wanted something, she wanted to know. The answer was obvious to everyone but her—she was a busy woman and working hours were not meant for socializing; she would have been the first to complain about people coming in just to chat.

Ellie was different. Her parents were very, very rich; and her boyfriend, whichever it was, Jones or Smith, was rich, too, or would be someday. Flo Boater had just heard about this development, from another good informant—Jay—who knew everything that happened on campus and told her about whatever he thought she should know; and, she suspected, he remained silent about the rest. All she could do, other than wonder whether to fire Jay, and, if she did, wonder how she could replace him, was to shake her head about the idiocy of nubile young women, then try to prevent Ellie's parents for blaming the college for her falling into the wrong hands! Fortunately, Ellie wasn't as useless as either Smith or Jones! When she wasn't under the influence of some chemical, legal or otherwise, or sleepy from reading too much, too late, she could study effectively and write good papers. Unfortunately, the first semester she hadn't as good at showing up for exams fully alert as she might have been, or turning in papers on time. This semester seemed to be different, though Flo Boater couldn't see why. Anyway that not an important matter—girls had their own priorities, and Ellie's included rarely missing a demonstration. This was the main reason Flo Boater wanted to see her—to learn what was the current protest really about? Ellie didn't need to buy grades, but she was there alongside Smith and Jones. Maybe she could tell her how to satisfy the marchers?

In the end Flo Boater was not able to get much information out of the young woman, who seemed bored and sleepy. Ellie wanted only to say that she and the rest of the student body supported Flechadoro. "The sooner our country is returned to its rightful owners, the better," she had said the one time her voice indicated passion. "And Briarpatch College should lead the way."

Flo Boater didn't understand. On a little matter like grades, she could understand Ellie supporting Flechadoro; after all, she was an A student or should have been—Flo Boater had never taught a class, but she was a keen observer of humanity and believed that she could tell by looking who was a good student and who was not. Ellie was a good student—there was something in her eyes that indicated disdain of the commonplace; that was a "sign certain" of intelligence. But on something as important as the existence of the college, Ellie was ready to give everything away. Could it be, she wondered, the Ellie had gotten sweet on the young Indian. God, she said to herself, I'm sounding like an old woman—"sweet," she had said, and "Indian," and now she was suspecting Ellie of being merely another silly girl. At least she hadn't used the word "squaw."

"Why am I unable to see to the bottom of all this?" Flo Boater asked herself. She didn't know. Maybe it was because when she had asked *Stan*, as she now preferred to think of him, about Ellie's views, she had been so distracted by his not moving his hand away when she had put hers upon it, that she didn't pay proper attention to what he was saying. Maybe she should call him in again, to get the story straight? Perhaps she'd even understand what some moving hand had written across the mural on the ground floor: *Many, many tickles upstairs.* She needed a Daniel to figure out what that meant, but all she could get out of Ellie was a giggle.

Chapter Thirteen

Dean Wooda sauntered over from his office, took a comfortable seat off to one side of the massive desk, an act that required Flo to give up her power seat to see him—she had installed low chairs in order to have a psychological advantage over visitors, but his leaning back and putting his feet up on a low table was an act of self-confidence that he had never dared before. She couldn't see more than the top of his head, but it was beautiful hair, she thought. Still, she wanted to see his eyes—"the mirror of the soul," she remembered—not his hair. She could have leaned forward, but that was just too awkward, and she recoiled slightly at seeing his shoes on her favorite antique piece. But she had no time to make a decision about what to do before he announced, "I just figured out how to blame the grade scandal on Lill and Lily!"

Flo Boater had not fully recovered from the two preceding conversations. Consequently, her reply was more caustic than she intended it to be, "How will you do that? It began when my husband was president."

This definitely did not have the result she wanted—he laughed, "Everyone will believe that your husband was too dumb to have thought the scam up." He closed his eyes even as he thought about how perfect the joke was.

Even she had to smile at this, "Okay, that part will be easy." Maybe, too, she thought, will be my plan if I don't rush it. Patience, patience.

Putting his feet down, he leaned forward to explain, "We'll portray the leather lesbians as a motorcycle gang, selling drugs and so forth. But their big scores come from changing grades."

She cast her eyes down, shook her head, then looked up at him, "That will be a hard sell. Everyone knows they are clean. No drugs, no money."

The dean explained, "'Everyone' forgets quickly. 'Everyone' only remembers the accusations."

"How well I know!" she said. "Well, go on."

"We'll drop hints that Lill is a mafia-style boss, working behind the scenes, selling grades for money." As he smiled broadly, he leaned back and put his feet up again. His head was invisible again, but she could not help but look at his feet.

"How appropriate for Theatre," she noted, emphasizing the British pronunciation, "and it might work. But will anyone believe an efficient person—and the mafia *is* efficient—can be found in any Theater department. I don't know." She meanwhile wondered how she could get him out of that chair—and his shoes off her furniture!

Wooda agreed, "The argument alone sounds so unlikely that people will believe it; in fact, if it's improbable, it's most likely true." After a pause, he noticed her starring at his feet and moved them, then explained, "It's the argument Tertullian used to prove the truth of Christianity."

She furrowed her eyebrows, "Tertullian?" she asked herself. "When did Stan start reading the church fathers?"

He jabbed the table with a forefinger, "Never make small plans. Never make a small accusation!"

"Goebbels," she thought. "The Big Lie Technique. Or was that Stalin?" But she contented herself with saying, "Interesting. But it has problems."

"Like?"

Standing up and walking over to the window, with Wooda following, she said, "The money. A Mafia head would have gotten rich." She noticed his arms were crossed over his chest. Touching would have been awkward—and would reverse their power relationship. Patience, patience.

"That's the clever part," he argued. "We suggest that she had been diverting the money into hidden accounts, under Dean Wooda's name... about which he knew nothing." He waited for her to see where his suggestion was leading. "That means that the late dean was innocent of all the charges! They were setting him up if anything went wrong."

She saw the weak point—rhetoric might be persuasive, but not if the bankers insisted they had never seen Lill and the accounts had been opened long ago, perhaps even before they were hired. But what she said was, "And then they would take his job!"

"Their next step was to discredit your late husband!"

"Very interesting! Very creative!" Where was this going?

"Even better," he boasted, "this will undercut the insurance companies' complaints that they were victims of fraud."

She frowned slightly, "Explain that, please."

"It's like this. They have argued that the dean's murder, and your husband's, were conspiracies by college officers to defraud them. Therefore, they don't have to pay." He paused. "However, if Lill and Lily appear guilty..."

"Wait a minute, why just *appear*?"

"That's the beauty of it. There's no way that they could be convicted, so they can't become martyrs. On the other hand, if it *appears* they're guilty... even their friends will abandon them." He almost strutted across the room, while explaining his plan. Obviously, his intestinal problem had vanished. "But doubt would be cast on any official involvement!"

The president scratched her ear, "I don't know that we should even bring the matter to anyone's attention. It will make the college look bad." And, me, she thought. I'd have to sell this idiotic idea! "Forget the drugs. That whole business could backfire. Concentrate on the grades." She threw up her hands, "Anyway, it's dangerous to make any of it public."

Stanley Wooda misread her body language. "It's going to come out anyway," he exclaimed. "We've got to get ahead of the story. Grades for sale. Why that's every adolescent college boy's dream, right next to a...." He almost said, "a hot teacher, hot to trot," but he glanced over at Flo Boater and realized that she might mistake his meaning.

She sighed. "So, the idea is that they were about to be exposed, so they..."

"They protected themselves...."

"So they had been running this out of the Theater department?"

"Why not? Who'd question good grades being given for acting or tech work? Besides actors and stage people are always shooting or snorting. Everyone knows that."

Flo Boater rolled her eyes, but she confined her response to, "And grades in other departments?"

"Lill was a faculty leader. She could have talked the registrars into, well, maybe some of the faculty, too, into cooperating. You know, for the good of the institution, and a sort of bonus to make up for the poor salaries. But when she became acting-president, this would have been too contrived." He paused, then almost added that additional income would have been unnecessary—as acting-president her salary would have been much greater than that of a Theater teacher.

She mulled the plan over, "Do you think you can sell that story?" As a rumor, it might have some value, but it wouldn't stand scrutiny.

Stanley Wooda had no doubts, "Newspaper people love conspiracies."

Flo Boater walked around, thinking aloud, "There could be an awful lot of people who bought grades from the late dean." She tried to visualize him doing that. It wasn't hard, and it helped her momentarily forget about Stan's gorgeous hair—the survival instinct can do that. "We'd be awfully embarrassed if someone showed up and said that he had bought grades from the dean, the late dean, not from her."

"How many were there? There couldn't have been that many."

"Then how was it a money-making proposition?"

"Oh, I guess that each transaction was expensive. How much money he made, I could only guess if I had better numbers. You sure you don't know how many we're talking about?"

"No idea, really," she admitted. "And most have probably graduated. They'd have no reason to talk, as long as they're sober. That's always a problem."

"Graduated? That's a problem for blaming it all on Lill."

He finally got it, she thought.

Then the dean furrowed his brow and thought out loud, "No, we'd have to suggest that someone else started it. Maybe one of those many registrars. Lill just kept it going or, better, revived it."

Flo Boater shifted her weight, wondering momentarily whether she had gained a pound or two, then explained that they were not going in that direction at all.

After thinking this over, Stanley Wooda began to have doubts, too. "That might start reporters looking deeper than we want."

She snapped, "And students might just talk if a reporter asks." She then walked over to the far window and crossed her arms. She rarely got to this end of the room in winter. It was cold over there, but it was far from Miss E's keen ears and no one could see in from that side of

the building. Slowly she relaxed. Should the proper moment come…
this was the place.

Following her, Stanley Wooda asked, "And incriminate themselves?"

Her response was, "If they were stupid enough to need to buy
grades, they might be stupid enough to talk about it. And the blame
would be back on the late dean, then on us." A memory of Smith's
newspaper articles flashed across her mind. Smith would do anything
for a moment of fame. Or was that JJ's idea?

He gave her no time to think about that or anything else. He
walked away, barking out, "It could affect their graduation! Or have
their diplomas recalled."

"Male antler rattling," she thought, using one of her favorite
phrases. But since he seemed to be showing less mating behavior than
silly posturing, she followed him, saying, "Honesty was always a stupid
policy."

"Especially being honest about cheating. I tell you, they won't
talk."

She stopped and gazed out on the campus to think better. Eventually,
she mused, "If only Lill and Lily weren't so honest." When a cold draft
reached her, she shivered slightly, then said to herself, "It would be just
like you said, their stopping the sale of grades was proof that they were
involved. There was no fall-guy, no dean to blame, in case somebody
spilled the beans." The more Flo Boater thought about it, the more she
liked the idea, and she liked it even more because it was so similar to
one she had used a year ago, "Yes, the fact that she didn't bring charges
would look suspicious."

Meanwhile, Stanley Wooda had taken up the other view,
symbolically pacing to the far end of the office again. The more he
thought about it, the more he worried about the rumor getting out of
control. "Who would believe that they only stopped the sales because
they didn't know what had been going on?" Having said this, he sensed
that she wasn't following him physically or mentally, hence, couldn't
hear. He tried again, louder, "They couldn't stop what they didn't know
about."

Flo Boater wasn't really sure, "Do you suppose she really didn't
know?" Something about the argument didn't make sense, but she

couldn't figure out exactly what. Stanley was such a good talker that one could be persuaded even when he argued both sides at once.

"The students knew," he said. "Surely the faculty knew, too. And surely Lill, or Lily would have heard."

"I don't know. Sometimes the faculty is the last to know anything."

"You might be right. If the faculty knew, at least one would have objected."

She agreed with this, "Moreover, if the faculty had been for sale, the students wouldn't have needed the dean."

"I believe we need to say, 'Lill and Lily'."

"Yes. We'd better get used to saying it that way. We wouldn't want to make a slip."

He laughed, "We just need to make it sound like a slip. Wink, wink." When she smiled, he moved to stand next to her, "How do you like the idea?"

Before she could respond, he slipped past her and resumed his seat, putting his chin in one hand. She sighed, then resumed her seat, too. "It has possibilities. Let's give it some more thought." What she meant was, "Deep Six it," though she wasn't quite sure what that meant.

He disagreed. "I don't think we should wait long. It takes time for a rumor to settle into a proven fact." He shook his head to indicate his agreement with himself.

So quickly had he returned to supporting the idea that it almost took her breath away. His self-confidence was so outrageous, she saw him becoming once more the ambitious young man who had so entranced her earlier, the personality that had caused her to envision him as her academic dean at age twenty. Smiling, she agreed, "I'll talk with the historian. He's good at passing on gossip." At that she indicated that their conversation was at an end. There was another appointment, she remembered—some upset parent to consol, as if Flo Boater had gotten her daughter pregnant. As Flo Boater moved toward the door, she thought about ways to make the Creep come up with this theory on his own, so that she would have no fingerprints on it.

Wooda, following her, said, "He hates Lill and Lily. With a passion."

Flo Boater agreed, "He'll never forgive them for some of the tricks they played on him. He could write a book on it." Maybe the idea *did* have potential. How dumb was the historian? That is, how overly sly was he?

"Within a few hours, he'll think he discovered the story himself."

Standing up, she said, "I'll speak with him right away. Just to lay the groundwork. Then you find an excuse to talk with him and slip it into the conversation."

With a wide smile, Wooda made his way toward the door, "Sounds great, boss!" But before he crossed the threshold, he stopped, "By the way, I've written out what I want to say to the editor of *The Journal of Obscure Cultures*. Just let me know when she mails the manuscript."

She was half-alarmed, "I had meant to say to call, not to write. Glad you thought of it, too."

With a wink, he agreed, "Never leave a paper trail."

She went over to him to put her hands on his shoulders, look him in the eye, and say, "Stanley, you are beginning to think like a real dean."

"Thanks, President..." he started, then finished "...Flo." He gave her another wink as he left.

When he reached his office, he remembered that he had forgotten to ask about the registrar. Again. Or mention the rumor about a ghost.

Dean Threshold wished that he could forget about this assignment. Dean C. Wooda's family history should have been easy. Miss E had given him a copy of the late dean's obituary, which included the names of his parents (both deceased) and where he was born. No siblings. Family—only his ex-wife, not named, but everyone knew it was Molly Dow.

Recent census records for his home town were still closed, but clearly his father was not in the records available. Awkward that, but since the census was always taken in the summer, anybody working out of town would have been missed. A call to the library resulted in a reluctant search through the old phone books. Nothing. No obituary collection, either, or index. Nor did the courthouse—this time the officials responded politely—have a record of deaths, births or marriages of anyone named Wooda. They had probably moved. His university records were rather sparse, indicating little more than he had earned all three degrees in swift order and that he had married Molly Dow shortly after finishing the Ph.D. Damn, if he only dared interview her.

Maybe Mabel could make discrete inquires?

That evening Chief Biggs gave Donahue a call, "I've heard from Ms. Hogg."

"She's okay, then?"

"Yes, but she doesn't want to come back yet."

"Why not?"

"Can't you guess? She thinks she's onto something."

"You'll call off the search for her, then?"

Donahue could hear the smile in the chief's voice as he replied, "No. I think I'll reduce the intensity of the search. But if people think she's still missing, she's probably safer."

Ellie, meanwhile, had persuaded Smitty to stay away from the demonstration, and Jones, not wanting to see their friendship deteriorate, agreed to do the same. Fortunately for Jones, there were still a few brave souls who loved the sheer extravagance of the demand to sell grades that they would have continued alone, even without a shirt if they could have found enough participants to spell out in body paint SELL GRADES. For a moment they thought they had recruited Ellie for such a stunt—which would have attracted enough volunteers for a much longer message—before she informed them that they were being childish.

Chapter Fourteen

Donahue entered the coffee house, looked through the crowd until he saw Mary, then waved. She responded by lifting her coffee cup and, by turning it almost over, indicated that it was empty. Once he had gotten coffee for each of them, reluctantly paying the higher new price, he sat down next to her, saying enthusiastically, "Hi, Mary! What have you learned?" He noticed that she was eating the mini-meal breakfast again. That was not a good sign. Her wry face at the taste of the coffee was another warning that she was not in a good mood. Discouraged, he guessed.

Her voice confirmed his concern, "Not much, DO. The students who know me well enough to talk, they say that they have heard of grades for sale." She put sugar and artificial milk into her coffee before she said anything more, then took a sip. It still wasn't very good, but a shrug of the shoulders indicated that it was okay.

Quietly, he asked, "But no direct knowledge?" His own first sip made him think that he might have to start using milk and sugar, too. Maybe real milk or cream would help even more, but on a Briarpatch professor's salary even cheap coffee was expensive. How do the others afford cars? he asked himself. And children? Then he blinked—those were questions he'd better not mention to Mary.

Mary, completely unaware of Donahue's train of thought, took one more sip, complained that they were cutting back too much on the ratio of coffee to water, then pushed the cup away, "Apparently, it's one of those rumors without a solid foundation."

"They can't even guess at a name? Someone I can contact?"

"None at all. They treat it like an urban legend… Must be something to it, but not even an idea about whom to ask."

He sighed, then said, "I've been asking our colleagues if they've had any strange experiences."

"No luck, either?" she inquired.

"None at all. Other than the choir director, and you know about that." Then, seeing that she was getting ready to leave, he asked, "Don't you have time for another cup?"

She smiled as she declined, "Not now. I've want to stay on the chase."

"Why don't you tell Chief Biggs about the grades?" Lily asked. "That student coming up to ask what it would cost to raise his grade, that was scary!"

Doubtfully, Lill answered, "I'm not sure he would believe us."

"Why not? He knows we are straight shooters!"

Lill stopped dead in her tracks to face her friend, "Lily, this would be the first time anyone called us straight."

Lily was, for once, not in the mood for banter, "This is no time for joking. Why don't we tell him?"

"Forget about the student. He'd just tell DO he was joking. We need real proof."

"The proof is in the registrar's office."

Lill was skeptical, "We can't get in there, legally. Ms. Hogg might cooperate, but she's gone, and the staff would be too cautious, or too talkative."

With a smile, Lily picked up on the key word, "Legally...."

At this Lill smiled, "I know where a key is."

"You do?" Lily hadn't expected this. "Jay?"

Lill waved that idea off, "No, not even he has a key to the records office." This was not an office that would be cleaned at night.

"Who does?"

Lill began to count them out, "Four keys: first, the registrar."

"Of course, but she's gone."

"Her staff, then."

"Irrelevant," Lily said. "We don't want to ask for it."

"Right," Lill answered, then continued, "Second, the academic dean."

"Which is how Dean Wooda got in to change grades."

"The late Dean Wooda," Lill reminded her.

"And the soon-to-be-late Dean Wooda," Lily suggested, "if I read the situation right."

Lill agreed, "Flo may need a fall guy." A moment later she added, "Though Ellie says there is some chemistry there."

Upon reflection, Lily shook her head negatively, "Ellie's got good instincts. Flo'll probably just get Stan a job. A move up."

This made Lill smile. She joked, "A job as a college president. It would be a feather in her cap."

Slyly, Lily observed, "They say that all a good college president needs is a good dean."

Lill gave her an affectionate push on the shoulder, "You just say that because you were my dean!"

"We were a good pair," Lily said.

"Yes, those were the days."

"Well, back to work," Lily groaned. "Who else had a key?"

"The Vice-President for Financial Affairs."

"That's three. But she left."

"Jenny's there temporarily, till the search is over. But I doubt they gave her a key to anything other than her office."

"Where's her key?" Lily asked.

"Probably turned back to Miss Efficiency."

"Well, that eliminates that one. Miss E. takes her job seriously!"

"So does Jenny. She'd like to keep hers, too."

"She's not there any more," Lily said. "It had slipped my mind. They moved her yesterday to help in the registrar's office!"

"She's moved?" Lill thought she would have heard. Secrecy was Flo Boater's strength, but why hadn't she said anything? Then it occurred to her—she had, only Lily had forgotten to pass it on. Dependability was not Lily's strongest characteristic. That is, she could be depended on in matters of character, but not for phone messages or mail.

Meanwhile, Lily had started to explain that Jenny wasn't trusted with keys—Miss E unlocked each morning—then interrupted herself, mischief in her eyes, "Maybe she could leave a door unlocked?"

"Miss E. locks up, too, no matter how late it is."

"No back door?"

Lill waved that idea off, "No restroom in that office with a second door to the hall." This sly reference to the way JJ and Smitty had broken in to the Finance Office last fall earned her a smile, after which she continued, "And in any case, should an 'unauthorized entry' be noticed, there'd be an investigation. Jenny couldn't lie her way past any direct question." After a pause, she added, "We can't involve her in any way."

Lily thought a moment, nodded her head, then said, "Well, there's the president."

"That's right," Lill responded. "All we need is one president."

Lily was mystified, "Flo wouldn't help us. There are only three keys out. How does having one in the president's hands help us?"

Lill leaned forward to whisper, "I was president."

At first Lily did not understand, then she asked, "You kept a key?"

Mischievously, Lill responded, "Yes."

"They didn't make you give it back?"

"I loaned my key to the registrar, who had left hers at her mother's. Had to get a temporary replacement."

"And later you only turned in one," Lily crowed. "Smart lady!"

"It wasn't deliberate," Lill confessed, "But it was lucky." They both understood that when Ms. Inefficiency ran the office, such oversights were common. "I intended to give it back, but you remember how Flo just packed up our stuff and put it in the hall. I haven't straightened that stuff out, but I believe I could find it."

"So we can get in after the office is closed!"

Lill nodded, "Let's get two flashlights. As soon as it's dark, we become the Pink Panthers!"

As they started to leave, Lily stopped her friend and said hesitantly, "Lill, I think the Pink Panther was the jewel, not the burglar."

"Who cares? At least pink is the right color."

Confused, Lily shrugged and gave in, "Pink leather?"

It was only later that Lily remembered to ask how they would get into the building.

"Jay'll take care of it."

"Jay?"

"Yeah, you know how often the building is left unlocked."

"Sure," Lily responded. "Student Service Empire wants students to have access."

Lill smiled, knowing that students rarely came in evenings. "Well, that's why Jay has been checking to see that the door is locked."

"Yes?"

"I'll tell him that we have students coming into the theater late at night, then ask him to watch it tonight, until we come back in to take over for him. That way we won't be interrupted, and he can honestly say that he knew nothing about our plans."

"Pretty good," Lily said. "We have so many keys out that chances are good someone will try to come in to work on a project. It'll prove that you weren't exaggerating."

Flechadoro had another vision.

Chapter Fifteen

Donahue was standing at the coffee bar, looking longing at a doughnut, waiting for the student worker to finish chatting with her boyfriend. He thought of Mary and her dislike of fat men, he thought of her not being *free* last weekend, and finally with a shrug, he said, "Old habits are hard to break," reached across the counter and took one. With only a dollar in his hand, he looked at the waitress, shrugged, reached for a second one and left the dollar. He sat at a small table, looking dismally at the three empty chairs and the tempting doughnuts, when he saw Sal enter. Waving to him, he asked, "How's it going, Sal?" Maybe he would not only be company, but would take the second doughnut.

"Nowhere," he sad, slowly taking a chair. "I talked with the president yesterday, with Jay Bird today." He declined the doughnut—he was Italian, he wanted to keep his slim build.

Donahue took a bite of doughnut and a sip of coffee, "No luck?"

"Nothing doing. *Mai.*" He sounded downright discouraged. "And the registrar's people were downright rude. Something about a new person in charge, how she'd have to decide." He made a gesture at leaving, "Well, I won't get anywhere here, either."

Donahue encouraged him to stay, "I don't know. Everybody comes to the coffee shop." He almost suggested that Sal get some coffee, but then he remembered that he was Italian and had higher standards. "You'll at least see some old friends, maybe some former students."

Relapsing into his chair, Sal reflected, "I never used to come here. I practically lived in my laboratory." There were a few moments of silence, then Sal excused himself and shuffled off. Donahue sat in silence, trying to warm his cooling coffee with his hands and wondering what he should have said. What do you say to an ex-con, especially to an ex-con who was really innocent? Every now and then he looked at the doughnuts, then remembered that his coffee was cold. His reverie was interrupted by Molly coming in. He motioned to her and said, "Sal just left, but join me for a few minutes." When she hesitated, he lied, "The coffee will do you good."

She returned with a steaming cup, but screwed up her mouth after the first sip. This was the moment Donahue chose to ask, "Have you seen Mary?" He held out a doughnut, suggesting that it would cut the edge of the coffee, but she waved it off.

When she said, "A few minutes ago," he was surprised. "What was she doing?" he asked.

"Strange. She swore me to secrecy, then asked if I had heard about grades being changed for money."

"Secrecy?"

"Well, I assume you asked her to check into it."

He smiled, confirming her suspicion, then asked, "Have you heard anything?"

"No. I've heard of grades being traded or sex, but not for cash. And I worked part-time in the Finance office for years, so I think I would have heard."

Surprised, Donahue asked, "You're worked in the Finance office?"

"Actually, I'm back there now."

"When did that begin?"

"Today, actually just a few minutes ago. I got a call some days ago from Miss E, asking me to assist in the Registrar's office. But I think you mean months ago, when Flo Boater became president; she asked each of us to help out during the financial crisis. Part-time. Anyway, after Ms. Hogg disappeared, they called me in for a couple hours each morning—rush hour, just before lunch—in the Registrar's Office. Then Jenny was put in the Financial Affairs office. Silly name, that. But we had already talked when we were both in Registrar's office, with nobody in the Business office, that is, acting-Finance officer, whatever the title is now. It's like nobody is in charge. We get moved around so much, that's what I told Mary, that we'd never notice if anything was strange. But we do hear gossip."

Donahue was almost dumbstruck, but managed to ask how she ended up with the finance job.

"Oh, Jenny and I talked it over. We decided that there was some type of snafu—you know that old word. Anyway, Jenny was not confident she could do a good job in the Finance Office, so we decided to act on the most recent order—for her to take over the Registrar's office. I'd go across the hall and work there.

"You're saying Miss E made a mistake?" That had never happened before.

"No, just that too many people are giving orders. I was really surprised that she didn't know I was already working in the Registrar's office. Anyway, I left a note for Flo Boater, telling her what we were doing, and saying that we would make any adjustment she wanted. But right now somebody needed to be in each office." She laughed, "This would normally foul up the bookkeeping, but since I'm in charge, I can just push the buttons—almost literally—to tell the computer to switch me and Jenny from one budget line to the other. That is, to reverse them."

If the room had been anything but cool, Donahue would have wiped sweat from his brow. Unable to do that, he took a deep breath and asked, "Did you tell Mary you were working in the Financial Affairs office?"

"No, Jenny hadn't come over to tell me yet. Well, you know that now. Why? Is that important?"

He rubbed his chin—an old professional habit, hard to break. "I had heard that Jenny was in the Finance office. You had been there before, too, so I remembered that right. I'm surprised that they didn't leave you there. They always need experienced help." He smiled before adding, "Somebody has to show the boss how the place works."

She smiled back, then said, "Yes, earlier I was there all the time. Floater had asked me, maybe ten years ago, to help when a financial officer, an assistant, left. I had been an accountant, well, a bookkeeper of sorts, before I went back to graduate school. I thought writing was more fun than entering figures. We had sort of a revolving door for business managers, that is, finance officers—the title goes back and forth—so I filled in all the time."

"Sounds like a good fit."

Thoughtfully, she agreed, "Yes, and the financial crisis was real. Rather interesting work" Then she added, a bit cynically, "But then my husband, the late dean, decided that faculty members—even part-timers like me—shouldn't be too well informed about the money situation. I'd already seen evidence of his philandering, and I wouldn't have been surprised by his stealing money." After a moment she added, "And, knowing Flo Boater, she may have been worried that I'd discover her affair with my husband and tell Floater. It was pretty cozy as far as she was concerned, and I could have been real trouble. She must be pretty desperate now to ask me to come back, or maybe that was just Miss E. or the dean trying to cover the paperwork there. Anyway, my time in the Finance office ended several years ago. I don't expect that this bit will last. Maybe to the end of the semester. I'm needed in English, so I expect to go back there—full-time part-time. Less pay and student papers to correct. Right now, since I started helping in the Registrar's office, I've been part-time, part-time. They've hired someone named Irene to take my two easiest classes."

"Odd," Donahue observed, ignoring the injustice of Molly's situation. "When Flo asked Jenny to work in Finance, she dropped her courses, but that was between semesters, so they had a couple weeks to find a temp. But Jenny had no background for handling money. Now that she's getting the hang of it, she's moved again, to another job she's not prepared to do."

Molly grinned at that, "According to Jay, she said that nobody in music could possibly to expected to understand anything about money." After a pause, she added, "Jay also suggested that Flo trusted him, and since he and Jenny were possibly getting married, she may have thought he could trust her, too." She looked at him a moment, then added, "He said this in fewer words, of course."

Donahue, ignorant of the musical chairs in the administration, grimaced, "Jay was a bit rough!"

"It's not as though Jenny would have become the permanent financial officer, the Vice-President, but there was plenty that she and I could have done while we made the search for a permanent appointment." She sighed, "Well, now I'm doing the Finance office bit as an overload, more or less, half my courses and the office full time." She glanced up at Donahue, "It helps balance my budget!"

"When will you hire permanent financial officer?"

"Not soon, but there's a committee now."

Donahue thought for a moment, "How do you like the job right now?"

"I don't really know. I've just stuck my head in. It doesn't look so bad, and I'm going to have plenty of company—all untrained, but we'll figure it out." After a moment's pause, she added, "Its much worse in the Registrar's office."

"Oh," Donahue said. "Who says?"

"My staff. They know what is going on across the hall. Regular bitching sessions. I guess Jennie will straighten it out, but it will take time."

"Can she do it?"

"Sure. It's mostly common sense, and no mistake will ruin the college credit line."

Donahue smiled, then asked, "Who else is working there now?"

"They used to have student assistants, just for clerical work." Her tone indicated that this showed how easy the routine work was.

"That's unusual," he commented, interrupting. He rarely did that, having known from his training that when people are willing to talk, it is best to let them ramble on. It was the "give them rope" technique— even with friends. But he was struck by the employment of students— was that the way grades were changed?

Molly explained that the late president, Floyd Boater, thought it was a way to cut costs, but Lill said that it raised privacy issues and therefore limited access to records to professional help. There wasn't enough staff and there was no money to hire more, so Flo had asked faculty to trade teaching duties for clerical work. Since enrollment was down, the small number of sacrificed classes made little difference. And some she persuaded just to take on extra work. "Of course, there are some she won't ask, like you, and some, like Stout, who would reject it on principle. And she asked us, sort of, not to spread the word around. Looks bad, you understand, like the school's on its last legs."

"So the work had gotten behind?"

"It had fallen somewhat behind while Lill was president, but became a serious problem once the enrollment increased—because there was more paper to process." She sighed, "In the Finance office we bill the students once, but in the Registrar's office they are always adding and dropping classes, getting mid-term grades, that kind of thing. Lots of paperwork."

"Why not buy computers?"

"They have a few, but, well, you know how the finances are."

"Who doesn't?"

"Also, the registrar had to be away more often, and Ms. Hogg, well, that's a problem. Gone already now, but still new. Well, you know all that." Molly stopped for him to nod agreement, then added, "Mary is supposed to start right away, too, to give Jenny a hand, but I don't think she'll have been told yet."

"Why is that?" It was a time-filler question while he thought. Donahue couldn't imagine Mary being asked to teach, to write a major article, to be on a new committee and then "volunteer" for clerical work.

"The registrar's staff is a bit distracted right now."

"About grades or about Ms. Hogg?" Donahue asked.

"Policy, actually." Molly said, "Flo Boater is concerned that the students will protest about the lost jobs. But it is awkward to not have Ms. Hogg to make decisions." At that she looked at her watch, glanced back up and said, "Well, I'd better run." She had picked up her bag already when she saw that Donahue had another question.

"Just a moment longer. Who is on the search committee for the new vice-president for financial affairs?"

"I think Flo Boater is doing that pretty much by herself." With that she started to stand.

Donahue, however, leaned over to touch her arm. As she sat back down, he indicated the other side of the building where Sal and Stanley Wooda had just entered. A moment later, they could not see them because of a column, but their voices were clear.

Wooda's was the first they could make out, "I told you, I don't know anything about grade changes."

"All I need is...."

"What you need is to get off this campus."

There was so noise, like a chair scrapping, but Molly stopped Donahue from standing up.

"I warn you. Get off this campus or I'll call the police."

Moments later they saw Stanley Wooda hurry past them and out the door. Following him slowly was Sal, who stopped, his hands on his hips and his teeth bared. But when he saw them, his mien changed.

Smiling, he joined them and explained that all he wanted were some records about grades, but the dean would not cooperate.

"So, what's new?" Donahue observed.

"What's new are some actually names to check. *Ma che fai*? He won't help at all."

Donahue and Molly exchanged glances. "Don't tell him," she whispered. "Don't tell him I'm working in the Finance office now. Or that I was helping the Registrar's office out."

Chapter Sixteen

Donahue left the coffee house in search of Jenny. Strange, he thought, how big a small college can be. "You'd think we'd all know all about one another. I don't remember her starting to work in the registrar's office. No reason to announce it, I suppose; and I haven't talked with her in a while. Not about what she was doing." Still, what did he really expect to learn? He was sure that Jay had kept her informed about everything that was going on, and that, if she had come across anything which would be useful, Jay would have contacted him or told Molly. Still, he didn't want to be seen contacting Jay directly. Maybe he could confirm what Molly and Sal had told him, and see if there was anything which did not seem important to them might just provide him some insights into the situation.

He thought of an excuse for calling her at work, just in case someone else answered the phone. Luckily, she did pick up, which allowed him to arrange to meet her in the coffee house during her break. It would appear to be a spontaneous encounter. Nothing to excite suspicion or wonder. She arrived first, and when she saw him enter, she waved, as would be normal, and indicated that he should join her. As he had anticipated, privacy was assured by the background noise and the empty tables around them.

No, there was nothing unusual to report in the registrar's office, she said. "Not for Briarpatch College. There's the excessive workload, the outdated computer system, the insane computer programs designed for multiple uses—for all administrative offices, as if they're all alike—and therefore useful for none. But nothing unusual."

"I'm familiar with that!"

"Unfortunately, I'm not. The financial records are pretty standard, I think, but everything else is… well, there could be irregularities everywhere and I'd not recognize them."

He thought a moment before asking a question that had been bothering him for some time, "How's the computer system for handling grade changes?"

"It could have been designed by monkeys at typewriters, monkeys with long lunch hours"

Sensing that Jenny knew almost nothing about computers, Donahue switched to the new line of inquiry, "You mean the office takes long mid-day break?"

"Yeah, from 11:30 to 1:30 every day. Started by Miss Purdy, a cost-cutting measure for all offices. Ms. Hogg decided to keep those hours, even though lunch time is convenient for students. She said she needed the time, uninterrupted, to work on special problems."

Donahue's ear pricked up at that, "What kind of special problems?"

"I'm not sure… She wasn't very communicative. And I was across the hall, so we didn't talk much." She added after a pause, "I use the lunch period to practice. I still have some music lessons."

Donahue's brow furrowed, "Ms. Hogg was new. Who did she ask for information?"

Jenny spread her hands, "Can't say, don't know. Not me."

Donahue thought a moment, "That long lunch break. Could the dean have come in at that time?"

Jenny thought about that before saying that it was possible, but unlikely. "Dean Wooda? Maybe the late Dean Wooda, but the new one hardly ever looks in. No more than Flo Boater. His office is just down the hall, but I don't know if the late dean ever 'dropped in.' I wasn't working in the building then. However, I understand that he worked nights, sometimes. The previous registrars did, too."

"Any one of them particularly close to him?" The implication that the late dean's womanizing ways might have been combined with changing grades hung in the air.

"Maybe, maybe even probably, but I don't even remember now what their names were, they changed so often. I'd have to look in a campus directory to see when they were here, and you know how hard those are to find."

"The library, I suppose," he answered. "I could look them up for you."

She laughed lightly, "Ms Gates puts all the archival material in big boxes, tapes them shut, and puts them in storage against the day she can catalog them." He though a second, "Probably Miss E. could come up with past directories." As she looked into his eyes, she sensed that he wouldn't want to call attention to his interest.

The question of when the dean might have had access to the system had bothered Donahue, and while he was vaguely aware of the office hours, until now he had never thought about them seriously, about the dean and registrars *both* working evenings. He had assumed that since the late dean had a key, he would simply have looked into the hall, then, if the way was clear, gone down to the Registrar's office and gone in. Coming out would have been more risky, since someone might have wondered what he was doing there, but in principle, coming out of an office is always less suspicious than pulling out a key and opening one. Bringing the new Dean Wooda into the calculations made it more complicated, and the incorruptible Ms. Hogg made it even more so.

As he was thinking he began to drum his fingers. At length, Jenny asked, "How's it going with Mary?" She knew the situation, she believed, but she wanted to hear his version. Anyway, the silence was getting boring.

He stopped to readjust his thoughts, then frowned slightly, trying to formulate an explanation that would not make matters worse if it got back to Mary via the campus gossip network. Finally, he answered her question with a question, "Jenny, back when I first met you, you said that working class men were less hypocritical."

It was her turn to think. "Yes, I remember now. Jay and I had just met. I had been divorced for a number of years and he had lost his wife, but the class barrier—I was faculty, he was a janitor—seemed awfully big. But Jay was a *genuine* person, not ambitious and backbiting like my 'ex.' You know what I mean, DO, not like some of our colleagues."

"Stout?"

"To name one, yes."

"Not everyone is like him," Donahue protested. "Some of those people have potential."

"No, of course not," she responded. "Heck, there are a lot of great guys around here, but they're all married."

"A few of us aren't."

"You put your finger right on it," she said. "You are, if you'll excuse the term, practically a baby." Seeing a protest coming, she continued quickly, "Okay, there's only a decade or so between us, and, technically speaking, that may be age discrimination. But that's the way it is, at least for me. And as for the other two or three men you can name, at least one is in love with his work. I'd have no more luck with him than poor Miss Brooks way back when. The others, well, I suspect they'd have more interest in each other than in me, if they had anything else in common."

Donahue smiled at the last comment, knowing that she had a body builder in mind—bald and waxing his chest—and a new fellow whose hobby was baroque music. Both nice chaps, even if the newcomer had, upon learning that he was single, made a pass at him. Donahue then admitted that he didn't know who Miss Brooks was.

Jenny explained that it was a television show long before his time. Before sex and violence. Before color. "She loved him, he loved science—totally hopeless. But he was her only chance. That is, only a man who wasn't particularly interested in women would be both unmarried and not bothered by her height, accent and personality. See what I mean? A decade makes a big difference, more so than class."

He observed that very few faculty women married working class men. Why was that?

She smiled, "You are out of touch."

"Faculty men marry women with less education."

She gave him a stern look, "Less is not the same as none. Where did they meet those women anyway? And think about the generations—I'll give you some of our older colleagues, but the younger ones have both been to graduate school. If we hire the husband, it's because he finished a year or two earlier and… well, you can figure all the rest."

"Distance, babies?"

"Distance, yes, either from the graduate school or, should she get a job, living in different cities. Adjunct work. Almost impossible to finish a dissertation."

He thought a moment, "So you don't think it's a class thing."

"Well," she admitted. "There's that. Women need to talk more than men, and educated women want husbands who, sort of, you know, know something about what they're interested in. Also, in our little community they're embarrassed to admit they couldn't land a man who was better than they were in some way—taller, richer, you know, a guy with status. And, of course, someone holds the right views on all the things we talk about."

"Is that *my* problem with Mary?" he wondered. His background, his views, his occasional lapses into conventional speech?

"Maybe a bit," Jenny conceded, "but it's probably not that important. You are, after all, one of us." As his brows contracted, she added, "You are a professor, you speak our language, you can, well, go to a party and talk intelligently….." At his demurral, she laughed, "Okay, you can listen intelligently about all the crap that everyone else thinks is so important."

At that he laughed, too. "Like the great right-wing conspiracy."

She smiled, "Think about where you're living. Middleville is Bubba-land, only with a losing football team. Well, the college team did better this year, but that won't last. Anyway, it's winter now, so it's basketball's turn to lose."

He tapped his fingers a few times before resuming the conversation, "Yes, but back to your point, you and Jay are making it, and he is working class."

"He does work for the college, so he can follow the gossip."

Donahue smiled. Jay was always the best informed person on campus.

"He doesn't go to many parties, you will notice."

"Neither do I, not many."

"Point taken," she replied, "but that's because we don't have many campus-wide gatherings right now. Flo doesn't like them. And those who want to talk politics don't invite you to private gatherings."

"I try to not be unpleasant."

"Of course you do, DO, but they can see in your smile that you know when they have said something idiotic."

"Maybe I should talk more?"

"It probably wouldn't hurt, but it's a moot point. You're not invited anyway."

He shrugged, "I get plenty of give and take with Lill and Lily."

"Exactly," she said, "they are willing to do more than nod and cite some article from the *New York Times*. And you," she laughed, "you would come back with something from *The Wall Street Journal*. No wonder they think you're a fascist."

"Back to the subject. You think it's a class thing. If you are not a professor, you're toast?"

"That depends," she responded. "We—the professor class, that is— we cut wives a lot of slack. At least the men do. I know it is sexist to say so, but we assume that their husbands married them because they were cute and funny, at least when they were young, and that if they don't have an idea past babies and babysitters, that's okay. We don't expect them to be able to talk about 'important things'."

Donahue smiled, "I knew a couple wives who are infuriated about that."

She smiled back, "How well I know. I was a trophy wife once." She straightened up and touched her hair. Then she laughed, "But, then, well, you know how my husband treated me. I didn't grow up until we got divorced. Now it's not so bad." She laughed again, "Older women have some advantages."

Donahue asked, "And husbands? How are they treated, or were treated. I don't know any right now."

"You're right. Job opportunities aren't great in Middleville."

"So the women either don't come or leave for a larger community?"

"Right on. We used to hold women to a higher standard, or, rather, we judged them differently. Like I said, we expect men to be as successful or more so than their wives, so a faculty woman married to a doctor or lawyer today gets nothing more than some sideways glances—a decade ago it would have approval or admiration! And the expectation that she would stop teaching. Nowadays they wonder why she didn't marry an academic. But put that aside. Should she marry, say, automobile mechanic, the eyebrows go right up. That's so *déclassé*! If you'll pardon my French. He could be a fine mechanic who spent more years learning his trade than we do in graduate school. In that case, as you know, most men would know enough about the subject to converse with him, even if they aren't experts. But few women my age know enough about cars to say anything. Besides it might look like they were coming onto him."

"*Lady Chatterly's Lover* syndrome?"

"Some women can be very aggressive, and some have stronger drives than others. Well, you're a sociologist. You know that's true in every class." She added with a tone of irony, "It's not just a case of man-emulating sex fiends." After a moment, she added, "Some hit on other women. Believe me, I know. But it's not something we talk about, and the men never notice."

Donahue smiled and noted, "You seem to be down on your sex."

"We call it *gender* now. But, yes, women have been discriminated against," Jenny said. "No doubt about that. But we can be our own worst enemies. Men can 'marry down,' but we can't, and its women who have made that rule. It's like a hundred years ago—respectable women marry the proper men, the others will, well, marry a laborer or clerk." She took a deep breath, "And it isn't easy. Men have their own macho beliefs, too, sometimes; and some want to earn more than their wife." She laughed, "In my case, that's not too hard."

He smiled, too, then asked, "Women are, you say, looked down on if they marry down?" He knew the answer, but he couldn't think of anything else to say.

"Oh, yes. Even the most enlightened woman has bought into the 'lady' business. We're too good for, well, you know...."

"Sort of," Donahue fumbled for the words, "that you are settling for less because there's..." His sentence daggled as he searched his mind for the right way to say it.

"There's something wrong with us," she offered. "Yes, that's right. We must be 'desperate' or something equally unsavory. Now, take Lill and Lily," she continued, "that's all right, because lesbians have it all together. They are the super-women, they have learned to get along without men altogether. So they are superior in some senses than married women, and far above those who have 'married beneath themselves'."

"But Lill and Lily," he started to say.

"Point made. They're not both women, maybe—I don't know myself and don't care—but you have to remember, they act as though they are and everyone accepts them as women. Rather exotic women, too." She smiled at this.

"And Mary?" he asked.

"Mary," she said, "is a different problem. And I don't know how to help you. But I am concerned. She needs someone like you. But it just isn't going forward. And a relationship, like mine with Jay, has to go forward or it dies."

"You and Jay are going forward?" he asked, suspiciously.

"One of these days, perhaps soon, you'll be getting a wedding invitation." She laughed when she saw him wrinkle his brows, "Oh, not a big affair. But Jay has some family in Zenith, and we want our closest friends there. You, for example." As he smiled, "And Mary. If we get married, maybe she'll get the idea." At that they both laughed.

He almost stood to leave, but sat back down for another question, "What attracted you to Jay. He didn't come courting you."

"Ah. If you had seen him when his wife was dying, you would have realized what a marvelous man he was. That was what I admired. He was a real man."

"Even though he wasn't educated?"

"He isn't stupid," she protested. "He follows the news, reads widely, and he asks intelligent questions. Not many, but good ones. He's quiet, but so are some intellectuals. Well, he's sure not one of them. But, believe me, my 'ex' was an intellectual. Being an intellectual is overrated!"

"How did you meet him? If I'm not prying."

"DO, you're a friend now. Nothing you ask is prying."

"Thanks," he answered.

"As to the question, I really don't know. We've known each other by sight forever. After my divorce, I never wanted to see another man again. At least not another one like my 'ex.' When his wife became ill, I told him how sorry I was. After that, whenever we ran into one another around campus, we'd talk a couple minutes. Nothing serious. A year or two after his wife's death, we'd talk longer. But he was, well, as we used to say, 'he knew his place' and never suggested that we'd ever become more than friends."

Donahue nodded, to indicate that he understood.

"One day, last year, I was complaining about the lack of public transportation. I had wanted to go shopping in Zenith. It was way early for Christmas, but you know how mad that season can be for musicians on campus. Anyway, he said that he was driving up to see his family and that he'd be glad to give me a lift, then meet me later to come back to Middleville. I accepted. The rest is… history."

"That was just before the dean drowned."

"And that's how I knew he couldn't have done it."

As Donahue walked across campus, he thought about the young woman who had frozen to death in the woods. How did she fit into Jenny's formula? The shock came partly from her being female. If a young man had gotten drunk and fallen asleep outdoors, how many people would have been surprised? The ways we think about categories of peoples—so familiar, yet always so… so what? Maybe there was an article in that.

A half hour later the coffee house was almost empty. Lill and Lily wandered in, looked for students to sit with, then shrugged and got their coffee. They could always talk to one another. After a few minutes the historian entered, nodded quietly at them, then got his coffee and sat alone, close enough to overhear if they spoke loudly, but not close enough to be asked to join in the conversation. Lily starred at him, but failed to make eye contact. At last, she whispered to Lill, "Is he here all the time?"

Lill laughed quietly, "No more than we are probably. But I've seen his office, and if we had that place, we'd be here more, too."

The historian sat reading mail and the *Middleville Moderate*, apparently oblivious of the whispered comments at the next table. Students wandered through, a couple joined at the arms barely managed to pour themselves coffee. When the class bell sounded, the historian folded up his newspaper with a snap and marched out.

"Thank goodness, he's finally gone," Lill sighed before adding, "How'd he get that newspaper to pop like that. Its pages are as pasty as its news."

Lily ignored the question. Exasperated by the need to whisper, she exclaimed, "I thought he'd never leave! I was ready to wring his scrawny neck."

"Save the thought," Lill said "We may need it later."

"Okay," Lily retorted. "What do you have in mind?"

"The key to this whole mess, Jay says, is the sale of grades."

"When did you talk with him?"

"He came back the theater—to 'check on' the fire extinguishers. You were in class. He didn't say very much."

"He never does," Lily interrupted.

"But he'd heard—didn't say when or what exactly—that Flo's sudden comeback hadn't been from the trustees' homophobia…"

"No?" Lily interjected.

"…but their fear that the rumors of another scandal might become public."

"Scandal? Grades?"

"Jay didn't know. But what else?"

Lily screwed up her face, "You think so?"

Reflectively Lill said, "May be something to it. I wondered why the trustees dumped us so fast. They'd known all along that we were a pair."

This got Lily's attention, "And you think…"

"…that Flo Boater somehow tied us together with the prospect of a scandal. After all, we were getting along well, then suddenly the trustees turned their backs on us."

"Makes sense," Lily said, "put that way."

"Flo's a crafty one," Lill agreed. "And she's capable of that subtle a plan. She knows the trustees wouldn't say anything, say, that could be bad publicity."

"Ah," Lily replied, "better to be thought homophobes than fools."

At that moment, Lill, seeing Donahue enter, said quietly, "Stow it for a moment." She then stood up to give him a hearty handshake, "Hi, DO. How's it going?"

This disconcerted Donahue somewhat, but not nearly as much Lily, who, though remaining seated, whispered seductively, "Hi, DO."

Recovering quickly, because he knew that Lily could be unpredictable, Donahue took a seat and exclaimed enthusiastically, "I spoke to Sal."

"And…?" the theater twins asked.

"He says that everything is fine."

"Fine?" Lill asked.

"Fine, how?" Lily echoed.

Slyly, Donahue observed, "It's what he didn't say that is interesting."

The indirect approach, the dog that didn't bark. Lill leaned forward to ask, "And..." And Lily, also leaning toward him, asked as well, "Yes, and..."

"He wouldn't talk about his meeting with Flo Boater."

Lily leaned back and thoughtfully observed, "Interesting."

"Very interesting," Lily echoed.

Donahue added, "When I asked about his visit to the registrar's office, he became agitated."

"Oh?" Lill found this *very* interesting.

So did Lily, "Oh. How?"

"He said that he had just wanted to check some grades, nothing important, but the assistant—some temp—wouldn't allow it."

"Some error in the grades?" Lill suggested.

"Somebody doing too well?"

Donahue wasn't sure, "He wouldn't say, and I didn't want to press him."

"You might well have Chief Biggs follow up," Lill said. "Since Sal isn't with the college, Flo can't complain."

"The chief can ask the tough questions," Lily said. "Why didn't you?"

"The chief gets along better with him. Spent more time—at the jail, driving him to Zenith, and so forth. Sal trusts him. But I still doubt he'll open up now."

"Why not?" Lily asked before saying, "Oh, I guess we all know why not. Sal is proud. He wants to resolve this himself."

"It's still worth a try," Donahue said, preparing to leave. "I'll talk to the chief. No problem."

Lill stood up, an old habit acquired from her parents, to see him off, "Thanks, DO. But while you're here, is Sal okay?"

Donahue turned back to her to give a thoughtful answer, "Not, he seemed a bit edgy. Real nervous."

"Good to back off then," Lill agreed.

Lily felt the same way, "Sal's had a hard enough time of it already."

Once more Donahue promised to give Chief Biggs a call. He also wanted to tell him that Sal had asked about the girl who had frozen to death in the campus wood. After he was outside he thought that he could have told Lill and Lily that, but it wasn't worth going back inside.

Flo Boater gave Stanley a call, "I just heard that Lill and Lily are up to something. No, I don't know what. But they are hanging around the coffee house. No students there. Just hanging out. Like... As if they were waiting for someone. Yes, I think so, too. We can't just wait for the ceiling to fall in on us." As she hung up, she involuntarily looked around her office to see if the restorers had done their work properly— they never show up on time, then they leave before they're finished. It's frustrating to live in a town like Middleville, where there isn't much choice in painters.

When Ellie asked Smitty why Professor Iva was asking about grades, he gulped noticeably, then excused himself, "I've got to talk with Jonesy. See you later?"

"Maybe. If JJ is more important than me...."

"Oh, Ellie. It's not that. But it's, well, I've just got to talk with him right away."

Chapter Seventeen

Mary swept into the coffee house with a wide smile, "Hi DO!"

Donahue would normally have brightened at her good mood, but now he could only turn and ask, "Any luck?"

"In a sense. I asked Jenny for a list of students who wanted transcripts last year. Then I began phoning graduate schools to check on grades in music, chemistry and philosophy."

"And?"

"You can't imagine how slow that process is! Oh, here's Mollly. You can ask her yourself."

"Molly?"

"Jenny was worried about being seen with us, so she asked Molly to talk with the staff—you know, to 'understand better' how the Financial Office and the Registrar's Office worked together. So she's as up on things as Jenny is."

As soon as the women had gotten their coffee and joined him again, Donahue asked how grade changes were recorded and stored, "Most importantly, what is the process for changing grades? And how can we look into the changes that were made."

Molly took a long sip before responding, "Recording you already know—you send us the grades, writing them out opposite the names. Changing requires a special form—only the blue form, so we don't get it mislaid. But checking on these changes might take forever, since each application is filed away, maybe even in separate buildings. I've never had to do it." She sighed before continuing, "I don't understand that. There is plenty of storage space in the Administration Building. Upstairs. Perhaps they are worried about putting any weight in the attic, but I think the practice began before the college acquired the building, so they just kept putting new forms where they had put them earlier. Maybe the last three or four years are still in the office."

"Not to hide them?" Donahue asked.

Mary added, "You can't imagine how suspicious they are! I couldn't get anyone except Jenny to talk with me, and you know how worried she is."

Molly looked about before explaining, "If you had asked about whether so-and-so had earned a degree, that would have been okay. But individual grades are a privacy matter."

"Yes," Mary responded, "there must be a major industry in people claiming degrees they don't have, while fake grades are confined to major university sports programs!"

Molly smiled at her passion, "If you had asked about a completely fake transcript, ok, but around her who ever heard of one or two grades being changed? For non-athletes?" With another smile, she added, "Or for ambitious politicians? Those who don't want their C grades revealed."

Roguishly Donahue laughed, "Apparently our college is ahead of the curve in something!" Mary cast a sly smile at Molly, then told Donahue, "When I inquired off campus, I didn't want to say who I was exactly, because that would tell the world that the college was looking into a scandal. Fortunately, Molly was willing to give me a hand—they could call her at the Finance Office to confirm that I was employed here and doing 'institutional research.' You know, being on Flo's new committee. The title, the CCPDC, sounded authentic enough."

"So," Molly added, "we made up a story about her being an educational consultant, then those which called me stayed on the line to answer questions."

"And?" Donahue asked.

Coyly, Mary responded, "We did come across a bit of luck, sort of."

Molly eagerly cooperated in dragging out the suspense, "Yes, one registrar."

"A medical school," Mary explained.

"She remembered getting two slightly different transcripts from one student. Apparently she wondered why one grade point average was 3.98 and the other 4.0."

Donahue calculated quickly, "A *summa cum laude*, either way."

"Yes," Mary said, "that was surprising. We had begun checking the weaker students first."

They hadn't expected a "summa" to be involved, Molly, explained. "We had thought we'd find evidence only among those who had been on probation at some point."

Donahue was intrigued, "What would the *summa cum laude* have changed?"

Mary whispered confidentially, "A volleyball grade. The PE requirement."

Molly, seeing Donahue's surprise, added confidentially, "From a B+ to an A."

"So we called her," Mary said.

"Wow!" Molly exclaimed. "Did she go off like a rocket!"

"Accused us of trying to destroy her."

"Threatened to sue," Molly said.

"Wept," Mary added.

Donahue sighed, "Sounds like a lot of guilt."

"Yes," Mary agreed, "and no reason for it."

Molly explained, "The registrar there had said that she was one of their top students. An excellent student. Going to be a great doctor."

Donahue was puzzled, "Why'd she do it?"

Mary looked at Molly before she answered, to see if she wanted to take this one, "Maybe she didn't. Said the instructor had changed the grade after graduation so she would have a better chance of getting into medical school."

"The one transcript went out in the last semester of her senior year," Molly said. "The other after graduation."

"Why'd the instructor do it?" Donahue asked.

Confidentially, Mary said, "Our college doesn't have the greatest reputation."

"Every little edge helps," Molly added. "There is a lot of competition for medical school."

Donahue shook his head, smiling, "It looks as though she learned something here."

Mary acknowledged this, "Chemistry has a good program."

Molly, who knew this was meant for her, said, "Sal was a good professor. She was one of his students. A lot of turnover in the department, of course, so nobody noticed when he persuaded the instructor to make the change."

"Does the outside world know it's good?"

"The chemistry department? Most people here hardly know it exists."

Donahue put up his hands, "I guess I hadn't heard myself. Not much at least."

Molly laughed ironically, "You're a true sociologist."

Mary agreed, "Sociologists never hear anything."

Pretending to be piqued, Donahue responded slowly, "That wasn't nice."

"But it was a good line," Mary said, "wasn't it?" She didn't often get a good jab in on him, but she enjoyed it when she did.

Then he spoiled the moment, "It's okay, Mary. When I was a cop, people said worse than that about me."

"And without a smile," Molly commented knowingly.

Donahue covered his mouth with both hands, then leaned toward Molly, "What about Smith and Jones. I remember the choir director saying that they had gotten credit for his class, but he didn't remember them ever having attended."

"That is awkward," she admitted.

"How so?" he asked.

The director didn't bother with the grade form. He just listed the students who deserved A's and said to give everyone else a C."

"That's unusual," Donahue observed. "Many get C's?"

"You just haven't been in the choir long enough," Mary laughed. "And you aren't enrolled for credit."

"I'll give you both points," he said smiling. His own attendance hadn't been good.

"The choir director does everything a bit 'differently.' I wouldn't be surprised to find more irregularities in his grades, but the records show that Smith and Jones were enrolled—under their right names, of course, which he wouldn't have recognized—and a C isn't much of a grade. Surely, if they bought grades, they would have asked for more."

"The late dean was too shrewd to call attention to the altered grades," he said. "That was the genius to the system. Who would care about a C in choir?"

"Also, it's only one credit hour."

"A little here and a little there, and creative advising as to the right courses."

"I suppose that it would be enough to keep S & JJ from flunking out."

"That and courses from Stout, that other new person in English, and PE—that's another area where a C is easily earned."

"I'm not very happy with any of them!" Indeed, Molly was not. "I'm old-fashioned—students should do their own work, because that is the way they'll have to do it after graduation. As far as I'm concerned, anyone who wants credit for group work should go out for basketball!"

"Uh," Donahue thought, "who was the instructor?"

"Probably Windy Gale. He has a soft heart."

"You would know it to look at him," Mary said, "Him and his dirty stories." Her deliberate copying of Windy's grammar accentuated her distaste for his influence on the students. Donahue, who liked Windy, changed the subject, "How about a bite to eat later?"

Mary was now suddenly in a hurry, "Not today, too much to do."

Flo Boater called her dean again, "Don't go out to eat tonight. Be where I can get hold of you."

Chapter Eighteen

Flo Boater entered coffee house, looked around and sighed. With a shake of her head, she went to the counter and told the student clerk, "Dark coffee, no sugar." Then, after a long stare at the offerings, she was about to order three doughnuts. She shouldn't eat even one, but stress made her hungry. No, she decided, not this time, but her reverie was broken by the historian tapping her elbow. Almost spilling her coffee, she snarled, "You oaf! Why don't you watch...."

The historian bowed his head, whining, "I'm sorry to bother you, President Boater. I was on my way to see you! It is hard to get an appointment. And I saw you here."

"See me about what?" she snapped, "And what's the problem? You know that I'm always here, where people can speak to me without an appointment." She then asked for the doughnuts.

As soon as the clerk had turned away for a clean plate, he whispered, "My subject needs to be handled confidentially."

She tossed her head, "Don't they all?" Then she indicated a free table, one where the students, though close, were facing away from them.

After they were adjusted in their seats, he looked around, then leaned over to whisper, "I am referring to a certain diskette belonging to the late Dean Wooda." He paused to see how she reacted. When she put down the doughnut and looked at him, he added, "A diskette, or several diskettes, hidden where he could use it quickly, but where nobody could find it." Getting no response, he added, "This is about grades...."

Brushing off doughnut powder from her lap, she half-whispered, "Yes. I see. That could be important. And confidential." Looking around at the nearby students, she concluded that they had heard nothing. Still, she suggested, "Let's go outside," and reached for her coat. Finding a quiet bench sheltered from the breeze, she contemplated putting her coffee and doughnuts between them—no point in getting too close—

but decided that whispering required more "intimacy." With a shiver, he put her snack down on the other side. When their shoulders touched, she shivered again. Taking up her second doughnut, she commented, "Cold here, isn't it?" Then she added, "There is so much noise in there. Now what was that? Something about a diskette?"

The historian brightened, then leaned toward her to whisper, "You know I've always wanted to be a dean."

"Yes."

"I know everything about this place. Somewhere else I'd have to start all over again."

Flo Boater put her doughnut down, then turned to face the historian, "We already have a dean."

"Stanley is only a boy. Moreover, he talks too much. You'll either tire of him or he'll move on. Anyway, the stress is getting to him."

"Yes," she admitted, "you have a point."

"He needs some help. Some mature help."

Sighing, she folded her hands and asked, "What do you have in mind?"

"Assistant dean right now."

She thought for a moment, "Perhaps, but we have no budget line for that right now."

He wheedled for a promotion, "A course reduction would be enough. Call it 'professional development'."

Flo Boater thought that this was reasonable, but she still responded very cautiously, "I don't know."

He suggested an alternative, "Perhaps chairman of the Theatre department again?"

She smiled at this, "Lill and Lily wouldn't be pleased." She wondered to herself if this meant in addition to Social Science or an exchange for Fine Arts? But she didn't have time to ask before he was gleefully rubbing his hands together, "Exactly, wouldn't that be perfect?"

Flo Boater tried to be non-committal. "Humm. And in return?" She looked at her coffee—it being too cold to drink, she carefully leaned back and poured it on the brown grass. She eyed the third doughnut, but decided she didn't need it.

"I find the diskette, or diskettes."

Flo Boater thought for a moment, then asked confidentially, "You know where it is, or they... you said 'they?'"

"I know that a lot of people are looking for it. I have my ways of finding out."

"I know that," she said. "And you apparently know how important it is." How, she wondered, did he come up with the idea that the information was on a diskette?

"More important," he said, "I understand *why* it is important *now*."

Flo Boater pondered this for a moment, looking across the campus, wondering if people found it unusual for anyone to be sitting outside today. Then she turned and said, "Let's put it this way. You find the diskettes and I'll find a new title for you..." She watched his sallow face for any sign of brightening, then added, "and perhaps more salary."

Smiling widely, but awkwardly, the senior historian answered, "That is an artful way of putting it. But my goal is to be dean."

Are you sure the faculty respects you enough to be dean?"

He dismissed this, "The faculty never respects a dean."

Flo Boater knew better, but realized that statistically he had an argument. This was not the time or place to discuss the matter, "I suppose you are right." Stanley Wooda had his allies, but it wasn't clear whether they respected him or not.

"Occasionally they like one," he offered as a compromise. "Certainly assistant deans."

Amused, Flo retorted, "You!?"

"Or *fear* him, which is much better."

Flo was impressed. Clearly the Creep had read his Machiavelli. So had she, since Stanley Wooda had recommended it so highly. She hadn't understood it all—too many references to Italian history, and Rome, while her husband's dissertation had been on Homer, not quite the same thing—but she found it interesting. She allowed herself to remember helping, actually more than helping, write *Agamemnon at Bay*; as a result she understood the stress of being expected to lead when nothing was going right. Reminded of Machiavelli's warning that a ruler, if forced to choose between being loved and being feared, should be feared, she answered, "I see your point." It was a lot like parenting, she thought. Though she had no experience with children, it must be a lot like dealing with faculty.

"After I fire a few people, the rest will respect me."

Probably so, she thought. Even an old dog is respected after he bites someone.

"I assure you," he said, "There will be order on this campus again."

Standing and looking around, she started to shake his hand, but decided that patting him lightly on the arm was sufficient. "We can call it a deal." As soon as she returned to her office, she hurried to her desk, got out the facial tissues and cleaned her palms. If despite only barely touching him, and that through his coat, her hands felt, well.... Then she hurried to the john.

Flo Boater was still shaking when she returned to her office. It was not, she told herself, the Creep alone and his information, but the stairs. She nodded at Miss Efficiency, who indicated with a movement of her head that she had a visitor. Stanley Wooda was waiting.

The president closed the door carefully, then sighed and asked what he wanted.

"What was that about?" he asked. "You know, the scene outside the coffee house."

Shaking her head, she said only, "You wouldn't believe it, but, believe me, it could solve a lot of problems." Covering her temples, she sighed again and walked over to the window.

He wrinkled his eyes—a rare show of confusion—and asked, "What is *it*?"

"That depends not on *what* it is, but *whether* it is."

"You lost me there," he replied.

At that moment she glanced outside, "There go Molly and Mary. Up to no good, I expect."

Wooda angrily exploded, "I know what they're up to! That's why I came over here."

"What's going on? I thought we had them isolated, one in Finance, the other in the Registrar's office."

"That was a mistake. They're working right across the hall from one another." He paused, "You remember the problem we were talking about. The one concerning the Registrar's office?"

She blanched, "They've found out!"

"No, but damn close. They're looking for evidence."

"How do you know?"

"The registrar at Zenith State University got suspicious. She was supposed to call Molly, but when she wasn't in, she called her dean, who he called me."

"What gave them away?"

"Caller ID! It indicated a private number. Mary's phone."

Flo's eyes blinked, "Can we fire them for this?"

He sighed, "Probably not. He said that they were doing some kind of research for a committee. The one you had me set up, that CPR-something."

Flo stood up and beckoned Stanley to follow her over to the far windows, "Okay, then that's out. But I've learned something new. That's why I was talking with the Creep. He says there is a program for changing grades. We've got to find it before they do, and destroy it."

"Program? I thought we were going to look through transcripts."

"No," she said, "it's more important than 'transcription errors.' It's got to be a program, maybe on a diskette—that's what the Creep thinks—for changing transcripts. Without the registrar knowing about it. Or, at least, needing to know about it."

"Why do you think there's a diskette?"

"Stanley, think about it. Did you really think that he would sit in the Registrar's office, call up the transcript and change it right there? No. He would, logically, download each transcript, make the changes in private, then put it back into the computer."

"On a diskette?" Stanley Wooda's computer skills were minimal.

"That's what I imagine."

He shook his head, "Do Mary and Molly know?"

"No, but it's almost the only logical way to keep track of the changes, other than keeping paper copies—and we'd have run across that. He didn't expect to drown, you know. They're sure of think of it, too."

After a moment, he replied, "You sure he couldn't have just cracked into the computer—he had access to everything, I thought. It doesn't take that long to make one or two changes," he argued.

"Look, Stanley, I knew the late dean intimately." She rolled her eyes, wishing she could rephrase that, then plunged on, "He was very careful. He would have kept copies of everything—the original transcript and each change—either on paper or, more likely, a diskette. If he needed to go back, to cover up his activities, he'd have everything at his fingertips."

"Sounds like he'd need more than one diskette."

"Maybe so, but if we find one, we'll find them all."

He thought for a moment, "You know where it is?"

"No," Flo Boater said, "But the Creep thinks he knows."

"You've asked him to find it for us?"

"God, no, Stanley. If he gave it to me, I'd have to do something with it or be subject to blackmail forever. We've just got to find it first. Then we can do whatever seems best with it."

He noticed the sudden change to "we", but only asked, "Why don't you just go find it?"

"Damn it, Stanley, I just learned about it. Besides, where is it? And is it really a diskette? The Creep didn't say why he thought that's what it was or even how he knew we were looking for something. I'm not even certain it isn't safer to leave it wherever it is, whatever it is, at least for a while. After all, I've been suspected of murder twice and each time my house was searched."

"No," he replied. "If the Creep knows somebody is looking for it, you need to find it first." He carefully did not say, "we?"

"You're right. But where to look? In the Registrar's office, I think. That makes the most sense."

"Not in my office somewhere? I'd have thought he'd hid anything important there or at home."

She snapped back, "You haven't seen it, have you?"

"No, but I'm almost never there, and I would have known what it was if I'd seen it. Besides, our secretary finds everything for me."

"Did Lily find it?" she asked, more to herself than of him. "She was very thorough."

He shook his head, "No, I don't think so. She wasn't dean very long, in any case. Not likely she ran across it, or we'd have heard. Besides, it was Mary and Molly who were calling around, not those two lesbians."

"But she went through everything, didn't she?"

"I guess."

"Then it has to be somewhere else."

"Your office, maybe?"

"Oh, God, Stanley. Did the dean have a key to my husband's office?"

"I don't think so…. I know I don't."

"Think about it," she said. "Would you leave something important where a secretary could come across it and want to file it properly?" Even her late husband's Ms. Inefficiency might have wondered that that diskette, or diskettes, might be for. Who knows what she might have blundered into?

"No, certainly not." That made sense. "Where could it be, other than the Registrar's office?"

"That depends on who knew about it?"

"Okay, suppose your husband knew."

She had thought about this. "If he knew about selling grades, it would be a first for him." He seemed to pick up everything about the college from the *Middleville Moderate*, and it only reported what he told the editor and activities open to the public, mostly sports scores. Moreover, if he knew about it, the transcript program would probably be at home. She was sure there was nothing there. She would have seen it, and if she had seen it, and not recognized it, it would have been in the dump months ago. Lastly… "he couldn't use a computer at all. He was barely competent at telephoning."

Stanley had a suggestion: "The late dean, did he know about computers? I mean, *really* know?"

She swung herself into her chair before answering, "Yes. He knew his computers. No doubt that he had the skills. But if he kept a diskette or tape in his home, it's long gone, too."

"Molly?"

"They were divorced, and estranged long before the divorce. She didn't want anything. Whatever wouldn't sell to cover the estate debts went to charity. Up in Zenith, I believe. Boxes of crap, stuff she didn't even look through."

"No point in trying to track down purchasers?" he ventured.

She nodded in agreement, then added, "Charities don't keep track of who buys what in their thrift stores."

"There's nothing in my office," he said, "but I can search it again."

"No point," she said. "I've already done that."

His mouth opened slightly. What did she think about what she found? Maybe she even checked his correspondence. But all he could only think to ask was a narrowly-focused question, "When did you do that?"

"When I was acting-dean myself. I went through everything. Threw most of his junk away. There was nothing that seemed to refer to selling grades."

"But not since I've been dean?" he asked after taking a deep breath.

"No. I've been too busy."

Involuntarily he left out a quiet sigh. Then he thought that she might just go through the office again now. Earlier she would not have known what she was looking for, maybe not looking for anything anyway. Just cleaning up. Now she would be more thorough. With a slight stutter, he asked, "Did he have a safe deposit box?" But he knew the answer to this, as she reminded him, that the late dean had several, all filled with money from the sale of the Latin American antiquities collection.

Stanley wrinkled his brow slightly, then asked, "You're sure this thing, this diskette or whatever, exists?" He was thinking of her habit of discarding letters without reading them. Diskettes could have gone into the trash without her remembering it.

"No, but we can't take the chance. Too many people are looking for it. If they find something, it would mean real trouble. If they do, I want at least to be able to pass a polygraph exam, saying that I had made a thorough investigation."

He looked at her silently, thinking that she could pass almost any polygraph on anything, but he said nothing. Instead, he walked over to the windows overlooking the campus.

Flo Boater thought for several minutes, joining Stanley in gazing out at the muddy campus, the ice having melted—a sign from the gods, she thought, and not an encouraging one. At last, she said, "If it's not at his home, not in a safe deposit box and not in his office, it has to be in some place where he could use it easily."

Wooda suggested, "Like you thought—the Registrar's office. Maybe not, but it's all that's left."

"That's what I've been saying," she sighed, "but where? In a file? Taped to the bottom of a drawer?"

"We could ask the registrar, or one of the temps, how the filing system works. You know, tell them that we just want to become acquainted with the process. He'd surely have put it somewhere out of the way, you know, where nobody would wonder what it was."

"We don't want help, silly! It would be suspicious, particularly if the rumor became public." She suddenly thought that the Creep might not be such a bad replacement dean after all—he wasn't very bright, but he was dependably dull. "Besides, the registrar was upset about something. She might have become aware of this. But we can't ask. We don't even know where she is."

"Yeah. Ms. Hogg is missing."

"Lucky for us," she replied, though she was wondering if that were just another scandal waiting to break.

After a moment he asked, "You mean we just go in?"

"We both have keys."

"I suppose so."

"Then you and I will go look for it tonight!"

"Tonight! Why not now?"

She explained that there are people around. This had to be kept absolutely secret. "That's why I told you to be free tonight."

"You knew we were looking for a program?"

"No, originally I thought we would be looking through transcripts. But it's the same thing. I don't want people knowing that we're nosing around."

"Okay," he said, warily.

"Come back at ten, no, ten-thirty. Bring a flashlight and your master key."

"Is this burglary? With my key?"

"No," she said. "We have every right to be there. It's just that we don't want to attract attention. If anything happened, say you break something… if the chief thinks it's burglary, that's his problem. As long as nobody thinks it's us. Ten-thirty. Call my house to confirm, then I'll meet you here."

At that same moment Max Stout was reading an essay. It was Ellie's. Had to be. Though she hadn't put her name on it, no one else had mastered the language of deconstruction. What puzzled him was the poem at the end:

> Everything is deep, everything but sleep.
> What is true, and what is not?
> Who knows best, and who knows less?
> I know a boy. He's not quite hot.
> He's not smart, not handsome,
> But he makes me laugh.

He'd never heard Ellie laugh.

Chapter Nineteen

The Registrar's office was on the second floor of the administration building, opposite the Financial Affairs office. Donahue had once asked why this was so, since it could have been easily fitted into the ground floor Student Services Empire.

"No money," Lill had explained. It would have been expensive to modify the original courthouse layout, so President Floyd Boater had taken one of the large second floor courtrooms for himself, then put academic dean's office across the hall, in what had been some kind of public service office, with storage rooms behind, rather than in the courtroom on the other wing. "The courtroom was too big for a dean, anyway, except maybe a dean of students, who preferred to have the entire downstairs to herself. Anyway, this left two large space open down the hall for the Registrar and the Business manager, and since the rooms facing the square had formerly been used for paying fines, it had a safe, thus making it more suitable for the vice president for financial affairs."

"Makes sense," Donahue had replied. "The old courtroom had lots of room, space for the filing cases."

Lill smiled, "Yes, it worked out well. Although there was no reason for all the filing cases had to be in the same room where students were served, a new wall would have been awkward. There was the great view of the campus through the high windows, lots of light, and on the second floor few flies came in during hot weather when the windows were open."

"Stairs bother some people. Wasn't that a problem when court was in session?"

"Good point, but the judges wanted their courtrooms on the second floor so that crowds could not look in—that had been a problem in the nineteenth century—and criminals had been known to jump through open windows after hearing the verdict."

"What did they use the third floor for?"

"Probably storage of records, but that didn't prove very practical. The rooms were small, with low ceilings, and the stairs to 'the attic' were inconvenient—entered through that side door at the back of the hall. You remember. Though not many people have been up there recently."

"Yeah, I'd wondered if the Latin American collection had been up there. Flo Boater, too, but she said that she felt the floors tremble under her feet."

"She did? She's not a heavy woman."

"No, by no means, no. And there wasn't anything particularly heavy. In fact, to judge by the accumulated dust, no one had been there in years. So I'd only looked in, then locked up again."

Lily had been listening, mentally drumming her fingers, but could not contain herself any longer, "DO, I'd have told you this long ago, if only I'd known about it. But only my friend here," whereupon she pointed at Lill, "has the patience to collect such trivia. Now, if I'd been involved in the decision, the dean's office would have been a lot nicer. As it is, it's a dump, and a small one. Barely room for a desk and an ante-room for a secretary."

Lill laughed, "A desk and a couch—for Stanley Wooda's *naps*." At that they all smiled. It was notorious that he used it for late night entertaining. "And he doesn't have a secretary right now." She had actually understated the furnishings. There were some file cabinets there, windows onto the square, a small adjoining storage room, and the tiny bathroom that nobody wanted to use.

Donahue's brow furrowed, "How did the real Dean Wooda, you know, the late dean, ever consent to such a small office? I'd have thought he'd have wanted some class, you know, like the college house he used. The one you sold."

Lill had to stop to think, "That might have been decided before he came. Lily, do you remember?"

"Lill, we weren't here then, and who gossips about departed deans?"

Lill laughed again, "You're right. Everyone talks about the current dean, and rarely in a positive sense."

"Oh, how well I know that," Lily replied. "How well I know."

At that moment, Flo Boater was looking around her office, without smiling. She noted that the large central doors of the courtroom had been locked permanently since perhaps the day the last of the furniture had been removed, unless maybe the day student pranksters had hauled that atrocious table into the room. On the hall side the doors had signs intended to discourage visitors from attempting to pass through them, but every so often someone shook them, believing that would somehow permit entry. The doors were, after all, right at the top of the stairs. She always hated those moments—it was like the building was falling down on her. In theory, a locksmith could have opened the door and made a new key, making the room usable for formal occasions, but so far no suitable event had presented itself. Everyone entered through the former jury room, which had been converted into the secretary's office—now Miss Efficiency's domain. There was another space behind it, the former judge's room, but nobody had used it in years except to go through the door into the antiquated men's toilet facilities; a large safe, once used for storing whatever it was that judges stored, was left ajar now. Her late husband, Floyd Boater, had kept liquor there for entertaining favored guests, but Lill had sent the bottles to him while he was recovering from his breakdown. Flo Boater had looked in once and, finding the safe empty except for some files, left it that way. The room was so abandoned that it might as well not have existed. In truth, Flo Boater feared a suggestion that she use it as her office. But that would have given the wrong impression—that she was the impoverished president of a small impoverished college. The large room at least had potential. She look around once, more, then said, "I did what I could for this office—new paint, curtains, restored the floor—and it still looks like an abandoned courtroom."

Dean Wooda, standing next to her, suggested that she bring the rest of her porcelain collection up for proper display. "The pieces you have look really good. They just sparkle in the sunshine." So did the smile he gave her.

Her more considered response was muttered. Visitors, like a couple bumptious trustees, were too dangerous. "I'd do better to get rid of that grotesque table and chairs." Then she smiled at remembering how most seated visitors couldn't reach the floor with their feet. Watching unwanted visitors squirm was always a treat, and it kept the meetings short.

"That would work," he replied. "You only use it now and then. We could move it." And there his imagination ceased to inspire. Move it where? And how to unlock the old doors? Getting them open would have been easy; but perhaps not without ruining them. He wasn't going to give some rube from Middleville the satisfaction of seeing how helpless he was.

"I suppose," she mused, "we could create a new room out of the corridor, with that great window looking onto campus." There had once been a crossway under the painted dome, but the side facing the street had long ago been made into a women's room. Restrooms once existed on either side of the alcove, but both had been so small that almost any use left them just nasty. The original women's room had been the exact counterpart of the men's room across the alcove, for exactly the same reasons, for the convenience of jurors and judge, but when women began to complain, it was converted for their use, only to discover that it was too small for reasonable privacy. Hence, the newer and larger women's room. Thanks to an inconvenient campaign by the *Middleville Moderate* for a larger jury room, the small women's room was dismantled and made into part of what became Registrar's Office. Male visitors continued to use the toilet that abutted onto the presidential suite until the lack of janitorial care combined with an ever-more bothersome noise to cause the judge to shut it down for everyone except his personal use.

"Yeah," he agreed. "I think there's just enough room. It would make a great dean's office."

Flo Boater shot him a disapproving look, "I think a new wall would make the corridor too dark."

Stanley Wooda thought about this when he returned to his small office. Plans to tear out the walls of what he thought of as a rabbit warren—not quite knowing was a rabbit warren was, but assuming it was a lot like his office—had always been put off for better financial conditions that never came. Consequently, his secretary's office was large—it had been somebody's office back when; right now it was empty, since he shared the services of Miss E—while he used the former storage areas for his own office and a place "to stretch out for a nap." The small toilet—an exact counterpart of the one in the other wing, in the Financial Affairs Office, accessible to the hall by a door that had not been used in years—was minimally suitable for female visitors, but it had so many recurring problems that he preferred to use the men's room on the ground floor. "Maybe, if we moved the registrar downstairs," he mused, "I could get that space." But the thought died. That office was far too large for his needs. If people joked about the president's office, what would they say about his?

Having nothing else to do, Stanley Wooda methodically checked behind every filing cabinet, knocked on walls for hollow sounds, lifted every ceiling tile. Nothing. Flo Boater did the same for her office, even checking Miss E's office when she was on coffee break.

The registrar's office was the mirror image of the president's, except that the large double doors were the public entryway. Students coming in for transcripts or information had sufficient room inside the double doors to look around before approaching a long table with wire baskets containing little booklets that summarized in complex language such information as was thought most likely to assist them. It was assumed that if students could not understand the contents, they were not smart enough to graduate anyway. What had once been the jury room, the judge's office and the women's restroom had been combined into two rooms, one for storage, the other for a safe. The outside doors had been walled shut and painted over, so that one would have to look carefully to see where they had been. Stanley Wooda's predecessor, he had once heard, had actually looked into opening them again, then making them into an office with a view onto the campus rather than looking into the trees that kept him from seeing the city square. Money, again, had intervened, and he could not persuade President Floyd Boater to accept a gift sufficient to pay for the work—"Woody, that is a magnificent offer. But I know how little we can afford to pay any dean, even any president." For the dean to argue that he had the money would make people wonder where he had gotten it.

In retrospect, it had been realized that the Registrar's office and Financial Affairs should have been switched. Instead, the VP for FA ended up with a small safe that had long before been damaged in a botched burglary—the money being blown up together with the safe's door. The large safe in the Registrar's Office—once believed less secure than the one across the hall—was now used for such records as needed to be protected from fire—mainly the oldest bound records and the newest computer disks—though everyone who thought about it realized that in case of a truly serious fire the safe would end up in the basement and the contents would be thoroughly destroyed. Middleville citizens, and especially the editor of *The Moderate*, had complained loudly about various errors way back when the courthouse was built, but in vain—the contractor had been related to the governor of the time, and the expense of redoing the project was beyond the taxpayers' desire to pay.

The downstairs Student Services Empire was confusion beyond description. When Flo Boater had first begun to wonder if the late dean could have hidden there something related to the grades problem, she had taken a brief "inspection walk" through the offices, but was overwhelmed by the number of student records; her dislike of searching through them was reconciled by the thought that the last Dean of Students had been at the college so long that Dean C. Wooda could hardly have hidden anything there; now that she suspected the records were on a diskette, not in a reasonably large file folder, she decided to go there again only as a last resort. In any case, nobody went into that area often enough that they could just drop in without being noticed, much less her.

By such a process of thought Flo Boater had concluded that if the late dean had hidden anything anywhere, it would have been in the Registrar's office, where it would also have been easiest for him to make the changes in the student records. Stanley's idea that he would have made the changes at home. Well, that might be true, but home was a poor place to keep anything. He'd come back from South America very ill. Suppose that happened again. Who knows who'd stumble upon the diskette? At least in the registrar's office there'd be nothing but fingerprints, and those could be wiped off.

It was just eleven-thirty PM when the president and dean entered the Registrar's office. She had been delayed by a telephone call from a trustee—he had wanted more information about the young woman who had died on campus, but she had nothing to give him but assurances that the death had no connection to anything at the college. After she locked the door behind them, they looked over the counter that served to separate students from the work area. The vast room was dark except for the light that came through the windows.

Stanley Wooda let out a sigh of relief, "That was easy."

"When you have a master key, everything is easy," she responded. There was a touch of exasperation to her voice. She was tired from her afternoon search and clearly in need of sleep. She'd be much better when this was all over—as long as they found the diskettes.

He replied, "I don't *use* mine very much."

"I don't *need* mine often, either."

"I'll look in the storage closet," Flo Boater said. "You check the file drawers." With those words she gestured toward the rows of files. As he started to shine his flashlight over there, she snapped out an order, "Keep that down. People might see it."

Flo Boater made her way across the room, bumping into a few chairs that were somehow not where she had remembered them. Stanley carefully maneuvered past several computers on high tables until he was almost at the windows on the far end of the office. Coming upon two large chairs, he asked in a stage whisper, "What are these things doing here?"

Flo Boater turned around to look, saw the chairs in the dim light that broke through the clouds for only a moment, then answered hoarsely, "Ms. Hogg needs a big chair. And it's more private back there. Sunlight comes in well, too." More than needed in the summer, less so winters.

"Why two?"

"They are of different hardness. It's good for her back to have a change."

"They look familiar."

"Miss Purdy had them. When she left, Ms. Hogg went over to her office and claimed them."

"Moved them across the hall?"

"Yes," she said. "They should have been thrown away. They are so old-fashioned." Flo Boater was a self-proclaimed expert on furnishings. "Everything up here should reflect the style of my remodeling."

To himself, Stanley murmured, "We should live so long as to see *that* finished."

"What? Did you say something, Stanley?"

"Nothing, just cursing the darkness."

"Turn on your flashlight then."

Shrugging, Stanley turned back toward the cabinets nearest the counter, then opened the first one at random. In a trembling voice, fumbling with his flashlight, trying to make it work while shielding it with the hand he needed to flip through the files, he said, "Dark in here!"

"Look in the cabinets over there," Flo ordered, flipping her light briefly toward the more distant ones. "I think you are looking at the more recent records, the ones they use every day. He wouldn't have put anything there."

Stanley Wooda did as commanded, still struggling with the light, which was beginning to flicker. A brief ray of moonlight gave him the courage to move ahead more rapidly than was wise, until he was suddenly in the dark again. "Oh, my God," he screamed as something grabbed his foot and pulled him down. He crashed hard, hitting a forearm and twisting an ankle. "Oh, my Goddd…"

Flo Boater hurried over and cast her beam at the hapless dean, who by then was sitting up, half entangled in what appeared to be a long, narrow fence on its side. He was rubbing his ankle and wanting to rub his head, but few people have the dexterity to do both at once—not even a good dancer. After a moment, he assured her, "I'm okay, I think." As she assisted him to his feet, he turned to look at the object that was still reaching for him. He exclaimed, "It's a damn ladder!"

He had seen ladders before, naturally, even in this very building. Flo Boater's first decision as acting-president had been to redecorate her office. A massive room, its high ceilings could be reached only by scaffolding, but often the plasterers and painters valued speed sufficiently to use long ladders. Modern ones folded up sufficiently to be easily carried, but they had left them lying about the president's office for months. The registrar's office was in need of paint, which might have accounted for the ladder's presence, but Flo Boater knew better, "I don't remember having authorized any repairs here."

"I don't either," Stanley agreed.

She shrugged, "I can't keep track of every detail of campus management. Anyway, this one looks awfully long." She went back to the storage area, where she began to inspect an old-fashioned desk, undoubtedly left behind when the courthouse was moved. It had small drawers, just right for diskettes.

The dean, however, kept staring at the ladder, "It's dangerous to leave things like this just lying around."

"Stanley, how many people come here at night with flashlights? It's just bad luck you stumbled onto it in the dark."

Stanley's thought was that it wasn't the first time he was in the dark regarding what was going on, but he was too wise to say anything. More seriously, his flashlight was not working properly. Intermittently, using both hands he could get the beam to flicker, but as soon as he took one hand off, the light vanished. How could he look through a file drawer while holding a flashlight with two hands? "Let's turn on the lights," he suggested.

"I don't want to," she snapped. "Someone might notice we're in the building.

"My flashlight doesn't work."

"Everyone on campus could see us."

"Everyone on campus can see the flashlights. Isn't that even more suspicious?"

"The campus is practically deserted after dark now. I may have been criticized for turning off the outside lamps across campus…"

"Yeah, putting money ahead of security," Wooda mumbled. "The rapists' paradise." After a moment he added, "In a Briarpatch winter rapists should get a bonus."

"I heard that," she snapped. "It did keep the women in their dorms. They needed to study more anyway." While saying this, she was trying to read the titles on various files. It was not easy. Her eyes were no longer good, and the penciled descriptions were faint.

He felt better about the danger once he began having more success with the flashlight. After taking out the batteries twice, spitting on the connections once (he had heard somewhere that this might work) and bending the contact to fit tighter, he got it to stay on long enough to read the labels on the first files before thinking that surely the late dean wouldn't have labeled his diskettes "fake transcripts." He needed to look into each file. The light then went out again. In frustrated fury he hit the flashlight against the file drawer. The light came on and stayed on.

After starring at it for several seconds, he was momentarily alarmed to see that he had aimed the beam at the window. He switched it off. Good enough. But it would not turn back on.

He stopped to think, asking himself, "Why are we looking in the file cases anyway?" Yes, that was the place one was least likely to look (on the principle of *The Purloined Letter*, putting it practically in plain sight), but with so many people having access, including students—at that time—the risk of accidental discovery was too great. He asked Flo Boater, "Where would confidential records be kept?"

She pointed with her flashlight beam, "In the computer over there."

"Do you have the password?"

She was disappointed in him, "Why would I have the password? If I had been given the password, why would I remember it? And, if I had it, why wouldn't I be sitting in your office, looking through the files."

He noticed that she had said *his* office. The computer center director could track everyone who signed into that account and which computer was used. Nothing would lead back to her. But all he said was, "Surely, there are hard copies."

She stopped, sighed, and pointed her flashlight over at a door which he remembered led into a storage area. She said, "Hard copies are in the cabinets you're supposed to be looking in. Old ones are probably in the vault. Or inside the storage closet. Probably in the vault."

"How do we get into that?" Wooda asked.

"Every president is given the combination," she explained. "Not a hard one." Even her late husband had managed to remember it.

"No?"

"Founder's Day date. March 19, 1848. That is 3-19-18-48."

"That's it?" Wooda asked, incredulously. But it all made sense— everyone wants a series of numbers or letters that are easy to remember. Birthdays are popular, but those change with every president. So why not the birthday of the college? But would the dean have left anything in the vault, where anyone looking through it would assume that it was important enough to investigate what it was? And four digits for the combination? That's a really old safe!

"This is a small college," she explained. "Yes, someone might guess it easily, but who'd break into the Registrar's office?"

As Wooda moved toward the main door, thinking he might use the restroom, or rather where he remembered the door being; suddenly he barked his shins against a chair, then bumped into what he realized was a desk. He cursed the lack of moonlight, then saw the outline of a desk light against the beam shot over by the president when she heard him knocking items onto the floor. He grasped the desk lamp and turned it on.

"I've got to see what I'm doing. This isn't anything like the main light," he offered as an excuse. "Anyone who sees it will think the registrar just forgot to turn it off."

Reluctantly, she agreed.

Stanley went through the letters and folders on the desk, stacking them to one side, then replacing them as close to their original positions as possible. Then he picked up the items from the floor and put them where he guessed they had been. Meanwhile, the president was becoming discouraged. At length, she turned to him and said, "We ought to look in the vault. That's where Chief Biggs would expect to find the program."

Stanley shrugged, then went to the large closet, turned on the interior light and asked, "Where did you say the vault was? I don't see it."

"It's to the rear," she said, coming to join him. "We don't use it much now that everything is computerized."

"Shouldn't we go to the computer center?" He knew it was a silly comment as soon as he said it—the dean wouldn't have hidden anything there.

"Not necessary. Everything is in cyberspace, wherever that is. Besides the director would never give us access to an encrypted system." Thinking that more likely he would wonder why she wanted the passwords, she opened the vault and stepped inside. The flashlight revealed stacked shelves and piles of boxes. "Good God, look at all the diskettes," she blurted out. It could take months, especially if they had to insert each diskette into the computer and read the contents. Also, the one they were looking for probably had a password. She wasn't sure about that, but she remembered being told how important security was, and how passwords should be composed of random letters and numbers. "Fat chance!" she whispered to herself. Whatever Woody used would have had to be easily remembered.

Stanley was impressed. He had envisioned a small safe, but this was indeed a vault. How had it ever gotten into this room? Switching on a light, he exclaimed, "Some of these are floppy disks. We don't use them any more."

"We've got to have some machine that takes them." She then stopped for a moment to think, "I didn't know we had a computer system back then."

Stanley Wooda looked at some of the labels, "Looks like routine stuff."

"What did you expect?" she asked. "That he'd write 'grades for sale' on it?"

He nodded, sighing, "I doubt we'll ever find it, even if it's here."

"We'll look anyway," she said, with a new determination.

"How'll we know when we find it?"

"It's got to have some type of title, silly," she responded. "Woody would have used something simple, something he wouldn't forget." Seeing that he was doubtful, she added encouragingly, "We'll know it when we see it."

"We still might not be able to read it."

"Perhaps not. But it's more important right now to make sure that nobody else finds it. Even if we have to destroy it, we'll be ahead of the game."

Wooda began looking along the shelves, asking only occasional questions such as, "You are sure the computer director wouldn't help us?"

Her response was to the point, "We wouldn't want to call her attention to our little project."

"In any case," he answered, "I suppose it's not in the computer system? Right?"

"Right. It is probably nothing larger than a diskette, maybe two or three, but not in the system permanently. That's why we are looking for something small." Within minutes it was clear to both of them that the vault which had looked so large was actually so small that they were getting in one another's way. "You go look around outside; I'll her search the vault."

He agreed happily.

After ten minutes, Stanley was at the door of the vault. "I don't understand," he complained, "Why would the dean keep the diskette or whatever in the registrar's office and not in his own office? If it's that small, surely he could find a hiding place." But he had just searched his office himself. Maybe he should pry open the floorboards—that's what they do in the movies. That might explain the strange noises at night.

The president stopped a second to think, then said, "He would have hidden somewhere outside his office so that he could deny knowing anything about if the scandal broke and it was searched. It makes sense to hide it here so that he wouldn't have to carry it in and out." She paused for a moment, "Also, I think the student records can be accessed only from here."

"That made sense," he said. But the details fascinated him, "Wiped off the fingerprints each time, I imagine?"

"Probably, but this is also a great place to hide one diskette, or two or three. There must be a thousand in the vault alone." Having said that, she brushed past her dean and went over to the shelves in the closet area that Stanley Wooda had been perusing. There were hundreds of diskettes in shelves there, too, piled in boxes. She studied them a moment, then said, "I wouldn't be surprised if he hid it here, just stuck in among the others."

"Why do you think that? There isn't anything important in these. Just daily reports. That sort of thing."

She wasn't so sure, "Everything in the vault might be important, so the registrar might have wondered what is was. But here, it's just junk. Moreover, he had a key and could have gotten in here easily, so if they changed the combination, he wouldn't have a problem."

Stanley Wooda liked that idea, "What would it be labeled?"

"Something that would not be suspicious, something no one else would look at. But something he would instantly recognize himself."

He held one diskette in his hand, "Perhaps something like this, 'Misc. expenses 1994'." When she glanced at him, he asked if he should put it in the computer and check.

"No. We don't want to log in. Besides, the registrar probably had a password. There might be an alarm if we tried to guess. Woody would have known it."

"What would he use?"

"The old registrar?"

"Who else?" he asked.

"Which one? That's the problem. Everyone uses something familiar, yet distinct."

"I don't know. I used to use *password*. Nobody ever guessed it. But this is different. If one than one person had to have access—and surely more people than just the registrar had to know it."

"The computer center director."

"No, the permanent staff had to know it. The registrar couldn't be here every day, every minute."

She agreed. "That makes sense. And I bet Woody had no problem persuading each registrar that sharing with just one more person wouldn't hurt."

"We already knew that he had access. He had to."

She reflected on this, "Something simple. He could never remember anything."

"Then I'm sure we can figure it out once we're out of here. If we can find the diskette, we can figure out how to get the password later. What's important is to find the diskette. No diskette, it doesn't matter if we can get into the computer program."

Taking the diskette from Stanley's hand, she put it back on the shelf without looking, in the wrong place, and commented, "I doubt it's this one." With that she walked back to the files. "I'll bet he left it out here. It might be suspicious for him to go into the storage area when someone is around, when he could pretend to look up a file without any problem."

"That's a good thought," Stanley agreed, following her after closing the vault and shutting off the lights. What he was thinking was that he probably didn't go back to the filing area during office hours—someone might ask if they could help him.

"There might not even be a program," Flo Boater commented. "He was such a liar. He could have taken the students' money and not done anything for them."

Stanley's flashlight inexplicably came on again. He returned to the ladder, threw the beam along it, then exclaimed, "That looks like blood!"

Flo Boater hurried over to join him, touched her finger in it and smelled. She agreed. As Stanley went one direction down the files, she went the other, until finally she asked, "Where's the body?"

Stanley Wooda swept his flashlight around the entire floor, then said, "I don't see one."

She exclaimed, "It can't be another damn murder! I can't have that again!"

"I don't see a body," the dean said, looking behind more filing cabinets.

"If the body isn't here, it has to be somewhere else. There was no blood in the hallway. We'd have seen it" Then her logical processes deserted her. She reflected, "Besides, the police chief always calls the president when a crime occurs."

The dean observed cynically, "He usually accuses you of it, too!" He almost remarked that it was unlikely that the body had been discovered yet. "The blood's still fresh."

"Yes, and now here we are in the middle of...." She hesitated, searching for the right words.

Stanley Wooda supplied the phrase, "Suspicious circumstances."

"This can`t happen, not again!"

"Well, it looks like it has."

"We can`t let ourselves be distracted. If somebody else is looking for the transcript program, we have to find it fast, before we report this!" At that moment, she heard a noise in the hall.

Stanley Wooda heard it, too, "We'd better get out of here."

"Damn it. Let's scram." In moments of crisis, the vocabulary of childhood friends reappeared. She was sufficiently alert to turn out the desk lamps, but as she heard the noise again, she retreated toward the window and fell down. Too late, Stanley whispered, "Watch out!"

She was up quickly, commenting acidly, "What idiot would leave a ladder lying about?"

They froze. There was the sound of someone at the door. Flo turned on her light long enough to ascertain where they were. She flicked the light along the floor toward the door, but Stanley pushed the flashlight down and whispered, "We can't go that way." He signaled to go to the window, which he tried to slide up quietly. Nothing doing. "Locked, dammit!" he swore quietly.

"I don't want to jump anyway," she said. Two stories high. Her eyes widening to the point that she could see around the room, she said in a hoarse whisper, "We'd better hide!"

"Why?" he asked, in a moment of lucidity. "We have every right to be in here."

She pulled him behind a file case, "Using flashlights? In the dark?"

"You're right," he agreed. Then, led by her to the closet, he heard her say, "In here."

She pulled the door closed behind them, then fumbled briefly with the lock before giving up, deciding that it would cause too much noise. Turning around to find some place to hide more fully in the blackness of the room, she bumped into Stanley and grabbed him to prevent falling.

He realized with fright that she had embraced him firmly, but once he realized it was panic, not romance, that possessed her, he relaxed.

They could tell by the light that swept briefly under the door that whoever had come in was using flashlights, too. Police?

Then they heard a voice, familiar, but not quickly identified, "I told you this would be easy."

They recognized Smith's voice, "I thought you were going to unlock a window."

"I did." It was Jones! "I even stole a ladder and left it behind the bushes, but somebody took it. But it didn't matter. I told you the doors would be no big thing."

Smith whispered, "I'd forgotten you could pick a lock like that."

"Com'on, that's why they call me Jimmy." He didn't bother to keep his voice down. After all, they were alone in the building.

"Yeah. But, still, how'd you do it?"

"The front door was tricky, but this door is fifty years old. The tumblers are so worn they fall right into place."

"Where'd you get that little pick?"

"Be prepared. I learned that when I was a boy scout for about a week." Jones then became sarcastic, "Some security lock. They don't even have a deadbolt." He then paused to ask, "I wonder where the ladder went." Shining the light up, he moved toward the window. Smith was following closely behind and whispering as loud as he dared to get him to douse his light, it could be seen all over campus. Jones did so, then went down, and Smith, too. Jones uttered a curse that Smith hadn't heard before (and he considered himself an expert). As they got up, Jones felt something moist on his hand. Shining his light on it, he saw a red liquid and began to whine. Smith studied the hand but could see no cut, "Shut up, you'll wake the dead." At that instant, his flashlight crossed the sticky pool on the floor, half-covered by a ladder. He was too shaken to say anything original or funny, only, "What's that? Paint?"

By this time Jones had wiped his hand on his pants and ascertained that the lack of pain was no accident. Turning his flashlight beam to focus on Smith's, he exclaimed, "My God. It's blood!"

"Blood? Whose!?"

Smith swept his flashlight around the floor, then realized that his batteries were dying. Cursing the pink rabbit and all his competitors, he looked around for the some illumination other than the ceiling lights. Spotting a desk lamp, he limped over there, realizing for the first time that he had sprained something in the fall. "Whose is this?" he asked.

"Probably the registrar's!"

Smith looked around long enough to determine that there was no body, and he thought clearly enough to realize that they were not going to be able to conduct a quiet search. There was only one conclusion, "It's Miss Purdy all over again! We'd better get out of here!"

"Damn straight," Jones agreed, but immediately froze at the sound of a noise outside. "Wait. Someone's coming."

"Into the closet!" Smith cried, and pulled open the door. However, before he could see Stanley Wooda and Flo Boater standing there, holding onto one another, Jones grabbed him and cried, "No! Over here! That's the first place anyone would look." He pulled him behind the rows of file cabinets, whispering "If we can get to the counter, it has a lip. You know, where people sit with their legs underneath. We can hide there. When they've gone far enough away, we can to slip out."

"We can't make it," Smith moaned, but he followed his friend from one shadow to another. Right behind them were Flo Boater and Stanley Wooda, their light footsteps masked by Smith's complaints.

When the newcomers passed down the aisle to the storage room, the president and dean looked at one another in the dim light provided by a moon ray that filtered through an opening in the clouds and somehow reflected right into their former hiding place. "They're right!" Flo Boater whispered, "We need to get out of here."

"But how?" Wooda asked?

"They didn't close the door all the way. We can crawl out!" Which is what they planned to do as soon as the newcomers were out of sight. Awkwardly, the space under the counter was already occupied, so they crowded under a desk. The fit was tight, but Flo Boater discovered that the physical proximity of Stanley Wooda offset her fear to a considerable degree.

"Who's the new group?" he asked.

"I don't know, but once they see the blood, they'll start looking around. I don't want to be here then. Is the door still ajar? We could crawl around and out."

"I think it's closed. Do you want me to look?"

"NO, stay down. Those boys may see you. Let me think."

"Well, think fast. They're coming this way." He would have liked to know who the newcomers were, but he was in no hurry to find out.

She gave him a squeeze, "Don't panic. Now, if the door is still open, the boys will slip out. We're okay if we wait a minute or two before crawling out, but not if we have to stand up to open it."

"What if those two idiots just sit there?"

"If they're that frightened, we can just crouch down, get to the door, sneak it open, then make a dash for it. The newcomers will hear the noise, but think the boys made it."

"A dash where? Our offices?"

"No, down the stairs. We'll have a head-start."

And that is what Flo Boater and Stanley Wooda did, more or less. As soon as they saw the shadows move to the far end of the room— actually when they saw the flashlights over there, they slipped out the open door and tiptoed away without attracting attention. What happened next they learned the next day from the Creep.

"As it happened, President Boater, I was just sitting in the coffee house when those two young rascals…"

"Smith and Jones."

"Yes, them. Anyway, they began to talk about an adventure they had last night. It was so ridiculous that I couldn't believe it at first, but nevertheless I began to take notes…"

"Notes?"

"So that I wouldn't forget any details. Actually, its pretty strange, but I thought you might want to hear about it. Before, that is, it gets into the newspaper…."

"Like those lies Smith wrote last time!"

"Yes, just like that. Truth doesn't matter to them. That's why it's important to know what lies are out there."

"Just so," she responded, "just so."

"Well," he answered, flipping a notebook open, "this is what they said…."

"Said?" she asked. "Why were they telling this to each other?"

"They were trying to impress Ellie," he said. Then, with a shrug, he added, "I don't think they were getting very far."

"Okay, go on."

"Well, Smith said—I think I got Smith and Jones right. Smith is the dumb one, I remember."

"The dumber. But don't say that to anyone else. Their fathers are trustees."

"Uh, yes, of course. Well, Smith said that as flashlights began to play around the floor, he had second thoughts about their hiding place. 'They'll see the blood soon', he said. "The first place they'll look is behind the files. This won't do!"

Flo Boater interrupted, "That sounds pretty literary for Smith. Does he really talk that way?"

"Oh, yes. Well, Jones does at least, though he doesn't always use the right word for what he wants to say. But let me read it to you. I wrote it out, you know, like a play. I thought it would be more effective that way. I almost went into the theater, you know. A playwright."

No she didn't know. Who could have imagined? But all she said was, "You wrote dialogue?"

"Oh, yes. That's why I was so pleased to be chair of the Theatre Department. I was, briefly, you remember, before Lill and Lily managed to…"

She broke that thought off. She never wanted to think about that again. She said, "Read. I'm listening."

He straightened up, took a deep breath, then after one false start managed to find the right voice:

"Where do we go, then?"
"There's a closet over there."
"I think we can make it. They're way over by the computers."
"What's there?"
"The computer disks in regular use. That's what I want to check."
"Check? I thought you were just going to make out a slip?"
"I think I know the password."
"The password?"
"Yeah, Ms. Hogg always called the president *Chicken Little*. I think that's what she'd use."

At that point someone came in with flashlights. They ducked down, then crawled over to the window, but couldn't open it. Then when the flashlights were at the other end of the room, they saw shadowy figures slip out of the closet. Two people went out of the room, shutting the door behind them, quietly. They were trapped.

Flo Boater shifted uncomfortably, but said only, "Go on." She couldn't tell who was who, but the historian's voice was getting on her nerves.

Smith started to panic, but Jones pulled him behind the nearest file cabinet. He put a hand over his mouth.

Flo Boater interrupted, "Smith admitted that to Ellie? I thought he wanted to impress her.

"Just so, just so, but it was Jones who said that. Anyway,"

…as the flashlights came closer, they saw feet; then they saw heels. That emboldened them to rise up. Just high enough to see X and Y.

"X and Y?" she asked.

"Lill and Lily," he responded. "I thought it might be wise to disguise their names."

"Oh," she sighed. "Just call them Lill and Lily"

"X… that is, *they*, were over by the computers, trying to read diskette covers; they were complaining about the crabbed handwriting, which made it impossible to know just what was on them."

"Well, here we are," Lill observed. She was trying to figure out how to read what the disk in her hand said. She had been in the registrar's office often. But she had never worked there, so she was unfamiliar with anything. She said, "The difference between 'having an idea' where particular files might be kept and 'knowing' is significant."

Lily realized this, too. "Now that we're here, what are we looking for?"

"Let's look for the original grade sheets," Lill suggested.

Flo Boater started with surprise. Why hadn't she thought of that? Lily had been similarly "in the dark."

"The originals?" Then she understood, "Oh, the ones we write the grades on. Aren't those discarded?"

"The registrar is required to keep originals for five years."

"Why ever for?" Lily asked. Mentally she seemed to be calculating the storage space that would be required. She said that she hadn't been told that as dean. But she had not been dean very long.

"In the past, everything was done by hand. It was occasionally necessary to check a graduating student's grades. Transcripts were not printed out. But the administration wanted to be ready in case. A student might argue that there had been an error in copying the grade onto his transcript."

"Makes sense," Lily conceded. "But why keep it up?"

"Tradition is very strong in higher education," Lill explained. "If storage space had been limited, the policy would have been different. But this is a big room."

The boys, crouching behind a file case, were very happy that Lill was correct.

Lily asked, "I thought we had a lot of off-site storage."

"Oh, in other buildings, yes. But my guess is that the dean would have thought it to inconvenient to hide anything important there."

The boys nudged one another. This was getting interesting. There was a moment of panic when Lily walked toward them, but she stopped in mid-step, turned and asked, "How will we know if anything was changed?"

"I am not sure. But there has to be a record of grade changes somewhere. Maybe just an unusual date on a new printout."

"Can we just check the computer?" Lily asked.

Lill shook her head, half sadly. How could her friend be so computer illiterate? She explained, "No point in even turning the computer on. We do not have the password for sure. Just a guess at it."

Lily understood that. But she would gladly have taken a chance rather than go through a lot of paper. She grumbled, but she flew into the work. She made rather a big mess of things.

After a few frustrating minutes, Lill exclaimed, "We might try to see what we are doing." She then turned on a lamp, then crossed over to the windows, then pulled down the blinds tight.

Flo Boater put a hand over her eyes. She thought to herself, "This guy teaches writing?" Then, noticing him hesitate, she signaled him to keep reading.

Lily asked, "Are we checking against clerical 'errors,' and if so, how are we doing that?" Getting nothing for her question, she said that she would "look for anything strange." She dived back into the folders. Her patience lasted only a few minutes; her back even less. Straightening up, she commented, "I have often wondered. Except for the grade hogs, who would check their grades?—except what is on the little summary we mail to them? How would anyone really know if a clerical error occurred after that?"

"If you do not ask," Lill suggested, "you probably would not. But that is why it would make more sense to change grades later rather than when they are mailed out."

Lily was not so sure. "I suppose a professor might notice an error on his advisee's transcript." She said that as acting dean, she had had similar experience with this.

Flo began to get impatient. A better reader might have made it endurable… how much of this crap could she believe? She knew that the Creep was an inventive story-teller, but this exceeded any performance he had ever put on before. She was about to say that when he anticipated her complaint, "The good part is coming right up."

Lill conceded the point, somewhat unsurely, "Some would, some wouldn't."

Turning to look at her, arms on hips, Lily commented archly, "That's pretty cynical."

Lill replied tartly, "Cynicism gets you through the day." But she did not pause in her search.

Returning to her work as well, Lily finally said, "Looks like some empty drawers here." Then she emitted a hushed, "Oh, my God." It was a Lily-pad-sized hushed exclamation.

Lill looked over, "Shush! You'll attract the watchman. If there is one…." They'd waited until the regular man had left, but there was always something one could not plan for. She was worrying about this when her attention was drawn to Lily.

Her friend had backed toward her, pointing away. She half-stuttered, "Lill. We've got a problem."

Lill's eyes followed the finger, but saw nothing. She took a deep breath. It was too dark to see anything. "Yes," she said impatiently. "How to find the files."

"No… Lill… We've got a real problem. Look." As she pointed her light behind the file case, Lill came over to look.

Lill stuttered, "Oh, my God. There's blood all over the place."

Flo sat up straighter. He was right. This was becoming interesting.

Lily joined her, then looked around all the file cabinets. "Where's the body?" she asked suspiciously.

At that they both began to look around carefully, taking special care not to step on the drops of blood. When Lily picked up a gigantic coffee cup from the floor and asked, "What's this?"

Lill almost had apoplexy. "Put that down! It's the registrar's coffee cup," she said loudly.

But Lily continued to admire it, "It's gigantic!"

"Ms. Hogg was a coffee addict. *Put it down*!"

Lily did so, reluctantly, and said, "She must have gone to the bathroom a lot."

Lill responded furious, "There was blood all over it, too, and now your fingerprints are on it."

This had not occurred to Lily, who asked, "Another murder? What do we do now?"

"Look around," Lill commanded. "Where there's smoke, there's fire."

"What do you mean?" She took this warning serious. She asked, "The alarm will go off?"

"Look around," Lill ordered. But after a brief search around the files, she said, "I do not see anything."

Wondering what she meant, Lily had looked, too. Until she realized, "No body."

"Maybe this is the vice-president's case all over again?" Lill asked. "Or what we thought happened."

"Maybe, but not necessarily. We were sure that nobody could have carried Miss Purdy's corpse out of the building. Not without a lot of help." Lily could see the humor in even the most ghastly situations. "This is not quite so certain, but it still would not be easy."

Flo Boater recognized this as a replay of last semester's suspected murder, when the overly large Miss Prudence Purdy had disappeared from the office right across the hall, leaving a trail of blood. But she let the historian drone on.

"If the registrar had been thin," Lill observed. "Even Ms. Gates could have carried her off." She paused for a moment, "Only a few years ago that would have been impossible."

Lily smiled at the thought of the prematurely elderly librarian totting off a body, any size of body. She barely carried a small pile of books. But fortunately, she did not have to do that. Not often, anyway. Briarpatch students rarely checked them out. Lily said that.

Lill suggested, "I guess we should get out of here."

Lily was meanwhile looking around suspicious, uh, suspiciously. She agreed, "I do not like this."

"Me, neither," Lill responded. "We must have left fingerprints all over the place."

"I do not know how we can clean them all up," Lily said. "Besides, what's the point? There must have been a million people in here."

"Yes, at least several dozen, but ours are on file."

"They are?"

"Do not you remember the motorcycle rally? The fight? We might as well tell the chief we were here."

"Tell? Why?"

"Suppose Ms. Hogg is injured and dies because we did not report it."

Lily nodded agreement, then went over to the largest patch of blood, "I wonder where she went from here."

At this Flo Boater interrupted, "They said all this? That is, the boys said they witnessed this?" She wondered why she had never heard about a fight at a motorcycle rally.

"Oh, yes. I believe them on that. When they heard the words 'the chief,' they must have gone completely pale. I believe that they started toward the door, which was closed, and they made enough noise crawling that Lill and Lily came over to investigate."

"Now, this is what happened? Not just your invention?"

He smiled, "Does it really matter?"

Lily, standing almost over them, whispered loudly back to Lill, "What are you doing over there?"

"Me, nothing," Lill whispered. "Stop making all that racket." She then busied herself by rummaging under the barrier that separated customers (that is, students) from clerks (that is, uh, clerks).

"There are all kinds of pigeonholes here," she noted, checking the papers and forms briefly.

"I'm going to look in the vault," Lily said and made her way into the ante-chamber, where she turned on the light, bringing a protest from Lill that it could be seen from the campus. Lily ignored her.

Meanwhile, Smith and Jones had slipped over to the window and tried to open it. Their fumbling with the lock, however, attracted Lily's notice. When she called out to ask what Lill was doing, Lill gave up her project and walked over to the window. She had heard the noise, too, but had been concentrating on a logbook that listed student requests for transcripts. "Too recent," she said. "Need an older book."

As soon as Lill was out of the way, the boys tried to slip over to the door, but when Lily came out and asked what Lill was doing, all they could do was crouch under the public side of the barrier and pray. Prayer normally came hard for each of them, but it seemed the most natural thing in the world right then.

In a loud whisper, Lill tried to hush her friend, "Stop making that racket. You'll attract attention."

"I'm not making a racket," Lily retorted.

"You cannot walk across the floor without making a racket."

Flo Boater relaxed enough for a smile at this. She even ran her hands down her hips, enjoying the contrast to the Leather Lesbians' more ample curves. The historian, noticing, stumbled over a few words, but proceeded manfully ahead:

"Maybe not, but I'm not walking around."

Smith took a deep breath, then sneaked silently past Lily when she turned to speak with Lill, then, seeing that Jones was lagging behind, had to hide behind one of the large chairs. Bumped by Jones's unexpected arrival, he uttered an involuntary "Dammit, Jonesy,"

Lily heard the noise, but could not determine where it came from or what it was. The chairs were too far away. When she went over to look over there, they moved to a window and pulled the curtain over themselves. There was a heavy curtain where the sun came in the strongest. Lily heard this movement, too, but thought it came from the chairs. After determining that nobody was there, she concluded that her nerves were on edge. "No point in checking the vault now," she called to Lill. "I think we should clean up and get out."

"What do you mean clean up? There is blood everywhere."

"Just our fingerprints. As many as we can. We do not want anyone to suspect we were in here." With that she pulled out some tissues from Ms. Hogg's giant-sized box and started to wipe off the counter.

Lill grabbed her hand, "Cut that out. I've already explained that it makes no sense. We're going to tell the chief. Besides, you'll erase the murderer's fingerprints, too."

"If there was a murder."

"You are right about that. If I was sure that it was serious, I would have called the chief already."

"I wondered why you were delaying."

"Let me think," Lill said. She walked to the far end and sat down in one of the big chairs.

As the chair gave a great sigh, two unidentified figures slipped out of the room. Hearing footsteps, Lill went to the door, "I thought we left this slightly open."

Hearing this Flo Boater made a low moan that momentarily stopped the reading, but at her hand signal—a slight outward wave of the fingers—it resumed:

Lily rose to follow her, "I did, too." She looked carefully inside.

"Nothing there," Lill said.

"Well?" Lily queried, "What do we do now?"

"Let's think this out logically. We cannot just run off and pretend it did not happen."

"We sure cannot just stay here and pretend everything will be all right."

"Maybe we should call the chief?"

Lily snorted, "We would be in deep shit! Breaking and entering at the least!"

Slamming one hand into the other, Lill exclaimed, "Let's call DO. Anonymously!"

Lily jumped up, somewhat awkward, and stopped her from pressing in the numbers,

"Cannot, uh, can't that be traced?"

The historian's voice was giving out. He almost asked for something to drink, but he saw Flo Boater's hand signal to move it along. Bravely, he swallowed, took a deep breath and continued.

"Sure. But no point. He'd recognize our voices, and, let's face it. He would not cover up a crime."

Flo Boater grimaced at this. "You want to bet?" she growled *sotto voce.* "How can the Creep be so naïve?" Sighing when he stopped to ask what she had said, she told him to read on:

"We have not done anything."

"We have not killed anyone," Lill said. "But we're *here*, and we have no right to be here."

"He would still give us good advice." Then she added, "I just hope he tells us to beat it."

Lill removed Lily's hand and began to dial, "Who would expect a murderer to make a call from the 'scene of the crime?' Or a burglar. Besides, we're not really burglars."

"I suppose you're right. It's only breaking and entering."

"Just 'entering.' We had a key."

"God, you make it sound worse and worse."

At this point the historian stopped.

What's the matter?" Flo Boater asked.

"That's all I overheard. The boys left."

"That's all?" She raised her hands to her head. "That's all?"

"Well, I did write a sequel. I do not know how accurate it is, but it's what I imagine was going to happen."

Flo Boater cast her eyes toward heaven. She had not attended church regularly since she was a child—and not often then, truth be told—but surely there had to be a court of appeal for human incompetence and stupidity. "You wrote what you *thought* would happen?" How often, she wondered was her historian's "information" based on nothing more than that. And how much of what he had told her was really true.

"Oh, yes. It was too nice a story to just break off like that. Life is like history—there is always more to say."

Flo thanked him and asked for the text. "I'll read this later. It looks very interesting, but I do not have the time right now to listen to it all." As soon as he left, however, she grabbed the manuscript and began reading:

Smith and Jones were now ready to panic. "What the hell's she doing that for?" Jones asked.

Smith replied, "Why does she have to be so honest? What's that business about 'entering' but not 'breaking?'"

Jones whispered, "We ought to get out of here."

"Let's slip out the door," Smith suggested.

"They would see us. The hall light is on."

"Then a window," Smith said. They slipped over to the nearest, which he tried, but could not make it budge without standing up. "It's too far to jump anyway."

"Be quiet," Jones whispered, as they tried to crawl back to the door. "They'll hear you!" Then he froze, chilled, as he heard Lill speak, "DO, this is Lill. Yes, it is late. But we're in a real jam."

Lily leaned over Lill's hand to add, loudly, "A real *jam!*"

"It's this way," Lill explained. "We're in the Registrar's office."

"And the Registrar may be *dead*!" Lily added, even more loudly.

Smith and Jones stared palely at one another. But neither dared move, or hardly breathe.

After a moment's quiet Lill said, "Yes, that is 'awkward.' The point is, what do we do?" Another pause, then "No, we do not have 'permission' to be here." Yet another, longer pause. "Okay, we will not leave till you arrive. I'll see that the door is unlocked." Then a thought came to her. "DO, yes, DO, I... that is, we, won't be here. No, we won't leave. But, if you understand, you won't see us. Okay." She then turned to Lily, "If DO sees us here, he'll have to make us stay while he calls Biggs."

"Why not just call Biggs?"

"I'm no professional. DO might look at this and figure it out immediately."

"Maybe," Lily said doubtfully.

"I do not know what else to do. We'll wait like DO says. I'll block the front door open. Then we protect the scene till he gets here."

Lily was not so sure, "So, now what do we do? Sit down? Where? Every place could have a clue on it."

"Let's go out in the hall!" Lill urged.

Logically, Lily pointed out, "We can't wait there! DO will see us."

"See us? No, we're just to *watch* the scene. He doesn't want to *see* us!"

"So, where do we hide?"

"How about the women's room? There's one almost across the hall. We could watch from there. Jump, if necessary"

Lily was reluctant, "I'd rather just get out of here." But as Lill pulled her in, she shrugged and said, "Okay, whatever you say."

Flo's eyes narrowed. Somehow this did not seem invented. In fact, the whole dialogue, the whole business seemed a bit too plausible to be something those boys would say—they were, as best she could see, not the kind to tell a coherent story. Moreover, it was too much like the eye of God in the sky, seeing everything. She didn't believe in God, but she believed that the Creep was capable of overhearing almost anything.

She remembered all too well the eternity it took to escape from the building. At one point she had actually said, "God, Stanley, this place is *full* of people!"

"We'd better get out," he had panted. "The chief is the only one not here, but I bet *he will be* soon!"

Flo Boater had grimaced and led the way, but at the head of the stairs, she had stopped short, signaling Stanley to stay back. There was a noise downstairs. "Who the hell is that?" Silently she waved toward her office. As quietly as possible they went to her office door, where she impatiently searched for her keys, becoming ever more nervous.

"There's no rush," he had whispered. "There's nothing wrong with trying to get into your own office."

"Don't be silly," she had responded. "You and me alone, in the middle of the night. And the registrar's office full of people!"

With regret he exclaimed, "They'll wonder why we didn't sound an alarm."

"Just so, Stanley, just so. At the least, they'll think…" That thought trailed off into an unvoiced disappointment about what might have been. Then with a grunt of triumph, she had brought her key ring out of her purse, opened the door, and both vanished into the dark waiting room of Miss Efficiency. Without turning on a light, they stumbled their way into her office and collapsed into the stuffed chairs.

Trying to shake that memory off, Flo Boater raised the manuscript again and read:

During these moments Smith had been trying to open the window. All the while urging Jones to lift the ladder, to shove it out.

"Forget that, Smitty, let's get out of here."

"Not that way, Jonesy, you saw how many of them went out that way."

"That's because that's the way out. They won't hang around to watch the door. Besides, we can't get the ladder out without it tipping up and breaking the window."

"Somebody pulled it up!"

"Yes, but the physics!"

"What?

"It's easier to pull it up than to push it out. It will flip up and break the window."

"We could jump."

"It's a long way down. I never planned to go out that way, anyhow. Too much risk of being seen." Jones was standing now; he was thinking the situation through.

"What the hell do you mean?" Smith cried; he was continuing to tug at the window.

"Going up would only take a couple minutes, and we'd wait until nobody was around. Leaving the ladder at the window, well, that was sure to attract attention. I planned to push it back, let it fall in the bushes, then go down the stairs. There's a crash bar—for fires and such. Just push it and we're out."

"The alarm would go off!"

"So? Who'd care?"

Smith was frantic: "They'd know that someone has been here."

Jones agreed. He pulled his friend to the door: "Okay, okay, but that'd be okay. As long as they don't know it was us, it won't matter."

But it was already too late. The alarm was going off. They heard steps; they ducked beneath the counter. Someone was outside the door, but only for a moment. The lights went on for a moment, then off again. The steps resumed, going directly over to the file cabinets. Whoever it was stopped for an eternity, then went to the telephone. There were two people apparently. Was the door open or closed? Neither could remember. Smith and Jones began to look for a better hiding place—if the owners of the footsteps turned on a light and turned around, they'd be seen instantly. But hide where? Where?

What a place to stop the story! She practically cursed. Why couldn't her information be in literature? Historians don't know how to finish a tale properly! They always want facts or other irrelevant information.

Chapter Twenty

What had actually happened was as good as fiction. When Donahue saw the chief, he exclaimed, "I'm glad you could get here so quickly. This looks bad."

When they studied the bloodstains, the chief agreed, "No body?"

"No."

"What happened?"

"This is all I know. The phone call. There's the blood. The small pool, smears all over the place, though it looks like they were made later."

"The phone call. Male or female?"

"Hard to say."

"Young or old?"

"A bit of both, actually."

"Any guesses?" the chief asked.

"Oh, I'd hate to point fingers."

The chief gave him a wary look, then shrugged his shoulders, took out a camera and shot several pictures. When he was finished, he commented, "Not too much blood, really." He bent over to inspect the site more carefully. "More like a bad cut."

"True, but there is enough; and it's smeared all around, like there was a struggle."

"Smeared then, or later?"

"Later, I think, but how much later, that's hard to say. Certainly the blood was on the floor first, then somebody got into it. A fight maybe, but only a short one."

"Any weapon, that can you see?"

"That big coffee cup there has blood on it."

Biggs found a pencil to lift it up by the handle, so that he could inspect it more closely, "Biggest damn coffee cup I ever saw." He began to get out an evidence bag, "Could be fingerprints, but how would one hold it to hit someone?"

"Lots of people like oversized cups," Donahue said. "They don't want to walk back to the coffee house for refills. And Flo Boater won't allow coffee pots in office areas."

"Not in a secretary's office? Not in the faculty lounge?"

"Floyd Boater did away with all coffee makers years ago. Cost saving measures." Conversation, he remembered from his cop days, relieved stress while investigating crime scenes.

The chief gave him a puzzled look, "I thought the problem was wiring, and Lill fixed that."

"Yeah, you're right. But Flo reinstated the policy." After a moment he added, "I don't know if all the wiring here was redone. Other buildings, yes."

"Why'd she do it then?"

"She said that we need to communicate more. If we have to go to the student center or the Japanese coffee house, we'll mingle more. Also, coffee producers take away land from subsistence farming, so we shouldn't drink it."

Biggs shrugged, "I suppose," then asked, "Buy local, too, I suppose?"

"Absolutely. Only eat what you produce yourself."

The chief had to smile, "Well, there go the student hamburgers. No tomatoes while classes are in session."

Donahue responded, "Don't use gas, either. Thing is, Flo Boater loves fine coffee—the kind Max Stout serves. She used to fly to Seattle just to visit the coffee houses, and now she complains that she doesn't have the time." He laughed lightly, "I'm sure she wouldn't like what is served at any police station."

"Ironic, isn't it?" the chief commented. "I bet she wants to cut down oil consumption, too."

"Sure, especially to limit air travel." Donahue smiled at this.

The chief grimaced in return, "Isn't education supposed to help people see connections?"

Donahue sighed, "We're all pretty complex people. But some of us can see our contradictions and smile at them."

The chief nodded agreement before saying, "Back to the question. Computers were installed almost everywhere, weren't they? They'd need power."

"Um, yes. I suppose they would."

Biggs continued to study the cup, turning it around to look at the stain, "It's pretty sturdy. Maybe it could be a murder weapon. But it looks more like it was dropped in the blood."

Donahue now looked at it, too, "No coffee stains. Must have been empty. Probably washed yesterday before everyone went home."

"Or earlier, if this was Ms. Hogg's."

"I think I've seen her holding it."

"This isn't the Miss Purdy case again, is it?" Biggs asked, suspiciously, referring to what some called "the case of the vanishing vice-president" and Donahue referred to as "the disappearing elephant act."

Donahue shrugged his shoulders, "No drips on the floor outside this room. Not even in the women's restroom, where one would expect the victim to wash up. So the registrar probably didn't walk out until she had stopped the bleeding. Or was carried out."

"Just the open window there. That's strange. It's cold out."

"Oh, the thermostats don't work. When a room gets too hot, people open the windows, then forget to close them."

"That must make for a big heating bill." The chief shook his head. Didn't the college have financial problems?

"Yeah. But nobody's figured out how to stop it. Lill used to go around and close windows herself. Of course, that's not Flo's conception of her office. Oh, well, I'd hope we'd find some blood here."

"Yeah, you'd think Ms. Hogg would go right to the women's washroom." After a moment Biggs asked, "You sure it was the registrar?"

"Who else? Besides, that's what the anonymous phone call said." He then began to scrutinize the area around the blood more carefully. "The caller said 'registrar,' too, not Ms. Hogg."

Looking along the most direct way to the door without finding any noticeable clues, Biggs remarked, "No indication that she was dragged or carried out."

"It's a puzzle," Donahue admitted. "And it wouldn't have been easy to do either one."

"Miss Purdy would have been a load," the chief observed with a smile. "But she was just on a trip."

Donahue nodded agreement before asking, "What do you want to do first?"

"First we search the building, then check her home again," Biggs said. "I'll go make a call."

What happened next is best understood by reading a creative writing assignment that Smith wrote that evening for his Honors course. That is, he wrote the first draft and Ellie put it into proper English. The next evening Professor Stout had lit his pipe before leaning back to read it. It wasn't often that Smith turned in an assignment. Looking forward to employing his red pencil, Stout began reading quietly aloud—a technique he had found useful for "hearing each student's individual voice":

The Pseudo-Burglary and Its Aftermath

It was a nightmare situation. The heroes of our piece, Rip Blouse and Dart Vader, had followed the suspect right into the heart of the secret society, a place so secret it was disguised as an ordinary office building. Yet it contained something so secret that everyone wanted to find it, and the word had gotten out that it was in a particular room. Something was amiss and Rip and Dart were determined to put it aright. If this meant violating an obscure law, they were responding to a higher law—the Truth. Also Justice and the American Way.

That it came to this was never expected, and certainly Dart and Rip never saw themselves as figures in a conspiracy that reached into the heart of the Capitalist Empire. They certainly never expected to get caught. But that was their dilemma—they found themselves trapped in this office late at night. Should they be captured, their opportunity to expose the villains of darkness would be lost; and they might be expelled from college as well. Their enemies were everywhere—two members of the Fascist party already hiding in the office, hoping to capture them unaware, and the newly arrived secret police, who opened the door stealthily.

When the secret police crept into the office, weapons drawn, Dart and Rip had no choice but to hide. Their only hope was in the darkness, that the secret police would not dare to turn on the lights and allow the proletariat laboring in a nearby building to see what they were up to.

Dart and Rip managed to wedge themselves in underneath a desk, right under the noses of the secret police. To make space for themselves, they had already removed several boxes, pulling them close. It was a perfect hideout—unobtrusive and implausible. But those were its disadvantages, too.

"Rip, I can't breathe!"

"Shut up, I can't either."

"It's too small."

"You're just too big."

"I'll diet tomorrow, but get us out now."

"In a minute, in a minute."

Stout sighed, took a sip of coffee, then noted in a margin, "Good effort at dialogue, but overly hyperbolic. 'Capitalist Empire' is unnecessary—you could just say 'America'." He thought a second, then amended that to read "American empire," then scratched it out. When he had written out "Capitalist conspiracy that reached into the heart of America," he smiled and began to read again.

Dart saw the head of the secret police move past their hideout. Only a few feet away stood his henchman, his back to them. The moment to slip out was slipping away. Then heaven answered the first prayer he had uttered time out of mind—the henchman walked over to the windows. Salvation was in sight!

Stout wrote in the margin, "Good figure of speech, but it might work better as 'A god—non-existent but conveniently ready to listen to requests for minor wishes—seemingly answered the prayer that sprang from the recesses of his childhood.' It qualifies as a 'minor request' because heaven never responds to important human needs like peace and election victories—thank goodness." He had almost written "Thank God," but he had caught himself. Yes, the vocabulary of childhood was hard to keep in check. As for prayer, the right people seldom prayed much. Good thing that God rarely answered the enemies of progress. He thought of adding that to his comment, but decided instead to work it into a lecture someday, maybe at one of the faculty symposia. With a smile he resumed reading:

Rip slid the boxes away and crawled out on his belly, followed closely by Dart, whose wheezing seemed as loud as thunder. The noise attracted the henchman's attention, but when he turned back, he saw the head of the secret police coming, "I thought I heard a noise, but it must have been you."

"I thought I heard something, too."

"Let me check something," the henchman said. He looked in the open storage area, scratched his head, looked in there again, then left the room.

The head secret policeman massaged his chin, shrugged his shoulders, then wandered toward the closet.

Our heroes, who had been hiding behind, that is, in front of, the desk for several seconds now, watched the feet disappear. Dart emerged, closed the closet door, then put a chair against it, angled against the handle. Winking to Rip that this would slow the enemy down, he indicated that they should sneak out. Rip, however, made a break for it. A noisy break. Dart had to follow. The scramble of feet was heard throughout the building, but the henchman emerged from the women's restroom too late to see anything. Looking down into the darkness of the stairwell, he decided that pursuit was hopeless, then rejoined his boss.

"Where were you?" the head secret policeman asked, puffing slightly from having forced the door.

The henchman explained, "I was checking the toilets when I heard someone running."

"Me, too. Whoever it was blocked the door, shut me in. I couldn't see anything."

"Two young fellows, I think. They just flew down the stairs. They must have been athletes, maybe track men."

The head of the police smiled, "I think we know who the most likely suspects are—Rip and Dart."

"Probably so, but they weren't alone. When I checked the women's room, the window was wide open."

"Could anyone have gone out it?"

"We're on the second floor. It's pretty high on that side of the building."

The head policeman shrugged, "I phoned the registrar's apartment. No answer. So I asked a patrolman to go over there personally to check, then told our lab specialist to come here. He wasn't particularly happy to get up at this time of night."

His henchman was impressed, "You have a lab specialist?"

"He's really the day dispatcher," the head policeman confessed, "but he is a photographer on the side. We sent him to the state police academy to learn how to take fingerprints and make crime photos."

Stout wrote in the margin: "You should emphasize the power of the Capitalist Empire, not make it seem like some rinky-dink operation." He smiled, then resumed reading.

"Is he good?"

The head policeman grudgingly admitted, "Probably not. He didn't do well at the academy, but he had managed to graduate from a hick college."

The henchman responded laconically, "Who can't?" That wasn't true, but it was the conventional wisdom. Even those who knew better repeated it, but usually—as in this case—as a joke.

"Well, he almost didn't make it." Thinking he heard a noise, he looked out into the hall. When he returned, he shrugged and said, "He'll be here eventually. Let's take another look in the women's room."

As they left the hall, two mysterious figures emerged from an office and slipped down the stairs, the noise drawing the attention of the Secret Police officers. As they reached the outer door, Rip and Dart heard the head secret policeman upstairs, saying, "I guess they got away. No point in looking farther. Let's check the ground under the window. Between the mud and the snow, there ought to be some footprints."

The way was thus cleared for our heroes to escape. They did not find the secret, but no one else did. Maybe it wasn't there. When they learned more, they would be able to continue their adventures in defense of *Truth, Justice and the American Way*.

Professor Stout was not impressed by the ending: "Overly melodramatic and totally implausible. Nobody would behave in this way, and surely these two improbable characters would have gotten caught. Besides, there is nothing to 'Truth, Justice and the American Way.' That is nothing more than a ruling class narrative to misdirect the people from their true interests. Good try. Better luck on the next essay."

Chapter Twenty-One

The next morning saw Chief Biggs, Mary and Molly looking through books and files, occasionally checking with the computer, looking for clues to the whereabouts of the vanished registrar. The chief said to the women, "I really appreciate your help. Coming in on a weekend. I may be all wet in thinking that the burglary is connected to her disappearance, and the rumors about grades is somehow tied to the blood on the floor, but those are the only ideas that come to me."

"Glad to help," Mary replied, barely looking up from the computer. "You've done plenty for us. I just wish I could get into the records we need. Jenny says she can't even help us unless it's directly connected with Ms. Hogg's disappearance. And if she came, too, it would look suspicious."

"That's one reason I came in," Molly added. I'm somewhat familiar with the place. And Sal has gone back to the state penitentiary, to visit his cellmate. So what have I got better to do? Grade papers?"

The chief smiled at that. He understood the joys of not having paperwork to do.

After a few moments Molly exclaimed, "I don't understand what the problem is. The staff has a password that works during business hours. I used it on this very computer just a couple days ago, but it won't go through now. I don't think it's been changed. Do you suppose there is a timer that prevents access weekends without an override password?"

"Looks that way," Mary responded. "I keep getting that request." Shutting down her computer, she said, "I guess we'll have to just look through the paper copies. Ms. Hogg is apparently the only one with the override password."

Donahue suggested the computer center director, to which they all gave a sigh. He continued, "Jenny said she didn't know, but couldn't give it anyway, without a court order. Privacy... again."

The chief responded that he didn't want to involve the computer director. "Let's keep this simple. The fewer who know what we're looking for, the less Flo Boater is likely to complain if the story gets out." When he moved from Ms. Hogg's desk to the nearest file cabinet, he added, "We're no worst off than we were, but on my own, I wouldn't have a chance with these records—even the paper ones. It's been too long since I was in college. I don't understand how all this works."

Molly smiled, "Probably about the same as then. It's just that students don't know what goes on in administrative offices."

Biggs nodded, then pulled out a folder and read. After several minutes he grumbled, "This is all very strange."

"How so?" Mary asked.

"We've been checking records without a system. Almost at random. Nothing makes sense."

Molly sympathized, "I know just what you mean. When I first began working here, I couldn't make heads or tails of anything. Now, some is very clear. Correspondence here, professors' grade reports over there, some transcripts farther over—most years old, before we had the computer. The really old stuff is all over the place."

Mary said, "Stuff seems to be all mixed up even just here. Like a mad registrar knew where everything was, so he could always find what he needed, but nobody else could."

With a light laugh, Molly replied, "I think that's the way it was. Registrars used to complain about the lack of file cabinets. I bet they just put folders wherever they'd fit."

The chief stood back to count the file cabinets, "Looks like there are plenty now. What's the problem?"

Molly smiled, "Lill ordered new ones when she was acting president. I think Ms. Hogg was on the way to straightening it all out, but she was very secretive. Then she was suddenly gone. Since she never explained anything to me, I can't help you much."

Biggs replied quietly, "It's understandable that faculty who fill in temporarily can't possibly find everything."

"It's the financial crisis. We all have to pitch in."

"What I don't understand," the chief said, is that students have told us they had heard of grades being changed, but we can't find any evidence of it."

Molly agreed, "Oh, grades are changed all the time, legally. Everything here seems straight-forward. Maybe we're looking in the wrong time period."

"You are saying, then," the chief asked, "that the sales may have stopped when Dean Wooda drowned?"

Mary interjected, "Hard to say. Students are persuaded that it's still happening."

"You mean the demonstration?" the chief asked. "I thought that was to start it up again."

"One group," Mary said, "wanted to stop it."

"The chief's right," Molly interjected. "How can it be that grades have been changed since Ms. Hogg took over? She's too honest and she may have been watching for it. Also, we've been checking computer print-outs, pretty scattered stuff, against the professors' grade reports and grade books, again hit-and-miss. Most are in ink; they'd be impossible to change. Pencil would be tough, too. Nothing suspicious yet."

"Yes," Mary conceded, "Everything seems correct. Even the occasional typo seems to have been corrected properly; and in both directions, up and down."

Biggs commented admiringly, "The previous registrars seem to have been competent, too."

Mary agreed, "That was their reputation, for whatever that's worth. Class lists got out promptly, but who checks to see if the grades were recorded right?"

"Advisors," Molly interjected, "if the student was in their class."

"Well, yes," Mary conceded, but if the dean had been selling grades, wouldn't he have taken that into consideration?"

"Smart people do dumb things," the chief noted. "Remember Watergate, or Whitewater."

At this Mary ventured a joke, "Water seems to bring out the worst in people. Isn't there some gate with alcohol?"

At that everyone laughed and turned back to the work until the chief spoke up, "The filing system is so complicated. We can't find all the class lists. Some are where I expect them, others are not. Do you suppose some were shredded? To keep someone from comparing them with the computer records?"

"Oh, they're probably around somewhere," Molly said. "The filing system is just odd, and we had student assistants. They just did what seemed convenient."

Mary snorted, "Filing the way they put their clothes away in the dorm."

The chief laughed, then asked, "Is there any way the registrar would have noticed something strange."

"Probably," Molly said. "For example, if a student on probation was suddenly in good standing, Ms. Hogg might have spotted that. That would be true for students she knew were on probation. But she's new, so she probably couldn't say much about graduates or upper-class-persons who bought grades when they were first year enrollees."

"When they were *what*?" the chief asked.

After Mary explained that the "gender balanced term" had replaced "freshmen," Biggs began flipping through small records books, trying to compare slips of records of grade changes to the instructor's handwriting. "Is this a B or an F?" he asked.

Mary looked over his shoulder, "An F, I think. Anyway, I know the student and I'd bet it's an F."

"Did you tell the professors what we wanted their grade books for?" Biggs asked.

"No," Mary said, "but most guessed."

Biggs sighed, "The professors seem to have cooperated?"

"All except Stout," Mary sighed. "Overly-intrusive government, police state, he said."

"The rest had no problem," Molly said, pointing at a jumble of small books on a filing case, "Those are their grade books."

Biggs looked through the pile of grade books, unable to find the one he wanted, even though Mary had put them in alphabetical order. "Where the hell is this one's?" he asked, pointing to a name on a faculty list.

Mary looked at the name, "Oh, he's left town. That's last year's list." Responding to his questioning glance, she explained, "The dean usually doesn't have a full list until late in the semester."

"How about the Financial Office? They should know who's getting paychecks."

"That includes staff, too," Molly said. "But I could just go through a list and cross off…"

"Forget it," he said. "We'll get along." After a minute, he turned to Mary, "How about this one?" he said, pointing to another name.

"We couldn't find his."

Molly looked over and said, "I suspect he never had any."

Biggs marveled, "Really!"

"He just makes up grades at the end of a semester. As long as the grades are high, nobody complains."

Biggs shook his head, "A system made to be exploited."

"That's a foundation stone of post-modern philosophy," Molly growled, "power and exploitation."

Smiling briefly at what he took to be a joke, Biggs asked, "How would it have worked, say, for a weak student to get a grade raised to stay in school?"

Mary answered, "If a student failed every class, it would have been too risky to raise every grade to passing."

"If the semester wasn't an absolute disaster," Molly added, "the academic dean could simply override the committee reviewing grades at the end of the semester."

Mary objected, "But that would only keep him in school, not change his grades."

Biggs asked, "Can he change grades?"

"Yes," Molly said hesitantly. "If a student complained of unfair grading and an investigation suggested the original grade was too low."

"Was that ever done?"

"Not often," Mary said.

Molly raised a finger, "There were a couple girls last year who complained about male bias."

"Their grades were raised?"

"One letter, I think," Molly said. "From a D to a C."

"Who was the professor?"

"Stout."

Biggs laughed, "I thought he was the biggest support of feminism on campus."

"Well," Mary said, "the word on the street was that the girls deserved F's."

Molly made a face, "Word on the street was that some got A's." After a moment, she added, "Everyone else in the class did."

After this the work went on without comment, the hands of the clock moving almost around until Biggs put down a grade report and commented, "Windy sure gives high grades!"

Molly looked over his shoulder, "Yes, but he says it is compensation for instructors who grade athletes down."

Biggs shook his head, then asked, "Does the registrar ever complain when grades seem out of balance?"

Molly smiled at his naiveté, "It's a courageous registrar who would do that openly."

"Well, how about privately."

"The dean was the final authority, and, in theory, he could override faculty if his experience or hunches suggested he should."

Mary commented, "DO says that the dean should just call those people in for a chat." She then frowned. She hadn't wanted to mention Donahue.

Biggs passed on the opportunity to discuss his friend's views, "In practice, did he?"

"Not that I've heard," Molly replied, "and it's the sort of thing that would get around."

"So," the chief asked, "there's no such thing as an 'average' grade that everyone recognizes."

Mary said, "Higher education is not higher mathematics."

At this Molly sighed, "Sometimes you stretch a point for a special student, sometimes you have a great class."

"Or a terrible class," Mary added.

"Is there no way to check on that?" he asked. "Perhaps run the grade point averages of the students against the grades in any one class. That would indicate who was too hard or too easy."

Mary stopped her reading to look up, "Strange you should suggest that."

"Why?"

"DO asked the same thing. He was told that the computer couldn't do it, and it wasn't worth the effort to do it manually. Besides, some classes are just harder than others." She then frowned again. Got to stop quoting him. And, worse, he had to be right—what administrative computer can't determine something as simple as the average grades of twenty or thirty students?

Biggs thought a moment, then asked, "Now, if you recognized the name of a poor student, as you did a minute ago, and saw a good grade in one of these lists, would you be suspicious?"

Molly responded first, "Sometimes a poor student gets turned on by a particular class or instructor. But, also, there are factors we can't always know. Poor students aren't usually dumb. They just don't know how to study, or they have personal problems, money problems, or just don't want to be in college."

Mary added, "And sometimes professors are just generous." When Biggs seemed to not understand, she explained, "Compassion, or whatever. That would be the way most explain it."

"In any case," Molly added, "some students look on grade point averages as some kind of black magic."

"Especially the weaker ones," Mary said.

Biggs persisted, "Yet the students believe that grades had been raised."

Molly supported him, "I don't think the students were imagining it. Not in every case, anyway. The stories are too widespread."

"Any truth to the stories?"

"Maybe not. Maybe just wishful thinking."

"What do you think happened?" he asked. "Mass hysteria? Urban legend?"

"Perhaps, but the students were persuaded, strongly persuaded," Molly said, "that grades had been changed. Still there's no evidence yet that the dean altered the registrar's files."

"Yet the students would have wanted transcripts mailed to graduate schools and employers." The chief thought this line of investigation might be easiest, since those students' academic records would be complete and most likely permanent.

Mary was skeptical. She commented ironically that there would more likely be altered transcripts for students who wanted to transfer, but didn't have good enough grades to get accepted—getting rid of JJ and Smitty would be universally applauded. That made sense to the others, since students with ambitions to go on to graduate school probably did not need to buy grades. Even more likely, of course, were the students who only wanted a BA degree and had no interest in ever reading a book again. Confessions from this group would be hard to get, however. They might have better luck among those whose purchased grades didn't get them out of academic difficulties. Some of these individuals might be just angry enough, angry at fate, at the dean, at the world, to talk. "But," she continued, "in the records we've checked, we've not found anything unusual. In fact, the two students who are most likely guilty refused to talk with me."

Molly broke in here, "Oh, they talked, but not about what we wanted. In fact, their grades were worse than they remembered. Now, what we really need are records of the hearings where the dean and the faculty committee decided who could come back, and who had to go."

"Yes," Mary agreed. "But we can't find any thing except the names and the decision. Otherwise, the dean had kept all the records, and they seemed to be missing. He probably destroyed them as part of a 'privacy' campaign."

Molly suddenly had an idea, "If might be that he didn't enter the changes permanently until graduation!"

Biggs looked at her questioningly, "I don't understand."

Mary explained, "No one checks grades for graduates, but undergraduates might have their transcript reviewed repeatedly. So he would make changes for, say, committee action, then collect the fake transcripts and destroy them." When the others did not comprehend immediately, she explained, "What he might have done is falsified the records repeatedly for committee work, for transcripts off campus, but left the originals on file. Whenever he needed a new transcript, he would get out his old program and update it. Except maybe for, well, I don't know, but he couldn't let the record look too black."

Molly and Mary saw how this scheme might work. Awkward, but possible. Almost with one voice they said, "Cut and paste."

"What?" the chief asked.

Mary explained, "He kept the altered transcript on a diskette or something, then just updated it by copying in the latest grades from the real transcript, then pasting them in, together with whatever new grades he sold."

Molly continued the argument, "And for committee hearings, say, for whether a student was kicked out of school, he would have a doctored transcript, too, but he'd never let it out of his possession. He could destroy it right away."

"Yes," Mary explained, "the registrar isn't usually at those hearings. And he could make sure that the junior instructors on the committee…"

"Wait a minute," Biggs asked. "What do you mean, junior instructors?"

Molly laughed, "Senior professors avoid that committee… It's a terrible job. And Mary is right. The dean could make sure that none of the changed grades were from their classes." She quickly added, "There are only two or three on the committee, and the director of admissions wouldn't look for reasons to kick students out of school." Seeing Biggs's puzzled expression, she explained, "Everyone who leaves has to be replaced. It's much easier to keep them in."

Biggs thought he was beginning to understand, "So, whoever organized this minimized the risk of getting caught?"

"Mary, I think you are right. It would be unlikely," Molly suggested, "that he would erase the changes completely. Surely he might need them again. Maybe he did leave the original transcripts as they were…. Unless we've missed something."

Mary explained, "A student in trouble once would pay even more for a second change of grades."

"Absolutely," Molly agreed. "Like a drug addict. That's where the safe money would be, too. Recruiting would be the dangerous part of the scheme."

"So a duplicate program might exist?" Biggs asked. "With the altered grades? Perhaps a diskette or several."

"Almost certainly," Molly said. "Ones that could be updated as needed, but the original transcript would remain essentially unchanged so that the registrar would not notice. The most anyone would wonder is why a student with such bad grades was still in school."

"It was a clever idea, if that is what he did," Mary agreed. "Even changing only a few grades would alter, say, overall grade point averages, but not enough to be noticed."

"Perhaps you are right," Molly said. "Grades are constantly being changed here and there. Incompletes, Fs turned into Cs."

"The students didn't have copies themselves?" Biggs asked. "That's a bit surprising."

"That might be the beauty of the scheme," Molly suggested. "Whoever did it, didn't want the students showing it to other students, or to their academic advisors."

Mary was frustrated, "If the students could only give us a name!"

"Come on," Molly responded. "Who are the two dumbest students you can think of?"

Mary replied, "Smith and Jones. That's why we looked for their grades first—Molly found a copy on Ms. Hogg's desk. If the 'burglars' had been looking for that, they'd have found them if they had more time."

Donahue smiled, "The two guys who flew down the stairs sure fit their description."

Biggs concurred, "Not their first break-in." But he and the others knew they had an alibi—drinking beer in their dorms with friends who didn't have watches. The dean of students had caught them when she got up for breakfast.

"So," Mary continued, "Ms. Hogg must have been suspicious of their grades, too. But nothing seemed out of line. On probation, off probation. The most we can think is that the dean persuaded the probation committee to give them breaks."

Biggs took it more in stride, "If we had more solid information, we'd have an arrest already." He hesitated before saying, "We already have one student trying to help us." He hesitated again before adding, "I can't say who."

Hopefully, Molly asked if he was likely to find something.

"Probably not."

Sighing, Mary looked at the others, "So we really should be looking for some 'duplicate' records? Not for evidence of changing grades."

"Probably, but any evidence is good," the chief said. "A paper trail is always better than personal testimony. We can't go to court without solid proof that a crime has been committed, then we can't get a conviction unless we link it to someone."

Molly broke in, "There's the problem. The dean is dead. That is, my ex-husband is, and he seemed to be behind all this."

"He may not have been alone," the chief responded.

"Changing grades is a crime, isn't it?" Mary asked. "But who's it against?"

"It's fraud," the chief answered. "Briarpatch College guarantees that it meets state and national standards."

"So," Molly asked, "where do we find the evidence? Neither Jenny or I have come across anything here in the Registrar's Office."

"Neither of you have been here long enough to look thoroughly," Mary said, "and you didn't know there was a problem." She looked around before continuing, "Anyway, Ms. Hogg limited everyone's access to the records. And now she's gone." She looked right at the chief, "Is there any connection here?"

Biggs almost flushed, "Maybe, but perhaps no more than to that poor young woman who froze to death."

That sobered everyone up. There was a period of quiet searching through folders until the chief asked, "Could the dean have just hidden his material in his computer files?"

"Probably not," Molly admitted. "In practice, yes, he could have done that because the director would never dare snoop around, but after he died, his files were transferred to his successor, that is, to Lily."

"Even private files?"

"I don't know, but the director wouldn't let us see them without a direct order from Flo Boater."

There was a moment's silence before the chief commented, "I don't think we want to go there, or Flo Boater either."

Molly suggested, "Perhaps he used a private computer."

"I imagine someone has already looked at his computer at home," Mary speculated, "to see if there were any college materials on it. It would have been Miss Efficiency's job to check that, and I can't imagine her not noticing files with student transcripts."

The chief asked, "She'd open the files to check?"

Mary laughed, "We don't call her Miss Efficiency for nothing."

"Moreover," Molly explained, "the seal is kept here and he would have to use it on any records he sent off-campus. Most likely, like we suspect, he had diskettes that couldn't be discovered except by accident."

"What if Ms. Hogg had come across the diskettes or the program, whatever it was?" the chief asked. "The dean hadn't planned to drown. He wouldn't have destroyed it."

Molly thought that he might have hidden it too well. The important thing was to keep its existence secret.

Mary interjected, asking, "No, he also needed to get to it easily. He could just go back and forth, and hide the diskette between uses!"

Disappointed, the chief concluded, "So it probably isn't even here; and if it is, it would look like something completely innocent."

Molly shrugged and said, "Probably so."

"According to the students," the chief said, "many of the phantom grades come from the music department. Why would that be?"

Molly suggested that Jenny might know.

"You can't guess?" he asked.

"I suppose I can. Probably, first of all, because almost everyone who shows up for choir or orchestra, passes. So it would not be a surprise if a weak student earned a good grade. Maybe not an A, but a B wouldn't be uncommon."

"Makes sense," he said.

"Some of those grades could be from courses that weren't offered."

This caused eyebrows to rise, "Oh?"

"If a department isn't very well organized, it is unlikely that anyone would check grades except those from their own classes. Who would know if a 'phantom class' was written in."

"You mean someone could just type in a class, an invented offering, on the transcript, say for history, and give the student an A?"

"Probably nobody would notice," she suggested, "as long as the student wasn't a history major. Or if the grade was less than an A. Even a D counts toward graduation."

"The Creep wouldn't notice?"

"Why would he? He'd only know about the real courses," Molly said. "But for true potential to add names to a class, you can't beat music, especially choir."

"The choir director wouldn't notice?"

Shaking her head, she explained, "All he thinks about are performances, and he's desperate for male voices. Everyone gets an A."

"Everyone?"

"A few B's," Molly conceded.

Mary objected. She knew about the choir. Some students got C's—the ones who were absent too often to learn the performance music.

Biggs thought about this for a moment, then asked, "Do a lot of athletes take music?"

Molly gave him a dirty look and responded, "Not many." She was not a supporter of college sports. They took up too much time, took students out of classes, encouraged the wrong values.

Mary felt the same way, but she thought about the question before answering, "Frankly, I don't think we know who is an athlete and who isn't. We don't go to the games, we don't read the *Penprick*—not the sports articles, at least."

Biggs wondered quietly if she just didn't notice see their impressive muscles—most women did, even those who disliked body-builders—but he only pointed at the printout, "What are all these grades? There seem to be quite a few A's.'

Molly looked over his shoulder, "Those are independent studies. A few A's there wouldn't attract attention. Weak students avoid that kind of work, so that's probably the standard grade."

Mary joined them, "That's a lot of independent studies."

Biggs came over to look at her book of entries. Turning over the pages, he noted, "The same thing seems to have occurred in Philosophy, Math and Biology."

Molly, who had moved to another file cabinet, observed, "Philosophy, yes, but they would be unusual in biology except for senior projects."

Biggs scratched his teeth with his fingers, a habit that helped him think through difficult problems, "So this would be an easy way to sneak in a high grade that would even out the poor grades?"

"Smith and Jones had independent studies," Mary exclaimed. "They said it was because they didn't like to get up for morning classes and professors didn't want to teach in the afternoon."

Molly looked at the transcripts for Smith and Jones, "There are some independent studies here, but mostly C's."

Mary almost laughed, "A C in an independent study is practically an F."

Molly interrupted, "That's not so important as that the classes are not from current faculty. We'd have to track these former professors down and hope they kept their grade books. Or find the grade lists here." Looking at the file drawers, she added, "Good luck."

Mary began to shake with excitement, "You're right! It wouldn't be necessary to change a grade. Just add a good one!" She then hurried over to rummage through a file cabinet. "God," she said after a moment, "I thought these were the lists for two years ago, but nothing. Just empty folders."

"Suspicious," the chief said.

Molly put her hands to her mouth, "So that's what has Sal so upset! He had wanted to look at the grades over the past two years. When I heard about it, I was going to check. Just not right away—you know how worked up he is. I thought they'd surely be here."

"Maybe Ms. Hogg?" Mary suggested.

Biggs thought for a moment, "You wouldn't show those records to Sal? In spite of your being engaged, more or less."

Molly stepped back to stare at him, "No. That wouldn't have been right. It was a confidential file. The registrar would blow her top! Besides, I really didn't know that was on his mind, so I never thought…. And we're really not engaged…yet." She paused for a moment, looking at the others looking at her, then added, "Besides, he didn't know I worked here, so he never asked."

Everyone sighed and went back to work, even Molly, who burned off her agitation by going through stacks and stacks of grade reports.

Biggs flipped through some of the other folders in the file cabinet, "There are quite of few of these empty. Molly, you said there were more independent studies than you think likely. How many does the average professor do?"

"Usually no more than one or two a semester for anyone, sometimes none. Perhaps a few more in philosophy than in math, but there has been so much turnover in those departments that nobody can remember more than a year or two back. I wouldn't have suspected so many."

"I see." Remembering that Molly had been working there only part-time for a short while, he discounted the estimate. Meanwhile, he studied the list she had given him.

Mary leaned over the chief's shoulder, trying to count how many were offered by any one professor. "I remember my first year of teaching. I was so busy getting preps done that I had no time for anything else."

The list looked long, but her count never came to more than a couple for each professor.

Donahue overheard this as he came through the door, "I'm still that way. But I'd make time for something else if I could."

Mary waved him off, but Donahue joined them anyway and asked, "Have you found out who got the altered transcripts?"

Biggs gave the list back to Molly, together with Smith and Jones's transcripts, "Maybe we can photocopy these? We can ask the professors later." Then he turned to Donahue, "We are still trying to figure out if anything was changed."

Mary pointed to another folder, "All these seem to have been students in the honors program."

"We don't have an honors program," Molly protested.

"Right, but Stout has his unofficial program. These are all his students whose grades have been changed."

"I'll check on that," Donahue promised. "I'll need copies."

Molly nodded and took both folders away.

Mary was meanwhile musing, "I know a couple of the students on that independent study list. I don't see how the late dean would have made any money out of them. As for the honors students, I can't see the dean trusting Stout not to check their records."

"Very good points," Donahue agreed.

Putting a finger to her lips, Mary wondered aloud, "The dean was very clever. What if he changed nothing but the total number of hours and the grade point average? That way he wouldn't have to change a grade, but the student would still graduate. Computers don't make those kinds of errors, so who would ever check?"

"That's an idea," Molly agreed. "Unusual, but possible." She pulled out a large spiral book filled with student grades, "We would have to add semester by semester."

"Why is that?" Biggs asked.

She smiled, "Our system has no subtotals, just semester grades and a grand total. The only registration system in America like that."

Donahue agreed, "The perfect system for a very simple fraud."

Mary disagreed, "But wouldn't one of the registrars have noticed?"

Donahue looked over to Molly, who explained, "The same reason that the computer center director didn't. 'Someone' in the administration decided to buy a non-standard system that did was simple, easy to work with, but difficult to check."

"Someone?" Mary asked. "You mean Dean Wooda!"

"Yes, my late husband. Floyd Boater wouldn't have known anything about computers!"

The chief pursed his lips, "That makes sense."

"And Floater was basically honest. An idiot, but honest. My ex-husband had to have done it."

At this Mary became excited, "You're right Dean Wooda was the first person on campus to buy a personal computer. He was very proud of it!"

"That's the one Miss Efficiency checked?" Biggs asked.

"Got to be."

The chief asked Molly, "Did he show you how to use it?"

"No," she answered, "He was even more secretive about that than about the rest of his life."

"You were suspicious?"

"I learned enough to divorce him! But it was all about him, nothing about computers."

After a moment, she added, "At the time I thought he was only interested in girls, women, whatever. It never crossed my mind that he was after money, too."

The chief persisted, "He still might have let something slip. Something that makes sense now, though it didn't at the time."

Donahue elaborated, giving examples, "Some off-hand comment, some joke."

Molly thought about this, "He was obsessed with privacy rights. Protect the students from snooping. Also, no bells and whistles. But he didn't talk with me much. You'd do better to ask his girl friends."

The chief shook his head, "I doubt that Flo Boater would cooperate." He barely hid his smile, then asked if she knew any names.

Molly shook her head, "He was very discrete."

Donahue agreed, "Not much chance, certainly not with President Boater, especially since she might have been involved." He then offered to follow the lead up, but the chief said he'd check it out himself—"That could be awkward for you if the dean found out."

This gave Molly an idea, "Flo once said that she was trying to learn how to use a computer. I don't like her, but I think she's smart enough to master anything she puts her mind to."

Following that line of thought, Donahue suggested, "If she was personally involved, that's an additional reason for her wanting to get rid of the evidence."

The chief agreed, "I'm surprised that she didn't break into the office, too."

Donahue thumped his finger on the desk, "Something's wrong here. If she had heard that grades had been sold, she would have started looking into it. It's unlikely that Dean Wooda would have left that evidence where someone might have stumbled onto it." He paused to look at the others' faces, "We do know that she is aware of the problem, and the number of ways to change grades is limited. If the program, whatever it was, diskettes or something else, wasn't in the dean's office, it was probably here." In his mind the burglary hammered for attention, shouting "Remember the break-in at the Financial Affairs Office." But he was determined to let the chief bring that matter up, not do it himself.

Mary disagreed, "This would a good place to leave it if the registrar didn't know. Especially if the dean was in it alone. His office would be such an obvious place to search. What if he became ill? He was a hypochondriac, and his replacement was more likely to stumble onto it than one of the new registrars.

"He did become ill," Donahue reminded her, "when he was in South America."

Tentatively, Molly offered a suggestion, "Maybe Ms Hogg was blackmailing Flo Boater."

Donahue doubted this, but wondered to himself how it all tied into the blood on the floor. Not seeing an obvious answer, he tried to get back to the earlier idea by teasingly suggesting, "Maybe she was another of Dean Wooda's mistresses."

"Fat chance," Biggs quipped. She had been heavier in those days.

Molly missed the joke, "I don't think so, but with him, who knows?"

That was the chief's thought, "We could ask her, if we knew where she was." Technically, this was not a lie, and he wanted to keep his secret secret.

Donahue was not so discouraged, "We have the blood, we have suspects."

Mary was less optimistic, "But no body. No relatives to compare DNA."

"That's really awkward," the chief agreed.

"There's a mother, I believe," Mary said.

"I've checked every Hogg in the state," the chief replied, blushing somewhat that he couldn't tell her the truth. "Even the marriage records, in case she changed her name."

"Looking wider?"

"There are more Hoggs in this country than you can imagine. And I can't ask the Feds till I have more proof a crime has been committed."

"You should be able to check by computer," Mary exclaimed. "After all, this is 1997!"

"Well," the chief replied, "there are a lot of things we *should* be able to do."

Donahue thought a moment before commenting, "What's really awkward is that none of the suspects had much time to get rid of a body!" It wasn't Ms. Hogg, so it had to be somebody else. He thought for a moment that they should check the woods. Who could tell what was under the snow? No, there had been thaws—colder in many ways than snow, but the wood was really too small to hide another body. But not all the snow had melted, and now there was ice on top. Bottom line: whose blood was on the floor?

"Which suggests," Biggs stated, regarding the presumed body, "that the registrar is still alive, at least until last night." He was relieved to step out of the swamp of fibdom or whatever it was when you didn't want to tell the truth, but he wondered if the others might be concerned about there having been another murder. He needn't have worried— they gave him fake smiles.

Mary made light of it, "With a giant headache." After the others smiled in recognition of the previous break-in, she added. "Like Miss Purdy, and no more dead. Just wanting privacy until she can thinking her situation out, or to escape." Then Mary sat down with folders in her lap, only to wish suddenly that she had a cup of coffee. The pseudo-breakfast had been too small even for her.

Biggs had meanwhile responded, "Probably no headache worst than mine."

Molly shook her head in agreement, "or mine."

Biggs and Donahue said their goodbyes, wished the ladies luck, then exited. Ahead of them, at the top of the stairs, they espied the historian, his head in bandages. With a nod at each other, they moved swiftly toward him, but he fled down the stairs with a surprising speed. Donahue started to chase after him, but Biggs laid a hand on his arm to restrain him, "Let him go, one of you might get hurt on the stairs. They're slick. We'll pick him up later."

Donahue reluctantly agreed, saying only, "That was really strange!"

Biggs, with determination, responded, "And I intend to get to the bottom of it. Later."

After a moment he added, "I want to know why is always showing up in unexpected places."

In the afternoon Donahue reached the chief by phone, "What did you see in snow where the ladder was set up?"

"Yeah, interesting question. As you remember, we couldn't see much by flashlight, so I put up the tape to keep people off and came back in the morning."

"Yes, not much time for sleep."

"No, I didn't sleep, my calls to the state police took up what remained of the night."

"And what did you find?"

"Ah," he sighed. "Sherlock Holmes couldn't have made sense of it. All sorts of people had been there. And some I hadn't remembered from last night. I had put tape up, but people just ducked under."

"Oh?"

"Yeah, remember we thought we saw three or four, maybe five different footprints?"

"Yes. I wish we'd taken more pictures."

"I used up all the film. Not many pictures left on the roll, anyway. The last thing I expected to need when I got the call was more film.

Well, I took pictures this morning and made some casts, but the footprints were probably more from curiosity seekers than suspects'. Probably students."

"Up that early?"

"Or still up that late. Word travels fast on a college campus, and too few use common sense. Nothing there, at least right now, that I could go to court with."

Dean Threshold found Ms. Hogg's ancestry within hours. His membership in the Latter Day Saints' genealogical society—obtained quickly, thanks to a Mormon friend who had a friend in Salt Lake City—provided her birth certificate, then baptismal records, then names and addresses of relatives. What he didn't understand was why the Creep asked him for this information on behalf of President Boater, and why he didn't seem to understand that associate deans report to the presidents rather than to chairs of Social Science.

Ellie told Smitty that she intended to transfer to Zenith.

"What?" he exclaimed, "Why would you want to do that?"

"It's pretty dull around here. Nothing going on."

"Nothing going on at Zenith, either, except big-time football and you hate that."

"More excitement, more…"

Smith cut her off, "Just hang around, there's a lot going on right here. Stuff you don't know about!"

"I suppose you have another documentary planned?" she sneered.

"You just might be surprised." After a moment, he added, "Just give me a few days. We might have another murder!"

She laughed. "Next you'll be telling me to stay around for you." As he blushed, she gave him a wink and said, "That's a better argument than a murder."

As she walked off, he stood there, shaking his head. "Women! Who can understand them?" And where had *this Ellie* come from?

Chapter Twenty-Two

"We've got a problem," the dean said to Flo Boater, after he closed the door, making sure that Miss Efficiency was not listening in.

"A new problem or an old one?" she snorted.

"A bit of both," he replied, uncomfortably. "It's Flechadoro."

"Who?"

"Golden Arrow."

"Ah, our Indian friend. What does the 'noble Red Man' want now?"

"I don't know exactly." Having said that, he sloped into a chair.

She sighed, then stood up. Moving back to the window, she looked out on the lawn. In spite of the frost and mud where students had made shortcuts, it had obviously been well cared for. "Stanley, you've got to be more efficient. Now, just look outside. Jay had no money to repair the lawnmowers, nobody available to ride them, the leaves came down every day in November and December, and, nevertheless, he got the job done. You have to learn to do the same."

He hesitated, "I'm not sure that this is the same kind of problem."

She turned to face him, "What kind of problem are we talking about?"

"Flechadoro knows we were in the Registrar's office."

"He knows? What do you mean 'he knows'?"

"He was there. He saw everything."

"I didn't see him. I saw Smith and Jones, then those two others, and heard Donahue and Biggs." She stopped to shake her head, then added, "I can't get past the feeling that the Creep was there, too. Just like I could smell him."

The dean objected, "You're exaggerating, Flo. Nobody bathes more than him, and he never wears any kind of scent."

"Nevertheless, nevertheless. I have my reasons—I'll explain another time. But he had to be there."

"Just like Flechadoro!"

"No. Flechado, or whatever his name is, couldn't have been there. There wasn't room enough for anyone else."

"He insists he was there."

"Tell me the conversation, word for word."

"That's a bit difficult. I couldn't admit that we were there, so it was a bit awkward to say that I hadn't seen him."

"I understand that. But how did he see us?"

"He says that he's one of the 'First People'. If he didn't want to be seen, we couldn't have seen him."

"You believe that?"

The dean rubbed his chin, "It could be true. It was dark in there. If he stayed in the shadows and moved about, we'd not have seen him."

"And what does he want?"

"I don't know. I couldn't ask him without admitting that we were there."

"He didn't give a hint?"

"Not really. I think he just wanted me to know that he knew."

"Softening you up?" There was a sting in her voice that she knew would not pass unnoticed.

"Maybe. It might have been just a bluff. We had very right to be there, but I'd rather not explain why we didn't turn on the lights."

Down in the coffee house, Donahue was talking with the chief. "I've just had a conversation with Flechadoro."

"Interesting?"

"Very, but also very mysterious."

"How so?"

"I think he knows where the dean kept his records. He may even have them."

"He said so?"

"No, it's the way he explained the dean's system."

"How did it work? We haven't been able to figure it out."

"Very simple, basically. The dean had access to the central computer. Probably a predecessor got it very early, years ago, probably a fall-back position in case something happened to the computer center director, with an automatic notification if the password changed."

"So that would have been sent on to the new Dean Wooda, too. Including the override password."

"Probably, but it's not clear that he knows he has it."

"So," the chief thought aloud, "he has the ability to change anything he wants."

"Yes, but there is always the danger that the computer center director could determine who has been in the records and what was done."

"So, it would be dangerous for him to make changes?" It was not a question.

"That's right. He seems to have been indirect. He would get into the system to check the student's grades, make a copy, then make out a change of grade slip and then leave it in the IN box. That way, if anyone checked, there would be a paper trail."

"Whose name would be on the request?"

"The instructor's. And that was the clever part—apparently he made Xerox copies of every professor's signature. He had a knack for counterfeiting them, so if the professor asked, there would be the proof he had given the instructions."

"Did that ever happen?"

"Not that we know. But since he picked people who were unlikely to check, it's unlikely that the matter ever came up."

"Why keep copies of the transcripts then?"

"That's the really clever part," Donahue explained. "If he ever did have to go into the system, he'd know what had to be changed."

"Was there even a diskette? If so, why?"

"To make fake transcripts, perhaps, then use the seal to emboss it. He could just drop the envelope in the OUT box for the staff to mail."

"I never thought about the seal. But you're right. Without a seal, it wouldn't be official."

"The seal is kept in the safe."

"Locked?" the chief asked.

"Supposedly, but TBCW."

"Ah, yes. The Briarpatch College Way. Nothing is ever quite normal here."

"In any case, the late Dean Wooda probably knew the combination."

Biggs pondered the matter for a moment, "But that's not what Flechadoro says?'

"Not quite. He suggests that the dean knew the combination, but not how to print transcripts. Special paper, a printer that only the registrar had a key for."

"You believe that?"

"Only partly, but I'd like to believe that the scam was limited to on-campus."

"On-campus?"

"Yes, without fake transcripts having been sent all over the country. Recalling those, well, that couldn't be kept quiet."

There was a moment of silence. Finally the chief asked, "Flechadoro can prove that?"

Donahue shrugged, "He was too canny to say so specifically, but I believe he's seen everything there is."

"He won't give it to us?"

"I doubt it. He'd have to explain how he got it." While the chief thought, Donahue added, "I suspect that the stuff is still right here. Our Native American is suspicious of us, even suggested that it wouldn't help to get a search warrant for his room or car."

"Interesting," the chief mused. "That's quite a lead. All we have to do is find evidence that might no longer be here. On the other hand, it might just be a ruse, to persuade us to give up. Then he could come back later."

Donahue agreed, "So we might as well keep looking."

"Uh, huh."

"However, until now we didn't know what we were looking for. If Flechadoro is right, it's a folder, a folder with a diskette."

The chief wrinkled up his face, "That's got to be a big folder. Hard to hide something like that where no one will stumble upon it." He paused before asking, "Is he just funning with us? Or does he really know something? Maybe something his uncle told him. You did say something about an uncle once, didn't you? An uncle close to the dean?"

"Well, he's not trying to be funny. He wants the college to flourish. Otherwise, it's not worth anything when he gets title to the land. On the other hand, if we get discouraged by following a blind path, the grade scandal may just vanish."

"Good points," the chief responded. "And we might get our hands on the folder, he might have emptied out all the good stuff."

"Could be," Donahue agreed. "As I remember, the tribe that sold Manhattan to the Dutch didn't live there. They were willing to take the money, though."

The chief laughed, "If there'd been a bridge, I imagine they'd have sold that, too."

Mary and Molly were meanwhile studying the newly cleaned floor. "Not a sign of violence now," Mary said.

"Cleaner than ever. Jay does a great job!" There was note of pride in Molly's voice. "The police work is all done, so now no one would ever suspect anything happened here. Even the ladder is gone."

"But no clue as to where Ms. Hogg is?"

"Her body, you mean?"

"Whatever," Mary responded, then winced at her colloquialism.

Chapter Twenty-Three

The next morning, Sunday, Donahue was in the registrar's office. It had taken Chief Bigg's most persuasive argument to get the president's permission to come back for a second day—if he had to get a search warrant, the entire town would know about it within hours, and within days the press would be swarming over the town, asking everyone in sight about the newest scandal—the break-in, the blood on the floor. One thing would lead to another—speculation about Ms. Hogg's absence, the young woman in the wood. It would be best just to allow the chief to look through the office, to see if he could find any clues. As long as she did not have to pay overtime to anyone who helped get this over with quickly! The chief avoided that problem by asking Molly, Mary and Donahue to volunteer their assistance, then let the president believe that only members of the police force would be helping. He knew that, since it was a weekend, she would not come into the building and stumble upon them. Presumably, neither would Stanley Wooda, who had let it be known that he had "personal matters" to deal with. While some hoped that it was an interview for another job, most guessed that it was a hot date in Zenith.

Flo Boater might have decided differently on the chief's request if she had realized that the only potential crime—the blood on the floor, the ladder indicating a burglary—would hardly have persuaded the local judge to authorize a search through personal records. He had been watching *Law and Order*, which could only recently be viewed in Middleville—cable had finally arrived for those with money. He was now persuaded that he was manning the last bastion of resistance against the forces of big government.

Molly and Mary concentrated on finding a folder large enough to fit the description given by the "anonymous tip," but within a few hours they had concluded that none existed. If it contained copies of pages with faculty signatures, it would have been sixty to a hundred pages long, more if it had multiple copies of student transcripts.

After checking the last file cabinet on the lower row, Mary straightened up, put her hands on her hips, and said, "I bet he cut and pasted, then Xeroxed." Stretching to work out the stiffness, she said, "That's what I'd do. It would cut the pages down to one or two. Much easier to hide." She then asked herself what DO would say about this idea—and decided that he would say that it was logical; moreover, that it could be put in the middle of something totally innocent, while the transcripts could be kept on a diskette. She frowned when he said exactly that.

Molly and Mary returned to Plan A, working together on looking through the hundreds of diskettes, sorting out those that looked suspicious and checking them; they weren't finding anything. Donahue discreetly found employment going through recent requests for transcripts and changes of grades. He became so absorbed in this mass of minutiae that he barely heard the women talking and eventually he lost all awareness of their conversation.

Mary made the last comment that he remembered, "I had no idea we had so many records!"

Molly had agreed, "Three of everything, it seems. No wonder registrars had a space problem."

"And no two organized the same way!" Mary pointed to two open ledgers from different years, and exclaimed, "It looks like each registrar changed the system."

Molly looked over her shoulder and agreed, "And in the end, each was so frustrated, he left."

"She," Molly corrected, "the last three, at least, have been women."

"Comparison is almost impossible."

Molly pointed to the papers from the folders she had been looking through, "On these handwritten grade sheets I can't tell a B from a D!"

Mary looked and agreed, "Or an A."

Molly asked what one letter grade was. Shaking her head, Mary said that she couldn't tell, "That could be an F or an A."

"It would be easier if we could use the computer."

"Yes, but we can't ask the computer center director to give us the password. Not without the registrar's permission or an order from the president. I just don't understand why Flo Boater wouldn't do that."

Molly didn't understand, either. After all, this was a special circumstance. Mary agreed, "The chief told her that as far as he could tell, the person connected to the ladder and the blood was dead."

"I bet he didn't ask her?"

"Oh, I imagine he did."

"And what did she say?"

Disgusted, Mary mimicked, "Show me the body and I'll give you permission."

"And the computer center director, I bet he wanted a note from the registrar."

"He did! He did!"

Molly laughed, "Fat chance of that!"

Mary laughed, too, "I can imagine Ms. Hogg saying, 'You'll have access only over my dead body'." After a moment, she added, "But Flo has a point. If we're looking for clues on the break-in, there's not much reason for our needing to look at transcripts. And the chief didn't want to tell her too much about someone selling grades." After a moment, she added, "I bet she already knows. I'd half bet she already has the diskette. Just laughing at us, ruining our backs here."

Molly put down the volume she was looking into to turn to Mary, "I never so much wanted to see a person dead as Ms. Hogg! And I don't even dislike her!"

Their work had practically ceased when Chief Biggs entered and, looking around to assure that they were alone, exclaimed, "Good news!" He had a bag containing a thermos and Styrofoam cups.

Exhausted, Molly said, "We could use some."

Mary, equally tired, agreed, "We sure could!" Donahue silently indicated his willingness to take a break. With a glance at one another, they marked the places they had left off and took seats around the registrar's desk, pouring themselves coffee.

The chief, in contrast to their phlegmatic mood, was practically dancing, "The registrar is alive and well."

The trio woke up immediately, "No!"

Molly corrected herself, "I mean, great!" And Mary added, "That's what I meant, too." Donahue merely asked how he knew?

"Her mother was ill, so she left in a hurry."

"Without telling anyone?" Molly asked. She remembered now that the mother was a domestic tyrant, who was constantly calling her daughter home to tend to her, though usually her ailments were imaginary. These outbursts usually took place during semester breaks or in the summer, so that only Ms. Hogg's vacation trips were ruined. This one, coming when the college was in session, was so unusual that the registrar had to take it seriously.

"But why didn't she tell anybody?" Donahue asked. "And why couldn't we find her mother?"

Biggs explained, "She says that she sent a note to the president. Delivered it personally to the office." He glanced around, with a smile, "Her mother lived too many hours away to come back, and she expected that she'd get a call if she was needed. Her mother spelled her name Haug. Never changed it officially, but if you wanted to find her through legal records, that's how it's been for years and years."

"Why didn't Miss Efficiency tell us?" Molly queried. Anything left on Flo Boater's desk was certain to end in the trash unread. Miss Efficiency, on the other hand, would have taken care of everything, or Dean Threshold.

"She was out," the chief said, "just for a moment maybe. The door to the president's office was open, so Ms. Hogg looked in. Some painters were there, putting covers over the president's desk so they could re-do a spot directly overhead. One of them said to give it to him, that he'd put it on the desk with the bill when they finished. So she assumed Flo Boater knew about her trip, and that it was all right with her." He paused before explaining, "The bill apparently got sent right down the hall to the Finance Office, but one of your assistants didn't realize there was a note attached. Anyway, it was set aside until the end of the month, that is, until a few days ago. That's when someone first noticed the note. It was sent back to the president, unopened. Dean Threshold read it only the other day."

"Dean Threshold?"

"Yes. Apparently that's the way it works. He put it on the president's desk with other important stuff, but she hadn't read it. When he heard of the apparent murder, he was worried, so he called my office this morning."

"Why didn't anyone see that the note wasn't part of the bill?" Molly complained. She had worked hard to train the staff to be more observant, more public-friendly.

He shrugged. "A little memo held to the back of a bill by a paperclip. Probably assumed the two were, well, connected." Seeing her disgust, he tried to consol her, "Just one of those things."

Mary was mystified, "So Flo really didn't know?"

"Good question," Biggs agreed. "I'm not sure. When I told her about the blood in the registrar's office, she didn't even seem surprised." After a pause, he added, "What bothers me is that I'm not sure she has read the note yet."

Mary's brows furrowed, "You mean that if she knew where Ms. Hogg was, she would have known the blood wasn't hers, but she didn't seem to know?"

"That's right."

Molly was outraged, "Why didn't you take her in for questioning?"

"I've arrested her twice for murder," he explained, "and each time I've had to let her go. One more time would seem like harassment. I am not doing to do anything now until I have solid proof. Rock solid proof."

At this moment Donahue entered and asked, "What did the lab technician find?"

"Lots of fingerprints. Too many. And DNA test on the blood can only be done at the state lab. That might take several days."

"Can't you match the blood type with the registrar's medical records?"

"It can't be her blood anyway. The registrar is alive and well and at her mother's."

Everyone gave a sigh of relief. Thank God, not another murder.

After a moment's thought, Mary asked, "If you knew the type, C or A or whatever, that would at least reduce the number of suspects."

"Yes," Molly agreed. "Narrow them down to those with the right blood type."

"Then see who is missing!"

The chief sighed, "We can't just rummage through medical records. Privacy issues."

"Privacy? Again?" Mary exclaimed. "You are looking for blood types, not STD histories!" She had forgotten that only a few days before she and Donahue had "discussed" this very issue, with her taking the chief's position, only more strongly.

Donahue sighed, then walked over to look out the window, "Snoopers always find an excuse for reading records."

Biggs explained, "The rules restrict everyone. I want a conviction to stand up, so I'm taking no chances." He then stepped back involuntarily as Donahue dashed by him and out the door. He moved over to the far window, trying to see below, at the side door used most often. After a minute he turned back to indicate with his spread hands that he had no idea what was going on.

Mary wanted to debate the privacy question more, but nobody else was interested. So the group stood in a circle, looking at one another, shrugging their shoulders, then waiting. Finally, Molly sat down, and so did Mary.

Minutes later Donahue returned with the historian in tow. He pulled him in front of him, then thrust him down onto a chair, "I think we have the 'missing person'."

It was the Creep, who began squeaking, "This is outrageous, just outrageous! By what authority does this, this "person" *haul* me here? He almost *tore my ear* off!"

Donahue bent over him, "Just assisting law enforcement."

The historian, who only now realized who was present, tried to shout, "Chief Biggs, arrest him! Arrest him!" His effort being more a whine than an exclamation, he took a deep breath to try again.

"Calm down. Calm down," the chief said. "That's right. Now, listen. Dr. Donahue is right to bring you here. He was just doing his duty." He resisted the temptation to remind him that he had run away once—better keep that in reserve.

Donahue shrugged, "I asked him to come along quietly. But he tried to run, so I tackled him—my football training came in useful. Scuffed his suit a bit—his Sunday best, he said. But since he would not come voluntarily, I pulled him in."

"By my ear! By my ear!"

Donahue ignored the complaints, "He was standing right at the door, almost out of sight, listening to us. He said he 'didn't mean anything.' But when he saw that I saw him, he ran down the stairs like a deer. He almost got away again, but his lungs gave out." After a moment, after catching his own breath, he added, "Look at his head. Quite a bandage."

Molly marveled at it, too, wondering who had made it, but all she said was, "The wound is too far from his ear to…."

Donahue interjected, "He's not hurt." There was no sympathy in his voice. With that he stepped back and allowed the chief to take his place standing over the bandaged man. "What are you doing here on a Sunday?"

The Creep squealed, "I saw the lights. I came to investigate." After a moment he added, "The door wasn't locked. I was going to call President Boater if I saw anything illegal going on." He rubbed his ear gently.

Biggs leaned toward the historian, asking calmly, "How did you hurt yourself?"

The historian looked around in panic, but when he tried to stand up, Donahue pushed him back into the chair, "Not so fast. We have some questions."

Biggs studied him until he was certain that he had his full attention, "It is time to talk, and I must warn you that anything you say can be used against you in a court of law."

There was a moment of shock, followed by, "I know my rights, and I don't want a lawyer." He frowned before explaining, "Lawyers are just expenses without doing anything."

"Where were you Friday night between eleven and midnight?"

"I was at home with my mother!"

Donahue shuddered in spite of himself, thinking that this explained much. But somehow he couldn't bring himself to believe him.

"Were you still up," the chief asked, "or already in bed? It was late."

"We were waiting until midnight to call my sister in Europe. The time difference is such that midnight here is early morning there."

Donahue was taken aback, "You have a sister?" He almost said that everyone assumed that he was an only child.

"She chooses to live as far away as possible. Mother and I cannot understand it."

Biggs absorbed that information before asking, "Any special reason to call?"

Drawing himself up to his full height and looking the chief squarely in the chin, the historian responded, "It was her birthday, as if that is any of your business."

The chief sighed, "I guess we can check that out pretty easily."

Donahue pursed his lips, "He could have hurt his head earlier."

With a slight frown, the chief agreed, "Might have." He then turned to the historian, "Now, how did you injure yourself?"

"It's too hard to explain." He shrank back down into his chair.

Biggs sighed, "Try me."

The historian squeaked out an explanation, "I was sitting at this table in the coffee shop, yesterday morning, minding my own business, when the two boys at the next table came over. One hit me with a huge bottle of carbonated beverage, a glass bottle, and they both walked out, laughing."

"Strange," the chief commented.

Mary grimaced, "Not to me." As she looked around, the others nodded agreement.

"Did it break?"

"No," the historian replied. "But it made me bleed."

"Much?"

More indignantly, he said, "It made me bleed!"

The chief shrugged, "Did the boys say anything?"

The historian wheedled now, "Only something peculiar, 'Now he can listen to the birdies for a while, not us'. I wasn't listening to them. What do football players have to say, and who cares which professors are 'hitting on girls'?"

"I get the picture," the chief said. Then he asked, "Why were you here yesterday?"

"To complain to the president. I heard about the burglary and thought she would be in her office. She wasn't."

"And when you saw us, you ran."

"Of course," he replied, straightening up as much as he could, "everyone knows that policemen are dangerous." Seeing that the chief was about to laugh, he added, "Donahue here, Donahue is proof of that!" Then he fingered his ear again.

The chief, turning to the others, said, "I think he can go now." With a gesture toward the door, he instructed the historian to leave. "Good grief," he uttered as the historian flew past, "I didn't think the man could move so fast."

"I didn't think he was a man," Molly snapped. "Nutcase."

There seemed to be nothing to say after that. Donahue offered dejectedly, "Now we have no suspect at all."

Biggs was even more discouraged, "I don't even have real evidence of a crime. Just some blood on the floor."

The semester break came, but there was no break in the case. Ms. Hogg conducted the business of her office by telephone, but she did not come to Middleville. Spring was approaching, but the end of winter did not have its usual allure—for her. For everyone else, it meant getting away from confinement in dormitories, classrooms and local bars.

In this short week set aside for recharging emotional and physical batteries, students head for beaches, lounge around in front of their parents' television sets, or gather in groups for idle amusement and alcohol. Faculty members who remain on campus use the days without classes and committee meetings to prepare for those tasks which lie immediately ahead. Most tire out after a couple days. Mary C was bored out of her mind.

Flo Boater, in contrast, was energized. She had come up with an idea: "Stanley, that course you made Donahue agree to teach next year, that 'Mexico before the Aztecs'."

"Yes, he taught it last year. It was his predecessor's course and he hated it, so I got the Creep to put in on his schedule again."

"Yes?"

"I thought that if he ever contemplated moving on, this kind of class just might encourage that thinking."

"Good plan. In fact, that fits right into my thoughts."

"Which were?"

"You know how we have been discussing, how the faculty needs to work on students' oral skills?"

"Yes, some of them can't get a full sentence out."

She agreed, "That's because in the dorms they speak in sentence fragments. And I had an idea about that. This is it in brief—that we have a pilot program, one where the students do all the talking, give all the lectures."

"That's a seminar. We already have those. Though usually the professor does most of the talking."

"Well, I'm not thinking about a seminar. A large class. Each day a different student in charge! Not conversation, but real lectures."

"That would drive a professor crazy! He'd have to spend a lot of time with each one, to get them ready. Five minutes they can do, but not fifty."

"That's the point. It will drive Donahue right out of Briarpatch!"

"Um, what about library resources?"

"We don't have any," she exulted. "That's the beauty of the plan, at least as it applies to this course. Donahue will have to give individual tutoring to each student. It will wear him to a frazzle."

"Exams.? Will the students learn enough to take an exam?"

"Probably not!" she exclaimed. "And that's perfect, too, because if we insist on using national exams we can blame him for any classroom failures. If half the class flunks, all the better."

"Interesting. Now, how do we justify this, uh, pilot program?"

"I've already spoken to the Creep, who ran it past Stout. Apparently, it is cutting-edge educational philosophy—*Learning Through Doing*. Some Ivy League universities are doing it, using graduate assistants. Donahue can hardly say no."

The dean smiled, "I'm sure he will appreciate the honor. And to being compared to graduate assistants."

Chapter Twenty-Four

When classes resumed, Flo Boater was back in her office, settled comfortably behind her desk. Though having reflected happily on her successful meeting with trustees and potential donors, she was still somehow uncomfortable. The contractors must have changed something she couldn't identify, but could sense. The feeling of discomfort was palpable. In fact, she remarked about it to Stanley Wooda, who answered that he had the same feeling.

"But I don't see any reason for it," he added.

As Flo Boater saw her visitor at the doorway, she stood up to wave her in, "Come on in, Mary." Then, perhaps realizing that her tone was too sharp, she added, "I was hoping to see you." There was something in the way she said it that made it seem as though Mary had asked for the interview.

"Yes?"

I hear that you have still been asking questions all over campus about grades being sold."

More meekly that she intended, Mary answered, "Yes. Chief Biggs asked me to help him."

"What the police do, that their business, unpleasant as it might be. But you were hired to teach Spanish, not to spread rumors that could hurt the college's reputation."

"But it's not a rumor!"

"It *is* a rumor, a nasty one," she growled. "And I'll have no more of it, you understand."

"Yes, ma'am," Mary responded, despondently. Her head was still hanging when she left. Miss Efficiency said goodbye, and she made no reply.

Almost immediately, the phone rang. Miss Efficiency straightened quickly in spite of herself. Jumpy, apparently. Something was indeed in the air. It was Jones on the phone. The secretary understood the importance of treating him well—his father, or his uncle, was a trustee—maybe both, they having that strange name even she couldn't pronounce—on and off, but every time he resigned, three times now, one of them, he or the other one, had been talked into coming back. (The president hadn't explained that very well. Like she didn't want her to know.)   Jones wanted to come over with Smith—again an important person, it being well-known that Smith's girlfriend, if that was what she was, was money-bags personified—no one had realized this until the break, when Ellie's parents had called to see where she was. When Miss E reported that she believed Ellie had gone to Europe, they announced their intention to come to Middleville themselves and see what was going on; money was not a problem, they had said, and they'd hire detectives to locate her if necessary. Miss E had talked them out of that, but she had reported the matter to the president and the parents hadn't phoned again. So, if Jones and Smith wanted to see the president, Miss E would find a place among the appointments, and swiftly. On Flo Boater's orders she cancelled a visit by a committee of nurses who wanted to institute a program to identify and cure STDs (sexually transmitted diseases, a new term replacing the awkwardly gyno-phobic "Venereal Disease"), penciling in a time for them a month hence, but warning them that if might take even longer, since President Boater was a very busy person; meanwhile, they could talk with the Dean of Students. "No, the dean does not have the authority to create such a program, but she will talk with the president about it, or leave her a note. A final decision can be made next month, and the program started in the fall, if it seems like a good idea that the college can afford." She then called the next person with an appointment and put them in the spot vacated by the nurses. With a sigh of relief at a job well done, she called Jones and told him that they could come over right away if that was convenient. It was.

Thus it happened that only a few minutes after Mary left, the two well-known students entered the president's office.

Insolently, Jones said, "We got the money."

Smith was equally superior to the situation, "Yeah, we got it."

"What are you talking about?" Flo Boater responded.

Feigning surprise, Jones mocked her, "You can't have forgotten."

Smith was more matter-of-fact, "The grades."

Flo Boater dismissed this, "Better grades aren't for sale now. Never were."

This statement caused the boys to smile. But Jones wasn't interested in her declaration, anyway, "We don't want no better grades." He was doing his Brando imitation, preparing the way for his friend's predictable next pearl of wisdom.

"We want worse ones," Smith explained.

She thought it was a joke, "With you two it's impossible to get worse grades."

Jones was now almost pleading, "We want the fake grades off our transcripts."

"The cops are everywhere right now." Smith indicated that he had dealt with the police before, but never when sober. "And now there's that Indian."

"We can't afford to be caught up in this." Jones had just attended a class in which Prof. Stout described American jails as places no sensible person would want to spend a night in. Donahue could have told him the same thing, but he would have emphasized personal responsibility, whereas Stout asserted that the individual was helpless against the organized powers of the corporate state, so that even the innocent use of harmless recreational drugs had to be done very quietly and discreetly. Jones preferred to believe that Stout knew more about policemen than Donahue. He wanted to be a victim, not a criminal.

Flo Boater, unwittingly in agreement with Donahue, asked, "Why didn't you think of that earlier?" What she wanted to ask was what had motivated him to attend a class.

"We was too young." It was Jones's best Bowery Boys imitation. No bad, either, he thought.

"We was just kids." Smith's effort was less successful.

"We was led astray." It was *West Side Story*, without the music. And without the excuse of poverty and racism. And the bad grammar was totally intentional—the boys lacked the natural rhythm of the New Jersey petty criminals. They wanted to sound like Rocky, perhaps, but only came off like what she imagined Sylvester Stallone's nerdy cousin might be.

She began thinking out loud, "To correct a transcript, so to say, back to its original state. I think we can work something out."

Jones immediately asked, "Do you want the money now?"

She responded cautiously, "No. I just need more information." After a moment she added, "I think Chief Biggs is looking into this. We can wait to see what he finds."

Smith looked at Jones, who then said very nervously "I can't raise any more." The Philly swagger had vanished.

She look at them, disappointed—she knew that their parents were loaded—then said, "I'm not shaking you down. I just want it to be safe for everyone." All at once, she gave a jump, then asked, "You aren't wearing a wire, are you?" She hurriedly sprang up, demanded that they stand and patted them down quickly. Shocked, they made no protest even when she touched what they thought she should have left alone. Satisfied that they were "clean," she dismissed them, saying, "I'll look into the problem. Dean Wooda will contact you."

Smith and Jones hurriedly left. They had barely started down the stairs before they were laughing to themselves, "'Never were changes, but we'll correct them', and feeling us up. Chief Biggs, what a crock! He can't prove anything."

Stanley Wooda entered, "What was that all about?" He decided not to repeat the boys' comment about the "dumb bitch."

She ignored the question, "Stanley, we've got to find that diskette. I think we are still in business, and better off than ever. This time there will be less risk."

"I don't know. Flechadoro is onto something, too. I think we're getting ourselves liable for blackmail from every side."

"Listen, Stanley, if we get the diskette, or diskettes, we can take care of the students we can trust."

"Trust? Smith and Jones?"

"Okay, not *trust*, but *handle*. They think they'll tough stuff, but mention jail and they fold."

"Jail? Why were you talking about jail?" Stanley Wooda asked, a light film of moisture forming on his hands and brow.

When Flo Boater had finished recounting the conversation, it took her a full minute of laughter to calm down sufficiently to wipe off her tears, "When I checked them for a recording device, their wieners shriveled up to Vienna sausages—or less. Real tough guys." She really didn't want to lose the time telling the story a second time, but it was a great stress reliever. "Almost as much as," she thought, looking at her young dean's sleek body, but she recovered in time to rephrase her words—almost panted out for lack of breath—as, "Stanley, what brought you in here just now?"

"Oh, nothing important, just a minor bother."

One of her eyebrows raised, "A minor bother?"

"Yes, it's Irene. She's ready to roll on the Co-curriculum thing. Mary and Donahue weren't getting anything done, so last week I gave her full authority. It hardly took her any time at all."

"Irene? I thought you'd take the leadership on that."

He hesitated, "I thought you'd want the cre…, that is, it would be more persuasive, to the faculty, coming from you."

"Me?"

"You talk with the trustees. Don't they have to approve it?"

She sighed, "You're right, in a sense. But I've had no time for that. In any case, we have to clear it with the faculty members who count. Have you done that?"

"Stout's aboard, the Creep has no objections, and Donahue thinks it's a dumb idea."

She smiled, "That 100% in favor of doing it." In the back of her mind was a memo to Donahue that his failure to cooperate would be considered when contracts were offered. She knew she wouldn't use the excuse to fire him now, but every negative report in his file would help build up a strong case for doing so later.

Stanley Wooda was cautious, "What do we do next?"

She smiled again, "Well, it's a curricular matter, so you should propose it."

He countered, "No, the CCPDC is a student services matter, the new student dean should handle it." He could see the proposal was a career breaker.

Flo Boater read his mind, "So she would be ready to take the blame, while if it worked out, you could take the credit." When he blushed, she continued, "Good enough. I'll tell the trustees about her proposal. You tell her that she's made it." When she saw his mouth open, she smiled again. "And I'll send a note to DO and Mary that they are on her oversight committee."

Donahue stood up when he saw Mary enter the coffee-house. He hadn't seen her since the semester break, so his smile was especially wide as he said, "Hello, Mary."

Her reply was disconcerting. She didn't sit down, but stood there facing him when she lashed out, "What the hell you think you were doing, DO?"

He didn't know what to say, since he didn't have a clue what she was talking about, moreover, he was very aware that several students had interrupted their own conversations to turn toward him and await his response.

Putting his hands up in a defensive posture as if she was ready to strike, as seemed likely, he suggested they sit down. This small change in their physical relationship calmed Mary sufficiently that they ceased to be the center of attention—except for one emaciated colleague who remained half-hidden behind his newspaper. His head had long since healed, but he no longer sat on an aisle.

"Okay," he said. "What's this about?"

She glared at him, swallowed hard, and asked, "What did you tell your mother?" Obviously, this was only the start of a longer discussion. It was also the continuation of many previous talks.

"Not much," he started to say. "And about what?"

"Not much! Apparently more than that."

"She wanted to know why we weren't engaged yet."

"And," she interrupted, "what did you say?"

With an effort to calm her by hand gestures, he continued, "I said that you weren't ready."

"That's all?" she asked suspiciously.

"Scout's honor," he said, raising his right hand and three fingers.

She leaned toward him before spitting out in clipped syllables, "Then why did your mother call my mother?"

"I didn't know she did," he said, horrified that she would mix into his personal life as though a man in his late Thirties couldn't handle his affairs alone. Though in their case, a courtship now two years old, he obviously couldn't.

"Well, she did, and now I have my mother on my case wanting to know..., well, you know what she wanted."

"What did you say?" Donahue responded, suddenly hopeful as well as interested.

"Same thing I tell you," she stated firmly, "That I'm not ready."

"And she said?"

"Same thing you do," she admitted, "I'm not getting younger and if I want children, I'd better get going. Okay, those aren't the words you use, but the thought is the same."

He sighed, then said, "Children aren't everything."

Indignantly, she responded, "She said that, too! Companionship and all that—that you don't know what you miss until you don't have it." It wasn't in a pleasant tone, either.

His eyebrows went up. She saw it and continued, "And you can't know what you're missing till you have it."

When Mary calmed down, tired out from her failed tirade, having forgotten the best lines she had prepared and frustrated for not being able to remember them, Donahue asked, "What did you tell her?" She didn't say anything, but just stared at her hands. He went on, "Am I bad company?... Bad habits?"

She looked up again, "She asked the same questions."

"And?"

"No," she admitted. "Nothing to complain about."

She caught her eye with a hard gesture till that she looked up. "Just nothing to get excited about, either?"

"DO," she said, "You'll be a great husband for somebody else."

"Is there somebody else?" When she indicated, no, he asked "Just what do you want?"

"I don't know. I'll know it when I see it."

With a sigh, he suggested that she might watch *Gone with the Wind* again. When he saw that she didn't understand, he did not try to explain.

A full minute passed before she spoke again, "It's even worse than you think."

What could be worse, he asked himself. But all he said was, "How?"

She shook her head, "She's coming here. To talk with us."

"And" he asked, not clear why that would make a difference.

"Your mother is coming, too."

"Uh, oh," he answered, "That changes everything."

She nodded. She hadn't met Donahue's mother, but she had heard about her. Mary had one more question, "How did your mother get my mother's telephone number?"

"I don't know exactly," he answered, "but how many Canarys are there?"

"You mean she just phoned till she found her?" She asked, unbelieving. "You'd have to know my mother," Donahue said. For the first time in a year he was optimistic.

Mary was meanwhile considering a return to the Amazon headwaters. Could Flo Boater arrange a grant as swiftly as she did last year?

Stanley Wooda almost shuffled his feet as he spoke to the president. Even though he was on the phone, he was momentarily intimidated. "Boss, I need some money. Cash money."

"Stan, I thought we agreed you'd call me Flo."

"Uh, boss. I'm in a bit of a rush right now."

She hesitated, "Okay, what's this all about?"

"I need some green, untraceable."

"I don't know," she responded. "Can't you just put in a request at the business office? Make up some story. Reimbursement for travel, maybe?"

"Molly's in charge there. She'd want receipts." Besides, he thought, she'd insist on writing a check.

"Molly's there?"

"Yeah, for a couple months. She said you knew all about it."

Flo Boater hesitated again, "That's a problem I hadn't expected."

"What do I do?"

"Tell me what it is."

"Uh, you said there were some things you'd rather not know about."

"Oh," she replied. "Well, I guess you'll just have to figure something out on your own." That's what deans are for, she thought.

"Ok, boss," he replied reluctantly. "I'll see what I can do." When he hung up, he was sweating again. Cold, but sweating.

Flo Boater, on the other hand, was merely shaking her head. "Boss, he said."

Chapter Twenty-Five

Biggs sat down laboriously, eyed Donahue carefully, and in an anxious voice confided, "I've got a problem."

"A big one?" Donahue asked.

"Couldn't be worse. My lab man messed up the fingerprints and the DNA evidence."

"Messed up?" This seemed incomprehensible. Fingerprints were easy. Anyone with some powder and Scotch tape could take them, and modern equipment was almost foolproof.

"The fingerprints are all smudged and he lost the DNA samples!" Apparently even the newest techniques could be botched by a determined fool.

"Why'd it take so long to find this out?"

"He thought I'd be angry, so he just delayed. He hoped I'd find another way to break the case, so the evidence wouldn't be necessary."

Donahue commiserated, "You said that he was really only a photographer." What else could you expect?

Biggs conceded the point, "His pictures weren't very good either. No better than mine." After a pause, he looked up at Donahue and asked, "So, what would you do in this situation?"

"Me?"

"You were a big city cop."

Donahue reflected a moment on his experience, then was sure of his answer, "Bluff. Act like you have the goods."

"And see who cracks?" The chief was not confident, but he said, half to himself, "Why not? If you don't have the cards...."

"You bluff!" With that, he smiled at the chief, who grinned back.

Stanley Wooda entered the president's office with a grin, "Good news."

Looking up, Flo Boater responded, "We need some."

"First of all, I've dealt with Flechadoro."

A frown crossed her face, "How? I thought he had you by the balls."

For an instant, his face darkened, then he responded lightly, "Easy. I persuaded him to major in Off Campus Studies."

She smiled, "Like you did."

"Yes."

"But," she asked hesitantly, "the lawsuit. The claim against the college. What about those?"

"The lawsuit will take at least three years. I persuaded him that while he's waiting for the lawyers to finish, he might as well get a college education."

"What about having seen us in the Registrar's Office?"

"I don't know about that. Not for certain at least. But he's decided not to go public."

"He's changed his mind? I thought he'd blackmail us for all we're worth."

"Maybe we're not worth enough," Wooda said, immediately regretting having said it.

"What does that mean?" she snapped.

"I meant that there is a price for him to pay, too. That's my guess at least. He would have to admit being in the building illegally. We could bring charges and expel him. That might have some influence on the lawsuit."

"I hadn't thought of that. Could we still bring charges?"

"There's no proof he said anything, and he didn't even make a threat. He just told me that he knew, but he didn't say how." He screwed up his mouth before adding, "I get the feeling that he knows much more than he lets on."

"Inscrutable red man," she commented.

He almost laughed, "That's what my Japanese friends used to say about Americans. But he's very 'scrutable', I think. He thinks he's got us. I just don't know how."

She reflected on this, "The grades?"

"Maybe, but more likely our being *you know where*."

"I suppose he could have seen us through the windows." She looked out onto the lawn and tried to imagine how that might have happened.

Stanley's mind worked faster, "On the second floor? Only if he was an owl."

"It's really not a very high second floor on that side. The courthouse was build into a hill, the old front was much higher. Remember, Jay cleans my windows with that ladder that was found *you know where.*" Second floor, not the dormers to the attic.

"It's a long ladder. But it doesn't matter. Our Indian friend's going to be out of the picture. He's going to finish here at Briarpatch, but he'll be off campus the entire time. Except maybe his senior year, and I can fix that if I have to."

"You couldn't persuade him to transfer?"

"Too expensive, he says." But Stanley Wooda's face indicated his doubts. "I'm sure he qualifies for all kinds of scholarships elsewhere. More important, I think, is his claim on our campus. His being here is sort of like a Spanish conquistador planting a flag in Queen Isabella's name."

Flo Boater half-smiled, then thought a moment, "Can he afford it here?"

"I offered him the same scholarships I got. That's the only way I could get him on those off-campus programs."

"Oh, a free ride!"

"Everything included."

"Can we afford that? The budget's awfully tight."

"We have to afford it. Besides, I know how to milk the feds to the max."

"Oh?"

"Native American, science student, international education…"

"I didn't know he was in science."

"He didn't either until I explained it to him."

"When does he leave?"

"Usually not till the end of the semester, but I arranged to use the grant you had just promised to Mary. He can teach about Native American science to the poor people of the mountains. I've enrolled him in an intensive language program over the summer. Almost on site. He'll pick up the language fast."

"Innovative! Does he know anything about Native American science?"

"Not much, but he's headed for home to learn all about it."

"His classes this semester?"

"Incompletes. He can finish them by mail."

"The professors agreed to this?"

"I'll handle the grading."

"The professors agreed to that?"

"After I revise his essays and exams, they'll be happy to pass him."

"Risky, isn't it?"

"They'll return the papers to me. Once grades are turned in, I'll shred everything. In the meantime, they won't be able to contact him, and as long as he doesn't get an A, they won't think about it again."

"Has that ever been done?"

"Oh, I talked them around. It's like the newest craze—internet classes—where professors and students never meet and nobody knows who writes the papers."

"How about the required courses? The faculty's sure to be sticklers there."

"As dean, I can certify that the transfer courses meet the requirements."

"Ms Hogg will agree?"

"Right now, with only temps there, I can arrange it."

"Temps? What about Jenny?"

"I've sent her back to the Music department."

"Huh? What will she teach? I thought her courses were given to temps?"

"No, she was doing the Registrar bit as an overload. Just a bit of extra pay. Not much of that, either."

Flo Boater thought about this before asking, "What if our 'Indian friend' doesn't pass the courses? Will he have to come back here?"

"Hey, I'm going to rewrite his papers, and if he doesn't send them in promptly, since he's an Off Campus Studies major, the committee that looks at grades, whatever we call it now—they changed its name again—will be understanding about extensions. Some of them believe that First People are always discriminated against, you know, by faculty who don't understand about the different concept regarding time and due dates, they'll be understanding." He smirked, "I can keep him eligible."

"Hm, I don't know." She scratched her nose and studied him sideways.

He hurried to explain: "Ms. Hogg won't complain, if she ever shows up. He was beginning to get on her nerves, always asking for credit for 'life experiences' and the like. Off campus will mean out of her office."

"So, she'll go along, too." There was some skepticism in her voice.

"She or her successor. I'll take care of it. Anyway, I can explain how he made the rumors about grades for sale go away. She'll appreciate that."

She breathed a sigh of relief, "Stanley, you're a marvel."

"More good news. We can sell the revised grades to the two students."

Flo Boater turned back to gaze outside, her chin in her hand, "Interesting idea, now that Golden Arrow is out of the picture. But how? We don't have the diskette."

"No problem, no danger. I think I figured it out. I studied the boys' transcripts very carefully and came to the conclusion that we've misunderstood what happened."

"Oh?"

"Usually the original transcript wasn't changed at all. Only in cases such as Choir, maybe, which couldn't be detected."

"How did that work?"

"Apparently, there were *some* changes made. For students the late dean trusted. But Smith and Jones were just too..."

"I understand—too...."

"In their cases, he probably did arrange for some C grades in choir, but otherwise he just printed up fake transcripts to show them, took their money, then shredded the fakes."

"How did you figure that out?"

"That was the easy part. Smith said something about having seen the changes—that's why he thought he had an improved grade in chemistry—but I could not find that on their transcripts. Just the suspicious choir grades, which the choir director admitted he couldn't remember one way or the other. Lots of students sign up, then stop attending and forget to drop. The only chemistry grade was an F."

"Smith went along with that? Just seeing the transcript? He didn't want a copy himself?"

"He asked, apparently, but went along with the dean's explanation that it was safer for everyone not to have any copies in circulation... just in case he needed to make more changes later."

She nodded, "Nice touch." After a pause, she asked, "And that was okay with Jones?"

"Must've been. He didn't complain. And I doubt either one checked the official transcript."

She thought for a moment before asking, "That transcript. Everything matched up with the rest of the professors' reports?"

"Yes. No problem."

"You're sure?"

"I had Ms. Efficiency contact the professors." He then smiled broadly, "Anyway, I gather that Donahue and Chief Biggs checked it all out, too, and couldn't find anything wrong."

She nodded approval, "Very smart, very effective." She paused to think, "The professors won't talk? To Donahue, I mean? If they think of anything else."

"I don't think so. Since everything seemed on the up-and-up, Ms. E was able to make it sound routine. And nobody is asking about the grade rumor any more."

"Not even the Creep?"

"Oh, him. Yes, but he's not getting anywhere, and he's being very, very discrete, like he wanted to become dean himself or something equally silly, so he won't say anything until he has real proof." Actually, the historian hadn't wanted to talk about anything. He had just clammed up.

"Clever," she said. "So even if DO and Biggs find out about the calls, there won't be any evidence of the late dean indulging in hanky-panky." Realizing suddenly how that might sound, considering his social habits, she changed the subject. "This *not changing* their grades, but making certain that there were no changes. Now, will that keep them in school? We can't afford to kick them out."

"Apparently he merely overruled the committee, said that he saw promise in the boys that others overlooked."

"Overlooked?"

"That's the best I can figure out. Out of prejudice, probably. Some excuse. But all the minutes say is that he overruled the committee. The point was, apparently, that in their cases he was merely exercising the legitimate authority of an academic dean."

"How'd you learn that?"

"Oh, the Creep was on the committee."

"He knew about it?" she asked.

"In a sense. He knew about it, but he didn't know he knew it." He saw doubt crossing her face and explained, "I didn't ask him. He volunteered the information. That the dean routinely overruled the committee. He had the minutes to prove it." He paused to smile, "He said that if he were dean, that sort of thing wouldn't happen except when absolutely necessary."

Flo Boater smiled.

"In short," Dean Wooda concluded, "we're in the clear."

"If I understand you," she asked slowly, "nothing illegal took place?"

"Not with them. The original grades are still in the computer. I checked."

She smiled, "So we can just tell them that we've made the changes?"

Grinning in response, he said, "And *take* their money!"

Putting a hand on his shoulder, she whispered, "Stanley, I think you have a great future in higher education."

Unbeknownst to them—a great phrase, Donahue always thought—Ms. Hogg was coming to the same conclusion: that nothing illegal had taken place; the stories were what most stories were—more imagination and hope and paranoia than reality. Moreover, if there was no scandal to be uncovered, it was safe for her to return to campus. At least, until the end of the academic year. But, she had decided, she was going to relocate. Why stay in a place where you might be murdered? Where people break into your office, when you see a ghost at night. And surely there was a job nearer to her mother. Or farther away. Maybe she could become an insurance agent? That surely had to pay better than being a registrar, and far better than being a part-time historian. There was that interesting job on an Indian reservation that a young student had told her about. His tribe was being ripped off by the government, he said. It needed someone skilled with handling records to assist in its lawsuits. There might even be a case involving Briarpatch College. That would be... a... a delicious irony.

She might even be living so far from her mother that communication might be difficult. Or impossible. Who knows? She might even lose a little more weight. She'd taken off another ten pounds during this ordeal. Maybe she could get down to high school weight, or junior high, or, maybe grade school. Anyway, she felt better than ever before. And she'd feel even better away from Middleville. Anyplace that wasn't Middleville.

Any place, too, where people wouldn't ask about the young woman found dead in the woods. They had, she remembered with a blush, been pen-pals, email style. It was almost a romantic relationship, one that was getting too torrid for Ms. Hogg, who had tried to break it off. Her trip off campus had seemed like a good opportunity to put some distance between them, but her silence had only panicked her friend, causing her to head for Middleville. Without money or car, she had gone the only way she could think of—by train. Apparently she had fallen in with a man, or men, who plied her with whiskey.

When Ms. Hogg heard of it in the papers, she was too embarrassed to tell anyone about it. And, anyway, what was there to tell? A sordid little love story that wasn't even a real romance? The gossip would never end. Maybe no one would ever find out, but the historian's mother was already asking questions. It was a matter of time.

There was also the deceased's connection to Professor Iva. He knew that she had learned of Briarpatch College through her brother, his cellmate. When a delegation of college officials had visited the prison to discuss expanding the number of classes for inmates, Ms. Hogg had represented Briarpatch—Dean Wooda was addressing a political rally for young people of color. Sal's cellmate had spoken briefly to her, mentioning his younger sister's interest in writing with a sympathetic woman. He was the only family she had, and almost nobody knew that he existed—he certainly didn't want the other children in the home to learn about him. Would she write? And now Sal was trying to find out what had happened, to inform his friend, who still had twenty years to serve.

Sal had been reluctant to tell anyone, fearing that it would ruin his last small chance to be re-hired, but at least had confided in Molly. How could they ever get married if he had to carry such a burden around with him?

Molly, of course, informed the chief. He quietly checked, then informed the state police that the matter had been cleared up—accidental death, from prolonged exposure to freezing weather while hitching a ride on a freight train. The state police, upset by reporters hounding them on another matter, chose not to share the information with the press.

Our world, Donahue told Mary, was small indeed. Almost too small to contain any secret, to which Mary replied, "Too small not to keep quiet as many as we can."

Chapter Twenty-Six

The next day Biggs, Donahue, Flo Boater, Stanley Wooda, Lill, Lily, Jenny, Mary, and Smith and Jones met in the president's office. All were seated except Biggs and Donahue. All were nervous, but all were trying in various ways to appear otherwise. Most looked around at the new decorations, trying to remember how it had looked before and wondering how much the renovations had cost and where the money had come from.

"You may be wondering why I brought you here," Biggs said, then felt very awkward. He sensed that he sounded like a television lawyer of his youth, Perry Mason, or that he was replaying earlier interviews. Nevertheless, he pressed on, "But if you are wondering, you are an exception. Everyone else knows why."

Flo Boater chose to assert her authority, "I would like to know why *I* am here."

Biggs explained calmly, "President Boater, there are several reasons to have you here. First of all, you *are* the president of this… excuse me, I almost say 'hick college'."

Flo Boater snarled, "That's a slander."

He smiled, having achieved one goal, to distract her. Raising a hand in apology, he proceeded to say, "and therefore, you have every right to know what is happening."

With a pseudo-sneer spoiled by a slight tremor in their voices, Smith and Jones asked simultaneously, "Why us, then?"

The chief was accustomed to adolescent bravado, "Let's just say that you have an idea why. And it's not in your interest that I explain it to everyone." He replied quietly, smiling at watching them slouch back into their chairs.

Mary clapped her hands, "Oh, this is just like on TV!" This embarrassed the boys more than anything the chief could have said, and as he became aware of this, he smiled once more.

Chief Biggs explained, "We don't have the DNA match on the blood yet, but the fingerprints indicated that four of you were in the Registrar's office." He gestured toward the dean and president, then as his finger moved toward Smith and Jones, their faces took on a mild blush.

Flo Boater shrugged, "Our fingerprints could have gotten there at any time."

Stanley Wooda hurriedly added, "Yes, we had reasons to talk to the registrar, too. Ours could have been left there days ago." At that he started to rise, but found the chief blocking him, "Don't leave yet."

As Stanley Wooda sat back down, Jones pointed to Lill and Lily, "Why are they here then?"

"Yeah," Smith said. "We've got privation rights."

"Privacy rights," Jones corrected.

Biggs smiled again, "Let's say that they know who was in the registrar's office that night."

"Oh," Smith responded.

As Wooda tried to hide his head in his hands, Jones spoke up, "Come on, it was too dark to see who was there."

The chief moved a step closer and warned, "That sounds like a confession!"

Jones's response was insolent, "You haven't read us our rights!"

As if on an ill-planned cue, Smith added his opinion, "Yeah, we can say anything we want and you can't use it."

Biggs coughed, "If you knew more about the law, you'd keep quiet."

When the boys hesitated, Flo Boater spoke up, "Listen to the chief. This is the time to remain silent."

Wooda interrupted, "Yes, shut up!" Then, seeing the others stare at him, Stanley became noticeably quiet himself.

Biggs looked around the group, "I want to leave the question of grades for sale until later. Right now I want to know whose blood was on the floor of the registrar's office."

The boys looked at one another, they shrugged.

At that instant there was a knock on the door. Donahue opened it cautiously, then led in Sal Iva, Donahue, "This is the man we've been looking for." Pulling up his sleeve, he pointed to a scar. Looking around, he shrugged, then turned back to Professor Iva, "Tell them your story, Sal."

"*Certo, certo. Un incidente.* I tripped and cut my hand."

Donahue explained that the ladder extended, and he had fallen on the guide for the extension."

Molly was holding Sal's other arm, "I told him to come in. It was just a matter of time, and we were actually on the way when DO saw us."

Sal confirmed that, "*Si, é vero.*" With Molly's help, he slumped onto a chair.

"OK, son," the chief said, standing over him, "Tell us what happened."

Sal coughed twice, then began to speak, "When I phoned the registrar weeks ago, she wouldn't help me. She seemed very distracted and had no interest in my questions at all. *Mai!*"

"That was before she disappeared?" The chief suspected that he had phoned from prison, which might have frightened her.

"I suppose. *Non lo sapevo*, that is, I didn't know before I got out that she was gone for good. All I could reach were students who didn't know anything."

Molly spoke up, "I have some information." As all heads turned to her, she hurriedly explained, "Ms. Hogg explained it to me on the telephone. Her mother was ill, and.." She turned to the president to explain, "That she couldn't reach you to tell you her plans."

"Couldn't reach me?" Flo Boater asked. "I never understood that. She could have left me a note."

"She said that you always throw notes in the trash. But, more important, that if she told you what she was doing, you'd tell her to leave it alone. So she told Miss Purdy what she planned—to contact students who seemed to have purchased grades. That was last semester, before Miss Purdy left. But more recently her investigation were getting nowhere, just frustration, and you kept putting off her appointment. Then her mother got sick."

"Ah," the chief exclaimed, "that explains a lot." The explanation had been jumbled, but he understood the key points.

The president and dean looked at one another, but it was Sal who voiced the question, "Explains what?"

Molly explained, "That she had the same suspicions everyone else did, only earlier. That, in fact, your call confirmed them."

This caused the chief to ask, "But why didn't she tell someone?"

"She tried to get a meeting with the president, but Miss E told her to write her a note, and she guaranteed she'd place it on the president's desk. When Miss E wasn't in, she just gave it to the carpenters to put there."

Flo Boater came as close to blushing as she knew how. No one had told her about that—maybe they had just sent another note?

Sal thought aloud, "I didn't know Miss Pig was worried. I thought she was just blowing me up."

Biggs nodded, "And then?"

"After dark I was walkin' by the building. I saw this ladder there, a folding ladder. A long one. I looked up. Not right up, but from the sidewalk. The window was open, just a bit; cracked, I think you say. Maybe a couple centimeters. I realized it was *her* office, and it looked like someone had used the ladder to go in, then—*forse per negligenza*—let it fall. It was like, like God had left it for me." He looked around, asking with his eyes for everyone to believe him. "Telling me to find out what was going on."

"Rubbish," Flo Boater snorted.

"Let him speak," the chief said.

"If there were *ladri*, burglars maybe, I'd catch them. If not, I'd look up my old grades. Anyway, *per forza*, I climbed up, came inside, pulled up the ladder... so it wouldn't fall again. I folded it back so that when I left, it would look like I was carrying a stepladder out." He paused, "But, you see, once I didn't see nobody there, I saw how awkward it look. It was big."

Biggs interrupted, "You turned on a light? To check?"

"*Non sono tanto...fesso!*" He paused to think, "I mean, a light would have been foolish."

"You weren't there to check the records?"

"Later I realized, *dopo*, I could have done that. I could have messed up my footprints in *la neve*, too. But then all I could, all I planned was that nobody would know I was there. *Nessuno, meno que tutto Molly.*" He stopped to look at Smith, who was nudging Jones.

Donahue turned to look, too. He heard Smith whisper something, maybe "Flechadoro."

Sal Iva ignored them, "But it didn't fold properly. So when I turned around after locking the window, I didn't see that it was partly open. It was dark. I tripped over it… "

Loudly, Wooda said without thinking, "So did I!" When everyone turned to look at him, he looked behind him, too, to see who had spoken; it was a gesture that had often worked in the past, provoking laughs, but was ineffective now. Biggs, however, calmly let him be for the moment. Speaking to Sal, he said, "It was dark in there. Go on, son." The encouragement worked.

"When I got up, I was a bit *confuso*…" He stopped to touch his head, like he wanted an aspirin. "My arm hurt. I was…."

Molly interjected, "dazed," after which he continued, "So after I stopped the bleeding, when I tried to get around that *cosa maladetta*, that thing, I fell down again. I grabbed at the table, only this time whatever was on it, some other thing, hit me on the head." When Biggs held up a plastic bag with the coffee mug, he continued, "Yes, *eccolo*, I think. That bled, too. I found something to put on the cuts. Tissues of some kind. When the bleeding stopped, I went to the washroom downstairs."

"It wasn't much of a cut on his head," Molly interjected. "See, you can't even tell where it was."

The chief ignored her, directing his next question at Sal, "Why not the women's room? It was close."

"It was the women's restroom! I could clean up in the men's room. When I came out, I went back upstairs. That is, I started. I was still *sulle scale,* on the stairs, when I thought I heard someone behind me, so I duked."

"Ducked," Molly said.

"Ducked into the women's room there."

"Upstairs?" the chief asked.

"Yes, upstairs. After I got upstairs."

"That's why we didn't see any blood in the toilet there," the chief noted. "You had washed off downstairs."

"Yes," Sal continued. "I put the tissues in my coat pocket. When I realized that whomever they were, they were coming up! They would discover me."

When he halted to look around at the company, Molly took up his story, "He could still hear them downstairs, there wasn't any point to hanging around, so he opened the washroom window and jumped out. It wasn't far."

"Five meters maybe," Sal explained. "A bit high, but there were tree branches I grabbed on. They bent. I went down soft. A few scratches, a tear in my coat. Nothing to complain about. It was old."

"That's why the window was open!" Lily whispered to Lill. But Lill was thinking how lucky Sal was. The old formal entry was right beneath that window. If the untrimmed trees hadn't spread limbs where he could reach them, he could have been badly injured.

"So," Flo Boater interjected. "What has all this to do with anything? Are you saying that this wasn't breaking and entering?"

The chief tried to calm her, "Only the District Attorney can bring charges, and he will do so only if he believes a jury would see it that was." After a pause he added, "And I don't see getting a conviction on this."

Flo Boater rejected this angrily, "He couldn't have seen anything in the dark, if it was as dark as he says. So why are we here?"

The chief turned to her, "Sal was not alone. You were there, too, and Dean Wooda also."

"We had every right to be anywhere we wanted, and in any case it was dark."

Calmly, Lill noted, "There was a security light in the hall, and it was *very* late."

The president spat back, "There was nothing unusual about our being in the hall!" At that she hesitated. What would people think about her and the dean being in the building that late? But she recovered quickly, "And Sal couldn't have seen us there. He just said that he had only heard *somebody* coming in, and he didn't know who."

"Ah ha," Lily interjected. "Sal didn't see anything, but we did. It must have been us he heard, not you." She then made a face at Flo Boater, who tried to make one back, but lacked the thespian training. "And you were there!" Lily crowed.

Flo Boater lapsed into uncustomary silence, moving only her lips.

Donahue ignored this in order to turn to Sal, "Why was the window open, the one in the Registrar's office? They are usually kept closed and locked no matter what the season."

"I don't know. I just saw the ladder and the window. And I went up… to check. And I'm so sorry that I did."

Biggs noticed Jones poking Smith as if to remind him of something. Moving to back to get a better view of everyone, the chief asked Sal, "How had you planned to get out? You say you would have walked right out with the ladder? Would you have been seen?"

"Maybe seen, but I couldn't go down the ladder. Someone would have noticed that the window was open. I could not, I thought, close it again. There was rain, too, or what you call it, not quite snow. Dangerous, anyway. So I made up my mind. Right out the front door with the ladder." Seeing a few inquisitive looks, Sal continued, "Nobody thinks it strange to carry a ladder out of the building. Not even in the middle of the night. The door has an automatic lock. No one would know I'd been there."

"And your purpose for breaking and entering, and I must warn you that your statement can be used against you. Moreover, I remind you that your actions could be a violation of your parole."

"I don't care," Sal said. "I didn't break nothing and I didn't think I was entering." He stopped to think, "I was convicted once, of conspiracy, though my co-conspirator," and he nodded in the direction of Flo Boater, "was found innocent. Now I'm told that my grades have been changed. I didn't want to be accused of that, too. Since Flo nor the registrar would help, I wanted to act on my own. I should have looked for the grades."

Mary jumped in at this point, "That's why everyone else was there!"

Biggs looked at Smith and Jones, "And that's what you boys were looking for, too." It was not a question.

Sheepishly, Jones admitted, "Sort of." And Smith agreed, "Yeah, I guess so."

"And you unlocked the window and opened it?"

"I guess so," Smith said.

"During the day, to go in later, after dark?"

When Smith nodded, Jones began to talk, "It was a great idea. The ladder and all. Professor S thought it was pretty good, too." He hurriedly added, "He didn't know anything about it ahead, if that's what you're thinking. He just liked our short story."

Smith interjected, "We didn't want to steal anything!"

"No," Jones said, "We only wanted our original grades back!"

"We'll deal with that later," Biggs said. Turning to Lill and Lily, he asked, "And that's why you were there, too."

They answered in unison, "Yes, sir."

And to the president and dean he directed the same question, "And that's why you were there."

The response was total silence.

Clearing his throat, Biggs summarized the situation, "It looks like multiple cases of non-breaking and entering." She smiled at his little joke.

Flo Boater objected to this, "Since Stanley and I had every right to be there, I think we could be left out of this. Lill and Lily are another matter, and they haven't explained how they got in."

Seeing that the chief was reluctant to respond, Donahue stepped in, "I doubt the newspapers will see it that way. Imagine the story: President and Dean enter registrar's office after hours with flashlights!" After a pause, he added, "Why?"

The whole ghastly affair passed before Flo Boater's eyes. It was a media dream—the headline would read, "Degrees for sale," with subtitles "college president, dean, faculty and students involved in scandal." It was awkward that they had come in before everyone else, but really dumb that they had tried to hide. If Biggs had made a threat, Flo Boater could have accused him of an ethical violation, but Donahue was an employee—and while she might think of him as a snitch, the media would call him a whistle-blower. It would be impossible to get rid of him. She was backed into a corner.

Stanley Wooda came to the rescue, "I was trying to get to the bottom of what could have been a nasty scandal. I didn't want even the registrar to know what I was looking for until I saw how big a problem as it really was."

Flo Boater followed along in his wake, "Yes, that's the truth. If it was just a rumor, we didn't want it to go any farther; if it was a minor business, we could deal with it in house; if it was a major problem, we would have called you." Wooda nodded agreement. "We only hid when we heard someone downstairs. We thought we might catch them."

Biggs considered the answer before asking, "Who was downstairs?"

"Probably the Creep," Wooda suggested. "He had probably seen the lights and was checking them out."

"But he was afraid to do more than enter the building and look around," Flo Boater said. "When he heard noises, he ran for his life." But she wasn't so sure—if that were so, how did he know so many details about that evening.

"The ghost of the dean," Stanley Wooda suggested. "He's returned from the dead."

Biggs ignored this little joke, wondering instead where Flechadoro had been during all this, then decided to keep the matter simple, "Which brings us to the heart of the matter—selling grades."

Flo Boater was unwilling to concede the major premise, "I think it is best to keep that rumor from going any further. There were no grades sold. It was simply a misunderstanding, and those who believed they knew about it are either dead or graduated. I regret having yielded to Stanley's suggestion that we set a trap for those attempting to buy their way through college, but his talks and mine, with various students intended to lead them on, were totally innocent."

Jones started to speak, "But…." He halted before saying "our money" when he saw the president glaring at him. Smith started to stand up to speak, but decided that it was unwise. He sat back into his chair, yawned and covered his face with his hands.

Once Flo Boater was certain that the boys were not going to speak, she stated for the record, "It is not in the college's interest to press charges against anyone. We shall treat this event as though it never happened."

Molly asked, "Even for Sal?"

"Especially for Sal." Flo Boater might earlier have thought that Sal could be put off easily or even sent back to prison, but she knew better now—if one story got to the press, everything would come out.

"In fact, in view of his enterprise in trying to uncover a potentially damaging scandal, I think we can find some employment for him."

Biggs indicated that his part in the affair was over, "If that is your wish, that is the way I will handle it."

Molly said, "Thank God!" As did Sal, silently.

The chief asked Dean Wooda, "And this meets your approval?"

"Of course. No hard feelings against anyone."

Molly, however, pressed the point—delay in such matters means their being forgotten: "What kind of job will Sal have?" But both the president and dean shook their heads, meaning that there was no way they would commit themselves without thinking it through.

Again it was Biggs to the rescue, "I think we can use a part-time chemist in the police department, if the college can give him a job supervising labs. Finger-prints and DNA, for us; buying supplies and cleaning up, for you. That sort of thing. Okay?"

Sal stood up and offered his hand to the chief, the other over his heart, "*Grazie.*"

Flo Boater and Stanley Boater looked at one another, then turned their heads to the chief and nodded their agreement.

Sal exclaimed, "*Che bella*! That's the second best offer I've had today, right next to *quella di Molly.*" He then held up her hand to display a modest engagement ring. Lill studied it from a distance—it was unusual, perhaps his mother's, or his grandmother's.

Mary stood up, indicating that the conversation had reached a good point to end, then observed, "Now I can work on my article."

Donahue joined her, offering his arm to escort her out, "Perhaps we can collaborate?" He had never been more hopeful.

She quietly but firmly rebuffed the gesture, "Maybe." Then, seeing the looks on the faces of their friends, she put her arm in his and said, "We'll see." Very quietly she whispered, "But first let's get our mothers to stay home."

He gave a silent sigh, masking it with a wide smile.

Lill winked at Lily, "We are back where we started."

But Lily was not sure, "What about the grades?"

"That will apparently remain an unsolved mystery."

Jones sidled up to the president even before everyone had left the room, "What about our money?" he whispered. "We want it back."

"You paid in cash?"

"Of course."

"There's a lesson in that—always get a receipt."

"The dean wouldn't give us a receipt! We didn't even ask."

"Did you get what you wanted?"

He hesitated, "I guess. I really don't know."

If you don't get what you paid for, come see me again. If not, never bring this up again. The store for grades is closed. In fact, it was never open."

As soon as the boys left, she whispered to her dean, "I just saved your ass."

"What about the Creep? He's still out there, and he wants my job."

"I'll see," she said. "He sees himself moving up step by step. First divisional chair, then associate dean, then...."

Quite unintentionally, the individuals who had gone down the stairs one or two at a time gathered just outside the main door to gaze at the beauty of the campus in winter. Watching Donahue and Mary walking off into the white mist, still arm in arm, Lily observed, "Real life is often a mystery."

Jones saw this as his opportunity to slip off. He whispered to Smith, "I'm just glad not to be in jail." And Smith agreed, "Yeah, even studying is better than that."

"The Creep," Biggs asked, "what's going to happen with him? He was in the building, too, and he kept information from both of us."

Flo Boater was dismissive, "I'm afraid there will be no promotions this year. Financial crisis, you know." She moved over to her dean and casually put her arm around his slim waist. Automatically, his arm went around hers—more substantial, but womanly rather than, well, really substantial.

"He's still to be chair of Social Sciences, maybe chair of Fine Arts, too?" The chief's face betrayed a slight smile, perhaps an indication that they had a common enemy, perhaps an indication that he understood how the historian's career was moving swiftly upward.

When she hesitated, Stanley Wooda gave her a quiet squeeze. It took her a moment to formulate her thoughts. "I imagine," she responded, "that financial limitations will require us to return to the traditional form of departmental organization. We'll have no money for released time for administrative functions. My dean, Stanley Wooda, will be able to manage everything by himself." At that she turned on her heel and left, with Stanley Wooda right behind her. As soon as they were out of earshot, the dean said, "I'm just glad we're out of this without somebody being murdered."

Flo Boater stopped and turned to face him, then said slowly, "I was wondering myself, when I'd be asked, how did you put it...?" She shook her head, "Just as I think we have the late dean buried, along with his... his shenanigans, he comes back from the dead." Once safely alone, she put her arms around his neck....

The new Dean Wooda understood just exactly what type of shenanigans he was expected to perform. He was to become a worthy successor to the first Dean Wooda in every way.

Smith persuaded Ellie to help him with his documentary. Though it meant working together late into the night, that was fine for her— she could sleep late in the morning. It was fine for Smith, too—she'd have no time to fill out the paperwork for transferring to Zenith. The state's third from flagship university was in the process of upgrading its reputation—first, by requiring faculty to publish, it could remove "dead wood" and hire more dynamic young people who would be too busy to publish, hence could be replaced by truly great scholars later on; secondly, by discouraging transfers from other universities and colleges in the state, it would suggest that they were not performing at the higher level that Zenith expected of its students. Meanwhile, more money was pumped into the football program and each time the coach lured a talented player away from a competing college, the event made headlines.

Mary and Donahue had not gotten to the end of their walk before she began complaining that the placement exam for Spanish 101-102 made no sense.

"How so, Mary? Isn't that designed to make sure that students don't waste their time repeating material they already know?"

"Oh, it works fine for that. But only a handful really want to major in Spanish. The rest want to fulfill the language requirement as easily as possible. They are deliberately flunking the exam." Seeing a question in his eyes, she explained, "101 would be a snap for them, while they'd have to work in 102." She saw the need for more explanation, "All they want is a review and an easy grade."

"I don't see the problem. I always have a few students with an instinctive understanding of sociological principles."

"That's different. I have native speakers of Spanish who need work, like… in grammar. But it's the rest of the students who are the problem—the ones who took it in high school, but never took it seriously. They know enough to be bored, then they disrupt the class; like, if they cut, they miss material they really don't know very well. If they really should have been in 102, they just fill up seats that others need, but might have to wait until the next semester to start, which really means like the next year, because we don't have many 101 sections the second semester."

"Do many flunk?"

"Not as many as should. It's like, we can't keep them in 101 forever, but they aren't really ready for 102."

"Why not just have them redo 101?"

"Like I said, we don't have enough sections, and it's really awkward. Like, we talked about having a remedial section for those who just won't work, but we don't have enough staff, and nobody wants to teach that kind of class." She frowned when she realized how often she had said "like."

"Um, I see. What's your solution?"

"That's the problem! If we get rid of the language requirement, which is the only way to get rid of those who don't want to take my courses, nobody will enroll!"

"Um, maybe they should be required to take a different language than they had in high school."

"That won't work. We don't offer much beyond Spanish, and that's the language they might have some chance to use. Besides, we are trying to recruit more Hispanics, and the test exempts some of them from the requirement."

"So the test works for some?"

"Yes, but... but, it's a lot of work, and it takes a full day to administer."

"Strange," he mused. "The Math department doesn't give credit for high school level work at all—you know, geometry and algebra. If they could fulfill the requirement with those classes, that's what they'd take, and somehow they'd loaf through. But since they can't, they work harder in the for-credit classes. At least, I think they do. Maybe we should treat Introductory Spanish the same way... offer it as remedial work, but no credit...." He couldn't finish—Mary had already turned her back and walked away.

She wished it were just the cold, but her fists were clenched almost as hard as her teeth. It was hard enough to think of their mothers converging on them, without Donahue coming up with so many silly unconventional ideas. Why couldn't he just be more imaginative? Without running against common sense?

Dean Threshold told his wife that they were opening a new business—genealogy.

"But, dear, I don't know anything about genealogy."

"That doesn't matter. I can do all the work."

"When? You have a job."

"Ha. It really doesn't take much time. I can do as much research on the side as I want and neither Flo nor Stan will ever suspect."

"Is that legal?"

"Legal, yes. Moral, maybe not. That's where you come in."

"Me?"

"Yes. You have to answer the phone, take information. Don't worry, I'll teach you what to ask. Everyone will think you are doing all the work."

"But I'm just a waitress."

"That makes it all the better. You know everyone in town who'd be interested and who'd have the money. And your training in Student Services makes you a good listener and, you know, how to put it all down and to explain it. Most of all, both that training and being a waitress has made you very, very accurate. That's what you need for genealogy."

"Do people really want that sort of thing?"

"You'd be surprised. I think we can make a bundle—people want to know if they're part Indian! I never suspected that there would be so many opportunities to get ahead as I see in Briarpatch College."

Flechadoro was packing his belongings. These were not numerous— he had adhered to his ancestors' belief that one should not own more than can be carried from one campsite to another. To these few shirts and pants he added a brown mailing envelope. He smiled to himself— this was the guarantee of his tribe's future prosperity. At such a moment it was right to break with the tradition of immovable facial muscles. It might even be a moment to celebrate by getting roaring drunk.

"However," he thought, wishing that he didn't have to say "how" so often in English, "who can celebrate alone?" And why should he? Weren't JJ and Smitty broke again? They were always good for a party, especially if it was on someone's else's dime. Stan had given him "traveling money." Why not use some of it for a few beers?

Hours later Flo Boater lay in bed, wanting a cigarette. "Threw them out long ago. Should have kept them around for an appropriate moment." Patting a still warm area next to her, she tried to reconstruct the events of that evening when the grade scandal almost got out of hand—who had come in when, who had left when, what each was doing. Finally, she gave up. "Can't figure it out. I doubt anyone really knows." Then she thought about Flechadoro. Had he really been there? Did it make any difference? She smiled—probably not.

Chapter Twenty-Seven

Flo Boater was in her office, admiring the new decorations. They had taken forever to finish. And the bills! Oh, how the trustees would complain. But she'd bring them around. Visitors with money would not be impressed by shabby furnishing, no matter how good the budget looked. She glanced up. "Hello, Max," Flo she said. "What brings you here?"

"Business, Flo, business. Important business."

She sat up, not because she really believed him, but because she had been taught from an early age to pay attention to men when they were excited.

"It's a speaker for your Gala Inauguration," he explained. "I think I can get us a good one."

Flo Boater nodded approvingly. Arcadia, though only a junior college, had been getting better speakers than Briarpatch. Still, she responded cautiously, "Who do you have in mind?"

"Billy Ayers! You remember him, surely. He was a big name in the Sixties. Now he's an important person in educational circles, teaches at a university in Chicago."

She grimaced, thinking, "How old does he think I am?" But she responded cautiously, "The name rings a bell, but I don't know why."

"Oh, it should, it should. He was on the FBI most wanted list for years and years, then was fully cleared. He'll be a big hit among the progressives on campus, he'll make up for that long list of conservatives we've had as Commencement speakers."

She grimaced again, "Two Democratic governors, a United Nations representative, a diplomat from some Third World country, and a presidential candidate of rather liberal credentials. Those are hardly conservatives."

He waved his hands at her, "Everything is relative. For real progressives, those people were true Neanderthals. They didn't speak about anything except what the students could do with their lives!"

317

"Max, that's what a Commencement address is supposed to be… inspiring, uplifting.…"

He cut her off, "Nobody can ever remember anything they say. They just repeat platitudes. Besides, this isn't for a Commencement."

She took a deep breath, recalling that she had been considering combining the Inauguration with Commencement—a cost-cutting measure that would guarantee some students showing up. The thought was cut off by Stout saying, "Lucy May Mankiller will have some exciting progressive for her Gala Inauguration, but nobody as good as him."

She sighed, thinking, "At least he didn't suggest her. That talk of hers, 'Never Get Laid Again,' that would be just the sort of thing she'd give." Then reflecting on the previous night, she decided that the title was really stupid. And she had expected that would be her fate. With a smile, she asked, "This Mr. Ayers will say something… more… *exciting*?"

"Certainly, certainly," he replied. "But even if he doesn't, he's a personality, he's well-known, and he's giving a talk at Zenith. It's *Dr.* Ayers, anyway—he teaches *Education*. You could drive up with me and see for yourself, then I could arrange an introduction. I'm sure I can." Seeing skepticism in her eyes, he continued, "He's a *progressive* educator. He's got all sorts of ideas for making education more *relevant*, more *effective*, more *central* to *everything* we do."

She thought a second, "Why is that important? More important than, say, someone who might contribute money." She was thinking of Ellie's father, who was put in a good mood by Stan locating her in France—he had simply asked the computer center director to check her emails and determine their origin. Using his fluent French—the most lasting product of his first off-campus experience, in France—he had called the police in Paris, persuaded them to get her to call, then talked her into coming home—home meaning Briarpatch College.

She tapped her fingers for a moment, wondering what his politics were. Ellie's father had money, but lots of rich men were very liberal. George Soros, any Kennedy, any Rockefeller, any Ford except Gerald. But on the average.…

He interrupted her thoughts, "Well, think about it, Flo. How many speakers have we had who were wanted by the FBI?"

"None, I guess." She could remember the one was arrested after he gave a dynamite speech about how essential honesty was for public service, then frowned at remembering that his promised gift never materialized. Pulling herself together, she asked, "What would the trustees think?"

"Screw them. All they think about is money. Here's a chance to talk about principles."

"That sounds like..., what do you mean by principles?"

"Well, revolution. You know, revolution is an act of education."

She stopped to think, "I thought it was 'education is a revolutionary act.'"

He smiled, "In our postmodern era, we are supposed to de-construct such mottos, to turn their simplicity into complex understandings, then get to the bottom of the meaning."

"So the bottom line is revolution?"

"Oh, no. You misunderstand. He won't say anything controversial— he's an educator, a highly respected educator."

"That's nice," she responded. "I thought he might be a community organizer or something."

"Oh, not for years, and not like you suggest. He doesn't believe in violence. Never did."

"As I remember, and I don't remember much, he planted a bomb."

"Yes, but it was just symbolic. It's not as though he wanted to hurt anybody."

"Didn't somebody blow themselves up? His girlfriend?"

"Pure accident, nothing connected to him."

"Why were they making a bomb?"

"To kill some soldiers. Nothing important. Just to make a statement."

She hesitated at this, "Now let me get this straight. He was associated with bomb makers, and you want me to invite him to give the address at my Inauguration? I was thinking of doing it myself, perhaps on the need to have more deans." Maybe that would slow Stout down, make him think!

But Stout didn't seem to have listened. He broke in," Absolutely... You'd be good, of course, and everyone would be fascinated to learn that deans were a necessary evil, but Ayers would be great publicity."

She sighed and said dryly, "I'll bet he would."

"He'll get our students out of their ruts."

"What does that mean?" How does this work? she wondered—he's not going to say anything controversial, but he'll get students "out of their ruts?"

"He gets students socially involved, involved in change."

"Involved?"

"Yes, under the right direction, of course. For social change."

"Max, our students already have two major demonstrations each year."

"Yes, but those are inconsequential. All they want are more parking places, that kind of thing. Never fundamental change."

Flo Boater sighed again, "Max, let's hope they never want fundamental change. Their first demand would be to shoot you and me."

"Me?"

"Anyway, do we need more demonstrations on campus right now?"

"That's the beauty of having him speak at the Inauguration—there wouldn't be any students around. And if we had him speak at Commencement, too, only graduates would be there; and they'll all be gone by nightfall!"

"Max, thank you for the suggestion. I always appreciate thinking outside the box. But for Commencement or my Inauguration, I need someone who colors inside the lines."

He thought before responding, "Maybe we could have him another time, but still give him an honorary degree."

She laughed, "A political radical would want an honorary degree?" Then she smiled—Briarpatch College was back to business as usual.

She then picked up the phone to talk with Chief Biggs about three intoxicated students. Nothing ever changes at Briarpatch College, she thought, nothing ever changes.